THE
BLOODY
BUSINESS
OF
LUCK

A novel by
Trine Bronken

PUBLISHED BY TRINE BRONKEN

Cover design by Katherine Norton
Cover images by iStock
and by Ervins Strauhmanis
www.flickr.com/photos/ervins_strauhmanis/

ISBN ebk 978-0-9951993-0-9
ISBN pbk 978-0-9951993-1-6

Printed in Canada

With thanks to:
Cathy and Rhonda for their friendship, support,
and terrific wine recommendations;
and to Mark, Rhys, and Logan . . .
What do you know? Here it is!

PROLOGUE

D etective Paul Lee brought his unmarked police cruiser to a stop at the scene of Vancouver's latest homicide.

"What've we got, Larsen?" he yelled to a hulking individual in black hoodie and backwards ball cap.

"Got a piece here. A piece there. Little pieces everywhere, Paul." Don Larsen lifted the crime scene tape over his head and ambled across to the senior detective's car.

Lee glared at his partner. "Bobbitized?"

"Not quite that up close and personal, but it's pretty gruesome." Larsen peeled the foil from a fresh stick of gum. "There are no signs of forced entry, but our vic's been shot twice and stuffed in a closet after having his lips, ears, and one hand excised."

"*One* hand? What's the point of that?"

"Good question. Of course, we could still get an excellent set of prints from the remaining hand." Larsen nodded to the attendants wheeling the body to the waiting van, then bent down to the open car window. "Another good question would be why we found the missing hand in the guy's cookie jar." He raised the stick of gum dramatically, as if he were proposing a toast, then added it to the tasteless wad in his mouth.

CHAPTER 1
Two Weeks Later

Three hours into her ferry journey up the coast of British Columbia, Kate's concentration was shattered by an elbow jabbed in her side.

"That guy over there is wearing that A'Climatize jacket I want. I'm going to go ask him how much he paid for it," Matt said.

She shot him a disapproving look.

"They wear the stuff on Everest, you know. I should start a company like that."

Kate closed her book and executed a surreptitious glance down the aisle. "What's he doing here?" she whispered.

"You know him?"

"It's Rhys Wilson. He's a reporter for the *Star*."

"Do we like him or don't we? I get all your reporters mixed up."

"We don't. He's fanatical about anything to do with gambling. He's the one who investigated the murder of that lottery ticket scammer a couple of weeks ago."

"The dismembered guy? Wasn't he re-selling old tickets to seniors or something like that?"

"He talked them out of their banking information and robbed them blind." Kate wrinkled her nose in disgust. "Of course, his business has fallen off since he was chopped up and stuffed in his closet." She nodded in Wilson's direction. "That guy made my life hell. I was really sorry those people got scammed, but it had nothing to do with Pacific Lottery. We're run by the government and there are all kinds of watchdogs and regulations in place." Her back to Wilson, Kate sunk a little lower in her seat and feigned great interest in her book.

Matt peered back down the aisle. "If you know him that well, maybe you could ask him about the jacket?"

"You seem to be missing my point." Kate glared at her boyfriend. "And I've never actually met him. I've seen him at press conferences though, and he constantly hassles me on the phone for info and quotes for his column. Now he's colluding with those crazy anti-gambling zealots that organized that protest last month."

Matt rolled his eyes. "Aren't you overreacting just a little? What are they going to do, flatten your tires or something?"

Kate stared at him in disbelief. "Those nuts are consumed with this. According to the police, they're right up there with the dopes that picket abortion clinics and shoot doctors. Maybe *that's* something you can relate to, *Doctor Brooks.*"

* * *

Angry at Matt and unsettled by Wilson's presence, Kate bought a coffee from the cafeteria and stepped out on deck for some fresh air. The drizzle had lifted and the clear blue ocean sparkled in the sunlight as the ship wove its way between islands thickly cloaked in Sitka Spruce, cedar, and hemlock trees. Gulls floated effortlessly alongside the vessel looking for easy snacks tossed by passengers. Alerted by an announcement from the bridge, Kate was lucky to catch sight of a pod of killer whales as they breached.

Kate had joined British Columbia's Pacific Lottery Corporation on a contractual basis, ten months before. Her responsibilities as Communications Manager included all internal and external corporate communication as well as facilitating the company's expansion into "Las Vegas-style" destination casinos. What started out as an exciting challenge, though, had turned into a nightmare for which years of experience had not prepared her. Plans to expand casino operations had been met with a huge negative outcry from volatile religious groups and from PAGE, People Against Gambling Expansion, who were concerned with gambling addiction. Reporters misquoted Kate and hassled her constantly at work and at home. Committees formed on all sides of the debate and changed the direction of the project as much as one hundred and eighty degrees from one day to the next.

Seizing the opportunity to get out of Vancouver and away from it all, she volunteered to co-ordinate the grand opening of the first destination casino at Dragonfly Lake in the province's northern Chilcotin region. A joint-venture between Pacific Lottery and the First Nations Native Band, on whose land the resort was built, it was to be marketed as a year-round attraction for the tourists who flocked to the area. The opportunity to take the scenic route to the resort, sailing up the coast to Bella Coola and then driving inland, was something she hadn't been able to pass up.

The area had been frequented by Russian furriers centuries ago, explored by Spanish mariners, and claimed by English sailors for their King. This spectacular morning, however, there was no sign of history's turmoil, no sign of development, and no other ship in sight. The deserted coastline looked like it had completely escaped the hand of man. As they motored by trees standing tall and proud, Kate leaned on the rail, sipped her coffee, and tried to forget the stresses of the past ten months.

CHAPTER 2

"Beautiful, isn't it?" Startled, Kate spun around to see Rhys Wilson standing behind her. "I spent a lot of time up here as a kid. It's always great to get back. Kind of therapeutic." He shrugged a well-travelled backpack off his broad shoulders.

She shot him a withering glance. "What are you doing here?"

"Look, I'm sorry if I've been on your case lately. It's nothing personal. Loosen up a little."

"Thanks for the advice. I'll try and do that." Kate turned her back to him and gazed out at the shimmering water. "You didn't answer my question," she said. "What are you doing way up here?"

"Looking into something for a friend. A tourist was murdered near Namu last week. The RCMP have a local in custody, but there's no way he's guilty."

"Isn't that a little outside your area of expertise?"

"Not really." He leaned on the rail beside her. "My mom was a member of the Heiltsuk First Nations Band in Bella Bella. I lived here until I was fifteen when my dad got a job in Vancouver and moved us south. I still have lots of family and friends on the coast, and the guy the cops have arrested is one of them."

Surprised at the emotion in his voice, Kate wondered if the arrogant Wilson might have a heart deeply buried in there after all.

"Where's Namu?" she asked. "Is it a fishing village?"

"Not anymore, but there was a big cannery there

4

in the 1800s. There were salmon canneries and company housing all along the coast years ago. My mother's family ran a floating dance hall for the employees." Wilson extended an arm and pointed to a bear ambling along the beach. "Things slowed down when the price of fish fell, and a fire in the 1960s pretty much destroyed anything that was left."

"So what was the murder victim doing there?"

"He was a guest at one of those posh new lodges that are hidden in the bays and inlets all around here. Some are built on floats and they tow them around to follow the fish. They cater to foreign tourists—super high-end."

Kate sipped her coffee and waited for him to continue.

"The only locals that can afford them are people like your ticket reseller friend." He flashed her a wide grin. "You know, the guy the cops found in the closet." He shrugged. "Rumor is they found parts of him in there, anyway. He and his buddies liked to fish up here."

"I didn't realize he was such a sportsman." Kate laughed in spite of herself.

"He preferred Mystic River Wilderness Resort, as did the murder victim. They have a private heliport. Only the best for your friends."

"Enough already. Just when we were getting along so well." She raised a palm in defense. "What's your connection?"

"My friend, Eugene Simon, was the guide who took the murdered guy out fishing early Tuesday morning. Eugene thought it was pretty strange that this guy, Vogel, insisted on going ashore to fly fish on Wild Blueberry River because he had told him there are no fish there." Wilson extracted a water bottle from his backpack and took a sip. He wiped his mouth with the back of his hand and continued. "As they had arranged, Eugene returned four hours later to pick him up, and Vogel was nowhere to be found. He searched up the river and six kilometers along the coast in both directions." Wilson flipped his wrist dismissively. "Nothing."

"Well, who says he was murdered? He probably got lost." She gasped. "Maybe a bear got him."

"Nope, because Vogel turned up. Thursday morning, a technician over at Thorsen's Aquaculture found him bobbing next to one of the fish pens. I don't know how he died, but the RCMP have arrested Eugene. Apparently he had the victim's A'Climatize jacket, which he says Vogel gave him for helping land a 60-pound salmon. The victim's buddies insist there was no salmon and that Vogel was wearing the jacket the morning he left to go fishing. The cops think Eugene killed him and stole the jacket."

"That's a hefty price to pay for a coat, even if it is A'Climatize. Personally, I think the stuff's overrated and way too expensive." Kate grinned, eyeing the expensive, sought-after label embroidered on Wilson's chest.

"Maybe. Anyway, that's why I'm here. The Simons are old friends and I thought I'd put those investigative reporter skills to work." Wilson looked at his watch, cringed, and glanced to shore. "Damn, I wasn't paying attention. We're getting close to my stop. It's a good thing Phil knows I'm on board or we might sail right by."

"Who's Phil? And I didn't think we made a stop until we got to Bella Bella."

"Sometimes it's more of a slowdown than a stop. Come on. I'll show you." Wilson hefted his large pack with ease and strode up the deck. "Look, there . . . " He pointed to a spot on shore. "You can see what's left of the old Namu cannery."

Brushing defiant strands of wavy brown hair from her eyes, Kate spied the remains of wooden outbuildings on crumbling decks cantilevered over the water. Rickety boardwalks still connected the wharves in places and old automobile tires, once used as boat bumpers, hung by chains along their sides. Just offshore, a water-logged fishing boat half-floated and half-sank. Further up the beach, Kate spotted the remnants of a large building, blackened by fire, its roof collapsed. A portion of the front façade still stood. On it, a sign hung by one corner and asserted in large, weathered type:

Pacific Spirit Cannery
World Famous Salmon
Namu, British Columbia
(established 1893)

Kate was thinking about the going concern the area had been, staring in silence at what seemed the final resting place of an era, when Wilson interrupted her thoughts.

"That wasn't here when I was up in the summer." He pointed to a sturdy looking dock and three motorboats largely concealed in a small bay. "Let's go ask Phil what's going on. He knows everything."

Kate followed Wilson inside to the customer service counter amidships where a tall, fair man in his early thirties handed out maps, earbuds, board games and travel advice. His ruddy face broke into a broad smile when they approached.

"How's it going, Phil?" Wilson asked. "Meet Kate Logan, government spin-doctor. Sorry...I mean Communications Manager and intrepid seeker of the truth in all things gambling."

Kate held out her hand. "Pleased to meet you, Phil. You have questionable taste in friends."

He took her hand in a firm shake. "I know, and I can't seem to lose the guy—always following me around."

"Tell me about it," she said.

"You've got me there," said Wilson. "Phil and I go way back, Kate. We went to school together in Bella Bella, fished, kayaked, played baseball, rugby—all the required stuff."

"Dated the same girls. Me first—then, when they met our scribe here, I became the third wheel with the great personality."

"That's not how I remember it, buddy." Wilson shook his head and changed the subject. "What's going on at the cannery? I saw the new dock."

With a nod of greeting, Phil handed a deck of cards and cribbage board to a pair of seniors and turned back to Wilson and Kate. "The cannery site was bought a year ago by some group that made a sweet deal with the departments of Economic Development and Native Affairs to develop the property and pay all the environmental cleanup costs." Phil's voice took on a noticeable edge. "They say their plan is to build a totally 'green' resort: no impact on the environment, solar power, home grown organic food, and composting toilets—which sound totally disgusting. All the bumf, man...Talk about spin doctors. With all due respect, Kate, you couldn't hold a candle to these guys."

"Another fishing lodge, another case of money versus tradition. We've seen it before," Wilson said. "It's tough to fight City Hall. Even I know that, although I try and talk tough." He looked at Kate. "Money versus tradition, newcomers versus old-timers, millionaires seeking recreation versus loggers and fishermen trying to eke out a living. It causes a lot of tension up here."

"But the whole process was a sham, Rhys. They didn't even have a business plan and they had a signed deal in a week." Phil shook his head. "Six months before this bunch parachuted in, your friend Wesley and I submitted a proposal for a unique wilderness resort at Namu which respected the area rather than strafing it to make a buck. It took us a year to put it together.

"We had people keen to illustrate local culture and the cannery's history, experts signed on to assist in raptor rehabilitation, bear mapping and the restoration of salmon habitat. The ferry corporation agreed to make us a port of call and to include us in their promotions. We even had permission to tour the archaeological digs." As he spoke, Phil ticked off each step in his plan with a vehement tap of his index finger.

"We knew we had to include the weekend warrior stuff, too, so we incorporated kayaking, sport fishing, non-invasive whale-watching, and gourmet food and good wine. And we paid in full for architectural drawings for a lodge and an interpretive center—both *very green*." He grinned at Kate, which lightened the mood a little. "Fourteen months ago, we signed a memorandum of understanding to proceed with the government."

Wilson, who had been waiting for his friend to pause for breath, quickly interjected, "The other group offered more money?"

"That's what's so strange," Phil replied, passing out a chess set. "They didn't. They got title in exchange for a profit-sharing scheme that kicks in way down the road. No money's changed hands and they haven't done a thing. No cleanup. No lodge. No jobs…One new dock, and it looks like somebody has moved in. I don't know if he's using a composting toilet or not."

"Kinda tweaks my spidey-sense," Wilson said. "I bet I could scam a little time off and do some nosing around up here." He winked at Kate. "And if I can work something into my column, I'll get to write it off."

Avoiding the taxman—more evidence a human being lives in there somewhere, Kate thought.

"Sorry to go on like that, guys. It's kind of a hot button with me," Phil said.

"We noticed," Wilson replied.

"Now, wait a second, bud. I've been keeping up with your columns. You're calling me hot under the collar? Talk about the pot calling the kettle black."

Wilson's handsome face flushed ever so slightly at the reference to his harshly opinionated columns on gambling and the lottery corporation.

As if recalling the accusations Rhys had leveled at Pacific, Phil took a step back. "You two aren't up here together—are you?"

"Oh gosh, no!" Kate said.

Wilson roared with laughter. "That reminds me, I never asked you what you're doing up here. My nosy reporter skills definitely need a tune up."

Not having much of a choice, Kate admitted she was bound for the grand opening of the Dragonfly Lake Casino.

"There's another shady deal." Phil pounded his fist on the counter.

"Hah! Touched 'ya last," yelled a wiry, curly-haired boy as he poked his companion and pushed past Kate and Rhys to escape.

Swack, came the retaliating hit. "Wow, I can't believe I touched you last," said the other boy, who barreled off in the opposite direction.

"Blast it. The Anderson brothers. I can't stand it when they play 'touched-you-last'. Excuse me for a minute, would you guys? It's movie time." Phil lifted a handset from its cradle on the wall.

"Good morning, everyone. This is Phil, your purser. In two minutes, our movie will begin in the youth lounge. Specially selected for our discriminating audience today is *Superheroes Two*. Don't miss it, kids. Back of the ship. Run! Now!" He returned the handset to the cradle.

"You have to time things just so around here," Phil said. "They get bored with one activity, I move them on to another, then another. If I'm lucky, I don't run out of activities before we get to Bella Coola. Listen, though, if you're getting off at Mystic River, you better get moving. I've got to put the movie on, so I can't see you off, but make sure you're ready or he'll sail right past. He's still pissed you know."

"Isn't Captain MacDonald on the bridge?" Wilson asked warily.

"No. MacDonald's on paternity leave. His wife had a baby girl last week. Your good friend Captain Haebler's at the wheel today."

"I'd better move it," Rhys said. "You coming down?" He elbowed Kate, grabbed his backpack, and took off double-time for the stairs to the car deck. Curious, Kate gave Phil a shrug and hustled to catch up, flipping a quick wave to Matt who seemed deep in conversation with a couple clad in matching outdoor gear.

CHAPTER 3

The *Queen of Chilliwack* had been built in Norway twenty years before to haul cargo. For its new role as a passenger carrier, the upper decks had been refurbished with a theatre, coin-operated showers, dining area, and reclining chairs so the passengers could enjoy the spectacular views in comfort. Although the vast area below, built to accommodate heavy equipment and supplies, had been renovated very little, its cavernous space was being put to new use. Impromptu games of football and soccer had sprung up. The ferry workers had even rolled out a length of synthetic turf and constructed a challenging mini-golf course on the port side. Happy to be released from the confines of their owners' cars, dogs of all shapes and sizes walked around freely. Closer to the stern, a group of people in wetsuits was going through a series of stretches. Kate noticed the huge doors at the back of the ferry were open and the lush scenery was moving by more slowly than it had before.

"Hurray for kayakers," Rhys whooped. "They're going to save me from soaking this new jacket that you so jealously admired." He approached a wet-suited woman who was fussing with her life jacket. "Are you guys getting off at Mystic River?" he asked.

"Yeah. Ten of us," she said. "And the weather is perfect."

"Couldn't be better," said Rhys. "Have a good time." He walked toward the stern and gave an exuberant wave out the back of the ship.

Following his gaze, Kate saw a small motorboat with two occupants bobbing in the ferry's gentle wake.

"You're getting off here?" she asked.

"Yep. Foot passengers only. So don't even think about following me."

"You're going to jump?"

"That's always a possibility, but I think I've been saved by the kayakers."

"What are you talking about?"

"Captain Haebler is not exactly a big fan of mine. There was a little misunderstanding years ago and he won't let it go. If I was the only one getting off the *Queen*, he wouldn't stop. It's happened before. He slows down a bit but won't bring her to a full stop. The Simon's boat is pretty small and, if the water's rough, it's tough to hit it just right from a moving ferry." He chuckled. "Last time, I damn near missed...But Haebler can't treat *real* passengers like that." He nodded to an approaching deckhand. "It'll take them a little while to launch ten kayaks. You might want to stay and watch. Red doesn't mind—do you Red?"

"Well, well, well, Rhys Wilson. Look what the cat dragged in," said the greying deckhand. Dressed in coveralls, he wore a leather tool belt around his waist and carried a coil of sturdy looking wire cable that he threaded through a large pulley attached to the deck.

"Heard you were aboard...Captain let it slip when I was up on the bridge this morning...Got lucky with the paddlers, didn't ya?" Red cackled and gestured to the kayakers.

"Remember last time. I didn't think you was going to make it. Lost a ten buck bet on that." Red winked at Kate. "'A course, I was on your side, son. It's just, the water was rough that day and the way the wind was blowing, when old Dodger Smith bet me ten you'd make Eugene's boat, I figured it was easy money you wouldn't." He hung his head sheepishly and tried to change the subject. "Look, they're getting the first guy set up."

The ferry was now completely stopped and out on the deck beyond the safety fence, deckhands were settling the first paddler and his kayak into a sling that hung from a crane. Kate watched as Red ran his cable through another pulley on the crane and back to a winch at an operations console. When his colleagues flashed him a thumbs-up, he pushed a button and the kayak and rider gently rose up off the ship's deck. With a turn of the wheel on his console, Red swung the kayak slowly out over the ocean and deposited it in the water. The boat floated free of the sling which was winched back aboard the ferry.

"Slick," Kate said. "Do you pick them up later?"

"On one of our return trips." Red skillfully worked the controls to lower the next boater. "Sometimes they paddle straight up to Bella Bella. Sometimes they explore around a bit and camp on shore for a few days...Not so much of that going on lately, though, 'cause of that thing that happened a few weeks back."

When he saw Wilson's puzzled look, Red explained. "Maybe a month ago, we let a group of kids from New York off, right here. They planned to stay for a week but when they went to put ashore down at the old cannery, somebody shot at them. They weren't hurt, but one of the kids' kayaks was dinged. They filled us in when we picked them up, so the captain radioed the cops, but I don't think they've done a thing about it. Everybody's pussyfooting around these new guys at Namu. I don't get it."

"Phil told us the same thing," Kate said.

"I think they're up to something, but Dodger tells me I read too much Jo Nesbo," said Red.

"Sounds pretty strange." Wilson stared thoughtfully back toward Namu, then started out of his reverie. "I'd better get going or Haebler'll fire her up again and get the last laugh after all. You guys are getting speedy in your old age," he said, referring to the fact only a few kayakers remained on board. Squeezing past the safety fence, he beckoned to the waiting motorboat, which sprang to life and motored up to the ferry, carefully avoiding the kayak pack. Wilson dropped his backpack into the boat.

"Rhys, wait." Red reached for a rolled ladder secured to the back of the operations console.

"C'mon, Red. It's a drop today, not a jump. Have you got a bet on with Dodger that I *will* make it?"

"Nope, no more 'bettin. When you made that last leap, I knew my betting days were over. Something's gonna kill you for sure, women, or that job of yours, but I don't want it to be jumping off the *Queen* on my watch."

Rhys laughed, reached over the fence and shook Kate's hand.

"Miss Logan, a pleasure to finally meet you. I'm sure I'll see you around." He crouched down and disappeared off the end of the ferry. Kate watched until the little boat and its three occupants disappeared from sight up the inlet.

CHAPTER 4

After exchanging a few words with Red regarding the foolishness of some people, Kate stopped at Matt's old hatchback to retrieve her book. Fluid from the car's engine had dripped onto the deck and was flowing in little crooked streams as the ship bobbed. Hoping it was something that could be easily fixed, she made a mental note to tell Matt.

The latest Jo Nesbo novel in hand, she ascended the staircase to the deck, annoyed to find Rhys Wilson on her mind. Unable to locate Matt, Kate returned to her seat in the bow. A thick mist had rolled in and the water had taken on a rough chop and turned a steely grey. On the port side of the ship, cloud covered all but the very bottom of a small island, making it look like it was wearing a fluffy white hat.

She shivered at how gloomy everything had suddenly become. Adding to her mood, the PA system crackled to life and Phil announced that in 1929, the lighthouse they were passing had been the scene of a grisly murder that had never been solved. Lost in thought, Kate didn't at first realize the man seated across from her had spoken.

"I like your trousers," he repeated, winking and pointing at the pants Kate had picked up at a sample sale in Vancouver. She was sure the price had been reduced to five dollars because everybody else had better taste than to buy them. The left leg featured the image of a galloping horse with MULE FEED emblazoned underneath. The vitamin and mineral content of the feed was itemized at ankle level.

"Thank-you. I thought they were kind of fun."

"Reminds me of the underwear my mother used to make us out of potato sacks." His mahogany brow creased as he thought back. "They were a little rough, but nice and warm. I noticed you talking earlier with my friend, Rhys." His eyes crinkled. "You better watch out for him." When Kate looked a little annoyed, the old man continued. "I'm sorry, my dear, but nobody tells me anything anymore, so I have to keep my eyes open. I'm the Chief you know." His gnarled, age-spotted hands kneaded the grip of his wooden cane.

"I'm supposed to know what's going on, be wise, offer advice, and all that, but absolutely nobody asks me what I think anymore. It can make a guy feel pretty useless. They're all busy YouTubing, texting, and tweeting." He flailed a hand in the air. "If I didn't spy on people every now and then, I'd never know what's happening. By the way," he leaned in conspiratorially, "do you know how to start a blog? I've got a few things I'd like to blog about and I think it would really impress my grandson, Wesley. Let him know the old man's not dead yet."

Thankful that she knew a bit about the subject, Kate explained the basics of blogging to the old gentleman, who introduced himself as Moses George, Chief of the Heiltsuk First Nations Band in Bella Bella. She also taught him some new terminology, suggesting he throw it into the conversation to really floor his grandson.

Moses was ninety years old and seemed happy to have someone to talk to. As the ferry plied its way north, he entertained her with stories about his people's complex culture, artistic traditions, and rich spirit life. It was only when Phil announced the cafeteria would stop serving lunch in half an hour that Kate realized how long they had been talking.

"I think I'll get myself a snack before they close," she said. "May I get you something?"

"You know, my dear, I don't have the appetite I used to, but a tuna fish sandwich would hit the spot." He fished a ten-dollar bill from the pocket of his sweater. "You take it," he said, pressing the money into her hand when Kate shook her head. "No tomato though, OK? I can't understand why they put tomato in a nice tuna fish sandwich. I should mention that to Phil."

Kate had missed breakfast and been so engrossed in the Chief's stories that she hadn't realized how hungry she was. When she smelled the delicious aroma of homemade soup coming from the kitchen, though, she decided she could use a tuna fish sandwich, too—tomato or no tomato.

She spotted Matt talking to the couple she had seen him with earlier. Wanting to continue her conversation with Moses, but knowing she should be social and introduce herself, she walked over to their table.

"Kate, you should listen to this guy. You might learn something," Matt said.

"I'll bet," Kate replied, accustomed to Matt's lack of tact.

Matt's lunch companion rose from his seat. "I am certain this lovely lady doesn't need my help," he said smoothly in accented English. "You must be the Kate we have heard so much about. Allow me to introduce myself. I am Hans Niedermeyer and this is my business associate Carla Roston." He extended his hand.

"How do you do?" Kate returned his firm handshake and took the proffered seat.

"Hans and Carla are going to the casino opening, too," Matt said. "Isn't that a coincidence?"

"I am in the same business back in Germany, but we don't have a location like this. You are very lucky," said Hans.

"This guy sells casino equipment all over the world," Matt exclaimed. "I should get involved in something like this. With all my years of post-secondary education, how tough could it be?"

"You must be with Vertex Gaming." When Hans nodded, Kate continued. "I've spoken at length to Ursula Bensch in your Public Affairs Department."

"Beautiful girl, Ursula. I know her well." Hans smiled widely, his super-white teeth in stark contrast to his deep tan.

"Vertex won the bid to supply all the video lottery terminals and software to the new casino," Kate told Matt.

"I know. Hans has been telling me all about it. These guys are into everything. Carla was just filling me in on her role securing joint venture opportunities." Matt nodded across the table to Carla who filled in the blanks for him.

"I find management opportunities for the company," she said.

"I didn't know Vertex was involved in casino management," said Kate.

"Mine is a relatively new division. With our expertise, you can triple or even quadruple a casino's current cash flow," Carla said.

"If it appeals to them, Carla and Hans may take on your Dragonfly Lake operation." Matt nodded his approval to Kate.

"Unfortunately, I don't think that's possible." Kate eyed them with doubt. "The lottery corporation's agreement with the government in developing these properties is contingent on managing the casinos ourselves."

Hans dismissed her remark with a flip of his diamond-laden hand. "Our professional advice is required to bring a junior property up to world standards in order to draw the serious player. I can tell you that this will not happen without our guidance."

"It will be interesting to see what happens, won't it?" Kate said, forcing a smile. Annoyed by Hans's condescending manner and Matt's blind acceptance, she explained she had to pick up some lunch for a friend.

"I'll catch you later by our stuff." Matt said. "I should have gone into business. I'm going to pick Carla's and Hans's brains a little while longer."

"That sounds like a great idea," Kate said, sincerely hoping the three of them would enjoy each other's company for the remainder of the voyage.

★ ★ ★

Armed with a tray too small for a pot of tea, cups, potato chips, and two tuna sandwiches piled high on thick brown bread, Kate made her way carefully back to her seat. She was relieved to see Moses hadn't tired of waiting for her. He had company now, though. Seated on either side of him were two native women who appeared to be in their early 50s. Both had dark hair fastened in a ponytail and wore baseball jerseys with "Bella Bella Orcas" printed on the front and "Whalesong Museum Collections" on the left sleeve.

"Let me help you with that," said the woman on Moses's left.

"Thanks," Kate said, and was relieved of the cups and heavy pot before any more tea could spill.

"This is the little girl I was telling you about," said Moses.

The woman with the tea-pot rolled her eyes. "Every woman's a 'little girl' to him—It's Kate, isn't it?"

"Yes. Kate Logan. Pleased to meet you," she said, handing Moses his sandwich. "No tomato."

"Wonderful," said Moses, picking up half of the big sandwich. "These two," he paused, "little girls, are my daughters."

"Pleased to meet you, Kate. I'm Tina," said the woman on the right as she poured a cup of tea for her dad. "I used to be little. I'm bigger now. Too big, really, but Alice has always been much bigger than me." She grinned at her sister.

"Thanks for putting up with us," Alice said, reaching over to shake hands. "Dad calling everybody a 'little girl' has become a running joke."

"See what I mean?" said Moses. "I don't get any respect anymore. When I get home, I'm going to vent about that in my new blog." He winked at Kate when his daughters flashed him surprised looks.

"Dad tells us you're interested in the history of the coast," Alice said, grabbing a potato chip. "Make sure you go ashore for the salmon barbecue when we dock in Bella Bella. The dinner's really tasty and you can take in my son's exhibit at the new museum up the beach."

"Wesley did a great job on that. I'm proud of him. And he had the good sense to go to the top and ask my advice on several things," Moses snickered.

"Is this the same Wesley that Rhys and Phil mentioned earlier?" Kate tucked into her own sandwich.

"I expect so. Wesley, Rhys, and Phil have known each other since they were kids. Thick as thieves, until Rhys moved away," Tina said. "Things started to fall apart a bit then." She cast Alice a knowing glance.

"He was just being a teenager." Alice returned fire with a steely glance back at her sister. "For them, it's all about pushing boundaries."

"I know I did," Kate said awkwardly.

Moses, in an apparent attempt to cool things down, said calmly, "Wesley's had his troubles, but it happened a long time ago and he's really cleaned up his act in the last few years. So chill, girls."

His attempt at peacekeeping made Tina and Alice laugh in spite of themselves and restored the levity to the group.

"Yeah, his Whalesong Museum Collections is going gangbusters and I still have hope the boys' Namu resort proposal will go through. That's the one that really excited him," Alice said.

"He's turned things around, that's for sure," said Tina. "You've gotta give his friend Rhys a lot of credit for that, though, don't you? He got him to stop drinking and was a godsend in that situation with Haebler's wife. Seeing the blank look on Kate's face as an invitation, she continued. "Haebler's a big bully that works for the ferries. Expects everyone to call him Captain, even when he's not working."

Alice nodded. "Absolute jackass."

"He used to beat up his wife. She was an old friend of Wesley's," Tina said.

Trying to lessen the stress she saw in Alice's eyes as her sister launched into the tale, Kate quickly swallowed her mouthful of sandwich and said, "I bet Wesley helped her out, didn't he?"

"He helped her out, all right," Tina said.

Alice interrupted. "Sarah and Wes had been sweethearts in high school. It was only natural that she came to him when she needed a friend."

"OK you two. If you're going to embarrass my new BFF with the dirty laundry, at least cut to the chase. I'm not going to be around forever, you know," Moses said. "To make a long story short, Kate—you're right. He did help Sarah out. Whenever Haebler got miserable, she'd hide at Wesley's 'til the storm blew over. It took the big dope a long time to figure that out, didn't it?" He grinned broadly at his daughters.

Alice's solemn eyes met her father's. "He figured it out, though, and one night he got all drunked up and went looking for them both."

Eager to tell the juicy part of the story, Tina interrupted. "By this time, Sarah and Wesley's relationship had picked up where it left off in high school—if you know what I mean."

"Oh, oh. What happened?" Kate asked.

"Luckily, Rhys was in town at the time. They were all partying over at Wesley's place when Haebler showed up," said Tina. "He had a knife and it could have been really ugly. Rhys was the least plastered of the bunch—largely because he had just arrived." She shook her head. "Anyway, he nailed Haebler with a right hook, knocked him out, and broke his cheekbone."

"Haebler went to the hospital and Rhys hid Wesley and Sarah down in Vancouver," Alice said.

"What did the police do?" Kate asked. "If he threatened them with a knife, surely they could lay charges?"

"Sarah never made a complaint, and he never accused Rhys of assault, either. Both sides knew they'd gone too far."

"It was a wake-up call," Moses said. "Everybody realized their lives were going to hell in a hand basket and cleaned up their acts. Rhys got Wesley and Sarah to go to

AA and he grew up and really started applying himself to that job with the newspaper. Started winning awards and the like. It was good to see."

"Speaking of awards—" Alice said.

"We've got a baseball team now." Tina gestured grandly to her jersey.

"Yup. My little girls won the tournament. Got the hardware right there." Moses pointed proudly to a trophy protruding from the duffel bag on the floor.

"The little girls are going to have to build themselves a display case if this keeps up." Tina rolled her eyes heavenward and the tension evaporated.

"You should show Kate those photo albums Phil has behind the counter. Give her a better idea of the way things used to be." Moses crumpled up his napkin. "He's got some pamphlets and information on art and festivals. Maybe you want to kayak with Wesley out to that rock Alexander Mackenzie scribbled on. City folks like to do that."

CHAPTER 5

For the next hour, Kate studied the brochures Phil had given her. The area had far more to offer that she could take in on this short business trip. She would have to return for an extended vacation. Her concentration was broken only when Phil interrupted with the PA system to ask the owner of four chickens to please return to the car deck. Apparently they had escaped from their cage and were nesting in the haunted house on the third hole of the mini golf course.

"There you are." Matt sat down beside her. "I'm so glad you dragged me up here. I'm having a great time."

"The scenery's gorgeous, isn't it?"

"I haven't seen much scenery, but I'm meeting some interesting people."

"Come out on deck with me. You won't believe the number of fish jumping out there."

"Actually, I just wanted to see how you're making out. I don't want you to think I'm ignoring you."

"Not at all," Kate said. "I've met some interesting people myself."

"Have you noticed the animosity the locals have toward developers? They'll learn though. There'll be lots of service jobs coming down the pike."

"Maybe they'd like a bigger challenge than flipping hamburgers and baiting somebody else's fishhook?"

Matt chuckled. "Pretty tough to compete with expertise like Carla's and Hans's. She's gone to get a portfolio of Vertex's properties. I thought I might buy them a drink for being so nice and showing me their stuff. You wouldn't have fifty bucks on you, would you?"

Kate sighed and passed him the money. "The local First Nations Band is hosting a salmon barbecue and cultural presentation for us when we land in Bella Bella. It sounds like fun. Shall we go?"

"I don't know. How much is it?"

"Twenty dollars each, according to my brochure."

"Let's think about it, OK?" Matt slipped the fifty dollars into his jeans pocket. "I'd better get back to Carla and Hans. Don't want to keep them waiting." Watching him hustle away, Kate shook her head and sighed.

★ ★ ★

Half an hour later, they docked at Bella Bella for a three-hour stay before embarking on the overnight portion of the trip up the inlet to Bella Coola. Kate, eager to do a little exploring, was one of the first foot passengers to disembark. Most of the children, including Phil's nemeses, the "touched-you-last" Anderson brothers, had been vacationing in the south for the summer and this stop was the end of the line for them. They flew into the arms of parents who bundled them into waiting vehicles and drove off. *Back to school next week*, Kate thought.

Impatient to get to the museum, she made her way up the beach, slipping and sliding on the strange rocks. Puzzled, she bent down and picked up a handful of the tubular brownish things.

"They're sea urchin spines," said a voice from behind. "Years of fishing for the Japanese market."

Startled, Kate looked up to see a puffing Alice slipping along behind her, an indignant red chicken under one arm.

"I didn't think I was going to catch you," Alice said.

"Your friend there probably slowed you down a bit."

"Darn bird. Houdini, that's her new name. Scared a few of the kids that were playing mini golf. Now who's afraid of a little chicken?" She patted the bird's head and it quickly nipped her finger. "Behave, or it's the soup pot for you my dear...I was trying to catch up to tell you that you don't need to walk. Wesley's got two vans at the ferry dock to transport everyone over to the museum."

They slipped and slid on sea urchin spines, back to the terminal where a group of passengers was hanging on every word an attractive dark haired man was saying. According to his mom, Wesley was 32 years old, but the fine lines at the corners of his eyes made him appear older. He raised his hand in greeting when he saw Alice then, pointing at the chicken in her arms, looked heavenward and smacked his forehead with the palm of his hand.

"Don't even ask," Alice said to him. "But it's a good thing Haebler didn't find out they were *my* chickens." She introduced Kate to Wesley as a new friend of his grandfather's, who wanted him to take special care of her. Alice and bird then made their way to an SUV on the knoll above, where Moses and Tina waved from open windows.

Wesley was warm and genuine and Kate liked him immediately. She was impressed with his museum's display of native art and artifacts, which was only a subset of a much larger travelling exhibition opening in Vancouver next week. The group enjoyed themselves for an hour at the museum before returning to a newly constructed longhouse near the ferry terminal, where they feasted on a delicious meal of salmon, roasted corn, and native bannock bread. Over dinner, Wesley had Kate in stitches with tales of the misadventures of Rhys, Phil, and himself. He also filled her in on the sites she would have to visit when she made her return trip. Throughout the evening, Matt and his two new friends were nowhere to be seen.

After thanking her host, Kate re-boarded the ferry with the others. According to Wesley, the scenery on the next part of the cruise was stunning but, as the late summer sun set behind the ferry, she knew it would have to wait until her next visit.

CHAPTER 6

T he next morning an insistent tapping from the PA system woke Kate. Phil apologized for being a nuisance at 5:30 a.m., but reminded passengers they would be docking in half an hour. He also recited directions to the Bella Coola office of "Fly and Drive Canada", for those continuing their travels by motor home. The cafeteria was open for coffee and breakfast and coin-operated showers were available on a first-come, first-served basis. He thanked everyone for travelling on the *Queen of Chilliwack* and said he hoped to see them on a return visit to the Discovery Coast.

Kate and Matt quickly packed up their belongings. She had just thanked Phil for his hospitality and purchased a souvenir t-shirt when she heard engines firing up on the car deck below and it was time to disembark.

Earlier, Matt had dismissed her suggestion that something was wrong with the car and written off the leaking fluid as, "Coming from the air-conditioner. They all do that." As they drove off the ferry, though, Kate noticed the old beater was making strange sounds—*new*, strange sounds.

A long line of passengers was making its way down the creosoted dock to the offices of "Fly and Drive" and, although it was still dark, Matt spotted Carla and Hans and honked and waved as he drove by.

"Don't worry about them," Matt said. "I told them we'd be happy to give them a ride to Dragonfly, but they have an RV reserved."

"There sure are a lot of people picking up a motor home."

"It's part of a travel package. I talked to a lot of Germans on the ferry and they've explored more of our country than we ever will."

"Where do they go?"

"They're almost all going to your casino at Dragonfly Lake to start with. The tour company's really promoting it as a destination. After, the ones that fancy themselves as cowboys drive through B.C. to Alberta, get some riding in, and fly home. Most of them, though, go clear across the country. They drive all day and cook and sleep in the RVs."

"I saw a lot of that type of thing when I was in Europe. Huge tour buses with sleeping bunks stacked on top of each other in the back."

"I think I'd like to have a shower and sleep in a real bed once in a while," Matt said.

Kate had to agree.

★ ★ ★

They stopped for breakfast at one of the few cafes in Bella Coola open so early in the morning. Kate climbed out of the car and was immediately struck by the crisp cool air and the salty scent of the beach at low tide. It smelled like adventure to her and she inhaled deeply. Inside the restaurant, a smiling woman in a blue uniform yelled a cheery, "Good Morning!" and plunked two steaming cups of coffee down in front of them before they could ask.

After a hearty meal of bacon, eggs, hotcakes, and lots more coffee, Kate felt refueled and ready to face the drive and tackle any glitches before the reception. She never expected things to go smoothly and she was never disappointed. Their fellow diners informed them they had three hours of driving ahead and to make sure they gassed up before leaving town.

They also cautioned Matt about the famous "Hill." Travelling during daylight hours was best, they said, as it reduced your chances of going over a cliff. It was also safer to be driving *up* the hill, rather than down, because there was less chance your brakes would overheat and you'd over-shoot a hairpin turn and plunge into a crevasse.

Kate had read about the notorious "Freedom Road" that the citizens of Bella Coola had constructed themselves when the government refused to help. She hadn't been too concerned at the time, thinking she was pretty comfortable with mountainous terrain. Now though, the condition of the car and the warnings from the locals had her worried.

They exited the restaurant and were approached by a middle-aged native with an armful of brochures. Grinning broadly, he proclaimed, "I am the one. Get your rental from me." He handed Kate some information and added, "Much better rates than Fly and Drive."

"Are you offering this generous deal because you saw us drive up in that old heap?" Kate laughed and pointed at their car. "I'm getting a little self-conscious."

"*That's* your car?" He stared incredulously at the rust encrusted bucket, then caught himself and apologized, saying he hadn't known they had transportation and had thought they needed an RV.

"Maybe we should rent something, Matt. Are you sure it'll make it up this 'Hill'?"

"There's nothing wrong with the car. It may look like hell, but I change the oil religiously." He turned the key and the car coughed a few times but eventually started. "It's not that old, you know. It developed those rust spots a month after I bought it. There was something wrong with the paint on this model."

CHAPTER 7

Despite grades of 18 percent, Matt's car tenaciously climbed the series of hairpin turns that eventually levelled off 5,000 feet higher on the highway leading to the casino. Once on the flat terrain, however, it didn't want to brake or corner. When they finally reached Dragonfly Lake, it groaned and swayed as Matt steered down the private road. Kate had worried they would miss the turnoff, but two TV satellite trucks perched on the side of the highway signaled they had arrived at their destination.

"That'll make Gregor happy," she said. "I hope the rest of the press I invited show up too, or there'll be hell to pay." An important part of her job was getting positive media attention for the lottery corporation, and she had been concerned this isolated location would discourage reporters. Company President Gregor Chernin delighted in seeing his name in the media and insisted that every mention of him or the lottery be clipped or recorded and presented to him each morning. Chernin kept score and was quick to reprimand Kate if his numbers fell off.

Any doubts she had, however, were put to rest when they swerved around the last corner and got a glimpse of the activity in the parking lot. Although the official opening wasn't for another six hours, the huge lot was half-full of guests' cars, media vans, and suppliers' vehicles. Twenty-five Fly and Drive motor homes were parked at one side, each bedecked with an "If You Drink—Don't Drive" bumper sticker. People bustled to and fro with dollies of chairs and banquet tables and Kate was pleased to spot her sound technicians toting cables and speakers into the building.

The resort was an impressive piece of architecture, constructed of huge logs and river rock with a First Nations influence. A dramatic porte-cochere graced the entrance, its roof supported by monstrous wooden columns carved into native totems. Suspended from the ceiling was a sparkling chandelier made of antlers. Six float planes were tied up to a long dock which extended out into the shimmering lake. When a large truck with "ABLE Party Rentals" stenciled on its side roared off from a parking spot near the front doors, Matt quickly pulled in.

Inside, a long line of guests was checking in and bellhops sped around delivering luggage. Beyond the front foyer, more antler fixtures lighted the way down a wide corridor flanked by ATM machines that led to the casino. Kate spied a western-themed bar separated from the gaming action by a totally believable indoor creek. Two stuffed Grizzly bears were fishing for salmon from the creek's rocky shore. Further on, a spacious restaurant with vaulted ceilings and huge picture windows offered a view of the lake. Inside the adjacent banquet room, members of the housekeeping staff were draping long tables for the reception.

"Kate! Where have you been? We've got a problem," shrilled a voice.

Kate spun round to see Pamela Luther, executive vice-president of Pacific Lottery, advancing toward her. Dressed impeccably, although in a manner more suited to a New York City boardroom than the Chilcotin Plateau, Pamela's curly orange hair flew back from her drawn, freckled face.

"Gregor missed the jet and the damn pilot won't go back to pick him up," she spat. "He's got to be here for the opening."

"How did he miss the plane? I booked it to fit his schedule," Kate said, referring to her chartering of the government jet.

"You know how he's always fashionably late," Pamela said. "But the pilot said he couldn't wait because right after he dropped us off here, he had to pick up the Premier in Calgary and fly him back to Victoria."

Kate took a deep breath, her mind already spinning with the contingency plans an event planner always has to have at the ready. She couldn't help but smile to herself as she imagined how Gregor Chernin must have spluttered when he found the plane had left without him. He was so accustomed to being catered to that this would be quite a slap in the face.

"Let me see what I can do," Kate said.

"Also, my ice sculpture is stuck in a broken-down van at the side of the road in Williams Lake and the champagne hasn't arrived." Pamela stuck out her chin and took a step forward until she practically stood on Kate's toes. "Make it happen." Stalking off, hair floating behind her, she paused to reprimand a staff member not draping a table to her liking, then turned back to Kate. "I'll count on seeing that ice sculpture centre stage this evening."

"Good God. What was that?" Matt asked. "She looks like she's been ridden hard and put away wet."

Kate roared with laughter. "She's told me several times she loves to ride, I just always assumed she was the one sitting in the saddle."

Unable to believe Pamela's rudeness, Matt stared after her, mouth agape.

"Hey listen," Kate said. "I've got to work fast if I'm to get Gregor's royal butt up here for the opening. Could you get my bag and laptop out of the car? I'm going to ask that lady over there if she's got a little space where I can work."

★ ★ ★

In half an hour, Kate had chartered a plane to fly Chernin from Vancouver to the local airport and located the people delivering champagne and hors-d'oeuvres who were en route, just a little behind schedule. They were happy to pick up Pamela's treasured sculpture from its disabled truck and bring it along in their refrigerated unit. She hung up the phone and wondered wryly what would befall her next.

CHAPTER 8

K ate had planned a menu featuring locally raised buf-
falo, fresh seafood, and seasonal produce over the
phone with Chef Gust. In person, she found the robust
German to be easygoing, yet extremely professional. He
was experienced at pulling off special events and things
were well in hand. Gust had already had a few run-ins with
Pamela and was quick to tell Kate about her meddling.

"That woman won't keep her hands off my food—
always sampling. I don't know where she puts it. Not to
worry, though," he flicked his wrist, "I've put up with worse."

Kate grinned and told him to text her if the sampling got out of hand. Checking next on the situation at the
expansive bar, she was pleased to see that they were also
ready for the number of guests expected that evening. The
only thing yet to arrive was the champagne for Gregor's
toast to the new business venture.

Mentally, she ran through her to do list: find president a plane-check. Locate champagne/ice sculpture-check.
Food/drinks-check. Nametags at the door, cloak room
ready, sound system working-check, check, and check
again. Gregor's banner up-rats! It had completely slipped
her mind.

Pacific's president thought himself quite a wordsmith
and wanted to make sure the catchphrase he had thought
up: "Looking for a Good Time? Want to Get Lucky?" was
captured in all the photos. Kate was on her way outside
to retrieve the risqué little ditty from the car when Chef
Gust's nemesis shrilled loudly from down the hall.

"Kate, I'm going to pick up Gregor at the airport and I want a driver and a car. I also want that hideous jalopy removed from the entrance before we get back."

Kate got Matt's attention, and pointed at him and then at Pamela as if to suggest he drive her to the airfield. Obviously panicked at the thought, he shook his head quickly and retreated to the warren of blackjack tables.

Final plans for the evening proceeded much more smoothly once Pamela left on her mission chauffeured by a brave volunteer. With some luck, Kate convinced Matt that anxiety over Gregor's absence had caused Pamela to unkindly insult his vehicle and he agreed to move it while she changed for the reception.

Kate had just finished dressing and slipped on her black pumps when Matt burst through the door to their room.

"I could've been killed...going up that hill outside Bella Coola, I could've been killed." He stumbled to the bed and sat down trembling.

When finally calm enough to speak coherently, he told Kate that when he backed the car out of its parking spot there had been a tremendous crash. Investigating, he found the car's engine had fallen out and crashed to the ground.

"If that had happened when we were driving...I could have been killed," he repeated.

"Not that it matters, but I guess I could have been, too," Kate said.

* * *

Outside, assessing the situation with the car and its regurgitated insides, Kate couldn't help but feel a little vindicated. She knew the car was dying. The problem now was how to dispose of the dead body when the wheels were pinned to the ground. She had to agree with Pamela this time. A car wreck blocking the main entrance to the building was not in keeping with the glamorous image they were trying to convey.

"Engine mounts, Kate." Gust had come out to see what all the fuss was about and now stood beside her in his white chef's coat and hat, stroking his chin and looking pensive. "Happened to me with a little compact in France." He gave the exhausted engine an obligatory kick and shook his head. "I'll bet the maintenance people can tow it somehow. Let me take care of it. You go do what you have to do. The guys delivering the champagne just arrived out back."

Kate was grateful for Gust's help; time was getting short. Racing to the loading dock at the rear of the building, she was alarmed to see Kevin, the bar manager, shaking his clipboard in the air, clearly at loggerheads with the deliveryman.

"They've delivered half the champagne we ordered," he said. "I don't know what we're going to do now." Kate didn't have to check his figures to confirm what she saw in front of her was never going to be enough for the crowd expected.

"The boss must have misread that digit there. It didn't print very well," the driver explained, pointing to the order form. "We brought along that sculpture you wanted, though," he said earnestly. "Still frozen and everything."

Silently cursing her life, Kate glanced at the paperwork and had to agree with the driver—it would have been very easy to misread his copy.

With the delivery driver gone and the sculpture in the deepest part of the freezer to firm up a bit before the big event, Kate and Kevin looked at each other dumbfounded.

The plan was for the local Native Band to bless the resort with a rather elaborate dance ceremony capped off with a champagne toast from Gregor.

"Could we mix it with something to make more? Make champagne sangria, or something like that?" she asked Kevin.

"This is premium stuff. That would be a disgusting waste," he retorted.

"What's the problem now?" Gust asked, pushing through the stainless steel doors. "Don't worry about the car, Kate. We used the little snow plough to tow it behind the maintenance shed." His eyes narrowed and his pleased expression faded when they filled him in on the champagne situation.

"Of course we can mix it with something," Gust said. "Sometimes you have to make do. What have we got a lot of?"

"Beer," said Kevin, still not inclined to be helpful.

"You know what I mean," Gust bellowed. "Let's get with the program here." He led the way to the bar where the three of them eyeballed the large selection of hard liquor and liqueurs on display.

"Cognac. How much of that have you got?" Gust asked.

"Actually, I ordered quite a bit." A clinking sound came from the cupboards under the counter where Kevin, now more interested in the challenge, was sorting through bottles. "I have a lot of schnapps. Do you think that might work?"

Armed with peach schnapps, cognac, white wine, and ginger ale, Kate, Gust and Kevin raced back to the kitchen and mixed and tasted until they had a large quantity of champagne cocktail that all three of them declared perfect for the occasion.

"It needs a name," Kate declared, brandishing her glass. "How about Dragonfly at Sunset?"

"How much of that have you had?" Gust demanded. "Dragonflies are blue; our drink here is orange."

"Spoil sport," she said. "I've got a great idea. Watch this." She dropped a little of the dry ice that had been packed around the ice sculpture into her glass and a spooky mist rose up.

"Dragonfly in the Mist. Even better."

"Yep, sounds good." Kevin nodded and sampled one of the marinated orange slices Gust had tossed into the concoction. "Let's go with that. I'm sure I've seen an orange dragonfly...Haven't I?"

"Dear God, save me from these two." Gust smacked his forehead with his palm and shook his head from side to side. "You're both cut off 'til the party's over. I'll save you each a glass."

"Make it a couple of glasses would you, Gust?" Kate asked.

* * *

Kate was distributing nametags to guests at the front door when Gregor bustled in imperiously with Pamela in hot pursuit. She was surprised to see Tom Berwick ambling casually along behind them. He smiled broadly when he caught sight of Kate. Tom was the overall boss of her department and one of her favorite people at Pacific Lottery. Whether she had a question concerning media relations, office politics, or how to calculate the odds on a lottery game, she could always count on him for direction.

Gregor's eyes, small and ferret-like in his florid face, darted about the venue, taking everything into account. Spying Kate, he whispered one last aside to Pamela then, waving with great fanfare, crossed the room and seized her in a big bear hug. The sour smell of alcohol on his breath was overwhelming, but Kate stood her ground. When he pumped her arm roughly up and down with his hot sweaty paw, though, it was all she could do to keep from wiping her hand off on her skirt.

"How about that great slogan of mine, Katie? I don't see it."

"I thought it best if I displayed it behind the podium Gregor," Kate said.

"And where is that, may I ask?"

"We're set up for the speeches and toasts down the hall in the banquet area."

"Oh," he said. "I would have preferred the formalities here under this magnificent chandelier."

"Exactly what I suggested," Pamela chimed in.

"Why don't we go see what Kate's got set up? I'm sure it'll work out fine," Tom said. "You know what a marvelous job she always does. Who else could charter you a jet on such short notice?"

"Anybody can make a phone call," Pamela said, lowering her voice when she saw Ron Boerner, the manager of the resort, and Charlie Elliott, Chief of the local native band, approaching. As Gregor shook his partners' hands and guffawed loudly at their jokes, Pamela multi-tasked—agreeing with everything they said while ushering them to the banquet area.

A lopsided grin on his broad face, Tom sidled his ample girth up to Kate. "Everything looks fantastic, kiddo... Happy to see us?"

"Always glad to see you, Tom. Not so sure about your travelling companions," she said, out of the side of her mouth. "I'm *surprised* to see you, though. Weren't you going into the hospital for some tests?"

"They cancelled at the last minute. To be on the safe side, the anesthetist wants me to lose a bit of my muffin top. Thirty pounds of it. That's a lot of muffin isn't it? That's why I was available when Gregor missed the plane. He was actually waiting around the hangar, convinced the pilot would see the error of his ways and come back to get him. I figured I'd better go over and buy the poor guy a couple of pops before he blew a gasket."

"You did a really great job loosening him up." Kate pinched her nose while giving Tom her most disapproving look. "He's got a speech to make, you know."

"Right. Good thing you mentioned that. He lost it. The speech, I mean. Sorry, kid. I got him to read it to me while we waited for the second plane...Terrific speech by the way. But we couldn't find it once we got on board. I think he dropped it."

Kate just stared.

"I was hoping you might have another copy?"

"You are going to owe *me* at least one 'pop' when this is over," she said.

"Always the consummate professional. That's why I hired you." He grinned. "Well, my job here is done. I'd better go keep the beautiful people out of trouble."

"I'm not sure you're a very good influence," she yelled, as his round body bounced down the hall. Kate flagged down one of the staff who agreed to give out nametags while she went to print off a copy of Gregor's speech.

CHAPTER 9

The reception finally began with a burst of colour and music as masked native dancers and drummers ushered in the speakers for the evening. Gregor, Ron Boerner, and Chief Elliott took their seats on the stage while Pamela, who had appointed herself Master of Ceremonies, leapt to the podium to introduce everyone.

The plan was to keep talk to a minimum, introduce the joint partners in the resort, toast the business venture, and let the guests enjoy themselves at the games. Kate felt more confident once things got underway, but realized she had been a bit hasty when, halfway through his speech, Gregor pushed it aside, plucked the microphone from its stand, and began detailing his career rise in the world of gaming.

"I'm so proud to be responsible for this opportunity for our native people and for the citizens of British Columbia." He bowed slightly. "I believe the champagne is being passed around now. Help yourselves to a glass for a toast."

"That's not the idea," Kate whispered savagely to Tom. "He's twisted everything around so they're going to toast him rather than the casino. I don't believe it."

Tom gave Kate a knowing grin and held his own glass high in a mock toast to Gregor. "Here, here," he said, then turned to Kate. "Honestly, he had the whole thing down pat in the airport, I swear."

Helplessly, she watched as Gregor snagged champagne for himself, Boerner, and Chief Elliott from a passing waiter. "He's supposed to thank the other partners, pull the drape to reveal his slogan, and propose a toast."

Tom watched Gregor's theatrics, sipped his drink, and shook his head pensively. "He's not going to do that. Nope, he's liking it too much up there. I don't think he's ever gonna get off the stage."

"Plans are in place to guarantee this beautiful site is a year-round entertainment venue. Snowmobiling, skiing, and snowshoeing will make it an irresistible destination for our visitors," Gregor continued. "I am so pleased we finally have some government officials who are not so, shall we say, colonial, but more sophisticated like we have in Europe."

The crowd applauded enthusiastically.

"Oh, terrific. Just what everyone needs to hear." Kate could tell by the elbowing and sniggering in the crowd that a number of guests had caught on to the fact the president was pretty pie-eyed. She spied the dancers in the doorway waiting to be cued for their final performance. "Tom, I've got an idea." She whispered it to him. "Wait here 'til I give you the signal." She wove her way quickly through the crowd towards the performers.

"In that regard, Mr. Chernin," came a confident voice from the audience, "I understand plans are in place to relax our current gaming regulations, as well as the structuring of developments like Dragonfly Lake. Is less accountability part of the sophisticated European system?"

There was an uncomfortable silence as everyone looked to Gregor for an answer. Kate, stepping back into the room to see what had happened, saw the lottery president, his own narrative forgotten, staring daggers at a dark-haired man standing head and shoulders above the rest of the guests.

Skilled salesman that he was, Gregor's mask of hatred faded immediately, replaced by a smile. "Excellent question...one that my communications manager, Kate Logan, will be happy to answer for you in the media room after the formalities."

Kate raised her hand to identify herself and Rhys Wilson met her gaze without a glimmer of recognition, before abruptly turning his focus back to the stage.

"My readers would prefer a quote from you, Mr. Chernin. You are, after all, the one with the global expertise."

"Ms. Logan, I can assure you, speaks for me and she has media kits available with more detail than we can go into right now." Gregor held his glass high. "Tonight's for celebrating." The crowd, well into their specially crafted, highly intoxicating Dragonfly Mists, raised their glasses with enthusiasm.

Seeing her opportunity, Kate gave the signal and the entertainers danced their way up to the stage, surrounded a tittering Gregor, and spirited him off with great ceremony. Cued by Kate, Tom clambered up on the stage. Seizing control of the situation, he saluted the departing Gregor and expressed his gratitude to Ron Boerner and Chief Elliott. To wind up, he invited a local elder in raven headdress onto the stage to bless the resort, while Boerner and the Chief pulled the drape to reveal Gregor's slogan. The audience, most of whom were finishing their second Dragonfly, clapped heartily and adjourned to the gaming tables.

Scurrying past Gregor, who was hamming it up for photographers with a vintage pull handle slot machine, Kate made her way to the media room where she answered questions for a number of the press. After an hour, there was still no sign of Wilson.

CHAPTER 10

Two Days Later

M onday morning dawned rainy and gray in Vancouver, but Kate easily spotted her lottery colleague, Charming Wong, waiting on the sidewalk, a take-out tray containing two lattes in one hand, the morning newspapers clutched in the other.

She angled her little red sports car into the curb and reached over to open the passenger door. "Good morning," Kate said, taking the hot drinks Charm passed her before climbing in. "Love the hair."

"Thanks." Charm primped her gelled, emerald green coif. "I did it myself, in honour of Pamela's latest fixation."

"What's she hung up on now? Green hair?" Kate pulled away from the curb and turned the car toward the lottery office.

"I forgot you were away for last Thursday's meeting. Pamela says it's imperative we 'go green' which, I agree, is a very fine idea. The fact that we spew out truckfuls of shiny cardboard tickets every minute of every day strikes me as a bit hypocritical, but it gave her the chance to stand on her soapbox." Charm paused to take a long drag on her coffee. "She also had me send out a media release detailing her environmental stewardship with you named as contact for further information."

"Excellent," Kate said sarcastically.

"Do you think she might be a little nicer to me? You know...now that I am actively promoting her cause." Charm tucked some green hair behind her ear.

"Not a chance." Kate stopped for a red light and eased her coffee from the cup holder. "I've had quite a weekend with the frantic little charmer, let me tell you."

"Well, do tell. How did everything go?"

Kate shuddered as she relayed the weekend's events. "I really think our liberal application of Dragonfly Mists saved the day. Everyone was so looped they wouldn't have noticed if a Grizzly bear gave the opening remarks...I must admit, I had a couple of Dragonflies with the kitchen staff when it was all over and they did go down quite nicely."

"How did you get home if the car broke down?"

"Tom insisted we hitch a ride back on the government jet. You can imagine how well that went over with your environmental stewardess."

Charm snickered. "Did Matt enjoy himself?"

"It's hard to tell." Kate braked as the two lanes of traffic merged at a construction site. "He spent most of his time with a couple of German gaming consultants and he seemed to really enjoy that, but he did lose his car. He flies back east Friday for a six-month course in GP Anesthesia."

"Well, that sounds like something he'll enjoy." Charm cleared her throat. "Now I've glanced at the papers this morning. Do you want the good news or the stressful bits?"

"Good news. I'm in the mood for good news today."

"Very well. Your weekend soiree got lots of press. Well done, Kate."

"Awesome. We like to see a happy Gregor."

"Yes, we do. However, there's this one column that may stick in the craw of our illustrious president, and it's taking up half the front page of the business section, with another excerpt promised on Wednesday. Pull over somewhere. I think you should hear this before we get to the office. It's written by our friend, Rhys Wilson, and if we weren't on the other side of the fence, I think you'd have to agree he's pretty informative, not to mention entertaining."

Kate turned onto a side street and stopped. Taking a sip of coffee, she regarded Charm with trepidation as her friend began to read aloud:

SPECIAL REPORT: WHAT ARE WE BEING DEALT?
A Three-Part Series by Rhys Wilson
PART 1: CLANDESTINE RESTRUCTURING

Last Friday, Pacific Lottery Corporation, in partnership with the First Nations Band at Dragonfly Lake, opened the first of many promised destination resort casinos. In his speech at a reception that evening, the president of the lottery corporation, Gregor Chernin, expressed delight with the magnificent 300-room complex and with the opportunities the venture affords the First Nations People and all British Columbians. (The expansion of gambling on native lands is driven by the rationale that it promotes economic and social independence.) Pressed for details concerning the structuring of the deal, however, Chernin had little to say and requests filed previously under the Freedom of Information Act have not been answered. His speech offered little information and was instead filled with his usual platitudes.

It's no secret that I am against the pointless expansion of gambling in this province, a bad accounting move because the costs outweigh the benefits. (More about this in Wednesday's column.) Adding to my concern, and that of groups such as PAGE, People Against Gambling Expansion, is the fact that as gaming expands, regulations and controls are becoming more secretive. Only hours after the resort opening, the provincial government announced the merger of the Gaming Commission and the

Gambling Investigation Office. The Commission had previously represented the participants in various gambling venues while the Investigation Office acted as watchdog.

"The purpose of this merger," says Tom Berwick, chairman of the new group and, coincidentally, a director of Pacific Lottery, "is to put the new Gaming Regulation Office in a position to keep gaming on a conservative path. We now have the best regulatory and gaming enforcement system in the country."

I think not. In the past, the gambling provisions of the Criminal Code and the regulations enacted have always been directed more at securing the government's monopolization of gambling than at preventing corrupt activity. The new situation is even worse than the previous model. Now, the individuals operating casinos and lotteries are regulating themselves. There are many opportunities for conflict of interest and no independent checks and balances.

For example, private companies may own casinos and supply personnel to operate the games, but the gambling equipment (roulette wheels, video-lottery terminals (digital slot machines), etc.), are owned by the lottery corporation. The private operators remit to the lottery corporation 30 percent of what they determine the casino's profits to be and keep the rest.

Not so widely known is that 20 percent of the remittance the casino owners pay the lottery is returned to them in the form of a Facilities Improvement Fee. Consequently, private casino expansions are being bankrolled by the lottery corporation and, in turn, the taxpayers. The Golden Fortune Casino funded $112 million in building costs in this manner. Situations like this, where there is such a huge potential for conflict of interest, demand the utmost in regulatory procedures.

The legalization of gambling tends to follow a pattern. First, government lotteries are approved and produce a lot of

revenue for the elected officials to play with. Over time, the nov-
elty wears off and competition increases as other jurisdictions
legalize gambling. When revenues decline, gambling-revenue
dependent governments seek to legalize other forms of gambling.
Government goes from a regulatory role to the role of gambling
promoter and politicians, who were voted in on a platform
denouncing the expansion of gaming, become "very excited about
our long overdue entertainment opportunities."

Our provincial history is typical of the legalization process.
When Pacific Lottery Corporation first got into the casino busi-
ness, there were no permanent casinos, only temporary events for
an approved charity, and a one-time special events license had
to be obtained. No alcohol was allowed and maximum bets were
five dollars.

Contrast then with now. One year ago, revenues were falling
due to increased competition from Washington State. The lottery
corporation responded by pressuring the Gambling Investigation
Office into raising the betting limit to $10,000. The 300 per-casino
cap on the highly addictive, highly lucrative, video lottery terminals
(VLTs) was also lifted, and the province-wide limit of 5,400 VLTs
was raised to 15,000. Alcohol now flows freely, bank machines pro-
liferate, and the hours of operation have been extended.

Is this what Tom Berwick's conservative path is all about?

Charm glanced at her friend. "Gregor is gonna freak."

Kate blew out a sigh. "I don't know where this is coming from. Wilson showed up at the resort on Friday night
and asked some pointed questions regarding regulations
and accountability. Gregor was pretty pissed at being put
on the spot like that and he basically blew him off.

"So Wilson's not far off with the 'usual platitudes'
bit." Charm grinned.

"That part's pretty accurate. What I'm getting at, though, is that this whole issue came up on the flight home, and both Tom and Gregor said Wilson was blowing smoke...Gregor actually said he was blowing smoke *out of somewhere*, if you get my drift. But both of them assured me there would be no loosening of the regulations at all."

"Wilson got some bum information?"

Kate shook her head. "He wouldn't print something he wasn't 200 percent sure of and he sure wouldn't misquote someone. Something's fishy. Let's go in and face the music; maybe there's an explanation." Plunking her cup back in the holder, Kate turned the key and they headed for the office.

CHAPTER 11

Having decided the best defense was a good offence, Kate and Charm marched into the foyer of the lottery building and swiped their key fobs for admittance to the sprawling warren of offices beyond.

"Lucas wants to see you as soon as he gets in," the guard manning reception told Kate. She grimaced. "He called from his car. Gregor, Pamela, and Tom aren't coming in today, so Lucas is in charge...sorry."

Kate had to laugh. It wasn't the guard's fault that Lucas Mardone was a calculating worm. Lucas was Kate's immediate superior and kept on a tight leash by Tom Berwick. He seemed to live for Tom's absences, when his narcissism reigned unchecked and he seized every opportunity to make the workplace hell.

Kate and Charm trooped down the long hall, past the vacant offices of Gregor, Pamela, and Lucas, to the area of the building designated for the communications department. Here, Tom's office with its large picture window anchored a bullpen formed by four cubicles: Charm's, two other colleagues', and a larger one for Kate.

Kate squeezed past boxes of promotional materials piled high in the doorway of her workspace and was dismayed to see her desk covered in pink message slips. She tossed Wilson's article down next to the phone, its blinking light indicating her voicemail was full. A super-sized sticky note marked "URGENT" was stuck to her computer monitor.

"I've been here since six o'clock and the phone hasn't stopped ringing." Kate turned as customer service representative, Jim Carver—telephone headset seated securely on his bald head, favorite coffee cup clutched in his beefy hand—struggled to steer his belly between the piled boxes. "I'm sorry, hon. Not much of a good morning, after the weekend you must have had."

Kate pointed her index finger as if it were a gun at the newspaper column on her desk and mimed pulling the trigger.

"Ah, you're up on the news." Jim grinned wryly. "I'm getting calls from across the country. The national papers ran something, too. In the column he wrote for them, Wilson focused more on how we're misinterpreting the Canadian Criminal Code. They all want to talk to Gregor."

Kate glanced at all the message slips. "Is there something particularly special about this one?" She plucked the urgent note from her monitor.

"Yeah, that guy was especially rabid—Doug McQuinn from NewsRadio. He wants Gregor on his program this afternoon to debate Wilson. Wilson has said he's available anytime."

"I'm sure he is," Kate said.

"But Gregor's not in today, Kate, and Tom's not either." Jim shot a look towards Mardone's office. "Lucas can't do it or we'll all wind up fired. Can you do it?"

"No way. It's not me they want to speak to." Kate shook her head vehemently. "Where are the two merry men, anyway?"

"Gregor's meeting with the party planner for his 60th birthday on Saturday. Apparently, it's going to be a real do." He sniffed dramatically. "Randy and I haven't received our invitation yet," he said, referring to his partner of ten years. "And I have no idea where Tom is."

Kate groaned and gathered up all the messages into a neat pile. She stared at the fat bundle in her hand. "If I was to get in my car and start driving, I bet I could be in LA by tomorrow night. Maybe I could get a job at Disneyland as a Goofy mascot. I'd fit right in at the Magic Kingdom."

Jim regarded her with concern. "C'mon back to my operations centre, kid. Randy made some of his special breakfast cookies. I think you need a couple."

"The ones with the white chocolate? That would put things in perspective." The two of them shuffled sideways out of Kate's office and back to Jim's customer service desk. "By the way, why were you here at six o'clock?" she asked.

"Tom wants me to come in that early for a while. He says it's for customer satisfaction reasons."

"But they can get the winning numbers off the Net."

"He's got a new way to record winning numbers and he says I should ease into it when it's quiet." Jim peeled the lid off a Tupperware container and held it out to Kate. "It works for me. There's no traffic at that time of the morning. I breeze right in and I beat the afternoon rush home in time to get dinner started."

Kate picked a couple of big cookies from the container. "He never told me anything about it." She took a bite and wondered what else she hadn't been told. Jim's change in hours didn't seem especially important, but there was also this issue of accountability Wilson had seized on that ran totally contrary to what she had been told.

Her thoughts were broken by a loud whistle. Looking up, she was less than thrilled to see Lucas Mardone had arrived. He pointed at her, snapped his fingers and pointed to his office. "Take another one for the road," Jim said. "You might need it."

Kate rolled her eyes and palmed another cookie. She retrieved the newspaper and message slips from her desk and walked to Lucas' office, smiling a greeting to his new secretary, Leah—the fourth since Kate had started at Pacific. *I bet the tooth fairy still visits this one,* she thought, referring to Mardone's penchant for young assistants.

Inside his office, Mardone was eyeing himself in the mirror that hung low behind his oversized desk, carefully smoothing his blonde mullet back into a curl over his collar. Unlike Kate's desk, his was devoid of anything save his slim leather attaché case, which lay unopened at one end.

"Gregor and Tom won't be in today," he said without looking at her, "so we can finally bring some efficiency to this operation." He leaned back in his chair and rested two highly polished Italian dress shoes on the open desk drawer. "Judging from what I read in this morning's paper, your junket this past weekend was pretty much a bust." He turned his beady-eyed stare directly on her. "This corporation doesn't exist to pay your travel bills, you know. I expect good press and lots of it. I, myself, will be going over your budget and expense reports with a fine toothed comb."

He removed his legs from the drawer and flipped open his briefcase, which he rifled through with impatience. "I have the performance evaluations for everyone in your group right here and they are not up to my standards. If Gregor would leave the marketing and the media to myself, rather than amateur hour here," he flipped his wrist in Kate's direction, "we wouldn't find ourselves in shitty situations all the time."

Although seething inside, Kate nodded her head in an attempt to keep from laughing as, from the reflection in Mardone's mirror, she could see the sole content of his briefcase was one banana. She glanced down at the stack of phone messages in her hand, knowing if she made eye contact with him, she would crack up.

"We've received a number of inquiries concerning this morning's column in the business section," she said. "A request to debate Rhys Wilson, live this afternoon over at NewsRadio, stands out as more urgent than the rest. Shall I arrange a driver for you, or would you prefer to take your own car?"

Kate watched Mardone's colour fade from blotchy red to deathly white. He stared at her for a moment and all was quiet save for the tapping of his pen on the desk. Then he shook his head and grinned. "You haven't a clue, do you? You really must grow a brain or borrow some sense from somebody. I don't go running after these people. They come to myself. If they're lucky, I'll talk to them."

"All the crisis management skills I was taught say to meet situations like this head on. If we don't respond to the media, they'll think we're hiding something. My problem is I don't know anything about it, nor where Wilson got his information, so I wouldn't be able to discuss it intelligently."

"No secret there," he snapped. "You have to understand that what you learned in school has very little to do with reality. You have no experience."

"I've worked in this field for seven years."

He gave her a condescending snort. "These things blow over. I can guarantee you Gregor won't lower himself to talk to this parasite. I'm not going to and I'm not authorizing you to talk to him either."

"So what do you want me to do with all the media enquiries?"

"I want you to deny everything. Right now, your focus is on completing your expense reports. I want them on my desk by noon."

Kate walked to the door and turned around in one last attempt to reason with him.

"We're done here. Noon. On my desk by noon." Mardone gave her a challenging stare, then eyed her up and down and his snarl morphed into an oily smile. "How old are you anyway?" he asked.

Her skin crawling, Kate managed to utter, "Noon, right," before ducking out the door.

* * *

Charm, Jim, and two temps obediently answered Wilson's inquiries and all the other media calls with "no comment" and took the resulting wrath. Wrapped up in his party plans, Gregor refused to come in or comment for the press. Tom, who Kate had always been able to depend on, seemed to have gone AWOL. Even his personal cell phone rang straight through to voicemail and she worried for his health as she felt there was more wrong than he was admitting.

CHAPTER 12

SPECIAL REPORT: WHAT ARE WE BEING DEALT?
A Three-Part Series by Rhys Wilson
PART 2: GAMBLING'S COST TO SOCIETY

Unfortunately, government's addiction to gambling has been transmitted to the public. Experts say gambling is North America's fastest growing addictive behavior and the number of addicts has not yet peaked. We need to consider if this is a wise way to raise revenues because the mounting costs far exceed the benefits.

The biggest cost is associated with players who are unable to control their urge to gamble. It is conservatively estimated that seven million people in North America have a gambling problem that is out of control, but the scope of the problem is tragically underestimated because so little research has been done. We do know, however, that the recent increase in pathological gamblers is strongly correlated to the increase in legalized gambling opportunities.

In 2003, a city councilor in Wildtown, Missouri, alarmed by what he perceived as an increase in crime since the arrival of small scale legalized gambling, conducted a survey that indicated two percent of the population were problem gamblers. A study three years later, after the town introduced riverboat casinos and casinos on native lands, showed the percentage of addicted citizens had jumped to twelve. These findings are consistent with those that show that when gambling activities are legalized, the number of addicted gamblers increases by 200 to 500 percent.

"The key to addiction is proximity," says Professor Ivan Yoblansky. "The more access, the greater the problem." This enormous burden is borne by governments, which increase taxes

to cover social-welfare costs. Yoblansky's 2012 study estimates addicted gamblers cost the U.S. between 33 and 54 billion dollars per year.

Every addicted gambler affects from seven to seventeen other people. (Compare this with alcoholics who negatively impact seven individuals). Shortly after the introduction of legalized gambling in the Canadian community of Four Rivers, child abuse cases increased 43 percent, police costs increased 90 percent, and domestic violence and assaults rose 80 percent. Problem gamblers suffer an inordinate amount of stress-related disorders and they are more likely to default on debts, pass bad cheques, lose their jobs, borrow money from loan sharks, and steal from family and friends. In addition, studies indicate that 15-25 percent of all compulsive gamblers attempt suicide.

When I raised the issue of the lack of gambling addiction treatment facilities in British Columbia, I was sharply rebuked by Pamela Luther, executive vice president of Pacific Lottery Corporation. Employing the credit-hogging lingo common to bureaucrats, she explained that she has established the "Challenged Gamblers Fund" to counsel those with "gaming control issues." Probing further, I discovered that the Fund's counsellors are expected to promote the services they offer the community, but are forbidden to mention the perils of gambling. (Compare this with a drug counsellor unable to discuss the dangers of narcotics with his client.) Failure to abide by the gambling-neutral directive results in an end to referrals from Pacific Lottery—the counsellors' only source of revenue.

Raising the provincial sales tax by one percent would raise more revenue than the proceeds of the lottery combined with all other legalized gambling—without the costs to families and society. But raising the sales tax, a political hot button, would demand government courage, and that is in very short supply.

"For chrissake." Gregor slammed his meaty fist down on his desk Wednesday morning. "What motivates this bugger anyway?" He hurled the newspaper containing Wilson's second column to the floor. "I want to know where he's getting these figures. I've never seen these figures." Kate opened her mouth to interject but was quickly interrupted. "Put out a press release refuting everything he says. And make sure you attach a photo of me—the new one with Mocha and the puppies," he said, referring to his Standard Poodle and her brood.

CHAPTER 13

The next morning, Kate had a problem. Following up on Gregor's demand for a media release, she had checked into the social costs of gambling and found where Wilson got his figures—from well-documented think tanks and well respected medical sociologists. The studies Kate tracked down concluded that gambling costs government at least two dollars for every dollar taken in. She stared at her computer screen and was grateful Wilson only had limited space for his column, because she was looking at a truckload of data that he could have included to support his argument. Sighing, she wondered how she was going to draft the release Gregor wanted. She pushed her chair back and stretched her arms out wide, making contact with someone in the process.

"Whoa. Watch out. Not after everything I did to get these just right." Kate spun her chair around to find Tom standing behind her with a take-out tray of drinks and a bag of something that smelled like fresh doughnuts. "It's Charm's that's the problem: half-caf, soy here, no foam there. I think I got it right. But by the time the barista guy got all the extra stuff in it, the coffee part had gone cold."

"No problemo. I'll nuke it." Charm pushed into Kate's office and took the cup from Tom. "What a treat, is this a half—"

"Half-caf, no foam, soy latte in an extra-large cup—with a shot of vanilla," Tom said. He put Kate's coffee and the pastry bag down on her desk.

"I like a man who pays attention. And in the bag, we have?" Charm took a seat on Kate's desk and made exaggerated sniffing noises. Tom rolled his eyes and opened the bag for her inspection. "Crullers. You remembered." She plucked one from the bag and took a bite. "So where've you been?"

"Yeah, where've you been?" Kate sipped her coffee and pointed at the computer screen. "You're going to need more than doughnuts to get out of this one, buster."

"Sorry about that. I know you've been busy," Tom said. Kate and Charm narrowed their eyes and shot each other a glance, exaggerated for his benefit. "I had some things to take care of that just couldn't wait." He shrugged off his coat, tossed it atop the mountain of boxes, then took a step back and eyed the pile. "What's all this garbage?"

"Advertising and counter danglers for Pamela's Valentine scratch tickets," Kate said. "When you scratch off the foil, the ticket smells like cinnamon hearts." Tom stared at her in disbelief. "She wants to keep it a secret until closer to February 14th, so she thought she'd store all the promo info here. That way, the warehouse guys won't let the cat out of the bag." Kate pressed her lips tightly together in an exasperated smile.

"She's fast-tracking another ticket—one with an environmentally friendly theme." Charm reached for another doughnut. "Smells like a pine tree when you scratch it."

"She can't leave this stuff here for four months," Tom said.

"I haven't had time to deal with it." Kate indicated the work piled high on her desk.

"Never mind. I'll get rid of it. Charm, can I ask you to take Jim his coffee and doughnut? Before you eat them all, that is." He grinned at her sweetly.

Charm glanced from Tom to Kate and licked the icing from her fingers. Raising a questioning eyebrow, she turned and left with Jim's treat.

Tom watched her walk to the customer service desk. "I think we should make sure all her drinks are only half-caf." He looked over at Kate and cringed when he caught the look on her face.

"I'm sorry I left you hanging out to dry. Believe me, it couldn't be helped."

As he stood with doughnut and coffee in hand, hair unruly, shirt hanging out, and sincerity coming through loud and clear, Kate sighed and couldn't stay mad at him.

"Next time, could you leave me a number where you can be reached? Some things came up where a little info from you would have been all I needed."

He nodded and squinted at her computer screen. "What are you working on now?"

Kate explained the situation she was in with Gregor demanding a press release contesting the facts in Wilson's column.

"The silly ass. He's got to learn when to keep his mouth shut. I'm going in to see him right now on another matter. Print me what you've got there and I'll straighten it out."

Grateful to have one thing off her plate, Kate made Tom a copy. "You're not going anywhere today, are you?" she asked. "I've got a few things to update you on."

"Nope, here all day. Let's do lunch at that new Chinese place. You can fill me in then." Grinning, he sidled his large self past the boxes, waving adieu with Kate's damning data.

Tom raised his teacup in a toast as Kate approached his corner table at Golden Happiness Restaurant.

"To you," he said. "Armed with your analysis, I managed to talk Gregor out of his self-incriminating press release." He hung his head slightly. "Of course, I had to promise you would destroy all the research you did and that we would issue something instead on how his expertise in the gaming world insures compliance and precludes crime."

Kate plunked down in her chair and stared at him.

"Come on. It'll be fun. Let's fit a bit on the smelly scratch tickets in there somewhere."

The waitress took their order and Kate pulled her to-do list from her bag.

Tom glanced at her lengthy notes. "Ugh, now I know why my doctor cringes when I show him my list of complaints." He shook two pills from a prescription bottle pulled from his jacket pocket, threw them to the back of his throat and chased them down with some water. "Excuse me," he said. "I forgot them earlier."

From his manner, Kate didn't know whether she should inquire about his health or let it go. Deciding to stick to business, she told him they probably wouldn't be in this situation with Wilson if the reporter's questions had been addressed in the past, rather than ignored as Mardone wanted to continue to do.

"I've never worked with anyone like Mardone," Kate said. "He makes up his own rules as he goes along—he lies, and he's rude. What's his problem, anyway?"

"He's short."

"He's not that short."

"No, really. I think he has issues with it." Tom signaled the waitress for more tea. "Lucas isn't really that bad a guy. He doesn't see himself as 'rude', he sees himself as—"

"A Type A personality. I've heard that a thousand times."

Tom laughed. "That's what he says he is. He's been with the corporation longer than I have and I think he's got a bit of a chip on his shoulder. He feels he should have gotten my job."

Kate shrugged. "Doesn't seem capable of taking the responsibility. He totally blew off this new situation with the Kinetic Keno software. Did you hear about that?"

He nodded. "The computer hasn't been drawing the winning numbers at random. I heard about it this morning. Who discovered that anyway?" Tom raised his eyebrows in appreciation as the waitress placed their food in front of them.

"I guess I did. Not rocket science or anything. I was reviewing those new reports you asked Jim for and something seemed a little odd." She squinted sideways at Tom. "Lucas got really worked up and told me I didn't know what I was talking about because I'm a girl and, consequently, can't add or subtract."

"Well, he's wrong—you're right. There's a glitch in the software and it doesn't draw any number between 50 and 60. Players can choose them, but they won't be drawn."

"But doesn't that mean we've been selling tickets with bogus odds for the last two months."

"Nobody but you caught on and the computer guys should have it fixed by tomorrow. So, Gregor says we keep it under our hat."

"I'm going to have to get a bigger hat." Kate tapped

her chopsticks on top of her head. "There's no more room under this one."

"Let it go." Tom flicked his chopsticks dismissively and winced when some chow mein noodles sailed across the room. He pressed his lips together. "Kate, have I not introduced you to my Code: 'How to Succeed as a Bureaucrat'?" He put down his chopsticks, extracted a folded paper from his pocket, and read:

'Go placidly among the politics and the decision-making.
Avoid ambitious and efficient persons;
They are a vexation to the spirit,
and many fears are born of overwork.
Always put *your* career first, and always take note of other people's mistakes,
for they can be very valuable.
Exercise caution, for the service is full of trickery,
But don't let this stop you from giving verbal orders,
Just never put anything down in writing.
When in doubt, speak convincingly and, when in trouble, delegate.
If you cannot convince others, try to confuse them,
and make sure they are less sure of themselves than you are.
Remember, with all its sham, drudgery, and broken dreams, government service offers a regular cheque and, undoubtedly,
things are unfolding as they should.
Always be seen with the right executives and strive to look important,
For one ounce of image is worth a pound of performance.'

He swept his arms open in a grand ta-dah gesture, stopping just short of knocking his water glass over. "Do you get the bit about working hard not being the path to success? Not in a government job, Kate. I appreciate your dedication, but quit knocking yourself out. That's not what we're here for." He beckoned to the waitress. "Just go along to get along...or they won't know what to do with you." He gave her a tight smile. "Life's complicated, huh?"

"Yikes, and I thought this was 'just lunch.'"

The waitress cleared their plates and returned with the deep fried bananas Tom had ordered for dessert.

Kate sighed. "I was saving the best for last. But I'm not sure if you want to hear it now."

He let out a bark of laughter. "Lay it on me kid. But don't forget what I said, OK?"

"Based on what you just told me, I guess Lucas was following The Code when he told me to ignore the press. But shouldn't we do something about this situation with Wilson? He's said some pretty inflammatory things about you, too."

Tom snorted. "You can't fault the guy for doing his job. The Code doesn't apply so much to private enterprise. And I've gotta give him credit for making some pretty good points." He nicked a fried banana off the plate.

"You're taking this far better than I would. Does your Code have that much of a calming effect on you?"

"It's a mantra-type of thing. I repeat it over and over." He waved his chopsticks dramatically, then caught the look on her face. "I'm kidding. But I'm not going to let Wilson raise my blood pressure. Gregor, on the other hand, figures it's war. He's in his 'never retreat, never surrender, never apologize' mode. This morning he called Wilson a slanted, supercilious little twit with the ethics of a cockroach, which I thought was pretty funny."

"That's something coming from Gregor, Mr. Ethics, who just screwed a bunch of people out of their Keno winnings."

"That's our Gregor."

Kate shook her head. "Oh, one other thing. I was surprised to see you quoted in Wilson's column Monday. When did you talk to him?"

"I didn't. Listen, don't get me wrong about the guy. He can't be trusted." Tom stared at Kate with an intensity that suggested something boiling just below the surface. "When he submits a request for corporate information, it goes straight to the bottom of my to-do list. I'll get something on him yet." With an effort, he stood up. "Tell Jim I want the winning number forms from the last few days, would you? He's late with them again."

Remembering the conversation she and Jim had had concerning Tom's new pointless paperwork, Kate nodded, nonetheless.

As they wove their way between the tightly packed tables and out of the restaurant, Tom said, "Always remember The Code—especially the part about noting other people's mistakes."

CHAPTER 14

Returning to the office after her baffling lunch conversation with Tom, Kate was delighted to receive a call from Wesley inviting her to the opening of his Whalesong Collections exhibit at the Museum of Anthropology the next night. The museum, world renowned for showcasing First Nations history, was housed in a spectacular concrete and glass building at the University of British Columbia. The recent interior renovation incorporated display units custom-built by the same firm that had worked on the Louvre. Floor to ceiling windows along the entire north side of the building provided a breathtaking view of Burrard Inlet.

Walking from the parking lot to the museum the next evening, Kate grimaced as the wind played havoc with her hair. She felt strange being a guest at an event, rather than the person doing all the planning and worrying. The wild breeze at the tip of the Point Grey peninsula smelled fresh and clean, however, and after last weekend's fiasco, she thought it felt pretty good.

Wesley greeted Kate at the entrance, looking especially attractive in a black suit, white shirt, and silk tie screened with a native design. He took her coat and, peering about the assembled throng a half-level below, beckoned to Tina and Alice who hustled over. The shorts and baseball jerseys she had last seen them in were long gone. Tina, her hair looped up in a dramatic updo, wore a violet and black floor-length gown from a native fashion designer whose work Kate recognized. Alice was dressed in a tailored black suit with a silver orca motif tastefully embroidered on the lapels of the long jacket. They looked fantastic and Kate was quick to tell them so.

Alice gave her a hug, stepped back, and eyed her from head to toe. "You are seriously gorgeous, yourself. Let's have a refreshment to celebrate us all looking *so* stunning."

"Any excuse for a party. That's what dad always says." Tina linked elbows with Kate and led the way to the bar. "I'm so glad you were able to come," she said, passing Kate and Alice a flute of champagne. "Wesley wasn't sure you'd be able to make it on such short notice."

"Are you kidding? There's no way I'd miss this." Kate scanned the carvings, totems, cedar baskets, and artifacts exhibited on the floor, then glanced up to take in the forest of colourful masks suspended overhead. "It's just spectacular. And I see you've got all the brass here." She inclined her head at the politicians and dignitaries in the crowd.

"He's really happy now, you know. After all these years, it's finally coming together," Alice said, watching the ease with which her son interacted with the guests. "He flies home Tuesday for three weeks and then takes the exhibit on the road to Ottawa and London."

"Dad was sorry he had to miss the festivities," Tina said. "He planned to fly down with us but had to cancel at the last minute. He's entered a backgammon tournament on the Net."

"He booked the flight figuring he'd lose after a game or two and get kicked out of the tourney early—but the old goat keeps winning," Alice said. "He's totally into it. He says his spirit helper is watching over him."

"To Moses and the Spirit," Kate said as she and the sisters clinked glasses.

"I want to show you the most recent addition to the exhibit." Alice hustled across the room to an illuminated case containing a small carved figure playing a stringed instrument that resembled the neck of a guitar. Alice explained it had been found by kids a couple of winters ago after a terrific storm uprooted a lot of trees around Bella Bella. "The carbon dating report just came back, and the little guy is from 2,000 BCE. The archaeologists say it suggests Chinese explorers were here 4000 years ago. Sheds a whole new light on history."

Tina, Alice, and Kate had leaned in for a closer look at the bewitching little musician when Wesley approached to steal his mom and aunt away for some introductions. A short time later, Kate's concentration was again broken by gales of laughter. She glanced toward the entrance and was surprised to see Rhys Wilson being greeted with great enthusiasm by Alice and her sister. They seemed to be kidding him along, or expressing concern, Kate couldn't tell which—especially since she was trying very hard not to stare. She could see he had dressed up for the occasion and guessed the sisters were ribbing him because they had caught him in a jacket and tie.

When he turned around to greet someone, Wilson caught sight of Kate and his expression changed from jovial to surprised. He descended the few steps to the exhibit floor, seized a glass of champagne from a passing server, and strode purposefully toward her, his broad shoulders slicing through the crowd. Kate, meanwhile, was trying to nonchalantly sidestep into a nearby washroom when she realized the sign on the door said "MEN."

"You seem to have trouble returning my calls." Wilson's voice had an edge to it.

She turned toward him, away from her feigned fascination in a map adjacent the Men's Room, and immediately saw the reason for the sisters' concern.

"What happened?" she asked, gaping at Wilson's swollen black eye.

Wilson returned her astonished stare with an inquiring stare of his own and was silent for a moment. "You don't know, do you?"

"Know what? What are you talking about?" She shook her head in confusion.

"Your goons at Dragonfly Lake 'escorted' me out of your reception. I'm told I ask too many questions." With Kate still staring at him dumbfounded, Wilson continued, "The three of them tried to beat the crap out of me and I'm pretty sure your friend, Berwick, put them up to it."

"Why would Tom do something like that? Besides, he was with me all night—helping me deal with our drunk president." She cringed. "I can't believe this. I'm so sorry. Does it hurt?"

Seemingly convinced of Kate's ignorance in the matter, Wilson shrugged. "It's much better than it was; it was swollen shut on Monday." Grinning slyly he said, "You should see the other guys," took a sip of champagne, and accepted an hors d'oeuvre from a waiter. "Of course, I wouldn't want this to tarnish my image as a model of decorum and respectability."

"I have an idea your image was already in need of a good polish." The corners of her mouth turned up just slightly.

"I thought you might be interested in what I found out about the murder in Namu, the one my friend Eugene was arrested for." Wilson swallowed the last of his canapé and reported the victim had died of a heart attack and must have fallen into the water and floated away on the tide. Unable to tie Eugene Simon to the death, the police had released Wilson's childhood friend.

"Ridiculous to think somebody would do that for an A'Climatize jacket," Kate said, helping herself to more food when a waiter approached.

"You are going to have to get yourself a jacket—maybe a green one to match those green with envy eyes," he joked, then his eyes grew darker. "Seriously, though, the poor guy's dead and I think the circumstances are pretty odd." Wilson looked pensively out the tall windows at one of the last cruise ships of the season to leave Vancouver harbor.

"A buddy of mine was hired to fly the victim's friends from Mystic River to your party at Dragonfly, and I hitched a ride with them. It's only a short hop as the crow flies. I talked with some of them on the plane and, with friends like that, Vogel didn't need any enemies."

Caught with her mouth full of smoked salmon, Kate nodded to encourage him to continue.

"Vogel was their boss. Maybe that was part of the problem. They all worked for a company called Vertex Gaming out of Germany. But none of them seemed to give a damn about Vogel, or the coroner's findings. I understand he had a family, but they didn't care." Wilson shook his head. "They seemed quite happy this would mean the end to his micro-management."

At the mention of Vertex, Kate choked on her cracker. The night before, Matt had pressed Kate for her opinion on investing in Vertex Gaming and seemed disappointed in her negative reaction. When she left their condo that evening for Wesley's reception, Matt had been packing for his six month's stay back east, thrilled he had made arrangements to meet Carla and Hans at a casino in Ontario.

Tuning back into the conversation, Kate heard Wilson say, "I did a bit of research and Vertex has got quite a checkered past, something for everyone: racketeering, bribery, fraud, extortion." He watched the last of the sparkling cruise ship disappear. "I think this deserves some looking into."

"While you do that, I'm going to find out who sicced those security guards on you," Kate said.

Wilson's brown eyes narrowed. "Leave it alone, Kate. Those guys weren't messing around and I don't want them coming after you."

"It wouldn't hurt if I asked a few casual questions. I could ask Tom—play dumb. He'll tell me if he knows anything."

"No offence, but you're not that good an actor." He shook his head slightly. "I saw you trying to avoid me by sneaking into the men's room. Promise me you'll leave it alone, OK?"

Taken aback by the conviction in his voice, Kate assured him she wouldn't say anything, but an uneasy silence fell between them. She was grateful when they were approached by Wesley and a gentleman she recognized as Richard Stahl, the government's Minister of Native Affairs.

The politician introduced himself to Kate, clasping her hand in both of his and holding it for longer than she thought necessary. She hastily complimented Wesley on the work he had done, deftly extracting her hand to indicate one exhibit in particular. Undeterred, Stahl turned his attention to Wilson, ribbing him about his black eye and asking if it was payback for his recent columns.

"You've been busy," Stahl said.

"I've been on a bit of a roll, lately," Wilson agreed. "Might be headed straight for a cliff." "You'd better watch out, my friend, with only one good eye, you might not see it coming." Stahl snorted loudly and Wilson laughed good-naturedly along with him. After some more bantering, he ambled off to the bar, shaking hands and patting the backs he met along the way.

"Sorry about that, Kate," Wesley said. "He's really harmless...He also happens to be really obnoxious. But maybe you're used to politicians?" he asked, raising an eyebrow.

"I'm learning more all the time," Kate said, recalling Tom and his precious Code.

Wesley gave a little finger wave of acknowledgment to the docent beckoning him from the podium across the room. "They want me to say something," he said. "I hate public speaking. I'm more of a behind-the-scenes type of guy. I need a preachy guy like Rhys to pinch hit for me." He grinned at the two of them. "On the other hand, with that shiner, he'd probably scare away all my honoured guests." He blew out a sigh of resignation and made his way to the podium.

Seizing the break in conversation to make an exit, Kate told Wilson she had to drive her friend to the airport, and immediately wondered why she hadn't said her "boy-friend." Turning to go, she was reminded of something.

"In your column Monday, you quoted Pamela Luther and Tom Berwick. When did you talk to them?"

"Last week. Wednesday...No, it was Tuesday morning. They said you weren't available."

CHAPTER 15

Charm climbed into the car and plopped the morning newspapers down in her lap.

"You never disappoint," Kate said, acknowledging her friend's latest hairstyle. "Did you do it yourself?"

Charm patted her handiwork. "I had to get my landlady to buzz the very back of the brown half."

"That would be tough to do on your own." Kate regarded the half of Charm's head that had been dyed brown and shorn off almost to the scalp. The other half was an inch longer, gelled up like a porcupine and retained last week's emerald green colour. "What's your theme this time?"

"Global warming." Charm made a "tut-tut" sound to signal her disappointment. "Kate, I'm shocked, a communications professional like yourself. I have deforestation on the one side, a greenhouse effect on the other. Isn't it obvious?"

"It was on the tip of my tongue, but you know how slow I am before coffee." Kate giggled and steered away from the curb.

"I was going to bleach the green side white to represent melting icebergs, but I ran out of time and decided to save a step."

"It's perfect the way it is. Your point is well made."

"Do you really think so?" Charm sipped her coffee and sighed. "No decaf this morning. Monday, it's just gotta be hi-test. Did Matt make his flight Friday night?"

"Yep. I left Wesley's reception early and drove him to the airport. So he's gone for six months."

"Doesn't seem like too much of a sacrifice to get that certification. Gives you the chance to get out and do something different, too." Charm glanced sideways at her friend to see if she got a reaction. "Speaking of different things, how was the reception?"

"I learned a whole lot and I'm not just talking native culture. I was checking out the exhibits with Wesley's mom and aunt when Wilson showed up." Kate shrugged. "I don't know why I was surprised. He and Wesley are best friends. I was just a little worried he might be annoyed at us for evading his calls and e-mails."

"I've talked to him on the phone," Charm said. "Does he look as good as he sounds?"

Kate changed lanes to avoid a car negotiating a left-hand turn. "I agree he can sound pretty good if he's trying to worm something out of you. But he wasn't looking very GQ Friday night." Kate recapped the story about the fistfight.

"Good God. Scary. I always thought the toughest part of a press conference was getting the press to turn up. Beating them up when they show up seems less than hospitable."

"I don't know what to make of the things he said. He told me he had spoken to both Tom and Pamela regarding his column, but Tom emphatically denies that. And Wilson would have no reason to make up the fist-fight story, and believe me, he was definitely in a battle with somebody. He's pretty confrontational and I can see how he'd piss people off."

Charm cleared her throat. "On that note, we both know we're avoiding the inevitable. Shall we bite the bullet and see how much he's gonna piss *us* off this morning?" She shook the business section free from the newspaper.

77

"I guess," Kate said with resignation. "Do you want me to pull over again?"

"Best if you do. It's the last of his special reports and if he winds it up with a real bang, I don't want you wrapping your shiny new car around a tree."

Kate stopped at the side of the road and killed the engine.

Charm scanned Wilson's article and sighed. "You're right. He's much friendlier on the phone."

SPECIAL REPORT: WHAT ARE WE BEING DEALT?
A Three-Part Series by Rhys Wilson
PART 3: A DARKER SIDE

This week, Pacific Lottery Corporation launched a major offensive to try and convince us we don't know what they know: legalized gambling breeds crime. Data from established gambling communities points overwhelmingly to a link between criminal activity and legalized gambling.

Three years after it legalized gambling, Atlantic City rose from fiftieth to first in per capita crime in the U.S.A., and the state of Nevada constantly ranks near the top. The crime rate in established Canadian gambling communities follows the same pattern, and newer gambling venues, limited, destination, or charitable, are no better. In Golden Oaks, Ontario, home of Canada's richest casino, rape, robbery, and car theft increased more than 400 percent in the two years following the casino's opening. Three years after permitting limited stakes casinos, serious crime in Harristown, Manitoba, leapt 93 percent. In every city in which casinos have been introduced, the marked increase in crime can be attributed to gambling.

Organized crime and money laundering typically go hand-in-hand with casino operations. Organized crime has successfully infiltrated ancillary businesses such as slot machine maintenance and been caught offering million dollar payoffs to legislators. Another tactic is offering operators kickbacks for allowing money laundering. In some areas of the U.S.A. and Europe, tax evasion and disguising the ownership of casinos through the use of nominee shareholders, have become rampant. Loan sharks lurking among the players run sophisticated operations with mobile apps. A shark might loan a borrower $10,000 with the provision he be repaid $20,000 in a month.

For law enforcement officers, the connection between casinos and crime is a no-brainer. In Golden Oaks, the casino pays for the salaries, bikes, cars, uniforms, and guns of thirty-five extra police officers to patrol the area around the casino. Some of these officers tell me the unconventional arrangements keep them from speaking freely about the impact of casinos on their city. Others are unwilling to go on record because they fear retaliation from the provincial government. "It would be career suicide," one officer states.

Seven years ago, an independent study commissioned by the British Columbia government, under pressure from anti-gambling lobbyists, concluded, "The introduction of casinos to the provincial gaming menu will result in an increase in violent crime, insurance fraud, white collar and juvenile crime, alcohol and drug related crime, domestic violence, and organized crime of all types."

Tom Berwick, Chairman of the Gaming Regulation Office, initially denied there could be an escalation in crime. When presented with the facts, however, he put some spin on his quote: "It would be a mistake to link the casinos to any increase in crime. Any escalation would be solely a factor of more people visiting these communities."

We have the potential for criminal operations in our lottery system and the officials at Pacific either have no sense of how *to prevent these problems or are willingly turning a blind eye. Something is fundamentally wrong, no matter how big a smoke screen they put up.*

★ ★ ★

Kate dumped her coat and bag at her desk, noted the light on her phone signaling her voicemail was already full, and decided she needed another coffee before making her first move. Coffee as a lifeline was concerning her lately but, as quickly as she entertained the thought of cutting down, she reminded herself that coffee dependency was pretty innocuous compared to the three martini lunches of old.

She was returning from the cafeteria, a hot cup clutched possessively in her hand, when she heard a loud, "Hey," and glanced towards Mardone's office, then gave herself a mental kick in the head. *Next time, Logan, keep right on walking.* She reluctantly approached Mardone's office where he refused to acknowledge her, instead giving Kate a full profile view of the new chunky blond highlights in his hair. He really should consult Charm the next time he has the urge to try something new, she thought. Somebody has totally overdone it in an attempt at "surfer chic."

"Glad you're finding some levity in the situation this morning," he said, apparently noting the beginnings of a smile. "Considering what I read in the paper, if I were you, I'd be concerned I might not have a job tomorrow." Kate's attempt to explain the situation was quickly cut off when Mardone shoved his palm in her direction. There was a cold silence as he slowly made a steeple with his fingers. "But what do I care? Media relations are your business. Yours and Tom's—so I'm told."

Recalling the Code Tom had recited to her at lunch

80

and his advice regarding working in a bureaucracy, Kate forced herself to remain calm. This was supposed to enable you to keep your wits about you and stop you from saying things you shouldn't. So she stood in the office as he raged, nodding in agreement, hoping she was projecting an empathy that she really didn't feel.

"Obviously you're spreading yourself a little thin, exhausting your efforts on other matters. I'm speaking, of course, of your investigation of the Kinetic Keno programming glitch," he said.

Kate let Mardone rant on, divulging more and more information as he became angrier. Her ears pricked up when he said he had been aware of the faulty Keno programming for some time.

"My door is always open. I don't understand why you didn't bring this to myself, instead of so obviously grandstanding. We are supposed to be a team here you know," he fumed.

"Lucas, I stumbled on some peculiar data that I wasn't even looking for and I dropped a quick memo to Gregor. I certainly wasn't insinuating you weren't doing your job."

Mardone stared at Kate. His eyes were wild and frightening and bore right through her. "You don't seem to realize that business is war," he snapped. "And in war, you get rid of incompetents. Unfortunately, this company is too soft and incompetents are permitted to stick around long after they should be dead and buried." His face took on an evil sneer and his speech an accent Kate couldn't identify. "They stick their noses where they don't belong and enable the media to prey on us." He stared at her with malevolence, his teeth clenched fiercely.

Probably because she had maintained her calm up to this point, Kate was still thinking clearly enough to remember reading that, "The victor in business *isn't* the person who yells the loudest, but the one who stays the coolest." Her problem was she couldn't remember what to do when you feared a colleague might leap over his desk and physically assault you. Tongue-tied and frozen in the doorway, Kate's eyes flicked to Lucas's secretary, Leah, at her desk outside Mardone's office. She had obviously been eavesdropping and Kate was aggravated to see her smirking as she pretended to organize papers. Thankfully, this galvanized both Kate's brain and her tongue into action.

She swung the office door closed on prying ears and, without apologizing, because she remembered it was a no-no, she told Lucas she understood why he was angry and that if a similar situation arose again, she would certainly bring it to him first. Surprisingly, the redness in his face began to dissipate and his neck muscles weren't protruding to the extent they had before. He seemed to accept her assurances as an apology, although he did make sure he squeezed in one last reprimand before Kate was able to hurry back to her desk to lick her wounds.

Sitting quietly in the safety of her cubicle, her heartbeat began to normalize and she reran this latest blow-up in her head. Although she was beginning to better appreciate the directives in Tom's Code, Kate didn't feel they had been responsible for resolving the clash. This latest blow-up had been truly frightening. He had gotten so worked up, Mardone seemed to have scared himself and calmed down of his own volition.

Concluding it was past time to search for a new position, Kate had just extracted a draft of her resume from her bag when Charm slipped furtively into her office, a large, rolled document in hand.

"You're the only one who hasn't signed," she said. Stretching up on tiptoe to peer over the cubicle walls, she seemed to decide the coast was clear and unfurled the document on Kate's desk. Utilizing her unique sense of style, Charm had photoshopped Tom Berwick's head onto the body of an extremely buff lifeguard in the smallest red swimsuit, reclining provocatively in a beach chair. She had decorated the border with a chain of circle and arrow male symbols and blown the whole thing up into a glossy poster. Written across the top was "Male Sex Symbol of the Year."

"What do you think?" she asked, placing a book on each edge of the certificate to keep it from rolling up. "I've got all of the girls and most of the guys to put down their birthday wishes." She indicated the signatures and funny comments she had collected.

Kate snorted and added her own signature. "It's perfect. Do you think he suspects anything?"

"I don't think so. He couldn't have seen us planning. He's been holed up in his office all morning."

"Probably stewing over your Best Phone Friend's latest lottery slamming column."

Charm shook her head. "I've only ever returned a few phone calls. Mr. Sexy Voice is your friend. You're the one he always wants to talk to. Besides, I wouldn't want to make Hank jealous. There could be bloodshed." She looked at her friend absolutely poker-faced and Kate burst out laughing at the suggestion that Charm's charming and zany, but very diminutive filmmaker boyfriend could possible beat Wilson in a fight for her honour.

"You never know. Still waters run deep." Charm rolled up the poster and secured it with a rubber band. "Seriously, though, we've got to hurry. Tom might come out for air at any minute and wonder what we're up to." She glanced at his closed door. "Jim's made a reservation for all of us at 12:30 tomorrow at that new fusion restaurant Tom wanted to try, Fabulously Fresh. If you could drive me over around 11:30, we can pick up the birthday cake, truck it over to the restaurant, hang up the poster and a few balloons and…Bob's yer uncle, we're all set." Looking pensive, Charm tapped the poster lightly on Kate's desk.

"One more thing—er, two, actually. Is there any chance you could dream up a short jingle to the tune of Happy Birthday?"

"I'll take a crack at it. But don't expect any miracles. I couldn't even think up something funny to write on the poster."

"Whatever you come up with will be super." Charm tucked the artwork under her arm and pasted a phony grin on her face. "The second thing is: take cover. Pamela was looking for you. Something about hosting a forum to boost employee spontaneity and self-actualization." She nodded. "Yup. I think that was pretty much the gist of it. Cosmic, huh?" Reacting to the dismay on Kate's face, she retreated to the doorway. "Don't shoot the messenger, she has to go order a birthday cake."

CHAPTER 16

Later that day, Kate received an e-mail from Pamela instructing her to attend a managers' meeting the next morning where counsellors from SAY, Self-Actualize Yourself, (which Kate thought a little redundant), would explain "How the conceptual core of the SAY movement teaches people to reach their goals and realize their full potential by working with their bodies to create something truly exceptional." Other benefits included weight loss, dynamic inner body cleansing and, potentially, contacting dead relatives.

Sighing in resignation, Kate keyed the meeting into her calendar and promised herself she'd get to work updating her resume that evening.

Tuesday began on a happier note than the previous day. The national Select Seven Lottery had been won the Saturday prior by four different people across the country who had chosen the same seven numbers to play and would share the $40 million jackpot.

Players often didn't want anyone to know they had won the lottery. However, a claimant could not collect his prize unless he allowed the corporation to publish his picture and name in the newsletter that Charm wrote. The information was released to the media and might also be used in future advertising. No publicity, no prize money.

Kate's job was to interview the winners so she could use their story in future promotions: How would the win change their lives? Do they have any plans for the money?

Do they often buy tickets? Where and when did they buy the ticket? etc.

Hidden behind the veil of congratulations, however, was another agenda. Lottery officials wanted to be sure the people presenting the ticket were its rightful owners. All the answers the prize claimants gave to Kate's questions were carefully evaluated by the corporation's security department of retired law enforcement officials.

Tuesday morning, the winner and her husband arrived at the Prize Payout counter dressed in hula skirts and leis. All the information they gave jibed with where and when the corporation's computers had already told Kate the ticket had been purchased and the claimant's name, and only her name, was signed on the ticket back.

Kate sometimes found when a jackpot was shared, the winners were more depressed they hadn't won the whole thing than happy with their portion of the prize, but this wasn't the case this time. The couple couldn't have been more thrilled about their quarter of the jackpot. They picked up their cheque and headed off to the airport for a long overdue vacation in Hawaii—stopping along the way to make a sizeable deposit.

Kate was happy for them and still laughing at how the winner had filled Kate's coffee cup full of champagne and orange juice from a bottle in her beach bag when she realized her meeting with Pamela and SAY was looming. She hustled down the long hallway, past Mardone's office, relieved to see his door closed and his smirking secretary away from her station. Palming a cookie from the container on Jim's desk, she caught his eye to say thanks as he patiently explained to a caller the answer to a question he'd probably been asked a thousand times before. She put her notes from the interview in Charm's basket and settled herself on the end of her friend's desk, waiting until she finished her phone call.

Kate gestured to the in-basket when Charm hung up. "Notes on this morning's winner for the newsletter. They were a really cute couple and we got some fun photos you might want to use for your cover." She took a closer look at Charm. "What's wrong?"

"That was the owner of Fabulously Fresh—where we were *supposed* to have Tom's lunch today. They had a fire in the kitchen last night. He called to tell me they're closed today to assess the damage. So lunch is off." She rubbed her temples. "Now what?"

"We'll just have it here." Kate glanced at Tom's office, where he was simultaneously punching away at his computer and talking into a headset. "It'll be a better surprise that way. We won't have to come up with something lame to trick him into going out for lunch." She snuck another peek at Tom and frowned when she saw him toss back some pills from a bottle on his desk.

"But everybody's paid for the buffet in advance."

"We'll decorate the boardroom, get pizza delivered and I bet we wind up with money left over which we can refund everybody. Nobody's going to argue with that."

"I guess that'll work. We've still got a cake—and it's a good one, too."

"I've got to meet with Pamela and her cult of lifestyle advisors. Why don't you meet me at the front door at 11:30 and we'll go pick up the cake?"

"Sounds terrific. In the meantime, I'll spring some of the girls from the sales department to help me hang balloons and streamers."

Kate stood to go. "Oh, I almost forgot…" She pulled a folded paper from the stack she was carrying and handed it to Charm. "The birthday ditty you wanted." She winced. "I warn you nothing ever comes together for me rhyme-wise. Maybe we can think up something better before the party. You know, like:

> *Don't give Charm and Kate the blame,*
> *Because the restaurant went up in flame.*
> *The first candle burned down before the last was lit,*
> *Even on your big cake, they wouldn't fit."*

Charm unfolded the paper and read the verse. "You're being too hard on yourself. It's perfect the way it is. I'll make copies for everybody and see you at 11:30."

★ ★ ★

Kate knew a bit about SAY. Her boyfriend, Matt, had participated in one of their Boot Camp Weekends at a downtown hotel. He later told her the participants were locked in a room where they were allowed to drink a little water, but not permitted to eat or sleep for 48 hours. They were constantly berated and ridiculed by SAY counsellors seeking to break down their weak societal defenses in order that they could be built up again in fortress fashion. Matt said he had experienced an awakening and realized what was truly important. Kate, on the other hand, was certain it was at this point that he changed from being carefree and thoughtful to intense and self-centred.

The sales presentation the SAY counsellors put on that morning reinforced her pre-conceived opinion of the "movement." The meeting was attended by Gregor,

Pamela, Mardone, Pacific's district sales managers, the vice president from the regional office, Kate—and Tom, who strolled in late. The first to arrive, Kate watched the SAY group assess each individual when they entered the meeting room. When Gregor arrived, the counsellor with the toothiest smile made eye contact with his colleagues and they all exchanged subtle nods. *They look like they're sizing him up for a tasty meal*, Kate thought.

The presentation was an hour long and very flashy, punctuated by the latest in computer graphics and techniques. Throughout, the lottery managers were complimented for the respect they obviously had for their employees, exposing them to SAY's cutting edge methods of introspection. Kate tried to get Tom's attention to share an eye roll. When he didn't acknowledge her stare, she hoped he was preoccupied with being another year older and not with the values of metacognition being preached from the front of the room.

When the talk finally came to a close, Pamela thanked the presenters and told them how excited everyone was to be allowed into SAY's exclusive club. She also told them not to hesitate to contact Kate directly as she would be handling all the arrangements. At this, Tom snapped out of his reverie and raised an eyebrow. The SAY team, too, turned their 200-watt smiles in her direction.

Thankful for the three cups of caffeine she was running on, Kate shut her mouth—which had fallen open when she heard she was coordinating the dog and pony show—and asked the question she was dying to ask. "How much is this going to cost?" She was pleased to see Tom nod and look to the front of the room for an answer.

Noting Pamela's reluctance and Gregor's insistence

that cost was not an issue, few in the group seemed to want to press for an answer. Tom and two district sales managers stood fast, however, and eventually Kate had the astounding answer: $500 per employee x 500 employees—a quarter of a million dollars. Tom glanced her way again and, this time, Kate's mouth fell open and stayed there.

* * *

"It's over there, the little shop with the striped awning. We're in luck. There's a parking spot right out front," Charm said.

Kate angled her car into the curb and they entered the small store where they were enveloped by the delicious aroma of fresh baking. A squat woman, dressed head to toe in the same stripes that decorated the building's awning, her dark hair restrained in a net, came from the back to assist them.

Charm told her they were picking up a birthday cake and the clerk hooked her thumb towards an adjacent cooler. "I didn't think you were coming," she said.

"Are we late? I thought I said we would be here between eleven and twelve o'clock?" Charm glanced at her watch.

"No," the clerk said with a heavy accent. "You said you had to have it by eight o'clock. So I arrived extra early to decorate it and have everything ready for you." She placed her hands on her hips and regarded them with indignation.

"I'm sorry." Charm walked over to the cooler. "I sure don't remember doing that, but I could have screwed up. I've had a lot on my plate lately." She looked down at the big cake.

"I have called the contact number you left several

times and there was no answer," the clerk said, increasingly smug.

Charm looked up from the case and over at Kate. "This isn't our cake."

"What do you mean? Of course it is." The clerk took her hands off her hips and trotted over to the case. "There was only one cake order today." Warily, she regarded the two women. "You are not from Dr. Tam's office?"

"I ordered a birthday cake for our boss, Tom," Charm said, evenly. "And I confirmed the order with you. Are you saying you don't have a cake for me?"

The clerk's eyes flipped quickly from Charm to Kate. "This is a very nice cake—a hundred dollar cake." Her lips parted in a thin smile.

Charm looked sideways at Kate who stared right back, neither knowing what the clerk was getting at.

"You have no cake. I have one I don't need." the clerk shrugged. "I will sell it to you for fifty dollars."

"I don't want a cake that says Happy Birthday, Dr. Tam," Charm said.

"Twenty-five dollars," the woman countered. She put the cake on the counter in front of Charm.

It was a handsome cake, as cakes go, and it was certainly large enough to feed the number they were expecting. "How about twenty dollars?" Kate asked.

Charm was appalled. "Kate, it has the wrong name on it—and little white things all around it."

"Those are teeth—little teeth made of icing," the woman said. "That's what took my time. Dr. Tam is a dentist."

Kate could hardly keep from laughing, but she was afraid Charm would cry if she did.

"Five dollars, it's yours," the clerk said.

Kate fished five dollars out of her bag and handed it to the women who quickly put the cake in a box and snatched the money before she could change her mind. Outside, Kate popped the back hatch on the car and set the box down inside. Charm, standing beside her, had disappointment written all over her face.

"This will work out just fine. Watch." Kate leaned over Dr. Tam's cake and neatly nicked off the top and the stem of the letter "a" in Tam with her little finger, pretty much turning the message into "Happy Birthday Dear Tom." She licked the icing off her finger. "Yum. That woman was right about one thing. It's delicious and I don't even like cake."

"You know, it looks all right," Charm said. She plucked two sets of wind-up, chomping toy teeth from the cake. "What's all that stuff around the outside?" She pointed to the reams of spun sugar that ran around the perimeter.

Kate wiped her finger off on a tissue and eyed the cake. "I'll bet Dr. Tam is an orthodontist and those are braces." She grinned. "Let's leave it. It's kind of decorative and, now that you've gotten rid of the toy choppers, nobody's ever going to guess the little rectangles are teeth."

CHAPTER 17

The party was a great success. While Kate and Charm were negotiating for the cake, the sales staff had decorated the boardroom and created a throne for the honouree, which bore a striking resemblance to the one in Charm's poster, which they hung on the wall behind. Tom was completely surprised, largely because Charm had miscalculated. His birthday was actually the following week. Nonetheless, he collected a good haul of gifts: a screaming rubber chicken, coffee mugs embellished with a variety of messages, a handy sock repair kit, a much needed tie tying manual and a potty putter containing everything needed to practice your golf game without leaving the comfort of your toilet seat. Gregor and Pamela put in an appearance, but didn't stay long enough to dampen anyone's spirits. The pizza arrived on time, the cake was delicious, and no one was the wiser to the spun sugar braces and the little icing teeth. Cued by Charm, everyone chimed in with Kate's birthday song:

> *Today is a Birthday,*
> *We wonder for who?*
> *Who's smiling and happy?*
> *My goodness—it's you.*

> *Happy Birthday Dear Tom,*
> *Happy Birthday to you,*
> *From old friends and new friends,*
> *Happy Birthday to you.*

Once a year we gather 'round,
With presents, cake—and soon,
Gifts and laughter do abound,
As we sing this joyful tune

Another trip around the sun,
Now you're one year older,
So Happy Birthday, dearest Tom
Now cut the cake. We're hungry!

Kate thought Tom looked suitably embarrassed seated on his throne with a paper crown perched on his head, but she wished she had added an extra verse about the restaurant burning down due to the number of flaming candles on his cake. He hooked his thumb over his shoulder to indicate the poster behind him, then grinned and pointed at her, as if to say he recognized her handiwork. Kate shook her head, but he seemed unconvinced.

The revelers had no problem letting the party run long once Gregor and Pamela had left the building. They finally decided the best use of the money Charm had refunded them was to continue the party after work at a little pub situated nearby on the river.

Kate, a recent cake convert, helped herself to a second piece complete with braces and teeth, and sneaked back to her desk where she found a sticky note stuck to her monitor. "Please Call. Urgent!" was written in bold black marker at the top. Underneath, she picked up the particulars. Wilson, tired of leaving messages all day, had negotiated his way through voice-mail jail to the Prize Payout Department, whom he convinced of the urgency of his call. With a groan of resignation, Kate punched in his cell number and connected on the first ring to a series of banging and clanging sounds.

"Kate! Don't hang up. Hold on a minute." After some time, the banging became more distant. "Are you still there?"

"I'm here. Where in the world are you?"

"I'm out in Delta, doing a bit of legwork for a story. Thanks for getting back to me."

"Something urgent you said?" She carefully scraped the leftover icing off her plate.

"Something's come up and I'm not sure whether it's relative to you or not, but I think you should know about it."

"So, tell me."

"Not over the phone. Can we meet somewhere? It won't take long."

Kate held the receiver to her ear with one hand and pinched the bridge of her nose with the other, trying to decide her course of action.

"I don't have anything else up my sleeve, if that's what you're worried about," Wilson said. "What do you say, six o'clock...six-thirty tonight? Some place public. No interrogating, no hidden recording devices or body wires, no supposedly 'off the record.' I promise."

Kate sighed and had to smile. The guy was a piece of work. "Oh, all right, as long as you're not wearing a body wire," she said sarcastically.

"Don't laugh. It's happened." Getting nothing but silence in reply, Wilson quickly said, "I won't. You can search me."

"Very kind of you, but I'll take your word for it this one time." He seemed genuinely concerned, but she was damned if she was going to jump at his every demand. "I can't make it today, though. How about tomorrow?"

"You definitely can't make it tonight?"

"No, tonight's out." She didn't feel compelled to explain she was meeting the more stalwart partygoers for drinks at the Flying Otter Pub.

"OK. Tomorrow's good. I'm playing soccer until about eight o'clock."

"Where do you play? I can meet you there."

"Works for me, if that's OK with you. We play at Andy Livingstone Park on the west side of Chinatown."

"I know where it is. I'll see you there at eight."

★ ★ ★

The next evening, Kate completed a final edit of her resume and sent it off to a job competition at the Department of Transit. Finished sooner than she had planned, she left early for the soccer field, parking in the pay lot under the Costco store, across the street from Vancouver's two pro sports stadiums, BC Place and Rogers Arena. It was a clear, cool night and a brisk two-block walk put her at Andy Livingstone Park at seven o'clock.

The park had previously been a bleak expanse of broken asphalt and garbage that property speculators were afraid to touch because the soil was so badly contaminated from years of industrial carelessness. When locals demanded the area be cleaned up, a local developer had partnered with the city to create a safe greenspace. Now a popular gathering place, the park was an oasis from the bustle of the city, boasting fountains and gardens, a playground, basketball courts, a skateboard park, and lighted soccer and baseball fields.

The game was in full swing when Kate arrived and she was surprised how professional they looked. She had assumed Wilson would be playing a pick-up game with a few friends, but each side had a full team of uniformed players and the action was fast and furious. She took a seat on the bleachers and spotted Wilson without too much trouble.

He was taller than the others and a pretty good player, moving the ball quickly, checking and intercepting passes. The teams were evenly matched and the score was tied at halftime—Wilson having scored two goals. Play had just resumed after sports drinks and strategy talks when Kate noticed someone in a blue uniform and black toque scaling the chain link fence that ran the perimeter of the field. He rushed over to the "blue" coach and, after some debate, pulled a pair of soccer cleats from his pack and laced them on. When the opportunity arose to make substitutions, the new blue man ran onto the field.

Kate thought she detected some laughter from the crowd when play resumed and she saw a few fans share a smile or a nod. Refocusing her attention on the game, she didn't know what she'd missed, but it was obvious the whole dynamic had changed. The new blue player seemed untouchable, running circles around his check, Wilson, and the rest of the red team. *And always with very nice ball control*, Kate thought, remembering her soccer playing days. He scored one goal and assisted on another within minutes of the substitution. When a corner kick was awarded the red team, Wilson received the pass—but the new guy easily got possession and took the ball down the field. Some of the hijinks at Wilson's expense were so effortless they were comical, and Kate joined the crowd in the good-natured laughter.

When the ref blew his whistle signaling the end of the game, the final score was seven to three, for the blue team.

Winded, sweaty players from both teams shook hands, red players congratulating the blues on their win. Kate made her way to the side of the field where Wilson was removing his cleats. His injured eye seemed a lot better and his dark hair, in need of a trim, curled slightly at his neck. Kate bit her lip, trying unsuccessfully to keep from smiling when she heard the ribbing his teammates were giving him.

"You enjoyed that did you?" he asked her.

"Number seventeen's a talented player." Kate said.

"Uh-huh." Wilson stood and turned his head slowly, then winced. "Damn kids. They've gotta learn a little respect for us old guys."

Confused, Kate looked more closely at the other players busy removing shin pads and boots and realized why the reporter was so much taller than everyone else. The players on the red team were adults, but the members of the blue team were kids. Kate had just looked questioningly at Wilson when number seventeen approached and the two opponents exchanged high fives. Seventeen reached up and pulled off the toque that had been restraining her mane of long blonde hair.

"Great game, Rhys," she said. "That was an awesome header."

"Thank you, Tory. It is my signature move." Wilson turned to Kate. "The last time I did that my head ached for three days."

At this point, a group leaving the field yelled they were off to Costco's food court for something to eat, each pausing to give an exaggerated bow to Wilson in mock deference to his soccer prowess.

"What do you think Kate? An expensive dinner at Costco? My treat? It's too cold to sit here and talk." Kate nodded in agreement. "How about you, Tory? Can I buy you a hotdog?"

"Thanks, but I've got a math test tomorrow and I haven't finished studying. Rain check?" she asked, slinging her pack over her shoulder.

"You bet," Wilson said. "Oh Tory, I've got two tickets to the game, Saturday. I can't make it and I wondered if you and your dad might like to go?"

Tory's mouth dropped open. "Would we ever." She took the tickets and gave Wilson a hug. "This is going to be a primo game. Nobody can get tickets. Thanks." She zipped them carefully into her backpack, said goodbye to Rhys and Kate, and raced off to catch up with a group waiting at the gate.

Wilson watched her go and shook his head. "I've gotta get that girl playing with a professional coach," he said.

"That would be nice of you. She's very good."

"Nice? This is about self-preservation—mine. She's killing me out there." He grabbed his duffel bag and the two of them set off, nodding to the few remaining.

"They're good players and the uniforms make you look very professional."

"A couple of years ago one of the sports reporters thought if we could get the inner city kids interested in playing soccer it might keep some of them out of the trouble they were getting into. A lot of them are from single parent homes and their mom or dad is working when they need somebody to talk to—so they start hanging out with the wrong crowd. The games caught on and it's a lot of fun—despite the physical damage."

"How old are the kids—fourteen, fifteen?"

"Yeah, around there." Wilson looked sheepish. "Tory, the keener, is only thirteen."

Kate laughed. "I'm sure she spends *a lot* of time practicing."

"Well…that is the whole idea. I guess my wounded pride and concussed head will have to take solace in that." They entered the Costco food court through the rolled up garage style doors. "Let's grab a seat away from the rest, so we can talk." He dropped his bag on the bench across from Kate and was soon back with two dogs, French fries, and soft drinks.

"They have the best hotdogs here," Kate said, taking the foil-wrapped package Wilson passed her. "But you absolutely have to doctor them up with all the stuff at the condiment bar." She gave him a disappointed look as he unwrapped his and prepared to take a bite. "You've gotta at least get some ketchup and mustard on that puppy—and onions. Never forget the onions."

He shrugged and followed her to the refrigerated unit beside the takeout window where they customized their dogs.

"Quite a bit of controversy associated with the origin of the hotdog," Kate told him, once they had returned to their table. "Most people think they were first sold at a Giants game in New York in the early 1900s. Others swear they were being sold in the 1880s in St. Louis."

Wilson, wrestling to hold his overloaded bun together, attempted a bite.

She washed down a mouthful with a sip of root beer. "When Charm and I went to the Festival of Comfort Foods, I learned all about the history of the humble hot dog. They originally served just the dog portion and customers were given a pair of white gloves to protect themselves from the hot, greasy meat. But people kept walking off with the gloves, so vendors started wrapping the meat up in buns."

Wilson wiped a blob of ketchup off his sleeve and glanced at her skeptically. "And they say I'm nuts."

"They say that and a whole lot more," Kate said, polishing off the last of her meal.

"How did you manage to eat that sloppy creation and not wind up wearing half of it?" He picked some hot pepper rings off his pant leg.

"Takes skill." Kate parked her elbows on the table and rested her chin in her hands. "So, what is it that's so urgent?"

Wilson scrunched his food wrappers into a ball and took a deep breath. "I don't want to scare you, but I've received some threats in the last couple of days. Now, this actually happens to me all the time—somebody blowing off steam in a childish way. And I've learned to take them with a grain of salt. This time it's different, though. These recent threats are much more menacing and are directed at me and my 'informant at Pacific Lottery.'"

Kate felt herself go cold. "What informant?"

Wilson shrugged. "People get funny ideas. The public sees *you* as the communications department and I don't want you blamed for tipping me to what's going on." His sparkling eyes grew serious. "Without repeating the colourful language, I've been warned to find something new to obsess about or suffer the consequences."

"Did you call the police?" Kate asked, grimly.

He nodded. "Unfortunately, my relationship with the Vancouver Police Department is tenuous at best."

Kate raised a questioning eyebrow.

"I may have publicly questioned their procedures on a few occasions," he said.

"How many occasions?"

"Enough of them for Detective Lee to tell me they're short staffed at the moment, but he will certainly file my complaint according to priority."

She shook her head. "Not smart."

"Well if you're not living life on the edge, you're taking up too much room." He tapped his fingers on the table. "I didn't want to discuss this over a lottery corp. phone because I'm concerned someone there might be behind the threats. What do you think? Tom Berwick and Gregor Chernin have got a good thing going. I don't imagine they like me stirring the pot."

"You mean you think my phone might be bugged?" she asked. "That's a bit James Bond, isn't it?"

"Not these days. Almost anybody can do it. And watch your hard drive, cell phone, and e-mails too. Password protected or not, they're all accessible."

"There's no way Gregor or Tom would be responsible. Gregor's an obnoxious boor but I don't think he's smart enough to be that wicked. And Tom is a rock. Everybody knows they can always turn to him for help." She smiled slightly. "When you were pissing me off a while ago, it was Tom who told me to cool it, that you were only doing your job."

Wilson allowed himself a grin. "Perhaps I've misjudged him. He's obviously an intelligent guy." He nodded goodbye to the members of the team who were heading home. "You haven't noticed anybody following you, or received any nasty phone calls lately?"

"Just you."

He laughed and pulled a business card from his bag. "Hopefully, I'm overreacting and there's nothing to worry about." He handed the card to Kate. "This is Detective Lee's contact info. I've written my work number and my private cell number on there as well. Promise me you'll call, anytime, if you think something funny is going on."

Kate scanned the card. "All right. I'll keep my eyes open."

"Good." Wilson's gaze met hers. "I'm accustomed to being in hot water myself—but it's very disturbing to think I could be taking someone else down with me. Puts me off my game a little."

His closeness and the intensity of his stare suddenly made Kate feel uncomfortable. "I think they're getting ready to close," she said. The other customers had left and the staff was rolling out wheeled buckets of soapy water to begin the evening clean up.

"Come on," Wilson said. "I'll walk you to your car."

"That's not really necessary."

"Yes it is."

"You just won't take no for an answer, will you?"

Wilson grinned broadly. "Then I wouldn't be me."

CHAPTER 18

C harm stuck her head into Kate's office. "It's Friday and we're overdue for a KALP session."

Looking up from her work, Kate saw her colleague and two of the more outrageous people from the sales department peering in at her. KALP, which stood for Keep a Low Profile, was a lunch group Jim and Charm had started a couple of years ago. Membership hinged solely on a member's ability to laugh and to keep a secret. Behind the group in the doorway, Kate could see Jim shrugging hurriedly into his jacket, obviously intent on joining the party.

"I'm going to have to take a rain check, guys," Kate said, indicating the paperwork she was reviewing. "Thanks for asking."

Jim pulled a toque onto his bald head and indicated with a sweeping arm that she was to accompany them. "You know what they say. 'All work and no play makes Kate...'"

"Sticks and stones," Kate said.

"What is it this time?" Charm asked. "Do you need some help?"

"Nah. Just Wilson again. He called earlier to say he's heard we're hiring Vertex Gaming to run the casinos." Kate threw her hands in the air. "According to what I've been told and what I read here in Tom's Vertex file, we're responsible for managing the casinos...Have you guys heard anything otherwise?" She glanced up and four blank faces stared back.

"And it's Friday." Charm pressed her lips together.

"Yep. He's looking to fill space in his column on Monday. Vertex is a hot potato. They've been in quite a bit of trouble in the past, and he knows it." Kate pressed the fingers of one hand to her brow. "He wants a quote from Gregor who, of course, isn't here, and Tom doesn't answer his cell, either."

"Gregor won't be back in the office until Monday," Jim said. "That doesn't do you much good, does it?"

Kate shook her head. "You guys go ahead without me. I'll keep trying Tom. If push comes to shove, I may have to ask Mardone or Pamela if they can help."

There was a sharp intake of air from the group at the door, followed by a melodramatic, "eww," before they left for lunch.

"We'll bring you back some sushi," Jim called over his shoulder as he hustled after them.

Kate leaned back in her chair and pondered her options. If she didn't protect herself by getting Wilson a direct quote from Gregor or Tom, they would blame her for whatever he wrote in his column—and she knew it would be a blistering expose. Her conversation with Wilson at the museum had prompted her to do a little research on Vertex's global operations and she discovered that they had indeed been charged with all the infractions he mentioned. Strangely, they usually escaped with a slap on the wrist.

Since their hotdog at Costco, Kate felt less ill at ease when Wilson called for information. At the soccer game, she'd been impressed by the interest the hard-boiled reporter had shown in the welfare of the disadvantaged kids. *More evidence a human lived in there somewhere*, she thought. When her thoughts turned to how concerned he had seemed for her welfare, Kate knew her mind had wandered too far and she reminded herself that was his "modus operandi." Once he ferreted info out of you, wove it into his column, and you read the rehashed version in the next morning's papers, you realized where his concern really lay.

She was still stewing over the situation when William, a retired postal worker who took his job in the lottery mailroom very seriously, arrived with a stack of correspondence.

Seizing the opportunity to procrastinate, Kate grabbed some iced tea from the cafeteria—which was now proudly exhibiting Tom's Sex Symbol of the Year poster—and returned to her desk to go through the mail. She worked her way through, sorting things based on urgency, until all that was left was one fat interoffice envelope. She unwound the red string securing the flap and inside found a manila envelope. Inside this was a small package neatly wrapped in colourful paper and bound with ribbon. Slipping the accompanying card from the gift, she read, "No special occasion...Just because." It was signed, "Love Lucas."

A feeling of apprehension came over her and Kate sipped her iced tea and stared at the parcel for a long moment. Curiosity finally getting the better of her, she cut the ribbon and lifted the lid on the box. Nestled in tissue paper was a black, lace-trimmed G-string. Stunned, Kate dropped it back in the box and then, just as quickly, recalled Tom's insistence she was responsible for the birthday poster that Charm had photoshopped. The corners of her mouth turned up in a smile. *That beggar, Berwick,* she said to herself. *I'll get him.*

CHAPTER 19

Kate stashed the parcel in her bottom drawer, her mind spinning with ways to retaliate. She decided to get Charm's input after lunch. She always had some evil pranks up her sleeve. Her thoughts returned to Wilson's inquiry and she decided that with Gregor out of town, she would have to consult Mardone or Pamela. Figuring Pamela as the lesser of the two evils, Kate stole carefully past Mardone's open door towards the vice president's office. She needn't have been so cautious. Mardone's office was empty and Kate realized she hadn't seen him since their confrontation a few days ago, which reaffirmed her conviction that Tom was the panty perpetrator. Unless someone had mailed the package for Mardone during his absence, he couldn't have sent the G-string.

Pamela's secretary, Tiffany, opened the office door a crack when Kate knocked and allowed her in only after receiving a permissive nod from her boss. The vice president sat behind her desk looking delighted. A package very similar to Kate's sat in front of her.

"Pamela received a surprise gift in this morning's mail." Tiffany nodded enthusiastically at Kate.

Recalling the vice president's fierce preaching against sexual harassment, Kate was confused by her pleased reaction to the package, since she was pretty certain what was in it.

"I had no idea he felt this way, but we have worked closely together for a long time," Pamela said, a coy smile pulling at the corners of her mouth. She made a show of suppressing a giggle and glanced up. "I know I can rely on you two to keep this just between us girls." She held up a racy red G-string and read from the card: "Looking for a Good Time? Want to Get Lucky? Love, Gregor."

"What a sweetie," Tiffany said. "Where's mine? I didn't get one."

Pamela giggled.

Knowing it wouldn't be conducive to her corporate health to tell them she thought the whole thing was a farce perpetrated by Tom, Kate managed to mutter a weak, "Wow."

"Do you think he intends to follow up with an evening out?" Tiffany asked. "I haven't seen him all day. Come to think of it, I haven't seen him in a few days. Where is he anyway?"

"He flew up north on Tuesday. He's entertaining some very important gaming people at Mystic River Resort." Pamela tucked her new lingerie away in the box.

Seizing the opportunity to get her business done and escape, Kate said, "Do you have a number where I could reach him? Something's come up and I—"

"I'm not going to let you interrupt him with your trivial problems." Pamela's eyes strayed from Kate to the package on her desk.

In her peripheral vision Kate could see Tiffany shaking her head at the notion of Kate contacting Gregor directly.

"It's not trivial. The media is saying we've signed Vertex Gaming to manage the casinos. I need some assurance from Gregor that this isn't the case."

Tiffany's head paddle-balled back and forth between Kate and her boss, ready to jump in at the first opportunity to agree with Pamela.

"I obviously would know if we had done that." The vice president regarded Kate disparagingly and snorted. An echoing snort came from her secretary. "Nothing has come across my desk."

"If I had his number, I could send him a quick text and get him to confirm it," Kate suggested hopefully.

Pamela wound the lush red ribbon back around the gift and shook her head.

Kate felt her bad angel alight on her left shoulder. "Don't feel bad if you don't know it. I'm sure he doesn't entrust his private number to just anybody. I bet his wife would know how to contact him. I could give her a call at home...but she's probably accompanied her husband on the trip."

Pamela froze for a moment, then tossed a handful of orange curls back over her shoulder. "Sharon doesn't understand him."

"Have *you* heard that, *too*?" Tiffany chimed in.

Getting more frustrated by the second, the bad angel still firmly perched on her shoulder, Kate strode angrily towards the door and spun around. "If Gregor's been out of town since Tuesday, he couldn't possibly have sent that by interoffice mail, could he?" She gazed at Pamela with what she hoped was a pensive expression. "Unless he had June do it for him, and I can't see that happening." A flicker of doubt wafted across Pamela's face. "Curious, huh?" Kate added.

Kate slammed the door behind her when she left. *That was childish,* she told herself; but it felt pretty good. The heels of her black pumps punching little holes in the plush carpeting, she marched over to Gregor's office.

Outside the president's office, his secretary, June, sat ramrod straight at her organized desk. Her long grey hair was pulled back into a tight bun and she wore a sensible navy blue skirt and collared blouse buttoned to the throat and tied with a ribbon. Holding the phone in her left hand while she methodically snapped the clasp of a clip-on earring with her right thumb, June was very succinctly informing her caller how misinformed he was and what was *really* going to happen next.

The staff treated June with great respect. The honest ones admitted they were afraid of her. Kate had always found her fair and generous, although she knew you had to tread carefully where Gregor was concerned. She decided to see how she rated as a judge of character and ask for the older woman's assistance.

Once the person on the other end of the phone saw the sense in coming around to June's way of thinking, she placed the receiver back in its cradle, snapped her earring back on, and greeted her visitor with a smile. Kate returned to her own desk five minutes later, knowing she had done the best she could. June had been unwilling to give her Gregor's cell number, as he had been adamant he not be disturbed. However, he called her every day at 1:30 and, when he called this afternoon, she would suggest he contact Kate. After insisting Kate help herself to a mint from the crystal dish on her desk, the older woman dismissed her with a curt nod.

June's professional assistance had somewhat alleviated Kate's anger at Pamela, but she wasn't yet feeling charitable when the mail clerk burst back into her office. His face was shiny and red, his tie askew and perspiration beaded his brow.

"Pamela wants that package you got in the mail today."

"What package, William?"

"That fat one. I brought it in with your other mail." He was almost bursting with the importance of the task he had been assigned. "And she needs the envelope it came in, too." He nodded his head vigorously up and down.

"Why? What's going on?" Kate asked.

William looked furtively left and right from the cubicle doorway then, hopping atop a leftover box of promotional materials, peered over the maze of office enclosures. Apparently satisfied no one was eavesdropping, he swept theatrically over to the extra chair and sat down.

"Evidently," he whispered, "Pamela and you, and Sabrina in IT, received something threatening in the mail and she's trying to get to the bottom of it. If the perp wasn't thinking and used an interoffice envelope previously sent to him, his name will be the one above yours on the distribution list on the front. She's smart huh?"

"For sure." Kate leaned back in her chair and rested her elbows on the armrests. "What makes her think I received one of these...packages?"

"I told her you did." William's head nodded up and down like a bobble head doll.

Kate shot him a glance. "William—'confidentiality'— isn't that part of every good postie's credo? I think it's right up there with 'neither snow, nor rain, nor heat, nor gloom of night.'"

William looked chagrined, then brightened. "In a case as serious as this, I know Pamela would say that rules and procedures should be thrown out the window. Besides, I told her you wouldn't mind."

"I see. Did you say Sabrina got a package, too?" Sabrina Szabo had warmly welcomed Kate when she started at the corporation and they had had a great relationship ever since. She had frequently been a member of the pack on Charm and Kate's after work happy hours until her husband deserted her a few months ago for his pregnant girlfriend.

William nodded again, even faster this time. Kate, fearful he might have a heart attack, wanted to suggest he stop talking and relax, but didn't want to stop the flow of information. His eyes almost popped out of his head when he told Kate that Sabrina had received something of a "sexual nature" in the mail. The accompanying gift card had supposedly been signed by her boss. When confronted, Sabrina's boss had roared with laughter and told her he couldn't believe anyone found her attractive enough to warrant such a suggestive gift.

"So, where's the present? Pamela wants it."

"Well she can't have it. It was addressed to me," Kate snapped.

William's mouth fell open. "Kate...it's for Pamela."

"If she's so interested in reading my mail, she can pop in anytime and tell me why."

William closed his mouth and rose from the chair. Perhaps fearing Pamela's repercussions when he returned empty handed, he shuffled away with his eyes downcast.

★ ★ ★

Charm darted into Kate's office and slid into the chair William had vacated earlier. Her face was a mask of grave concern that told Kate the eyes and ears of the office knew something was up.

"You have a question?" Kate teased.

"What the hell's going on? Are you all right?"

"How was lunch and where's my sushi?"

"Jim's bringing it in. For Pete's sake, quit trying to bug me."

"This is killing you, isn't it?" Kate clicked her tongue in dismay. "Your gossip detection skills are slipping, you know. This all happened a couple of hours ago."

"Extenuating circumstances. I was out for lunch. Come on, spill it. I want to know if you're OK."

"What do you mean, if I'm OK?"

"William's telling everybody there's a sexual predator on the loose and that you and Sabrina went to Pamela in tears."

"What a pile of..." Kate stared evenly at Charm. "Do I look tearful to you?"

Charm eyed her friend intently as if seriously assessing her mental state. "No you don't. And I know you. You're more of a get even type, than a get emotional type."

"Thank you. I'm very proud of that reputation." Kate relayed the true chain of events, including Pamela's elation when she thought she was the object of Gregor's affections. She handed the offending panties to Charm for inspection.

"Tom's done it," Charm said.

"Absolutely."

"Apparently Pamela's thrilled no longer. William told me she's going to see the offender pays for this *assault on the virtue of all women*." Charm opened her eyes theatrically.

Kate clicked the refill in and out of her pen. "Pamela was really flattered when she thought Gregor had sent her the G-string."

"Oh, and excuse me. What's up with that? Gregor?" Charm put a finger in her mouth and feigned gagging.

Kate waved her hands back and forth in a "pipe down" gesture. "Now that others have received panties with cards that are obviously forged, she realizes the whole thing is a farce and that she's the butt of a joke. To save face, she's going to go on the offensive and turn the whole thing into an opportunity."

"And, thanks to William, she knows you received a pair and didn't tell her."

"Yeah, thanks a lot, William."

Charm looked wistfully at Kate. "How's that resume rewrite coming along? Maybe you should consider dropping Pamela as a reference. What do you think?"

"That's one of the many reasons I like you. You're always full of helpful hints."

The abrupt ringing of the telephone stopped Charm before she could bestow any more advice.

June was calling to say she had only a brief conversation with Gregor while he and his guests boarded a plane to Dragonfly Casino and he would be unable to talk with Kate that afternoon."However," June continued, her words clipped, "I impressed upon Mr. Chernin that I thought he could be a bit more accommodating and that you can't be held responsible when the press insists on a quote from senior management." Kate was trying to imagine the look on Gregor's face when his secretary laid into him.

"Mr. Chernin does not arrive back in Vancouver until just before his birthday celebration tomorrow. I suggested he spare a few minutes for you during the party. You should have enough time to make Wilson's nine o'clock deadline."

Kate was speechless. Only June could have persuaded Gregor to do this.

The secretary relayed the time of the party and Gregor's home address to Kate. "I know what you're up against, dear. This Wilson fellow—he's a hard-ass. Just the same, he can put his boots under my bed anytime."

Kate almost choked but managed to squeak a heartfelt, "Thank you," before hanging up and snorting with laughter. "I'm in. June got me an audience with the almighty one at his birthday party tomorrow night."

Charm's eyes widened. "And I'll be hearing all about that at brunch Sunday morning." She pointed to the panties. "Good quality. That's French lace. I wonder why he didn't pop a pair in the mail for me?" She feigned disappointment and sniffed. "It's just nice to be thought of sometimes."

"You know, you're right. They're not exactly my style, but it's the thought that counts." Kate shrugged. "And it's a whole lot more than I've ever received from Matt—on any occasion."

CHAPTER 20

After a crippling aerobics class Saturday morning, Kate limped her way down the hill to the beach. It was a beautiful day but long past summer and the sand was deserted except for die-hards walking their dogs. Grateful for a moment to de-stress, she took a seat on a log and watched in amazement as a three-legged dog swam, fetched sticks, and dug holes, frantically running circles around his teenaged owner.

Kate stretched her tired legs, knowing she was going to suffer for those last few sets of leg lunges the aerobics teacher had coaxed from the class. The mindless jumping around had cleared her head, though, and the loud music had removed any opportunity for communication, save for the occasional eye-rolling between participants. Still, Kate caught herself mentally checking her to-do list.

She hoped she had all the bases covered. After taking a rain check on Friday night drinks with Charm and the gang, she texted Wilson, telling him he would have a quote from Gregor Chernin before his deadline Saturday night. She tidied up a few other loose ends and tucked the G-string into her bag. Alone in the office, she had also grabbed Tom's file of information on Vertex Gaming and stuffed it in her case next to the panties. At home that evening, she poured over the material and formulated some pointed questions to ask Gregor the next night. If the international gaming group was involved with Pacific Lottery, she could see why Wilson was intrigued.

Leaving the correspondence and clippings from the file on her desk, Kate poked through her closet for something appropriate to wear to Gregor's party, finally deciding on a favorite multi-purpose little black dress. She hung it on the back of her bedroom door, smoothed some wrinkles, and consoled herself that, dressed up or dressed down, it always seemed to work.

The next morning, perched on her log and enjoying the salty breeze, she felt her mood lift as she watched two seagulls engage in a furious battle over an old French fry. She squinted into the autumn sun as the seagulls took their French fry, and their battle, into the air. *I'll have just enough time tonight to get the info I need from Gregor and pacify Wilson,* she told herself. And a new pair of earrings from one of those shops on Fourth Avenue would give her dress some needed zing for the evening.

The three-legged dog's owner was now trying to calm the energetic animal, who bounced around and darted at the ball in the kid's hand. She caught the boy's eye and waved goodbye, a little retail therapy in her near future.

At 6:30, Kate realized she had left her best shoes at the office. She kept a nice pair under her desk in case she needed to be on camera unexpectedly and had forgotten to bring them home. "I'm wearing a recycled dress," she grumbled. "I've absolutely got to have the new shoes."

She buzzed the lottery building's door open with her key card and walked into the silent front foyer. Her security card allowed afterhours access as she had to resolve communications crises at all hours. She padded down the carpeted hallway and past the door to the warehouse from which she was sure she could hear laughter. Unmarked armored trucks came and went from the warehouse all night long, distributing tickets, terminals, software, Charm's lottery magazine, promotional materials, and other supplies. Because the tickets were as good as cash and the hardware and software vulnerable to theft and tampering, the warehouse was a high-security area. Her access card didn't allow her to enter that part of the building and that was just fine with Kate.

The ceiling lights glowed overhead, but only dimly, another step towards energy conservation. The buzz they emitted, coupled with the hypnotic blinking lights of telephones and electronics in the vacant building, was a little unnerving. Ghostly images reflecting back from the huge picture windows adjacent Tom's office did little to ease her discomfort. Kate retrieved the shoes from under her desk, straightened up, and was surprised to see the screensaver furtively darting about her monitor. She was sure she had shut the computer off in accordance with a recent reminder from the IT department to conserve energy and guard against malware.

She jiggled the mouse, which brought the monitor to life, revealing her desktop and shortcuts. Sometimes the IT people would update a program or install new drivers during off hours, but Kate had never known them to leave the machines on since a virus had infected the company's network a few months ago. She shrugged and with a couple of mouse clicks powered the unit down. Glancing at her watch, Kate inhaled sharply and raced toward the foyer. Despite cozy hot dog dinners, she knew she was naïve to expect special treatment from Wilson. If she didn't get him a quote by nine o'clock, he'd write that Pacific Lottery had refused to comment, which always had very guilty connotations.

As she hurried down the long hallway, the warehouse door swung open and a laughing Lucas Mardone stumbled out, a girl on each arm. Seeing Kate, his eyes registered surprise for a moment, but he quickly flipped his streaked hair from his eyes and his poise returned. Secretaries Tiffany and Leah, equally self-assured, stared defiantly.

"Ah, forgot my shoes," Kate said. She held them up to prove her point and immediately felt silly.

Mardone, apparently not at all worried he had been caught taking people without security clearance into the warehouse, smirked. "Big date tonight?"

As Kate excused herself and side-stepped past the two girls, who did nothing to make it easy for her, the three of them broke into gales of laughter.

* * *

Kate turned right off Granville Street onto wide, tree-lined Angus Drive. Tall wrought iron gates barred the drives of monstrous homes built for forestry and railway magnates at the turn of the 20th century when Vancouver was a young boom-town. In the hundred plus years since, the homes had lived many lives: high society party houses during the Roaring '20s, bank repossessions in the 1930s, and rooming houses and hospitals for soldiers during the war years. Torn down, propped up, added to and divided up into apartments and condominiums in later years, some still stood defiantly, thanks to the quality of their original construction. Recently, many had been returned to their initial glory by a different breed of magnate—energy tycoons and technology moguls.

Despite the fact that the homes were concealed by towering cedar hedges, Kate spotted Gregor's with ease; ten foot tall gates stood open to the driveway of a huge palace ablaze with lights. At the top of the drive, valets in black pants, vests, and white dress shirts helped party guests from their cars.

Hemmed in by the German sedan in front and the behemoth SUV crowding her rear bumper, Kate and her red compact were drawn through the gates and up to the head of the line. She climbed from her car and surrendered the keys to a smiling valet. Glancing at the black tie and long dresses the guests wore, she hoped she was dressed appropriately. She proceeded up the wide stone stairs and identified herself to a chicly-dressed sentry who verified her story via the communications device tucked discreetly in his ear and directed her to Gregor's office.

Kate stepped through the leaded glass doors and was relieved of her coat by a uniformed maid. She took a moment to adjust to the opulence of the interior. Colourful artwork hung all around the marble tiled entrance hall, which was filled with raucous guests. A staircase rose from the far side curving about a monstrous crystal chandelier. Kate wove her way between the guests to the next room, bigger than the last, with pale, glossy floors of a different type of stone and a high domed ceiling. Incongruous for a residence, at the far end of the room, was what appeared to be a stage, raised a few feet above the floor.

A maid told her she couldn't miss Gregor's office at the rear of the house, two doors past the Games Room. The mansion seemed to go on forever, though, and just as Kate was thinking she must have taken a wrong turn, a series of jeers and cheers drew her attention to a room with double doors flung open. Inside, two dozen men writhed in agony and ecstasy, cheering a soccer match on the largest TV Kate had ever seen. The signed jerseys of four NHL players, which Kate recognized as among the most popular of all time, hung above the bar. Suspended from the ceiling, a mini JumboTron, identical to those in professional sports arenas, broadcasted the scores of other games. Figuring she was close to the prize, Kate stepped gingerly past the man-cave, passed another closed door, and peeked hopefully into the next room where Gregor sat behind a large desk looking very irritated. He was dressed in a tuxedo and a glass containing the remains of a cocktail rested near his right hand. He impatiently snapped a pen back and forth between his index and middle finger.

"So Wilson thinks he's on to something?"

"Excuse me?" Kate said.

With an impatient gesture, he indicated she close the door. "June told me what the issue is. I swear I don't know where that spineless worm gets his information." Gregor stared hard at Kate. "Do you?"

"Excuse me? Of course not." Kate buttoned her lip and sat down on the sofa, wondering what was to come.

"You know the extent of Vertex's involvement with our operation," he said. "They supply software and VLTs. That's it. Anyone who says anything else is a liar." He slammed the pen down and drained his glass. "That's what I want our communication with the media to reflect." He pointed a pudgy finger at her. "Nothing else. Do I make myself clear?" He swiped at the liquid that dribbled from one corner of his tightly pressed lips.

Kate, frozen on the couch throughout this tirade, was suddenly angry. Angry she had put herself in this position. Angry that the president treated her so rudely when she was trying to do her job and make him look good. And angry because she felt so powerless. Tossing aside all the questions she had prepared, she said instead, "I can quote you on that, then?"

"You go right ahead and do that," he snarled. Dismissing her with a vehement wave, he turned his back on her and stared out the window.

Dumbstruck, Kate retraced her steps past the Games Room, where the fun was obviously continuing, and down the hall to the room with the stage. She was eager to leave and was alarmed to see escape via the front doors was effectively blocked by a huge throng of partygoers. Casting her eyes about the room, she spied a pair of patio doors and stumbled outside, hoping the fresh air would help her process the conversation she had just had.

A waiter approached with a tray of wine and lifted an inquiring eyebrow. Nodding her thanks, Kate helped herself to a glass. She had one hour before she had to contact Wilson; a glass of wine couldn't make the situation any worse. She took a sip and glanced across the pool to where a group was taking little care to conceal the marijuana they were passing around. She had met Gregor's stepson once before and recognized him as one of the smokers. Kate was trying to see if she could identify anyone else when she sensed someone behind her. Startled, she spun around to see Tom, cigar in one hand, drink in the other, looking disdainfully at the group puffing away so brazenly.

"Amazing," he said, shaking his head.

"Jeez. Don't sneak up on me like that." Kate steadied her wine glass and dabbed her napkin at the small spill on her dress. "Aren't they afraid Gregor will catch them?"

"He doesn't care. Rules are made for the little people." Tom's tone was angry. He took a step back and eyed her from head to toe. "Nice dress, by the way. Suits you."

"Er, thanks."

"I would have said hi when you arrived," he continued, "but Sharon was telling me all about the stone countertops she has 'personally sourced' and had shipped from Italy." He winked. "It's hard to break away when Sharon's telling you a story." He nonchalantly indicated a tanned middle-aged woman with long straight hair bleached to the blond hue popular with those over a certain age. Bejeweled hands gesturing dramatically, she was telling an animated story to a clearly captivated audience.

"Have you met Gregor's better half?" Tom hailed a passing waiter, plucked several canapés from the tray, and lined them up on his palm. "You may know her better as Elsie."

Kate gave him the eye, knowing he had more to tell.

Tom placed his cigar and glass on a nearby patio table and polished off a shrimp, rubbing the tips of his fingers together and brushing the little critter's tail to the ground. "She explained to me that she changed her name to Sharon because you would never see an 'Elsie' in the society column."

Kate smiled. "You are putting me on."

"Nope." He made an unsuccessful attempt at crossing himself, spilling some wine in the process. "Swear to God. There's been a secret Sharon inside all this time, just waiting to make her debut."

"It's the perfect place for a debut. I didn't realize lottery presidents did so well."

Leaning toward her, Tom whispered that Gregor had recently purchased the house to keep Sharon happy. "Did you see the stage?" he asked. When Kate nodded, he explained Sharon has decided she's going to host charity balls and the stage gives her a 'pulpit' from which to address her minions.

"Unbelievable. What's the charity?"

"She's not particular. As long as it's one that 'needs a ball where the ladies get to wear gowns.'" Tom grinned at Kate's reaction. "Sharon owns a home accessories store that's going gangbusters. That's where most of the money's coming from."

"Must be some business."

"What brings you to Chez Sharon, anyway? No offence, but I don't imagine you were invited."

"Well thanks a hell-of-a-lot. And, no, I wasn't." Kate took a sip of determination from her glass. "I'm here to get a newsworthy quote from Gregor. But, now that I've found you, we're going to discuss a couple of things, too."

"Oh, oh, that doesn't sound good." Tom plucked Kate's half-empty glass from her hand and exchanged it and his own for two full ones as a waiter passed by.

"I've been trying to get hold of you for days."

"Sorry, kid. This problem with my gut again. Had to take a bit of time off. And that reminds me…" He pulled a bottle of pills from his jacket pocket, shook out a couple, and chased them down with a swallow of wine.

She winced. "It's none of my business, but is it good to take them with alcohol?"

"It all gets mixed up down there anyway, right?" He slipped the pill bottle back into his pocket. "Now, what are we discussing?"

"All right, easy one first: I got a strange present in the inter-office mail."

"Yeah? What'd you get?"

"Well at first I thought it was a pincushion. But it's a pair of panties."

Tom grinned.

"I thought you might know who sent them?" Kate grinned back.

"Whoa. Ladies' un-der-gar-ments?" he asked, drawing out each syllable. "Why would I know anything about that?"

"I just thought you might warn the person that sent them that the red-haired battle axe is on the warpath."

"Why? Didn't she get a present?" Tom roared with laughter.

"Oh, shut up, you fool." Kate glanced around, hoping they hadn't been overheard.

"I wish I could help you warn the gift giver, but I'm afraid I don't know anything about it."

Kate didn't know whether to believe him or not. When confronted, Tom was usually quite proud to fess up to his pranks. Exasperated, she checked her watch. She had a half hour before she had to call Wilson.

"Someone's taking dangerous liberties on my pranking turf, though. I've obviously been spending too much time away from the office. What's our second topic du jour?" Tom asked.

"What do you know about Vertex assuming management of the casinos?"

"Oh...that." Tom cleared his throat.

Kate's eyes narrowed. "You had better tell me. Wilson's got a source that says we're breaking the law by hiring a management company."

"What did Gregor say?"

"He told me Wilson's wrong and to tell him to go to hell."

Tom stroked his chin with his free hand. "I'm afraid Gregor's more or less feeding you a load of shit, Katie. That woman from Vertex, Carla Roston, has talked him into a partnership deal."

"But he can't do that."

"He's going to. Vertex is relentless in finding neat little loopholes they can take advantage of. They go in, fill their pockets, and get out before the curtain falls." He sighed. "Gregor's going to be pissed the media knows about this before he's got all his ducks in a row."

Exasperated, Kate tapped her fingers on the deck railing. "I told Wilson I'd call him by nine o'clock. What am I going to say?"

"If you want to keep your job, tell him what Gregor told you. If you want to have some fun and rock the boat, tell him what I told you."

Kate felt like a puppet having its strings yanked.

Tom reached out and clutched Kate's arm, turning her around to face him.

"I'm sorry, kid. I didn't intend for you to be pulled into this. I've always had Gregor under control. He's impulsive and not the brightest bulb in the box, so it hasn't been much of a challenge, but it's always been quite fun."

"It's not your fault, Tom." Kate was having a hard time following his rambling and when he tightened his grasp, pulling her toward him as if to confide something, she was actually thankful that Lucas Mardone, Pamela, and a pack of hangers-on arrived from the direction of the garden.

"You just turn up everywhere, don't you," Pamela said, eyeing Kate. "We'll have to get you a bell." She sandwiched Tom's arm under her own and he quickly regained his composure. "Come along, Thomas." She glanced back at Kate. "Time to go, or you'll turn into a pumpkin, or something worse." Tom, feigning helplessness, shrugged with his free arm.

"Yeah." Tiffany clung to Mardone's arm, apparently none the worse for wear from her adventures in the lottery warehouse. "Go home and organize your panty drawer."

CHAPTER 21

Arriving at their favorite brunch place the next morning, Kate spied Charm nursing a large coffee. She was settled deep in an overstuffed armchair, a baseball cap pulled low over her brow.

"You don't look all that well. Tough night?" Kate sat down opposite her friend.

"Please do not talk so loudly to people with exceptionally bad judgment," Charm whispered. She planted her elbows on the table and used her hands to hold up her head. "Hank and I went to check out some new Indie bands at the East Side Festival last night." She yawned. "They were terrific. There were drinks and dancing and then…even more drinks. You were supposed to come. Remember?"

Kate bit her lip to hold back a smile. "That's right. Sorry I had to miss it."

"I bet you are." Charm lifted the brim of her cap and peaked out. "Never mind. A little breakfast and I'll be good as new."

The waitress took their order and Kate gave Charm a rundown of last night's events.

"But Gregor knows he can't outsource the casino management," Charm said.

"It's even worse that he's doing it with Vertex. They've been involved in all kinds of bad stuff. I don't know anything about the loopholes Tom mentioned, but I'm going to check it out." Kate paused while the waitress set down their eggs benedict, then quickly resumed her tale. "And speaking of Tom, he was acting really bizarre last night.

One minute laughing like everything's fine—the next minute, I swear, I thought he was going to cry. He's washing his medication down with booze and I think it's screwing him up—"

"Slow down my spin-doctor friend." Charm held up a palm, gesturing for a halt. "Remember you're dealing with a person short a few brain cells this morning."

"Right. Sorry."

"I want to hear more about Tom, the house, and Elsie-Sharon, but first—tell me what you told Wilson."

Kate took a deep breath and exhaled loudly. "I lied to him, Charm. I told him what Gregor wanted me to."

Charm regarded her thoughtfully. "You don't know for sure Gregor was lying. Tom might be lying."

"Nah. Wilson knows his stuff. He's had all kinds of lawsuits and accusations levelled at him, but nobody's ever proven him wrong." She shook her head. "I did some research on him, too. That, coupled with Tom telling me pretty much the same story—and an overall feeling of doom—tells me I bet on the wrong horse." Kate took a long sip from her cup and peered over the rim. "He told me if I was going to stick to my story, I was leaving him few options."

"What does that mean?"

"He's threatening me. He's going to print whatever he wants and when Gregor's quote is added, Gregor will look like a total liar and so will I."

Charm paused, a forkful halfway to her mouth. "He's not threatening you, and he doesn't print *whatever* he wants. You said yourself, he's a stickler for accuracy. He's reminding you he has a job to do and giving you another opportunity to come clean which, I bet, he doesn't do for everybody."

"I guess so. But it isn't going to be pretty. On a cheerier note, did I tell you I've applied for a position with the Department of Transit? Seems they've come up against quite a bit of opposition trying to blast a new subway line underneath a residential community and they need a public relations manager to head off community opposition."

"Kate." Charm shook her head.

"I know. You've told me. Everybody's got a complaint about transit."

"Even people who don't use it...Especially people who don't use it. I swear the five years I worked there took fifteen years off my life. Besides, don't you have a contract with Pacific?"

"It terminates in a month."

Charm stuck out her lower lip. "It won't be the same without you and we'll have to hold an election for a new KALP. chairperson." She finished her eggs and dabbed the corners of her mouth with a napkin. "That hit the spot. I almost feel human again."

They nodded their thanks to the waitress who refilled their coffee and removed the empty plates.

"We'll deal with whatever Wilson prints in his column," Charm said. "We always do. Worrying and second-guessing yourself is going to spoil your day and give you wrinkles." She stirred some sugar into her cup and grinned at Kate. "And ruin the great idea I've just had.

"Let's go visit Elsie-Sharon's store. There was a rumor at the office that she had some sort of business. Jim, Randy, and I had promised ourselves a visit one day." She squared the cap on her head so she looked determined, rather than wretched. "I hate to leave out our dear friend Jim, but there's no time like the present. We'll fill him in on all the juicy details later. Let's go see how the president's wife manages to afford a house like that."

"You're on." Kate plucked her jacket from the back of her chair. "I'd sure be interested in knowing."

"And let's not waste any time, OK? I'm feeling a lot better." Charm looked at Kate sheepishly. "But I'm not sure how long it's gonna last."

★ ★ ★

Sharon Chernin's store was in an old warehouse in the area of Vancouver first carved out of the wilderness by European pioneers. Known as Gastown, the area was named for "Gassy Jack" Deighton, a boisterous saloon owner in the 1800s, who stepped ashore with a barrel of whiskey and told the mill workers he'd serve them drinks if they'd build him a saloon. He was in business the next day.

As the city grew and the centre of business and commerce moved away from Gassy Jack's fiefdom, the area fell on hard times. It rallied for a while when the hippie movement parachuted in during the 1970s, bringing new energy, peace, love, vegetarianism, and incense to the area. In its most recent rebirth, many of the brick warehouses and factories were restored, brought up to code, and turned into pricey shops, restaurants, and trendy loft living units. In the evenings, the cobblestone streets and courtyards teemed with shoppers and nightlife. Real estate prices were sky high.

Rusty old pulleys, once used to fabricate logging equipment, hung from the ceiling of the store. An assortment of pinecones, seedpods, feathers, shells, sticks, and wooden bowls filled with stones and items culled from nature were artfully arranged on the floor below.

"The owner has a passion for imperfect things. She's

very tactile," said the sales clerk. "She has been known to cause her friends and family great embarrassment," the woman chuckled, "by openly fondling their towels and sheets."

Kate glanced at Charm and knew she was going to laugh and spoil everything at any second. Desperately trying to salvage the situation, she strode over to a display of birds' nests. "You have a marvelous collection. Have you been in business for long?" Thankfully, the woman trotted after her, leaving Charm on the other side of the store to regain her composure.

"We've been in this location for a year." The clerk held one of the desiccated bird homes aloft for Kate to admire. Mud and sticks dropped all over the floor. A poorly concealed snort told Kate that Charm had witnessed the demonstration. "We're expanding next month, though."

While the clerk focused on settling the nest back in the display, making sure the $175 price tag was tucked underneath, Kate made a "zip your lip" gesture at Charm.

"The owner has purchased the entire city block and we'll be contracting with architects and designers and tearing down a few walls to get the space we've always wanted," the clerk explained. "Our colour palette will be made up entirely of greens, blues, and subtle browns drawn from nature. Very relaxing and organic. The display fixtures will be crafted from found items, harvested from the forest to specifications that allow these belongings to breathe." Pausing for breath, she gestured like a game show hostess toward another table, inviting Kate to take a look.

The more the woman talked, the more trouble Kate was having restraining her own laughter. When the clerk slyly kicked the mud and sticks from the broken nest out of sight under a table, Kate truly thought she was going to lose it. Instead, she reminded herself she was on a fact-finding mission.

"I'm glad to hear your business is going so well. An entire block in this pricey neighbourhood. That's really impressive."

The saleswoman nodded modestly. "It's tough to educate people in a new concept. But consumers are catching on and business is booming. They're finding it's calming to live among reclaimed items." She smiled intensely at Kate and tapped her lacquered nails on the table. "Reduce, reuse, recycle. Find that diamond in the rough." The manicured fingers flipped out in a dramatic "aha" gesture. "Our owner is European. They're always way ahead with everything. She is never tempted to buy anything new."

Kate's gaze had drifted over to Charm, who was spinning an antler above her head, seemingly trying to decide which way it fit on the animal's head. The clerk's statement, however, refocused Kate's attention, for stuck vividly in her memory was the lavishness of Sharon and Gregor's mansion—everything brand new and over the top—and Tom's tale of the rare Italian stone, specially quarried and shipped.

"That's so important these days," Charm said, inserting herself into the conversation. "Reducing your carbon footprint. Isn't that what we're talking about here?" Kate stared at her blankly and the clerk stared suspiciously. "Just trying to get with the program. Obviously I'm one of the ones that's been caught out of the loop, but I think I can become an educated consumer." She smiled widely at Kate, who knew there was more to come. "Seriously, I'm hungry for knowledge." Charm nodded appreciatively at the antler. "I'm a work in progress really."

Far from being offended, the clerk cocked her head to one side and nodded. "We are always trying to deepen the information while maintaining its accessibility," she said.

"That's the only way to go, you know," Charm replied amiably, plunking the antler down with a gusto that made Kate wince. She glared at her friend. Charm, however, was on a roll and would not be put off.

"I have always admired people who can pick up a piece of junk and make it work. This is the epitome, though." She nodded cheerfully at Kate who was inching towards the door. "I mean, it's working here. This is truly the point at which J-U-N-K becomes J-U-N-Q-U-E."

"Exactly," the clerk exclaimed, apparently proud to have another disciple.

"We'll certainly have to come back when we have more time," Kate said.

"How about this afternoon after we meet your sister for lunch?" Charm said. "Wow. I just remembered your sister's name is Karma. She's a natural."

"We're open 'til nine," the clerk called as the two friends made their way out the door. "Remember to like us on Facebook."

"You are an ass," Kate said as they trotted down the old uneven sidewalk, distancing themselves from the store. "And who in the world is Karma?"

"I have no idea. It just fell off my tongue," Charm chirped. "I got going there and kinda couldn't stop."

"That woman sounds exactly like Matt after he took that SAY course." Kate shuddered. "I'd like to hire her as dedicated media liaison for Wilson. He'd never get anything useful out of her."

"Oh, to be a fly on the wall. She would drive him insane and we could watch."

They reached Kate's car and climbed in.

"I don't get it though." Charm reached for her seatbelt. "That store's supposed to be the goldmine that's supporting Gregor's lifestyle? Antlers, sticks and birds' nests... and we were the only customers in there for what, thirty minutes?"

"We are the only customers they've had for a year." Kate turned the engine over. "Did you see the amount of dust on that floor? Ours were the only footprints."

CHAPTER 22

PACIFIC LOTTERY PARTNERS
WITH NOTORIOUS COMPANY
By Rhys Wilson

Thirty years ago, when our politicians turned the Mob's favorite racket—gambling—into government-run lotteries, many foresaw profits from a cleaned-up centuries-old vice being used to benefit the community. Others predicted new moral lows.

In the decades since, provincially-run lotteries have proliferated and both the believers and the cynics have been proven right. The government has hauled in a truckload of cash. But the fact that the costs of gambling exceed the revenues collected and that they are robbing Peter to pay Paul seems to have sailed right over their heads. There have also been a few spikes on the dishonesty meter: lottery retailers winning more often than they should, sports lottery players beating the odds time and time again and, most recently, an anomaly in Pacific's popular Kinetic Keno game which has prevented some numbers from being drawn. Whether or not it has "enabled" the drawing of certain numbers, we will leave for another column because these infractions are mere speed bumps on the morality highway and pale in comparison to the corporation's latest plans.

Sources tell me that, in contravention of the Canadian Criminal Code, Pacific Lottery will engage Vertex Gaming of Germany to manage their new casino resorts and equipment. Contacted Saturday, Kate Logan, Communications Manager, Pacific Lottery Corp., denied any wrongdoing. And, according to the always passionate company president, Gregor Chernin,

"Vertex Gaming only supplies software and video lottery terminals to our casinos and anyone who says anything else is a liar."

Vertex controls 60 percent of the world's gambling and is engaged in every aspect of the business, from writing computer code and sales of video lottery terminals to developing and operating gambling venues. They brag that no company is quicker at setting up lottery systems and running them smoothly. Credit is also due Vertex for their proficiency at extracting the maximum amount of cash from the public. During fiscal year 2012, Americans spent a staggering $78 billion on lottery tickets. The Canadian public spent $9.3 billion.

What the company doesn't brag about is the number of criminal charges levelled against them. In 2010, a probe by U.S. investigators revealed Vertex had paid $5 million for non-existent services to a Texas company that proceeded to divert the funds to a private bank account in Switzerland. Vertex has admitted to making several million dollar payments to a paper stock supplier in Argentina for materials that were never delivered. The same Argentinean company has been found guilty of money laundering charges three times in the past decade. The gambling conglomerate was also questioned regarding a non-collateralized loan of 40 million dollars, which they made to the Russian Federation, just prior to their negotiations for a lottery deal in that country.

Most recently their 60-year-old vice-president, Johan Schultz, was convicted of bribing the director of Britain's Lottery Corporation into awarding management of the world's most lucrative gaming contract to Vertex.

Shocking? Well, yes and no. Shocking because Schultz was convicted. Vertex has an intriguing history of beating the criminal allegations laid against it. Similar bribery charges in Texas and New York resulted in complete exoneration for the company and job loss for the accuser. Charges of orchestrating kick-back schemes, bogus billing, illegal lobbying, and uttering threats have been similarly dismissed in European and U.S. courts of law.

Commissions, job opportunities, political contributions, wining and dining, partnerships with obvious conflicts of interest—the message is clear: good things happen to those who play ball with Vertex. Job loss, prosecution, and public humiliation are often the result if you cross the company.

The company's bread and butter is developing gambling properties, and they have made a bundle in the U.S. partnering with Native American groups to develop and operate gaming venues. Vertex typically takes 40 percent of the revenues, while the natives and the regulating body receive 30 percent each. Because financial independence is portrayed as a huge step toward native self-government and responsibility, and because Vertex's management routinely doubles revenue figures each year, they have been extremely successful in finding business partners. Their website describes in great detail the extent to which they go to address the "profound financial and social needs of our Aboriginal partners."

When pickings get slim, Vertex gets creative. A recent partnership required creativity as well as legal wrangling. Two years ago in South Dakota, Vertex's scouts located a choice piece of land. Not a problem that it wasn't a reservation. They moved in a few natives and had it declared a reserve. Today, a 300-room casino resort stands proudly on the "Klahanee Reserve." Three years ago they partnered with the ETOK of Arizona. The band had only one member but lots of land and the looser gaming regulations to which native bands are entitled.

There's one problem that even Vertex's highly paid lobbyists can't circumvent, however. The U.S. strictly enforces a law prohibiting outside management firms from operating tribal casinos for more than five years. At this time, the reins have to be relinquished to the band's board of directors. Consequently, Vertex *moves in fast, milks a venue for all it is worth, and bugs out when their five years are up.*

Enter the neighbour from the frozen north and our loosely enforced gambling regulations. Vertex has been courting Pacific Lottery for the past four years, ever since Johan Schultz and Hans Niedermeyer, a longtime Vertex employee, and their wives lavishly entertained President Gregor Chernin and his wife at the international gaming convention in the Netherlands.

No stranger to the courts, Neidermeyer was found guilty of distributing illegal video lottery terminals in England in 2013, but he struck a deal to testify against his boss, Johan Schultz, at his bribery trial, and did no jail time. During his testimony, Neidermeyer admitted he had pocketed five million dollars in "side deals" the previous year. Having helped incarcerate Schultz, Niedermeyer moved up the food chain and is now Vertex's point man in wooing Pacific Lottery.

Interestingly, Pacific's Director of Sales, Lucas Mardone, worked as a sales manager for Vertex from 2005 to 2009, leaving the company when he was accused of taking kickbacks. In true Vertex style, he did no jail time. In 2010, apparently unconcerned with Mardone's past, Gregor Chernin hired him.

CHAPTER 23

When she arrived at the office Monday morning, Kate found Wilson's column spread out on her keyboard. Five minutes later, June called to say her presence was requested immediately at a strategy meeting with the president. She was savagely reprimanded during the explosive hour-long meeting occasioned by Wilson's latest column. As his agitation grew, Kate's attempts to defend herself were vehemently shot down, and the colour of Gregor's bald pate rose like a thermometer to a bright cherry red. Had the circumstances been a little different, Kate might have found it entertaining; however, it was no laughing matter. Gregor blamed the situation entirely on her and accused her of misquoting him. The first to escape the boardroom, her eyes burning, she hurried to the privacy of the women's washroom at the far end of the building before her emotions boiled over.

Adding to Kate's distress was the behavior of her colleagues. Usually in these meetings, there was an unspoken camaraderie among the underlings: "We're all in this together. Humor the old fool in charge and we'll make things right later." This time, perhaps afraid he was going to turn his wrath on them, members of the other departments joined Gregor in his condemnation of her.

Alone in the vacant washroom, she splashed some cool water on her face, did some deep breathing, and reminded herself she had other options. She had stuck it out at the lottery corporation because managing crises was an inherent part of the job and she wasn't a quitter.

However, despite her contractual obligations and Charm's opinion on public transit, it was obviously time to make a move. Cheered by her decision, and another few minutes of measured breathing, she was feeling much better when she heard a tentative tapping at the door.

"Kate," whispered a gruff voice. "Are you in there?"

Her eyes darted to the door in surprise. "Yes," Kate said slowly.

"Are you all right?" The voice was stronger this time. "Oh screw it. I don't care." Cautiously pushing the door open with his left hand, a plastic container clutched in his right, Jim stole into the women's washroom, his eyes darting around furtively for other patrons.

Kate snorted with laughter. "Don't worry. It's just the two of us," she said dramatically.

"Oh, be quiet." He peeked in the stalls to make sure they were empty. "I was worried about you." He rapped her on the shoulder. "You didn't come back." Jim peeled the top off the container. "Cookie?" he asked. "Randy's trying something new—carrot, orange, and coconut. Very good for breakfast."

"Another job hazard," Kate said, reaching in for one of the iced golden mounds. "Cookies for breakfast. I'm going to be a blimp."

"We've gotta keep your strength up." Jim grabbed one himself and snapped the lid on the box.

Kate eased herself up onto the marble countertop and bit into the cookie. Pacific had won an interior design award for their last office renovation; even the toilets were plush. Doing his best to keep his large frame perched on the glossy surface beside her, Jim listened with rapt attention as she told him what had transpired that morning and at

Gregor's party. By the time Kate finished, they had polished off three cookies each and she was tensing up again.

"Now kid, I can see you're concerned Randy will be pissed you didn't invite us on your mission to Sharon's nest and antler shop." Jim flipped his hand dismissively. "Believe me, I know better than anybody how excited he gets when he thinks he's been left out. But not to worry. It'll be our little secret."

Kate laughed in spite of herself, then bit her upper lip. "We'll go again. I promise. We just need somebody to impersonate my imaginary sister, Karma."

"Randy's your man." Jim nodded confidently at Kate. "Seriously. He's got this great getup from last Halloween, hair extensions—the whole shebang. You've got to see it to believe it."

Picturing the masquerade, Kate choked on her cookie. Jim hastily reached out and pounded her on the back.

"Wilson called while you were in the meeting," he said quietly.

"What in the hell for?" Kate's eyes widened. "To see if they've shot me yet?"

"No. He was inquiring about the 'sexual harassment' taking place at the corporation," Jim said, making little quotation marks in the air.

Kate let out a sigh. "The panties. How did he ever hear about *them*?"

"I have no idea." He cleared his throat. "But I took the opportunity to let him know what I think of his column and his methods."

"Good for you. What did he say?"

"Not too much," Jim admitted. "But I did get my two cents in."

Kate smiled and they both started when the washroom door was pushed open by an unsuspecting female employee.

"Give us a moment, would you, Lucille, hon?" Jim asked.

She nodded and backed out the door without a word.

Jim turned his attentions back to Kate. "The long and the short of it is you're doing a great job. 'Illegitimi non carborundum.' Don't let the bastards grind you down. Oh, speaking of bastards, Wilson wants you to call him back right away."

"His every wish is my command." Kate hopped off the counter. "Let's go."

"You're not serious."

"In his dreams." She heaved the door open, then stopped. "Hey Jim, you've never told me what happened to the old Communications Manager. The one you had before me?"

Jim paused for a moment before answering. "No one ever knew. He just stopped coming into work."

CHAPTER 24

The next morning, Kate and Charm stopped to clarify a few issues with the graphics company designing some promotional materials and arrived at the office a little later than usual. Kate was feeling better about her situation. After the ruckus yesterday morning, things had cooled down considerably and the rest of the day had passed relatively calmly. Reminding herself she was leaving also helped put a positive spin on things.

They had entered the building, fobs poised for swiping, when Charm spotted her prey. Her step quickening, she trotted up to Garth, the guard on duty. The two of them had a long-running friendly feud. He teased her about her crazy hair. She harassed him about the "soul patch" he had been trying to grow for four months. The reception she received this morning, however, was different and definitely chilly.

"What's up with him?" Charm asked Kate as they made their way down the hall. "I was going to tell him his beard was looking pretty good. The whiskers are all starting to point in the same direction. Did you notice?"

"It's coming along nicely," Kate said absently. "I know security is short-handed. Maybe he can't leave his post to get a coffee and that cinnamon bun he likes every morning."

Drawing closer to the communications bullpen, they were startled by the sound of raised voices. Cautiously rounding the corner of a padded office partition, they spied Tom at Jim's desk, fingers pointing and arms waving. Jim was dishing it right back.

Tom spun around to face the late arrivals. "Charm," he barked, "where in the hell have you been? Get over here and help Jim with this winning number info. I need my reports right away."

Tossing a questioning glance at Kate, Charm hustled to Jim's station.

"Kate! I want to see you now." Tom yanked open the door to his office and disappeared inside.

Kate peeled off her coat and hurried over to see what was going on.

"Close the door," Tom growled. He tossed the morning paper across the desk at her. "I assume you've seen this?"

PANTYGATE: LOTTERY EMPLOYEES RECEIVE OBSCENE MAIL
By Alastair Fawkes, Staff Reporter

Vice President, Pacific Lottery Corporation, Pamela Luther, says she and two other female employees were "terrified, disgusted, and upset" when they received a pair of heart-shaped, G-string panties in the inter-office mail last Friday. Each "gift" was accompanied by a handwritten card, supposedly from a colleague.

"We all took it hard," Luther says. "One of the women broke down and cried."

Luther was heading a meeting in her office early Friday morning when Manager of Communications, Kate Logan, burst in bearing the package she had received and broke down in tears.

"You can imagine their embarrassment," says Luther. "Young women attending a serious meeting in their business suits, faced with this. As senior representative, it is up to me to defend them."

Luther has hired a detective agency to find the perpetrators.

"I don't care how long it takes or how much it costs, I'm going to bring them to justice," Luther says.

So far, the culprits remain at large.

144

Kate felt backwards for a chair and sat down abruptly. "What in the hell is this pile of crap?"

"You don't know anything about it, then?" Tom asked. "Looks to me like you've had quite a bit of input."

Kate sat up straighter. "I thought the panty thing was a joke. I told you that Saturday night." Tom stared at her impassively. Becoming more upset by the second, Kate wondered for only a moment if she should say what was on her mind. "As a matter of fact, I think you sent them and I warned you Pamela was going to make a big deal out of it. Certainly you don't think *I* made an issue of it?"

Tom leaned back in his leather chair and regarded her with suspicion. "The taxpayers are going to think we've got a lot of free time to spend joking around."

"I never mentioned it to anyone," Kate emphasized, "and I don't appreciate Pamela using me to make her mark as a savior of womankind." She stood up. "You should know that." Slapping the newspaper down on his desk, she stormed out the door.

Ignoring the stares she received along the way, Kate stalked down the hall to the washroom. *This is beyond ridiculous,* she thought. *I might as well set up shop in the toilet.* However, she needed some privacy. She was so angry she thought she was going to cry and that would play right into Pamela's hands. Alone in the washroom, she collected her thoughts.

What she had just learned explained the reception she and Charm received from the security guard that morning and the stares and sniggering she thought she had been imagining. Pamela had a great many detractors at the company. The way the column read, many of them would think Kate had grabbed this opportunity to brown nose and make points with the boss.

Having regained her composure, Kate was returning

to her desk, now fully cognizant of the snickering, when she spied Sabrina exiting Pamela's office. Kate waited until her friend was well clear of the vice president's office then quickened her step to catch up.

"Hey," she whispered, "can you meet me for lunch?" Kate was startled to see Sabrina's face was tear-streaked, her mascara smudged.

"Please, Kate. I can't be seen talking to you." Sabrina continued down the hall but Kate increased her pace and gently took her arm, forcing her to stop.

"I'm sorry. I didn't know you were so upset over this," Kate said.

"I could care less about a stupid pair of panties," Sabrina whispered. "But I can't lose this job. Jeremy is making things really difficult and he won't pay any child support." Two people approached them and she immediately began making vague references and gesturing to the reports she had under her arm. When the coast was clear, she gave Kate a quick squeeze. "I have to go along with her. I'm desperate and she knows it." Her face began to melt again. "I'm sorry," she said and hustled away.

★ ★ ★

The rest of the day was strangely quiet, almost like the calm before the storm. At one point Jim stole into Kate's office to check on her. But he was too busy compiling Tom's reports to go for lunch where they could have hashed things over and compared notes.

"Tomorrow for sure," he said.

Charm wasn't available for intelligence gathering, either. Pamela had made her Chief "Metacognition Coordinator" instead of Kate and sent her over to the SAY offices to plan the upcoming session. And Kate could get no satisfaction from Pamela, herself, as she was "away for the rest of the day, at very high-level meetings", according to her smug secretary.

★ ★ ★

Kate got up early the next morning, threw on warm clothes and boots, and trotted through the blackness to the newspaper boxes on Granville Street. She popped her money in the slot, grabbed a copy of the paper, and was dismayed to see she was still making news.

SEXUAL HARRASSMENT AT PACIFIC LOTTERY: OTHERS VICTIMIZED BY PANTY PRANKSTERS
By Alastair Fawkes, Staff Reporter

Women were not the only victims in last Friday's Pantygate debacle. Lucas Mardone says he was shocked to hear that the gift card accompanying the G-string panties received by Kate Logan, one of the women complaining of sexual harassment, was signed "Love Lucas," apparently indicating him.

"I had nothing to do with this matter and I am extremely grateful to our Executive Vice President, Pamela Luther, for taking immediate action to identify the perpetrators of this crime," says Mardone, Director of Sales.

In case you missed it, three employees of the taxpayer funded Pacific Lottery Corporation received a gift of lacy panties in the inter-office mail on Friday and are complaining of sexual harassment. Besides Communications Manager, Logan, Luther received panties with a card indicating they were from company president, Gregor Chernin. Sabrina Szabo's panties were accompanied by a card suggesting they came from her boss, Julian Henry.

"This could have a very damaging effect on my career and

147

professional standing," Mardone says. "My wife is devastated. We are relying on our Faith and each other to keep it together."

Please see today's "Letters to the Editor" for a sample of the overwhelming response we have received to yesterday's story.

Stunned, Kate tucked the newspaper under her arm and self-consciously peered left and right. "Letters to the Editor" would have to wait; the day was brightening and the streets coming alive with commuters. She was getting more than a few odd looks, pouring so raptly over a newspaper atop a vending machine. Pulling her jacket closer, she hustled for home and wondered at her own sanity when the first thing that came to mind was: Mardone has a wife? Who would be that stupid?

She had just entered her condo and kicked off her boots when the phone rang. Kate was surprised to see Matt's number in the call display window. She was even more surprised to realize she was glad to hear his voice. Her attitude changed when he started to talk.

"Here I've been bragging about my girlfriend and how she's got an in with this global gaming corporation. Imagine my surprise when a classmate sends me a link to an article about you making a big scene over underwear." He raised his voice to drown out Kate's explanation. "It was in the national paper and there's more this morning."

"That's not what—"

"I hope you're enjoying all the attention you're getting. You look totally ridiculous."

Kate's eyes darted to the newspaper on the couch and back to the telephone she held at arm's length. She punched "end," grabbed the paper, and opened it to "Letters to the Editor."

CHAPTER 25

To the Editor:

I am appalled at the hypocrisy of Kate Logan and Pamela Luther. They have no qualms signing their names to a "Male Sex Symbol of the Year" poster where their boss's head is photo-shopped onto the body of a young hunk, but when the shoe is on the other foot, who's the first to cry foul? As far as I am concerned, they are the ones guilty of sexual harassment.

Name withheld, Vancouver, B.C.

To the Editor:

Is this the same Pamela Luther who's always telling us the important roles Pacific Lottery plays: providing entertainment, enriching communities, providing for healthcare, education, and sports, blah, blah. I don't see tracking down "panty pranksters" as one of them. From what I have read, Pacific Lottery should clean up its own backyard.

Obviously this is a tasteless act, but: How old are these women? Aren't they all senior managers? What are they getting paid? Get a grip and get on with it. You're being paid to do a job and this isn't it.

R. Cuthbert, Coquitlam, B.C.

To the Editor:

How did these women get their jobs? They're just a bunch of publicity seekers. I've never heard of such a waste of taxpayer money in the seventy years I've been around. Government people in highly paid positions never fail to amaze me.

S. Brown, Victoria, B.C.

To the Editor:

"Young women sitting around in their business suits."
Imagine. Would it have been any different if they were sitting
around in their birthday suits? Obviously, business attire does
not a professional make, Ms. Luther.
C. Dowd, Prince George, B.C.

Kate felt tears welling up in her eyes. How could this be happening? Matt was right. She looked like an ass—and she hadn't even done anything wrong. The professional problem solver and spin doctor felt absolutely helpless.

She pulled her laptop out from under the file she had been reading on Vertex, lifted the cover and opened her e-mail. She had thirty new messages—some from well-wishers, others from individuals obviously hungry for gossip. Three were from Wilson: "Call me," "I'm getting concerned. Call me," and "I've tried texting. Please call."

Concerned? I'll bet, Kate thought. *He just wants fodder for his column.*

The most recent message was from a name she didn't recognize. Kate knew she should delete it unopened for fear of viruses, but curiosity got the best of her. Sent only minutes before, it was from the human resources manager at Transit. She thanked Kate for participating in the recent competition for Communications Manager, then went on to say an applicant had been chosen that they deemed more suitable for the position.

Kate felt like a lifeline had been pulled from under her. She had been counting on the Transit job. Matt had not only left all his belongings in the condominium when he went east, he had left Kate with the mortgage payment and the monthly bills as, he explained, he wasn't in fact living there.

She walked mechanically into her small kitchen, spooned out the beans needed for a few strong cups, and flicked the coffee maker on. As the machine hummed and sighed, Kate gazed out the window at the grey day. Rain had begun to fall and a strong wind was blowing the first leaves off the trees onto the street below. She stood there until the ready beep of the coffee machine startled her out of her trance. Only after she had consumed an oversized cup of the brew did her mind begin to function again and she returned to the living room, pulled her laptop closer, and began to write:

Editor, The Vancouver Star
Dear Sir:
I was surprised to read in your paper of my emotional collapse upon receiving a joke gift at my place of business. Apparently, I was so "horrified, disgusted, and upset" that I burst into tears.

To set the record straight, when I received this "gift,", I took it exactly as it was intended—as a joke. I have never considered this incident to be anything more than a prank and have never made an issue of it. Despite what has been reported, Pamela Luther and her detectives have not spoken to me about this incident, asked me if I was upset, expressed any interest in my state of mind, offered to console me, or anything else. I have no idea how any spokesperson at Pacific Lottery can presume to know how I feel and am curious to know who burst into tears. It certainly was not me.

Consequently, I am finding it difficult to read myself portrayed in your paper as a humorless fool with so much time on my hands that I can dwell on silly matters like this.

I am engaged in a business where my ability to deal competently with issues and to quickly make complex decisions is key. I do not appreciate having my livelihood threatened by those who, to further their own ends, misrepresent my actions and words and infer that a little prank is too big an issue for me to handle.
Sincerely yours,
Kate Logan,
Manager of Communications, Pacific Lottery Corporation

If it accomplished little else, writing the e-mail helped Kate vent her anger. When she was satisfied it said what was on her mind, she clicked "send" and got dressed for work. *I'd better "walk the talk,"* she thought. *Failing to report for work would give them a legitimate reason to penalize me.* And she grimly reminded herself of one of Jim's pet sayings: "If you're not *at* the table—you're *on* it."

* * *

Aside from the snickering and whispering which had ramped up significantly, the atmosphere in the office was calm. Everyone seemed to be walking on eggshells, which made Kate wonder when the other shoe was going to drop. Tom and Gregor were absent for one reason or other. Lucas was taking a couple of days stress leave after the horror of learning his name was attached to Kate's gift. Pamela was holed up with the private detective she had hired and Charm and Jim were worried about their friend—Jim having brought a huge assortment of fresh cookies, in case the need arose.

"Wow," Charm said. "There're some fancy ones in there today."

"What can I say? Randy read that bit about Kate in yesterday's paper and he just started baking." Jim held out

152

the decorated box and Charm snatched up one of each cookie. He narrowed his gaze. "Yep, Randy said this situation was going to upset Charm, so he'd better bake loads."

Kate grabbed a handful. "Well, she's going to have to fight me for them this morning." Taking a seat on her desk where she had an unobstructed view of anyone approaching, she polished off a cookie and told them about the call she had received from Matt, her e-mails from Wilson and Transit, and the letter she had written to the editor of the paper.

"So, which one of our colleagues is the anonymous chicken that tipped them off about Lucas's signature on your gift card, and Tom's poster?" Charm whispered. "And what's the big deal? We all signed it—the girls and the guys. Tom knew it was just for fun. He told me it was the best present he got."

"But that was before he lost his sense of humor." Jim shook his head, undoubtedly recalling the battle over the customer service reports. "Do you think it's something in the water? Everybody around here's losing their marbles." While Charm and Kate chewed thoughtfully, considering the tainted water angle, Jim told them the latest rumor was that Garth, the security guard at the front desk, had a hand in the panty prank.

"I don't know if Pamela and her detectives suspect him," he added, "but it's all the talk around the water cooler."

Kate nodded to Charm, recalling how Garth's behavior had changed since the panty incident.

"Why don't you call Wilson?" Charm asked. "You might just find you've misjudged him and he genuinely wants to help."

Jim and Kate stopped mid-chew and frowned at her.

Charm cleared her throat. "Only a suggestion. I never took you two for glass-is-half-empty kind of people." She dabbed at the corners of her mouth with her fingertips. "How about a little levity? I have gossip on Lucas."

"I already know...he's married," Kate said.

"No way," Jim exclaimed. "Who'd be that stupid?"

Kate shrugged. "It gets better. Apparently, he's a man of Faith."

Jim shook his head. "Do you think?"

"No, no. This is even better." Charm lowered her voice. "He's been seeing a plastic surgeon. According to his jilted girlfriend over in advertising—who's bitter as hell and brimming with information—he's already had his eyes done and now he's going in for a procedure called a Y-lift."

"That might explain why he's looking so wild lately," Kate said.

"Yeah," Jim concurred, waving a cookie at Charm. "I'd say the eye 'lift' thing turned out to be more of an eye 'wrap' on him."

"Very scary," Charm agreed. "Anyway, that's where he is today. He's not on stress leave at all. These Y-lift procedures are done in a doctor's office and you can go out in public pretty much right away. He's getting himself all prettied up for when the press wants a photo of the injured man."

Once her friends had left, Kate wondered what to tackle first. A bundle of advertising copy had been dropped on her desk for final approval and Charm needed e-magazine copy signed off. Lucas wanted a speech written for a convention at which he was key-note speaker, and Tom had left her a voice mail changing the format of the winning number reports. She had a mountain of calls to return to reporters and a demand from Gregor for a press release on the phenomenal success Dragonfly Lake Casino had been in its first few weeks. When her phone rang, she snatched it up. Although she wouldn't admit it to Jim or Charm, she hoped it was Wilson.

"Thank you for taking my call. How are you bearing up? Do you feel sexually exploited?" began Alastair Fawkes. Sincerity not being his strong suit, however, it quickly became apparent whose side he was on.

"What makes this situation any different from you endorsing the 'Sex Object' poster? I trust this incident is not indicative of Pacific's professionalism in dealing with the millions of taxpayer dollars you take in every year? How much time and money are being squandered by Pamela Luther on this 'investigation,' anyway?"

Kate did her best to remain calm answering Fawkes's barrage of questions, but when she hung up the phone she was badly shaken—and angry because of it. *Note to self,* she thought: *Media liaison becomes a totally different ball of wax when you are personally involved.*

CHAPTER 26

K ate set off to grab a copy of the paper as soon as it hit the street the next morning. A pair of joggers ran effortlessly past her and she speculated how early a person would have to get out of bed in order to already have their second wind.

She peered into the vending box and felt her spirits rise. The headline, although it caught her interest, was not about her. She extracted a paper and read that an elected official had been caught using his expense account to pay for prostitutes. She had her first real laugh in some time when she read that the penny-pinching philanderer was the boorish Minister of Native Affairs she had met at Wesley's reception. "Roxy", the escort, had been running Richard Stahl's government credit card through her mobile credit processor for over a year.

The phone was ringing when Kate arrived home and when she spied Charm's number in the call display, she quickly answered.

"Have you read today's Opinion page yet?" Charm asked.

Kate sank onto the couch and closed her eyes.

"I didn't want to face it on an empty stomach and coffee's not ready yet. Judging from your tone of voice, maybe I should make it a scotch."

"You might find it upsetting." Charm was fuming on the other end of the line. "Damn that Pamela and who is this Fawkes, anyway? We don't know him. I'm going to phone Wilson and find out what this guy's problem is."

"Not yet, OK? I'm still working out how to handle this." Kate pulled off her boots with her free hand. "I don't imagine they printed the letter I wrote to the editor?"

"I checked every page."

"There's balanced reporting for you." Kate sighed. "I keep reminding myself Pamela looks like an even bigger fool than she's made me out to be, and I don't feel so embarrassed."

There was a long moment of silence. "Maybe take a look at page six before you go to work...Or better yet, don't go in at all," Charm said.

"I was going to give Jim some help with the winning number reports. Tom is changing things again and—"

"I'm not telling you what to do but, if Lucas can take days off for plastic surgery, you're entitled to a legitimate mental health day with all this mental stuff happening."

The way Charm was carrying on, Kate knew an extra strong pot of coffee was called for, and that she would be wise to down most of it before tackling page six. She scowled at the photo of the Minister of Native Affairs on the front page, grinning confidently from a less stressful time in his life. The phone still to her ear, she walked into the kitchen and put a pot on to brew.

"I know you're going to go in no matter what I say," Charm continued. "I have to go downtown to see if the meeting rooms at the convention centre are suitable for the SAY event." She groaned loudly. "If you need me, promise you'll call my cell."

Kate told her not to worry and disconnected. She put the phone in the charger and flipped to page six, which was half filled with scathing letters from readers and an editorial by Alastair Fawkes calling for the taxpayers to make examples of Pamela and Kate and fire them. It wasn't the written word that was the most shocking, however, but the black and white image that filled the top half of the page. Beneath a headline that read, "Shut up Already— This is a Waste of Taxpayer Money," was a hideous caricature of Pamela and Kate with pairs of G-string underwear stretched across their mouths like gags.

★ ★ ★

Kate knew Jim was at the end of his tether where the winning number reports were concerned. When Tom had thrown fuel on the fire by insisting Jim use a new computer program to speed things up, she knew her big buddy was going to snap. He was a hardworking and dedicated employee, but a technological whiz he was not. Unable to sleep, Kate had mulled the problem over and came up with a solution that she thought would work perfectly. Her desire to relay this to Jim, plus her desire to confront Pamela for lying to the media, overrode Charm's grounds for taking the day off, by a slim margin.

Jim quickly grasped Kate's data reporting scheme and was grateful for a solution to his problem. With this first item off her to do list, she moved on to the second and was disappointed to discover Pamela hadn't yet arrived. Returning to her desk, Kate tended to a few pressing issues and retrieved her e-mail, including another from Wilson:

> *Please call me on my cell.*
> *R.W.*
> *P.S. Charm tells me you're receiving these messages.*
> *So no more stalling. Call me.*

Damn that Charm, Kate thought, although she couldn't help smile, even with the government rake grinning back at her from the newspaper atop her in-basket.

"Who in the hell is Alastair Fawkes?" she asked when Wilson answered his phone on the first ring.

"He's a narrow-minded jackass."

"There, you see, we can agree on something."

"He can be prejudiced—doesn't consider all sides of a story."

"Who accused him of that?"

"I did, actually," Wilson said, faltering slightly.

"Kind of a 'pot calling the kettle black' situation, wouldn't you say?" Kate asked, only half joking.

"I think, 'it takes one to know one', is much kinder," Wilson replied. "I knew something was up. He's been pumping me for information about you and Pacific."

"And you said what, exactly?"

"Nothing. You won't even return my calls. I don't know anything worth telling…I do know that a few years ago Fawkes was in the running for the VP position at Pacific and he lost to Pamela Luther. When he heard she was involved in sexual harassment at the lottery, it was like manna from heaven."

Eager to get her position on record, Kate quickly summarized the real course of the panty events.

"How are you making out?" He paused. "I've seen the recent articles."

"I'm OK." Kate spoke with more conviction than she felt.

"Have you received any strange e-mail or texts?"

Kate forced a laugh. "My admirers aren't that cheap. They know to send gifts, preferably racy lingerie."

"That's good, I guess," Wilson said hesitantly. "But be careful." He cleared his throat. "I'm afraid I haven't shopped for gifts and I don't want to imply you're a cheap date, but would you be interested in another Costco hotdog tonight?"

There was an awkward silence while Kate considered his offer. "Could I take a rain check? I don't think I'd be very good company tonight," she said, meaning every word.

★ ★ ★

Just after lunch, Kate was hashing through material for Lucas's speech when John, her building manager, called to tell her that her condo had been broken into.

She arrived home as the police officer was climbing from his patrol car and they walked in together. Inside, the frail eighty-year-old building manager stood at attention outside her suite, apparently on guard against further trespass. Expecting the worst, Kate walked through the splintered doorway and into the living room. Her desk drawers yawned open and had obviously been rifled through. Items protruded and papers littered the floor. She immediately noticed her new laptop was gone, but nothing else seemed to be missing. This did little, however, to alleviate her fear.

"I know it's small consolation," the officer said, "but don't take it personally. A break-and-enter like this is strictly a crime of opportunity." He pulled a pen and notebook from his cargo pants. "He was probably in here for less than a minute looking for something small enough to carry and easy to pawn. You might want to see if any small electronics or jewellery are missing."

Kate nodded and walked into her bedroom where her attention was immediately drawn to something in the middle of the bed. Approaching with apprehension, she took a closer look and screamed. Lying atop her white duvet was a dead rat, its brown fur matted with blood, the long, ribbed tail sticking straight out behind. Beside it on a piece of cardboard was a message in red marker:

"This is what happens to rats!!"

With this new development adding a personal component to the crime after all, the investigation took on a new dimension. More officers were summoned, some to take photographs, some to scoop the grisly evidence and check for fingerprints, and some to take Kate's statement. All the while, John stood by her, his bony, liver-spotted hand resting on her shoulder for moral support.

When the rat was disposed of, the police had departed and John reluctantly returned to his suite for a much needed nap, Kate put in a call to Matt. She had been unable to find their theft insurance policy in the desk or among the documents thrown on the floor and she hoped he had filed it elsewhere.

"Are my snowboard and bike still there? I know they'd want those," he blurted.

He was oblivious to the fact the burglar hadn't been in the basement storage room and that Kate had assured him nothing of his was missing. When, close to tears at the recollection, she told him about the rat, he told her to wash the sheets in hot water and to quit being such a drama queen.

"Property crime is common in the big city. It's not like they targeted you personally." Once he had put forward this earth-shattering piece of information and was convinced his belongings were safe, he had one final piece of advice.

"Now that I know the bigger items weren't stolen, I'm thinking we don't want to make an insurance claim for your computer. It will only raise our rates for next year. Why don't you just pick up a new one and pay for it yourself. On the other hand, do you really need a computer? You can use the one at work."

Kate slammed the phone down, scooped the papers up off the floor, and tapped them into a neat pile. Sliding the desk drawers closed, she sunk into the couch and eyed the door to her bedroom warily. One of the detectives had done his best to clean up the mess, stripping the sheets from the bed and disposing of them. Still, Kate didn't know how she could ever sleep in that bed again.

She crossed the room to the kitchen, ignored the coffeemaker, pulled a glass from the cupboard and poured herself a measure of the scotch she had joked about with Charm that morning. *God, the stuff is awful,* she thought after taking a sip. But there was something *'bracing'* about it.

After a few fortifying nips, she was feeling more decisive and knew that polishing off any more would be counterproductive. She considered giving Charm a call, realizing that if she didn't, she would suffer for it later. She put down her glass, reached for the phone, and punched out a number.

"Hi," she said, her voice breaking. "I'm hoping I can still take you up on your offer for dinner tonight?"

CHAPTER 27

K ate stepped from the shelter of the overgrown laurel hedge when she saw the approaching Jeep blink its lights. When it pulled to a stop at the curb, she yanked the door open and quickly hopped in.

Wilson reached forward and turned the stereo down. "I thought we would have more privacy if we ate at my place," he said. "OK with you?"

"Sure," Kate replied.

He put the vehicle into gear and sped north down Hemlock Street. "Did you get the locks changed?"

"Locks changed, alarm installation next week," Kate replied, hoping she sounded brave. "Your friend, Detective Lee, called the locksmith for me. He also got rid of the rat."

Wilson braked for a red light and turned toward her, a look of disbelief on his face. "Paul Lee? You're putting me on?"

Kate shook her head. "He spotted his business card— the one you gave me—stuck to my fridge. When I told him I got it from you, he couldn't do enough to help."

"If you say so." The traffic began to move and Wilson signaled a right turn onto Seventh Avenue. Little else was said until they parked in front of one of the condominium complexes on the hillside. "This is probably as close as we'll get." Wilson climbed out of the car and hastily crossed Seventh heading towards the pedestrian overpass spanning the road below. Old, woody, rhododendrons grew along both sides of the narrow walkway. Undoubtedly intended to camouflage the ugliness of the concrete bridge, they would have been beautiful adorned with their vibrant blossoms—in the spring—in the daylight. Tonight, as their scraggly branches reached out and swallowed Wilson up, they looked grim and threatening.

"Hey, what's going on?" Kate yelled as he disappeared in the darkness.

"C'mon. It's not far." He emerged from the tangle of vegetation and motioned her to follow.

"There are no houses down there."

"I live on a boat. This is the closest we can get to it by car." He advanced toward her and continued more quietly, "I thought I'd told you about my boat."

"No, you didn't." Kate backed toward the safety of populated Seventh Avenue.

Wilson stopped in his tracks.

"Kate, I can't help but think your place was broken into because of your association with me." The faint glow from the streetlights barely illuminated Wilson's face but Kate sensed his distress was genuine. "I'm afraid it's distracted me a little. I'm sorry if I scared you."

A car sped down the street with its stereo booming and Kate jumped. "The last few days have been pretty rough and I'm trusting you here."

"I know," he said. "And there are some things we should discuss. Would you feel safer if we picked up Charm and I took you both out to a restaurant? We could talk there."

Kate regarded him warily and fumbled for her cell. "I think I'll just give her a call and tell her I'm with you and where we're going."

Despite a torrent of questions, Kate managed to make Charm understand the situation. She then slipped her cell into her bag, took a deep breath, and followed Wilson across the bridge to where the path branched in two different directions. He grabbed her hand and proceeded down the right-hand trail. Kate stumbled along blindly, afraid if she let go she'd lose him in the inky darkness.

Wilson crossed a shaky bridge over a small pond and pressed on confidently when their pathway was bisected twice by other trails. They finally emerged at a rocky beach bordered by prickly blackberry bushes. Kate could hear the water lapping quietly in front of her, but could see little. The overgrowth blocked the lights of the city and what little moonlight there was only cast spooky shadows.

Trembling, she struggled to gain a foothold on the slippery rocks. "Where exactly are we going?"

Wilson's loud whisper came from a jumble of brambles and shadows to her left. "In my line of work, I find it's safer to live on a boat. It comes with a built-in moat."

Kate clambered towards him over the mussel and barnacle encrusted rocks. Avoiding the blackberry vines, he moved two dilapidated dinghies off of a third one, which he flipped over. He threw in a pair of oars that had been concealed in the undergrowth, dragged the rowboat to the water, and helped Kate in. Once she was seated, he pushed the boat out a little deeper, jumped in himself, and shoved off with one of the oars.

They rowed out to a small group of boats in various states of disrepair. When they bumped up against a vessel with "Rock'n Roll" stenciled on the stern, Wilson hauled in the oars. "We made it," he said. He tied the dinghy's rope to the larger boat. "How are you doing?"

When her eyes met his in the moonlight, she could no longer contain her anxiety. She felt the corners of her mouth turn down, a sure sign tears were to follow. Wilson wrapped his arm around her shoulders and pulled her close.

"Damn it," she said, between sobs. "I feel so stupid." Tears now streamed freely down her face.

"Come on inside," he said. "It'll be all right. We'll have something to eat and figure out our next move."

He helped her aboard and across the back deck to the cabin where he opened the door and snapped on the lights. Although the boat had definitely seen better days, Kate was surprised to find that it was clean and classy—in a nautical kind of way. Smelling faintly of varnish, the interior gleamed with polished teak and shiny brass fittings. She recognized an assortment of marine equipment. The small galley held a fridge, a two-burner stove, and a built-in dining nook already set for two.

"I was kind of hoping you'd say yes to dinner on board," he said, sheepishly. Kate laughed despite her tears and took a seat in the upholstered chair he indicated. "That's the most comfortable seat I've got, providing the King isn't asleep in it." He handed her a glass of red wine. "I wonder where the little beggar is. He better not have fallen over-board again. That really pisses him off."

"What in the world are you talking about?" The wine was a nice choice for a cool evening, full and robust and, after a couple of sips, Kate began to relax.

"Ah, here he comes now. Kate, meet Elvis, the King of Rock 'n Roll." A big tortoiseshell cat sauntered up from below decks. "He used to be a pretty good guard cat, but I'm afraid he's getting soft in his old age." Elvis rolled onto his back at Kate's feet. "Give him a scratch, would you? Besides being sloppy when it comes to security, he's also cranky as hell if he doesn't get his belly rubbed."

Kate obliged and Elvis began to purr loudly. She grinned at Wilson. "How long have you been living like this?"

"Like this? You don't like...?" he asked, feigning offence.

"I think it's a terrific set-up. Although you had me worried for a minute."

"On occasion, a few of the city's more *colourful* businessmen have disagreed with some of the things I've written about them and, when they would still talk to me, the cops told me I'd be smart to watch my back. So, I came up with the *Rock n' Roll* solution. Only a few good friends know where I'm anchored at any particular time. If I think anybody else is on to me, I move to a different location. There's a lot of coastline to hide in."

"Are you allowed to just park a boat in False Creek?"

"Most of the time. Every now and then, some city councilor decides he's going to make a name for himself and gets the Harbor Patrol to kick out the floating village. Everybody moves away until it's blown over, then we all move back."

"It suits you. It's...quaint."

"Quaint?"

"Eccentric is actually the word I had in mind."

"Hah!" Wilson reached for the wine bottle and topped up their glasses. "It was my dad's boat. He used it to get away, go fishing, clear his head. I do too. Despite outward appearances, this tub's seaworthy and I've got a brand new engine under the hood."

"Does your dad go along?" Kate leaned back in her chair to accommodate Elvis who was settling himself down in the lap of his new best friend.

Wilson regarded the dark wine thoughtfully as he swirled it in his glass. "My dad's dead, Kate. He committed suicide when I was seventeen."

Stunned, Kate quit fussing with the cat. "I'm so sorry," she said softly.

"He's the reason I'm so *obsessed*, as you put it, with gambling addiction," Wilson explained. "Dad was a compulsive gambler. He couldn't stop. He got in so deep, he lost his job, his family, and his self-respect. He finally couldn't take it anymore and he killed himself."

An uncomfortable silence fell over the cozy cabin.

"I had no idea . . . " Kate mechanically patted the cat. "Some of the things I've said must have sounded terribly cruel."

"Forget it. You didn't know, only a few old friends do. And I don't act with much *decorum—most* of the time." He grinned. "I know I can't stamp it out on my own, but I tell myself I'm educating people about gambling with my column.

"How hungry are you? I hope you like steak." He eased himself out of his chair and monkeyed with a small propane tank until the burner of the stove burst into flame. "Small problem with the pilot light," he said. "I've got to fix it one of these days." Wilson removed two thick steaks, salads, and a bottle of dressing from the small fridge. He put a bowl of salad at each place setting and a basket of French bread in the middle of the table.

"I'm hungrier than I thought," Kate said, sliding into one side of the dining nook. "This looks delicious."

"Three peppercorn, cranberry, vinaigrette." Wilson rolled his eyes. "According to the clerk at 18 Carrots: 'It's excellent for dressing a perfectly plated salad of 100-mile locavore greens'—whatever that means. I've used lettuce here, the regular stuff. I hope it works on that, too."

"*You* went to 18 Carrots?" Kate asked, referring to the pricy, upscale market frequented by the "my body is a temple" types.

"Absolutely," he nodded. "And, for being a first time customer, I got a reusable, eco-friendly shopping bag."

Kate waved a slice of bread in his direction. "I've got a bunch of those bags, but I always forget to take them with me when I go shopping."

"I'm glad to hear you've got some extras because I went back to get us some dessert—took my bag—but I got so distracted discussing the merits of Omega-3 fatty acids with the nice wellness clerk, that I lost my dessert and my new bag somewhere in the shuffle."

"Omega-3s, eh. I'll bet that's what you were discussing."

Wilson dropped the steaks into a cast iron pan that had been heating on the stove and seasoned them generously. "I kid you not. Rather impressive research. I did wind up buying a bottle of it." He stepped over to the table to retrieve a slice of bread. "In fact, you can have a teaspoon of cod liver oil when you've finished your steak. I never did find our dessert."

He flipped the sizzling meat over and a delicious aroma filled the cabin. Once the steaks were cooked to his liking, he slipped each one onto a plate and added a baked potato extracted from a microwave Kate had failed to notice.

It was a delicious dinner and Kate filled Wilson in on the specifics of the robbery between mouthfuls. As she drew to the end of her account, she noticed lines of tension growing around his eyes.

"You said Paul Lee was there?"

Kate nodded. "I think he figured it was pretty odd that he comes to investigate a burglary and finds his card hanging on the fridge."

"There's something a little strange about that." Wilson gazed out the porthole. "Lee's a detective. He isn't a beat cop…I don't mean to minimize what you've been through, but Lee investigates major crimes—extortion, murder, and gang activity."

Kate chased down a mouthful of steak with some wine. "He wasn't there to start with. He arrived when the first cop radioed for help—after I found the rat. Maybe he was in the neighbourhood?"

Wilson nodded his head. "That might be it. Routine property crime doesn't come accompanied by dead rodents bearing threats."

Kate felt a chill that the buzz of the wine couldn't dull and leaned back in her seat. "They told me not to take it personally—that break-and-enters were escalating and until they started happening to the judges, the police were fighting a losing battle."

"Did Lee blow the situation off like that?"

"No." She faltered. "The first officer on the scene told me that. Now that I think of it, Detective Lee took things much more seriously. He wanted to know how long I've lived there? If I live alone? Where I work? Do I work routine hours? And he asked where I got his card."

"So you told him you knew me and you work for Pacific?"

She nodded and drew her legs up onto the bench seat. "He didn't think much of the lock on my door. He told me I needed a secure deadbolt."

"You told me he called a locksmith. That's good." Wilson cleared the plates from the table. "What about living alone?" he asked. "Do you?"

Kate felt her face flush.

"Obviously safer if you don't." He sat down and fixed his dark eyes steadily on her.

Annoyed with herself for being embarrassed by the question, she told him about her relationship with Matt, pointing out that because he was out of town for the next six months, he didn't rate as much protection.

Wilson broke the awkward silence. "We're sort of stuck for dessert, unless you really would like a spoonful of cod liver oil? Or, maybe I could interest you in finishing off the wine out on the back deck? It's a bit chilly, but I've got a space heater and lots of blankets."

With the heater on, it was very cozy outside and the weather had cleared enough that the lights of the city sparkled all the way down to Science World at the end of False Creek. While Wilson went inside to retrieve the wine, Kate settled down in a deck chair and tucked a blanket around herself. She had just gotten comfortable when Elvis leapt onto her lap and began circling to find the perfect spot.

Stepping back outside, Wilson took one look and chuckled. "Are you good and comfortable?" he asked. "Tied up in a blanket? Imprisoned by a fat cat? Glass full?" He poured some wine in the glass Kate waved in his direction. "And," he grinned, taking a seat opposite her, "ready for my next line of interrogation?"

As Elvis purred contentedly, busily kneading her leg with his paws, she laughed and said, "I give up. Lay it on me."

In answer to Wilson's questions, Kate admitted the public backlash from the panty incident was getting to her.

"Alastair Fawkes is spinning Pamela and Mardone's self-serving lies into a tale of his own that's making me look like a fool." She emphasized she hadn't mentioned the panties to anyone, there had been no tearful counselling sessions, and that Pamela was intimidating Sabrina in order to make herself into a hero.

"Sounds like the Pamela we've all come to love and *disrespect*," Wilson said. "Remember, I've known Pamela, Gregor, and your friend Tom a lot longer than you have. I've been a thorn in their sides for years...some of my prouder moments actually."

Kate raised her glass in salute.

"For what it's worth, I agree with a lot of what Fawkes has said about Pamela." Wilson cupped his chin in one hand. "I think I told you that Fawkes thinks Pacific's VP position should have gone to him?" She nodded, listening intently. "He's right. It should have. Do you know how she got that job?"

Kate shook her head and pulled the blanket closer around her shoulders.

"Pamela was given that job as payment for taking the fall for something that our Minister of Native Affairs, Richard Stahl, did."

The boat rocked slightly when a series of small waves hit the port side and Elvis lifted his head, instantly on the alert. Kate patted the cat until he settled back down, her gaze fixed on Wilson.

"I guess it would be around seven years ago that Stahl had the province's electoral boundaries redrawn on some pretext. His point, of course, was to make sure his new constituency included an additional area of guaranteed support. If you look at a map, all the constituencies have pretty regular divisions—like postage stamps—except Stahl's, where this appendage that looks like a big thumb protrudes from the west side. We started calling it 'Dickie's Digit.'"

"Didn't anybody notice?"

"Not until six months after the election, at which time the media jumped right on it. Our editor at the time was a stubborn old friend of mine. He knew Stahl did it and he was damned if he was going to let it go. Stahl even got all juiced up one night at a sister-city junket down in Los Angeles and bragged about it. You saw the guy in action at Wesley's reception. He can't keep his mouth shut."

"Or his hands to himself, according to this morning's paper."

"That's Dickie."

"What's that got to do with Pamela?"

"Long story short, Dickie kept his seat. He swore he knew nothing about it, but was quick to point out it was the fault of a junior bureaucrat, Pamela Hirsch."

"Hirsch?"

"That's her real name. Dickie made a huge show of firing her. Meanwhile over at the paper, Alastair Fawkes thought he had a big scoop and was judiciously reporting all the details of Pamela's bad deed, as laid out in the press releases he alone was receiving from Dickie's office." Wilson grinned. "You couldn't make this stuff up, could you?"

She frowned and made a hurry-up gesture with her hand.

"Dickie had so distinguished himself in sourcing out the culprit that he wound up looking like a hero and an innocent man. He kept his seat and the story faded from the headlines. Pamela, however, was never fired. She stayed in the background and continued collecting her full paycheque. If they needed an extra hand in the office designing invitations for a government function, they would call her in. I hear she's magic with a glue gun."

"That's unbelievable."

"You haven't heard the best part. The reason Pamela took the blame for Dickie's Digit was because she was promised a trophy job in return. After suitable time went by, she reappeared with a new job and a new name. The incident had pretty much been forgotten and no one took any notice."

Kate snorted. "Have I got a lot to learn."

"Fawkes eventually wised up and realized he had been used to circulate the phony story. At around the same time he interviewed for Pacific's VP job—he actually has a business background. When it was awarded to someone with no qualifications, who looked suspiciously like Pamela Hirsch, he really got his nose out of joint.

"So, you really can't appeal to Fawkes's better nature to set matters straight. He doesn't have one, and he's been accused of media bias before and is still given carte blanche because he sells papers." Wilson shook his head. "If the truth runs contrary to what he's decided his storyline is, he's not going to print it—and you might aggravate him further." He gazed across the water, his fingers drumming out a marching beat on the arm of his chair. "There is someone who would be interested to hear what you have to say." He drained his glass and grabbed his cell phone.

After a ten-minute conversation with Wilson's mentor, Colin Jones—the editor who had mysteriously been made redundant after his dogged pursuit of the Dickie's Digit debacle, Kate found herself feeling cautiously optimistic about future press coverage. She hoped the wine wasn't making her overly confident.

"It's getting late and I should go." Kate lifted the sleeping Elvis from her lap, stood up and placed him carefully back on the chair. "Thanks for listening, the delicious dinner, and introducing me to your buddy." She indicated the contented cat.

"Why don't you stay?" Wilson stood up and laid a hand on her arm. "I'm concerned someone might be lurking around your apartment. You'll be safe here."

He caressed her cheek softly and she looked up into the brown eyes she had once thought arrogant and callous. Wilson kissed her gently. Her brave façade crumbling, Kate wrapped her arms around him and returned his kiss. After too short a time, she forced herself to step back.

"I'm sorry. I just can't...not tonight," she said. "So much has happened lately—and there's Matt."

Wilson brushed a lock of hair from her forehead.

"You're right," he said quietly. "I still wish you would stay, though. I really am concerned for your safety. Trust me. Nothing will happen."

Kate realized that only a few hours ago, she would have regarded this last comment with total skepticism. Now however, eyeing the boat's tiny sleeping quarters and the way Wilson's t-shirt stretched over his broad chest and shoulders, she realized she probably trusted him more than she trusted herself.

Kate awoke with a start, fists clenched for battle. She had dreamed she was paddling a kayak, fruitlessly trying to outrun two armed men in a Zodiac. When she screamed, no sound came from her mouth. Heart pounding, she jerked her head off the pillow and was relieved to find herself fully clothed and wedged in Rock'n Roll's small bunk, Rhys Wilson's arm wrapped protectively around her. She nestled back into his embrace, closed her eyes, and, after a time, slept soundly.

CHAPTER 28

Wilson refused to drop Kate at home the next morning before checking to make sure it was safe. The two of them had just padded quietly past John's door when it swung open and he stumbled out, baseball bat in one hand, cell phone in the other. Recognizing Kate, the old man stopped and scrambled to reposition his glasses. He assessed Rhys silently and gave him a slight nod, which Wilson returned. He then scanned the hallway in both directions and retreated back into his apartment.

Embarrassed at being caught returning home in the early hours with a man in tow, Kate fumbled with the new lock and recalled that the building super never had cared much for Matt.

A smile crept over Wilson's face. "I bet he watched all night to make sure nobody bothered you."

"Huh?" Kate said, moving aside to let him go in first.

"It's a guy thing," he whispered, stepping past her. He checked the condo and the new deadbolt carefully and, after satisfying himself no threats lurked, cautioned Kate to be careful, and left for work.

Doing her utmost to avoid the site of rat sacrifice, Kate showered and dressed and arrived at the lottery corporation right on time. She passed several employees in the hall who seemed to be grasping at any pretext to turn away and not acknowledge her. Feeling like a pariah, she glanced cautiously at the newspaper in her in-basket. She knew Colin Jones wouldn't have had time to get a column to press and she wasn't feeling as confident that he could level the playing field as she had been last night.

Fearful of running into frosty colleagues, Kate was reluctant to venture to the cafeteria for the cup of coffee she desperately needed. Opting instead for the safety of her cubicle, she grabbed the newspaper and shook it open. Pleased to see there was no mention of Pantygate on the front page, she breathed a sigh of relief, plunked down in her chair, and flipped to the employment section.

In four full pages of career advertisements, she found nothing that interested her or that she was qualified for. Kate was realizing how slim her prospects were when someone cleared their throat loudly. She peeked over the top of the paper and spied a group of SAY disciples engaged in passionate discussion outside her cubicle. Hands flew in excitement, heads nodded in agreement, and faces shone with self-confidence. The only impassive member of the group was Charm, who stood with her back to the crowd, arms laden with SAY propaganda, eyes boring a hole through Kate.

Kate raised her brow in a questioning, "Who? Me?" gesture and Charm pointed at Kate, then herself, and mimed eating. It was clear the two of them were on for lunch to discuss her evening with Rhys Wilson. Kate spun around to face her computer monitor and laughed to herself, grateful not everyone had retreated to the dark side. Her e-mail inbox was full of requests and demands, and Tom, who was at Dragonfly Lake with Gregor and Pamela, had forwarded his edits to a press release Kate had drafted on the new casino.

He wanted her to incorporate two quotes. The first, from Gregor: *"I am pleased to confirm the exciting rumors are* true. Pacific Lottery Corporation, in conjunction with Vertex Gaming, is developing another unique entertainment facility. The 700,000 square foot complex in downtown Vancouver, comprised of casino facilities, restaurants, retail, and boutique hotels, will be a huge boon to the city and to international tourism." The second quote Tom wanted attributed to himself: "The complex is expected to generate $200 million dollars in gaming revenue and a further $100 million in visitor spending in its first year, all to benefit the people of British Columbia."

Lastly, he wanted Kate to add some words on a subject he and Gregor agreed had to be addressed: "Senior management at Pacific Lottery takes exception to recent stories in the Vancouver Star. Our valued guests and customers might mistakenly conclude from the inaccuracies that we are misleading them. This is not the case. People are under no pressure to purchase tickets or enjoy themselves at our new casinos. We are a team of experienced professionals providing the entertainment our customers demand and we always have their best interests at heart. We have the greatest respect for our players and the citizens of this province."

Kate inhaled. Rhys was right all along, she said to herself. Gregor's gone into partnership with Vertex and I'm supposed to slip it into a release as if it were a win-win. I've got to tell Charm. She had the draft release open on her monitor and was looking for the Vertex file to check some facts when the phone rang.

"You're late for your meeting with Trevor Edgar. I e-mailed you your appointment time," said Tiffany. "Don't you check your messages?" Kate could hear her viciously snapping her chewing gum. "Pamela won't like it when I tell her."

While the caustic girl continued snapping and criticizing, Kate searched her inbox and discovered she had an appointment at nine o'clock with one of Pamela's private detectives. Speaking in a higher octave than her norm, but managing to keep her temper in check, she interrupted Tiffany's vitriol to say she was on her way.

* * *

Dwarfed behind the massive table, a person who looked barely out of his teens was reviewing a stack of files. Kate stood uncomfortably in the boardroom doorway for a full minute as he worked his way through the pile. Feeling foolish, she finally cleared her throat. "Excuse me, I understand we have a meeting."

She saw his shoulders tense, but he kept his head down until he had vetted the last document, then regarded her disdainfully. "You would be Kate," he said, turning his attention back to the file.

She nodded, hoping she may have timed this just right, missed her interview, and it was somebody else's turn.

"Respond," he said, without looking up.

"I beg your pardon?"

He leaned back and was swallowed up in a massive leather armchair Kate recognized as Tom's.

"Respond to my question. Are you Kate?"

"Yes. Kate Logan. How do you do?" She extended her hand, which he shook with his fingertips.

"When Ms. Luther is away, I see punctuality falls by the wayside," he said with a smirk.

Kate drew a thought clearing deep breath, took a few steps to the side of the room to retrieve a chair she hadn't been offered and discarded her intention to apologize for keeping him waiting.

"I am Mr. Edgar, senior associate with Edgar Security

and Investigations. No doubt you have heard of us. ESI has been assisting the police and providing security to the people of the Lower Mainland since my father founded it over twenty years ago."

Kate assumed as unimpressed a demeanor as she could muster.

He explained his firm had been engaged in connection with the recent incident where pairs of underwear had been used as objects of terror.

Kate answered his questions honestly and concisely, hoping to wrap things up fast and get out the door. The black impatience on his face, however, told her that Mr. Edgar did not consider honesty to be the best policy if it was contrary to his opinion.

"I imagine a certain class of people is accustomed to receiving G-strings, prophylactics, vibrators, or bondage paraphernalia as gifts." He nodded understandingly. "Saves you a trip to the store at an inopportune time." He slapped his pen down hard on the desk, making Kate jump and totally blow the display of ennui she was trying so hard to put across.

"Kate...Kate, I know you know more than you are telling. You refused to surrender the evidence to Ms. Luther and have been completely uncooperative. In addition, I understand you 'hang' with a group that finds things of this nature quite amusing. For the sake of Ms. Luther and Ms. Szabo, moral women, perhaps you can set your own proclivities aside and tell me who you are protecting."

He used his arms to push himself out of the chair and stood up. Kate was waiting for the rest of him to stand up, when she realized that's all there was. Swinging bowed arms at his sides, weightlifter fashion, all five foot two of him sauntered across the room to the chairs against the wall. Not a small feat on legs that short, Kate thought. Grabbing one of the chairs, he spun it around backwards, threw a leg over and straddled it, which also couldn't have been easy.

"I've told you everything I know," she said angrily. "And I have work to do."

"You have the opportunity to do the right thing here, Kate. Think about it."

Livid, she stalked to the door.

"I understand your condo was broken into yesterday."

She froze, then turned around to face him. "How do you know that?"

"It's my business to know." He removed both hands from the chair back and raised them in a shrug. This earned him a look of disdain from Kate and caused him to lose his balance and fall to the floor. Red in the face, he leapt up, put a foot on the seat of the offending chair, and rested his arm on his bent knee.

"Whoops." Kate felt the corners of her mouth turn up in a smile. "I asked you how you knew about the break-in at my house."

"You'll find very little gets by me." His confidence fully regained, Edgar continued, "Should you have any further problems, feel free to call ESI. I'm available for moonlighting, no job too small." He pulled a business card from his shirt pocket and waved it in her direction.

Kate's mouth dropped open in disbelief. The little ferret who had called her a sexual deviant now wanted a job. Speechless, she spun on her heel and stormed out.

"It's not like what the cops tell you," Edgar yelled. "You should take these things seriously. Very seriously."

At noon, Kate was putting finishing touches to the press release she had been working on earlier when her jacket was draped over her shoulders.

"I don't care how important that is," Charm said sweetly. "Don't even think of trying to avoid this lunch."

"I second that motion; we want all the dirt on Wilson." Jim stepped in behind Charm. "Hang on a sec, you two. I'm going to get my coat."

"Er, James." Charm put her hand on Jim's shoulder. "This is a girls only luncheon, big guy."

"Since when doesn't that include me?" Jim asked, crestfallen.

★ ★ ★

Kate was still incensed at Trevor Edgar's rudeness when she and Charm arrived at Mr. Foo's Great Two Lunch Express. "I'm told I hang out with a group of sexual deviants. I imagine that includes you."

Charm laughed. "Forget it. He's an idiot." She hung her bag on her chair and sat down. "You didn't tell me much about the burglary on the phone last night and, speaking about *last night.*"

It was while Kate was explaining that only her laptop was missing, that she realized the Vertex articles had not been where she left them in her condo.

"That's why I couldn't find it in my office earlier today," she said. "I took the file home." Exasperated, Kate rubbed her temples. "I remember leaving it on my desk, but it wasn't there after the break in."

"Who'd want that?" Charm filled their cups from the teapot on the table.

183

"I have no idea. But somebody's going to notice it's missing."

Charm shook her head. "I'll come over tonight and help you search. You've probably misplaced it. Hey, why don't you stay with me for the weekend? I've got the whole joint to myself. Hank's gone back home for a few days. His dad's in the hospital—nothing serious. We could go for brunch, catch a movie." She peered accusingly at Kate. "Unless you have *other* plans?"

"If it's Wilson you're getting at, smartie, he's away for the weekend—soccer tournament in Seattle." Kate poured a puddle of soy sauce on her plate. "I was planning on cleaning up my place. I just want to scrub absolutely everything that guy might have touched."

"Here's a better idea. You come stay at my place and hire some professional cleaners to go in and do it for you."

Kate deliberated for only a moment before nodding her head. "I know someone who could do it on short notice."

"Settled. Now, on to the good stuff."

Kate rolled her eyes, then filled her friend in on the details of the previous evening.

Charm was impressed with Wilson's cooking and boat, more impressed by the fact he had a cat—shows he cares about someone besides himself—and extremely impressed by the fact he hadn't pressured Kate into sleeping with him. "Truth be told, though, I don't know if I'm proud of him or disappointed he didn't try a little harder."

"Careful, you're letting your deviant side show," Kate said.

"Right, my bad." Charm gazed out Mr. Foo's window. "But you have to admit, a little sexual deviancy on his part might be interesting."

CHAPTER 29

The Star, Monday's Opinion Page:
SO, FIRE THE HYPOCRITE, MR. PREMIER
by Colin Jones

Fire Pamela Luther. Show some backbone, Mr. Premier, and fire this hypocrite who insults our intelligence.

For those of you who have had their head in the sand this past week, let me briefly summarize for you the depths to which the civil service and the media in this province have sunk. Last week, Pamela Luther, Executive Vice President Pacific Lottery Corp—a taxpayer owned corporation—and two other employees, Kate Logan and Sabrina Szabo, each received a pair of flashy, lace trimmed G-string panties in the interoffice mail. Someone's idea of a joke.

Always one for the spotlight, Luther vaulted to the soapbox, surpassing her performance seven years ago, when she and this reporter first butted heads. In a clandestine agreement at that time, she agreed to take the rap for the Honourable Richard Stahl when he engaged in gerrymandering, redrafting his constituency boundaries to include a thumb-shaped pocket of guaranteed support–a debacle which came to be known as "Dickie's Digit." What you may not be aware of—as Dickie and the party-faithful went to great lengths to cover it up—is that Luther agreed to take the blame, provided she was gifted with the VP position at Pacific Lottery.

I don't want you to think this column is sour grapes on my part, even though, when I refused to suppress the facts seven years ago, I was fired from my posting of 20 years. On the other hand, you are certainly entitled to your own opinion, which is more than employees of Pacific Lottery are entitled to. Luther wants everyone united against the panty perpetrators. That means no matter what their own feelings, the other two panty recipients are expected to agree with the boss. To her credit and her boss's irritation, Kate Logan didn't.

"It didn't bother me at all," says Logan. "We always joke around here."

Although Luther says Logan came to her office in tears to "seek counsel," the truth is Luther has never discussed the matter with her. There are, however, only so many hours in a day and much of the busy Executive VP's time is undoubtedly spent managing the private detectives she has engaged to track down the panty culprits at taxpayer expense.

She may also be allocating some of her time to papering the lunchroom walls with creative posters. As reported in Alastair Fawkes's column last week, Tom Berwick, Director, Pacific Lottery, was awarded the special honour of Male Sex Object of the Year at his recent birthday luncheon. Among his gifts was a poster of a VERY scantily clad male physique onto which Berwick's head had been photoshopped. Ms. Luther's signature and generous words of physical admiration were boldly emblazoned on parts of "Berwick's" torso where most folks would fear to tread.

When reached at Dragonfly Lake Casino, aggrieved panty-recipient Pamela Luther informed me that the poster was simply given in jest to a lovable old gentleman.

Hmm?

Hypocrites like Pamela Luther, capitalizing on inconsequential issues to advance their own agendas, undermine the credibility of genuine victims, victims like Ms. Szabo and Ms. Logan. So, fire the hypocrite, Mr. Premier. You missed your opportunity seven years ago.

CHAPTER 30

Kate smiled as she came to the end of Jones's column and wondered for a fleeting moment if she was being vindictive. It was gratifying to see the truth finally come out, but she knew the column sounded the death knell for her job at Pacific.

Paging absently through the rest of the paper, she saw that her press release last Friday had resulted in an article on the proposed downtown casino. To her surprise, it expanded on the economic benefits that would result from the development. "Already, Jackpot Manufacturing of Delta has been awarded a substantial contract to manufacture video lottery terminals for the new entertainment complex," Tom was quoted as saying.

Kate was pondering the fact that Tom had again cut her out of the communications loop when Sue, one of the Prize Payout clerks, phoned to say a couple had arrived to collect a half-million dollar prize from last Wednesday's draw.

A $500,000 win was not as big an event as a multi-million dollar payout, but Kate still had to administer the standard battery of questions in an upbeat manner to ascertain the people making the claim were the rightful winners. She glanced over at Charm's desk where her friend was fussing with the important task of slotting seminar attendees' nametags into the official SAY nametag holders.

"You look like you need a break," Kate said. "Come help me interview a couple of winners."

"My knight in armor, come to rescue me from this challenging mental task. I'd let down my golden hair—if I had any." Charm flicked her hands to free up the plastic tags, which stuck tenaciously to her sleeves with static cling. She grabbed Kate's upper arm and steered her towards the hallway. Bowing her head close, Charm whispered, "Pamela wants to turn this SAY thing into a sleepover." A slow smile spread across Kate's face and Charm shook her head vehemently. "Don't even think about it. If I'm bunking out on a concrete meeting room floor for the weekend, you're right there beside me sister."

"Have you read Colin Jones's piece this morning? Pamela will have me out of here long before your slumber party." Kate finished filling Charm in just as they arrived at the Prize Payout counter where a woman and an impatient looking man perched on the couch.

"Exactly how long do we have to wait?" the man snarled, ignoring Kate's outstretched hand. "We've got the winning ticket right here. All signed and everything." He shook the ticket in his right fist. "I've got a very busy day ahead of me."

"Now, Dwayne." The woman tugged timidly at his sleeve. She had stringy bleached hair and wore an excessive amount of smeared mascara. Kate wondered if she had been crying or unsuccessfully trying to adopt the heroin chic look popular in some fashion magazines. "This is just a formality, like the lady at the counter said."

"I will do my best not to keep you any longer than necessary." Smiling reassuringly, Kate said, "Now, which of you is the winner?" When Dwayne growled in the affirmative, she exchanged glances with Charm, kicking off a process they had employed many times before.

Charm stepped forward to address Dwayne's companion and brightly said, "While Kate completes the forms, would you care for a croissant and a latte in the lounge?"

After receiving a nod of permission from her companion, the woman shuffled down the hall behind Charm, who chattered away in a friendly fashion. Meanwhile, Dwayne grew more agitated.

"I want you to know I'm not one of those losers who buys lottery tickets all the time." He handed the ticket over to Kate and grudgingly took a seat. "Only if I happen to be at the gas station where the tickets are right in your face, am I going to buy one."

Kate nodded, as if agreeing wholeheartedly that they certainly weren't pulling the wool over his eyes, and casually asked, "Is that where you bought this one?"

"Yeah. I filled up with gas on my way to work Tuesday last week, and picked up the ticket for my wife's birthday."

"Well you sure made the right choice that day, didn't you?"

Dwayne regarded her for a moment and an oily smile spread over his large features. He settled himself back onto the couch and confidently crossed one cowboy booted leg over another. "I guess I did."

Kate flipped through the paperwork in her binder while trying to maintain her best poker face. She had checked the lottery corporation's vast computer system before the interview and knew the winning ticket had been bought on Sunday evening, at a gas station in Whistler. Not only was Dwayne claiming winnings that were due his wife, he didn't know where, or when, the ticket had been purchased. He got the gas station part correct, but that was about all.

Kate asked a few more trivial questions, chosen not to raise his suspicions, then excused herself and walked to the boardroom, past the glass-walled lounge where Charm was brilliantly playing her role as secondary information gatherer. A minute later, Charm, carrying a plate recently emptied of croissants, strode into the boardroom where Kate waited.

"Little Miss Perky reporting in sir."

"Things aren't adding up on this one, are they?"

"Looks OK from my end, Chief." Charm pointed at Kate's wrinkled brow. "Don't do that. You'll need Botox."

Without thinking, Kate lifted her eyebrows to relax her expression then shook her head to restore sanity. "It's not their ticket. He says it is and his signature's on the back, but he doesn't know where or when it was purchased."

Sensing something shady, Miss Perky kicked into serious investigator mode. "She told me they spend $50 every week betting the same lucky numbers."

"*He* told *me* that only losers play the lottery and it was just a fluke he bought this ticket."

"Got lucky this time didn't he?" Charm's eyes narrowed.

"Seems that way. We're going to have to get some direction on this," Kate said anxiously. "I've never had a suspicious winner."

"Gregor, Tom, and Pamela are still at Dragonfly. Lucas is the only one in."

Kate pressed her lips together in a tight line. "Well, he's going to have to take responsibility for something for a change. I think Dwayne could get miserable and I'm tired of taking all the heat." She reefed open the heavy door and stalked towards Mardone's office.

"You go, girl. And don't worry—I've got your back." Charm tucked the platter under her arm and hustled to catch up.

They blew past Leah into Mardone's office where they found him seated behind mountains of paperwork. Two things struck Kate immediately: his face did look different—although she wasn't sure the Y-lift was an improvement—and he appeared to be working. His tie hung loose and his brow was bedecked with little beads of sweat. He was not at all his cool, overconfident self.

Thinking she had caught him with his political gamesmanship hat off, Kate hoped she might get a straight answer. She explained the situation quickly, unwilling to give him the upper hand and time to scheme. Charm confirmed key points with a nod.

"Maybe they didn't steal it," Kate added. "Maybe they forged it somehow. Either way, shouldn't we hold funds until we check into it?"

"This guy's shifty and he looks like he could get mean," Charm said.

Mardone eyed the two women for a long moment, then leaned back and rested his feet on the desk. When his mouth widened into a lipless smile, Kate knew his political hat was back in place. He extended his arm and snapped his fingers for the ticket, giving it a cursory glance before tossing it back. "Seems OK to me. The guy's probably so excited he forgot where he bought it."

"And when," Charm piped in.

"*And when,*" Mardone mimicked.

"But..." Kate began.

"Approving these things is Tom's job, not mine. Obviously he's too busy for that, and *everything* else," he said, indicating the mountains of paperwork. "I'd say give them the money."

"It's half a million dollars," Charm said, aghast.

Still smirking, Mardone made a dismissive motion with his hand.

Realizing how things were going to go down, Kate asked evenly, "Will you sign to authorize release of the money?"

"Nope."

Kate heard a snort of laughter and turned to see Leah leaning against the doorjamb.

"But Kate could get into big trouble if—"

"That's what he's counting on, Charm," Kate said.

★ ★ ★

"I am *so* stupid," Charm said when the two returned to Kate's office.

"No you're not. You just have more faith in mankind than you should." Kate dropped her binder on the desk, made a quick call and learned Dwayne was in a much happier place now that Sue was plying him with champagne and orange juice. She thanked her, explaining a small computer glitch was delaying things. Next, she asked Charm to keep Dwayne's companion occupied. "I think it's a good idea to keep them separated to prevent them from comparing stories."

While Charm served celebratory drinks to the wife in the lounge, Kate tried unsuccessfully to reach Tom on his cell. She knew she could just wash her hands of the whole thing, walk out the back door, and let nature, too much champagne, and Dwayne's temper take their course. But, if it was the last thing she did at Pacific, she didn't want Mardone to get the best of her. She quickly composed an e-mail, hoping Tom would break with tradition and check his messages, then went back to her inbox where she spotted a housekeeping message to all staff from Gregor's secretary.

"I wonder…" she said aloud, then raced down the hall to Gregor's office.

Always the professional, June agreed that when Gregor touched base with her that afternoon, she would tell him it was imperative Kate speak to him.

"Tom should be with him, so, one way or the other, we'll get an answer for you." June sipped her tea then set the cup down on the matching saucer. "I'm afraid I can't get hold of him any sooner. He's only turning the goddamn cell on when he calls me in the afternoon."

Kate did a double take at the unexpected expletive.

"Sorry you had to hear that, dear, but he's got to get with the times. It's just not efficient."

"Men." Kate shook her head.

"You said it, missy." June indicated her dish of candies. "Mint?"

Kate popped a candy into her mouth and was rising to leave when the phone rang. In one fluid motion, June removed her earring, waved goodbye to Kate, and pressed the phone to her ear.

"Yes, she's right here. One moment please." June passed Kate the receiver.

"Hon." Jim sounded agitated. "I've got some loon on the phone wants to talk to Tom about the story in the paper today. With him gone, and Gregor too, I'm sorry kid, but you're it."

Kate was scanning the phone for the button to transfer the call back to her own desk when June indicated she was going for more tea and pointed her towards her empty chair. It was a plush chair and Kate was glad she was seated when Jim put through the call from the owner of Jackpot Manufacturing who wanted to know when he was going to receive the lucrative contract the paper reported he had won.

"I know nothing about this or any other contract with you people," he raged. "I do know, contrary to what you tell everybody, that you don't put your jobs out to tender as you are required to and that any time I deal with you, I have to put up with incompetence and dishonesty."

Kate tried to break into the conversation, but was outgunned.

"I'm sorry now that I gave the bum's rush to that Star reporter when he came to see me. He was more of a straight shooter than the bunch of you could ever be."

He stormed over past incidents were he had been treated badly, including the contract for manufacture of the VLTs for the Dragonfly Casino. Kate promised to check into today's matter immediately and, because she was so upset, slipped into offering up some of the usual bromides, which he immediately called her on and hung up the phone. She was reminding herself not to take the caller's attacks personally when June's phone rang again. Spying Jim's local in the display, she snatched up the receiver.

"Sorry to bother you again," he said, "but Wilson called while you were on the line, so I took a message. He wanted me to tell you that he's back from Seattle but has to fly to Bella Bella. Some guy named Wesley went kayaking a couple of days ago and hasn't been seen since." Jim paused for breath and what sounded like a bite of cookie. "Apparently, an important event this guy was involved in was cancelled. Wilson says when something gets Wesley down, he retreats to this little island and that's where he'll be. His mom and grandpa are worried about him, though, so Wilson's flying up to find him and knock him senseless for worrying everybody."

CHAPTER 31

With champagne and the treats the Prize Payout clerks had specially delivered from Gourmet Obsessions, Dwayne remained remarkably happy while waiting for his money.

"Can those two put away the bubbly," Sue reported to Kate when she phoned. "They've gone through three bottles."

"He's not getting miserable?" Kate asked.

"Lord, no. He's totally buying the computer glitch excuse. He went into a long spiel on why we wouldn't have this problem if we used Macs. Seriously, what is it with these Mac people? Don't you think they're a little culty?"

"They do love their computers." Kate forced a laugh. "Thanks for babysitting him, Sue. It shouldn't be too long 'til we get an answer from Gregor and Tom."

"Uh-oh. I have to go. Dwayne's dancing this way with his empty glass. I've got the guys from the production department coming over," Sue whispered. "We've asked him if we can feature him in a couple of TV promo spots."

"Oh no," Kate said.

"No worries. He's a natural." Sue giggled. "Gotta go."

Kate hung up, apprehension settling over her like a thick fog. Her impression of Dwayne was that he wasn't a very nice person and she worried Sue might be putting herself at risk if things went sour. It seemed to her that she was the only one considering the fact that Dwayne might not get his money. Not a pretty possibility.

He may have been a little behind the times, but Gregor could tell time with the best of them and he phoned June at 1:30 as promised.

While Kate waited anxiously for them to conclude their conversation, she marvelled at June's old-school professionalism. From her perch on the secretary's desk, Kate watched her jot down a list: pick up dry cleaning, check shipping status/ kitchen countertops, hire new dog-walker, call tailor re tux, schedule tune-up-Sharon's Mercedes/G's Beemer, book Maui flight-second week December. When Gregor instructed her to confirm the puppies' vaccinations were still on for Friday, June deftly redirected the conversation, telling him there was an urgent matter to discuss.

Kate's brief summary of the situation was made even briefer when Gregor silenced her and passed the phone over to Tom. Starting from the beginning, she once again relayed the circumstances of Dwayne and the suspicious ticket.

Her faith in Tom was somewhat restored when he apologized profusely for not being available and told her not to worry, the responsibility was his. Kate heard some discussion between the two of them and then Tom came back on the line.

"Gregor and I agree it's OK to release the money," Tom said.

Kate couldn't believe what she was hearing. There was definitely something amiss with Dwayne's claim.

"I remember that half mil prize from Jim's Winning Numbers Report," Tom continued. "I already verified the information. That's one of the reasons I ride you guys so hard for those reports, my friend. I know you think they're a waste of time but, with them in place, we're prepared for things like this." He chuckled. "Tell Jim, would you? Maybe we can avoid future blood baths."

"So you'll sign to release the funds?"

"Sure. That's cool. I'll get the office here to fax the paperwork down to you right away."

She put her hand over the mouthpiece and whispered to June, "They say it's OK." June never lost her composure, but her eyebrows shot up and that said it all for Kate.

"I saw a real positive article online, on the new downtown casino. Nice work," said Tom.

Kate turned her attention back to the phone. "Don't thank me. I'm not the one who promised huge economic benefits and I'd never even hear of Jackpot Manufacturing until today."

"That was my bad, kid. I should have run it by you. These projects are so exciting, I'm afraid I ran off at the mouth."

Kate felt herself softening a bit. "I'm just so programmed to worry about what's printed in the media."

"I know, and you do a hell of a job. We've got to get you back up here, Katie. The place is packed. Vertex has brought planes full of Chinese people in from the Pacific Northwest and they're having a ball. When I get back, what do you say I buy you dinner to make up for my verbal diarrhoea?"

She laughed. "You're not getting off that easy. And before I forget, what is going on with Jackpot Manufacturing?" She filled him in on the heated phone call.

"That bloody guy is a piece of work," said Tom.

"He says we gave the Dragonfly VLT contract to Vertex without putting it to tender and he's never heard of this contract either."

"What did I tell you? He's nothing but an injustice collector. I'll check into it. Probably something as simple as purchasing being behind notifying him. Hold on a sec, would you?" There was a sound like papers being shuffled and he came back on the line. "My brain's starting to kick into gear and I've actually remembered to check my notes. About that dinner I owe you...you may decide I owe you a new car instead."

Kate eased herself off the desk and gratefully sat down in the chair June rolled up.

"We've hired Gregor's stepson, Jack Stec, to do a little consulting for the Communications Department. With Charm so busy with the SAY conference and you *crazy busy as always*, we thought we could use a little extra help."

"You're not talking about the poolside pot-smoker from Gregor's birthday party? What in the world is he going to do for us?"

"At Vertex's suggestion, we're going to implement a study of the Chinese market. These people love gambling. Did you know that? Jack is going to come up with some new ways to target their market segment."

"Didn't you find out a while ago that gambling can be an Achilles Heel for some Chinese people and decide the moral thing to do was to leave it alone?"

"That's a pretty racist attitude. You can't generalize like that. They don't have to play if they don't want to. We just want to offer them entertainment options."

Kate tried to recall what she had read in the report on Chinese gamblers.

"Jack has lots of experience in market research and—"

"The kid from the *pool*?" Kate interrupted.

"Look, he starts Thursday. Make him feel part of the team. He's Gregor's stepson for Chrissakes."

CHAPTER 32

K ate accomplished little at work over the next two days. Such a high priority had been placed on accommodating Gregor's stepson, there was time for little else. The IT guys worked double-time setting up his computer, while HR fretted over office furnishings and the maintenance folks shuffled cubicle walls to create an office with a window. Unfortunately, Charm—absent from the office at SAY headquarters—became the first casualty of the nepotism, when her office space evaporated and her belongings were carted off to the boardroom.

Wednesday night, Kate, Jim, and a few colleagues made their way to the Flying Otter Pub to compare notes and commiserate.

"Kate, did I tell you I caught June trying to jack your desk chair for the hero's office?"

"June wouldn't do that to me."

"I know." He shook his head. "Lucas must have manipulated her somehow. If her heart was truly in it, I never would have gotten the chair off that wiry old woman."

They ordered another round just as the pub's heavy doors crashed open and Charm blew in.

"That bag, Pamela. She kept us all until 6:30." She tossed her purse in Jim's lap and shrugged off her jacket. "The SAY people suggested a few changes to our conference agenda, and now she's thrown all our plans out the window and we're back to square one." Fuming, Charm regarded everyone at the table, hands on her hips. "What?" she asked, suddenly wary. "What did I miss?"

"You haven't read your e-mail," Kate said, eyeing her over her glass of beer.

Charm pulled up a chair and sat down. "The SAY zombies blocked my e-mail. Apparently it allows negative energy to permeate." She punched Jim on the shoulder. "Bet you didn't know that was your problem, James." She kicked her bag under her chair. "So quit beating around the bush. What's happened?"

When the gang at the table had finished conveying the latest goings-on, Charm signalled the waitress for a drink.

"They just took my desk away?" she said, obviously wounded.

"It's not all bad," chirped one of the maintenance people. "You've actually got the biggest office of them all now—the boardroom."

"And it's got a door on it, love. Those chintzy cubicles haven't got a door," said another. He nodded smugly and tried to tempt Charm with a yam fry from the platter in the middle of the table.

"But what happens when they need the boardroom for a meeting?" she asked.

Everyone exchanged glances.

"If that happens, you're supposed to gather up your stuff and come on back and share with me." Jim was drinking mugs of beer instead of glasses like the others, and his face was florid and full of emotion.

"But you don't even have room for your cookie tin with all that phone equipment and odds charts and stuff," she said in a small voice.

Kate put her arm around Charm. "I'll find room. You can move into my office. As a matter of fact," she chuckled, "you can have my office. I hammered the final nails in my coffin today. I won't be around long."

"Where were you today, anyway?" Jim dipped a couple of fries in the chipotle dip and made quick work of them.

"Bob and I," Kate lifted her glass to the rumpled gent at the end of the table, "spent the day with Lucas and the promotions people discussing the Chinese marketing campaign."

"Isn't that what we've hired the hero for?" Jim asked.

"Guys, I don't know what we've hired him for," Bob said quietly. "Jack Stec isn't doing any market survey. Our research department completed that project a year ago and it's not like it needs updating already."

Kate frowned. "Lucas told me he got the statistics he was referring to today from the thesis Jack submitted with his resume."

A severely coiffed woman sitting opposite Bob shovelled up the remaining dip with a fry and cleared her throat. Kate recognized her as being from Human Resources. "Look," the woman said, in a voice even softer than Bob's, "I shouldn't say anything—but I'm going to say it anyway. For what we're paying Mr. Stec, he had better be doing something...and he'd better be doing it well." She enunciated each word slowly and clearly.

"So he's getting paid major coin, Samantha?" Charm asked.

Samantha tucked a loose grey lock behind one ear. "I'm not telling any tales...except I've been around for a while and I think the Communications Department should watch their backs."

Kate looked sideways at Charm, and they both exchanged glances with Jim.

"Damn," Jim said. "I've only got two more years 'til I retire."

"As my grandson says, 'I'm just saying.'" Samantha sipped her drink and her corporate-hardened face creased with a glimmer of compassion. "Keep your eyes open. And a little ass-kissing wouldn't hurt."

Jim sat bolt upright. "*That's* out of the question."

Charm shook her head. "It's just not his style."

"Or ours, either." Kate elbowed Charm.

"I'm just—" Samantha began.

"You're just saying." Charm nodded absently.

Samantha tossed a twenty dollar bill onto the table and stood up. "My fellow colleagues, I leave you with this: Although I was told not to, being an irreverent non-ass-kisser myself, I fact checked Jack's resume. The university from which he claims he received a degree has no record of him even attending. I could not locate any of the personal or business references he listed, and the evidence I *can* find indicates he may not have graduated from *high school*." She shrugged her shoulders, pushed her chair in, and was gone.

The rest of the group sipped in silence for a moment and then all began to talk at once. Kate was trying to make out what Jim was saying over the ferocious din when his focus seemed to shift, his eyes darting furtively toward the door. Someone's boot delivered a quick kick to her shin and, without his facial expression altering one iota, Jim casually interrupted his ramblings to announce that Tom had just walked into the pub. He reached across the table and slapped Kate on the arm, as if emphasizing a point. "Yup, he's spotted us. He's coming this way."

"Kate, Jim, everybody. Fancy meeting you here," Tom said. He stopped behind Kate's chair and massaged her shoulders with his beefy hands.

Kate stared wide-eyed at Jim, then sideways at Charm. After a moment's hesitation, and hoping she appeared suitably nonplussed, she pivoted round in her seat and out from under his busy hands. "Welcome back. How did it go at Dragonfly?" she asked.

"Good, good," Tom said quickly. "Barkeep," he yelled, "another round for this table. On me, please." A cheer went up from the crowd and Tom bent down to Kate's ear. "Can I talk to you for a moment?" he whispered.

* * *

Back at her apartment later that night, Kate mulled over the strange conversation that had ensued. Much to the disapproval of Jim, who was still stewing over his recent run-in with the senior manager, Tom had insisted he "talk shop" with Kate in private. The gist of the disjointed conversation that followed seemed to be an apology for circumventing media protocol and especially for being rude—"just plain rude, damn it"—so often, lately.

Kate had known he was tired. He stayed on at Dragonfly to deal with a few issues and had stopped in at the Flying Otter on his way home from the airport, hoping the gang from the office would be there. There were big black circles under his eyes and he seemed stressed.

"How are you feeling?" Kate asked. "Any word on when they can operate?"

"I'm still working on whittling down the muffin top, my dear." Tom stared theatrically at his big mug of beer. "Whoops," he whispered, then his face became serious. "I don't think these pills I'm taking in the meantime are doing me a lot of good, though."

"Well, I don't think you should mix them with beer, buster," Kate said, pursing her lips in disapproval. When he attempted to argue the point, she interrupted. "Yeah, yeah. I've heard that from you before. I don't think it matters that everything eventually winds up in the same place."

He hung his head in mock remorse.

Kate grinned. "You'd better join us and finish off that ONE beer." She shook her finger at him. "Only one, though."

When the evening broke up, Jim and Tom seemed to have mended fences and forgotten office politics. To keep things on a positive note, Kate had been careful to guide the conversation away from Jack Stec.

At home later, she made herself a cup of camomile tea and perused the *Star*. She hadn't had an opportunity that morning to check on her current standing in the public eye. Letters to the editor continued to pour in. Many still insisted the panty recipients were looking for publicity and made Kate's blood boil. A growing number, however, were in her favour. Maybe Colin Jones's piece had had the desired effect after all.

She put the newspaper down and glanced around her apartment. Shadows seemed to lurk everywhere and she suddenly felt very alone. Kate reminded herself of the new deadbolt on the door but knew she would never feel safe there again. On a whim, she picked up the phone and tried Wilson's cell. When it went straight through to voice mail, she hung up.

Jack Stec's arrival was anticlimactic. He remained holed up in his new office Thursday and Friday, ostensibly vetting resources and setting a budget. When he emerged to go to lunch with Tom and Gregor, Kate caught a glimpse and had the opportunity to confirm that he was, indeed, the poolside pot smoker. Even dressed in what appeared to be a brand new suit, there was no hiding those tattoos and the fact he'd look so much more at home in rapper jeans and a hoodie.

★ ★ ★

Mid-morning Sunday, Kate received a call from Jim.

"Not that you're second banana or anything, but our brunch this morning has been cancelled and Rand and I are looking for something to do. We're wondering if you'd like to come with us to snoop around Sharon Chernin's store?"

Kate heard Randy yell, "We'll pick her up at eleven-thirty."

"Eleven-thirty, how's that sound?" Jim asked.

"OK," Kate replied. She couldn't stop dwelling on the robbery and welcomed a diversion. "Wait a minute. Randy's not getting dressed up as my sister, is he?"

"Oh," Jim trilled. "I'd forgotten all about that."

Kate groaned and hung up the phone.

The guys picked her up promptly and the three shoppers snagged a prize parking spot on Water Street, the main thoroughfare in Gastown. Their luck ran out, however, when they found Sharon's store closed for renovations. "Check us out in the New Year—And Prepare to be Amazed!" read the huge banner in the front window.

205

It would be an understatement to say Randy was disappointed. "It took me forever to find these heels," he said. "And I gave everything the once over with an iron, too." He flashed Kate a full wattage smile. "I wouldn't want Sharon's people thinking your sister is a frump."

Since Randy had gone to so much trouble and they had plugged the parking meter with all their change, they decided to go for lunch to salvage the day.

Kate returned home in much better spirits than when she had left. Hearing the phone ring inside her condo, she quickly turned the key in the tight new lock and bolted inside.

"It's the first chance I've had to call," Wilson said. "I knew you'd want to know." There was a pause. "Wesley's been murdered."

CHAPTER 33

K ate gasped. "What happened? Where are you?"
"Flying into Vancouver harbor. The cell reception
in Bella Bella is sketchy." Wilson's voice faded in and out.
"This is the first opportunity I've had to call you."

"I can't hear you all that well now."

"I'm going to get my cousin Brad to bring my boat over
from his marina in North Van. Could you meet me at the
government dock on Granville Island in a couple of hours?"

★ ★ ★

Kate rounded the corner of the Granville Island Market and
scanned the newly refurbished dock in front of the building. It provided handy moorage for boaters for up to three
hours while they shopped for provisions. Wilson stood on
the dock beside his boat. Suddenly afraid to hear the news,
Kate stopped and drew in a breath. She watched him bend
down and stroke Elvis the cat who was busily threading
himself in and out between his owner's legs.

Because the tide was out, the ramp down to the
dock was steep and Kate held on tightly to the railing as
she descended. She made her way along the floats, calling
Wilson three times before she got his attention. He had a
grim set to his jaw and grief etched all over his face. He
raised one hand in greeting and, with the other, pulled the
boat into the dock. Elvis obediently leapt aboard. Kate ran
the last few steps and wrapped her arms around him tightly,
tears streaming down her face. He cleared his throat and
again drew the boat in snug against the dock. She tossed
her bag of sandwiches aboard and climbed on.

It was a short, conversation-free ride to Kitsilano Beach where they dropped anchor. He glanced at the little dining table where Kate had laid out the sandwiches and soda and managed a half smile. He hugged her to him.

"It's good to see you," he whispered.

Afraid to let him go and afraid to hear the news, Kate held on without a word. After a long while, she broke their embrace. "What happened?"

They sat down at the small dining table and Kate took his big hand in her two.

"The government reallocated their funding and cancelled Wesley's Whalesong exhibitions in Ottawa and London. I knew he'd be upset and I figured he'd go out to Blackfish Island to get his head together. We used to hide out there whenever we were in trouble...I spent the better part of two days looking for him." He rubbed his forehead with his fingers. "There was a campfire, and signs someone had recently been there kept me going." He paused. "Stupid of me. I shouldn't have wasted all that time on the island. Maybe things would have turned out differently."

"He wasn't there?"

He shook his head. "Thursday morning I paddled back to Bella Bella to see if there was any news." He lifted his eyes to meet Kate's gaze. "Around five in the afternoon a friend came over to Moses's house and told us he and his kids had stumbled on some new petroglyphs down by Namu. He said Wesley had been really excited to hear this and he thought he might have gone to check them out." Wilson sighed heavily. "We all headed down there in the Coast Guard boat thinking maybe a high tide had floated his kayak free and he was stranded." Wilson smiled as Kate tried to blow an errant curl of hair out of her eye without letting go of his hand.

"I'm sorry," she said. "It drives me insane lately. I'm going to cut it all off."

"Don't you dare." He tucked the misbehaving lock behind her ear.

"Where did you find him?"

"We didn't. We combed the beaches and searched inland by the petroglyphs, but there was no sign of him. That night Moses had a dream that we had to look even further south. So the next day we went down the coast and we found him."

Kate swallowed.

"We found him on the beach south of the old cannery." Wilson paused. "Shot." He cleared his throat loudly a few times and stared out the window. "Of course we called the cops and the Coast Guard who seem to think I'm the chief suspect. I spent all day yesterday, and most of today, filling in reports and answering question after question. It's just about destroyed his mom and Moses. I swear the old man has aged twenty years and you can't afford that, you know—not when you're ninety," he said matter of factly.

Kate gently turned Wilson's face towards hers. If he was trying to joke to ease the situation, his face showed no signs of it. She asked him when he last ate.

"I don't remember, but I'm not hungry."

"It's important that you eat something. You'll feel better."

They found they were much more able to cope after they had tucked into the sandwiches and several cups of hot tea which Kate put together with the help of an old electric kettle—the boat stove still being a bit of a hazard. They rehashed the details again and again, discussing the alternatives the cops might explore. Rhys also reminded Kate of the murder at the fishing lodge only a few weeks before.

"That was the first murder on the coast in fifty years," he said.

"And now there are two within a month. What's going on?"

His eyes met hers. "This kind of thing is supposed to get a reporter's juices flowing. When others are grieving, we're conditioned to give ourselves a kick in the ass, get out there, and find out what happened...But I just can't motivate myself."

"I don't think the 'kick yourself in the ass' directive applies when the murder victim is your best friend," Kate said softly.

* * *

They talked far into the night on topics ranging from gambling and harassment at Pacific Lottery, to Alastair Fawkes, friends, and boats—anything to get their minds off the situation.

"I should go," Kate said when she realized the time.

Wilson pushed his cup towards the centre of the table, stood, and wrapped his arms around her tightly.

After a long while, she leaned back, looked him in the eye, and cleared her throat with a loud "ahem."

"I wish you'd stay," he said.

They stared silently into each other's eyes for what seemed like an eternity to Kate. Gently she traced her fingertip over a faint scar on his cheek that she'd not noticed before. Then, embarrassed, she lowered her gaze and laid her head against his chest.

"But I parked in a three-hour zone," she argued without conviction.

"I park there all the time...They won't tow you." He kissed her neck softly.

CHAPTER 34

"Coffee?"

Kate snapped her eyes open to find Rhys, in jeans and t-shirt, standing beside the bed with a steaming mug in each hand. The boat rocked gently back and forth in the harbor waters.

"Oh, yes…Thanks." Last night had ended on a romantic note. In the harsh judgmental light of morning, however, Kate was deeply embarrassed waking up in his bed. Clutching the bedcovers tightly to herself, she sat up and took the cup with a sheepish grin.

"I think we got distracted before we came to any conclusions last night." Wilson perched on the side of the bed.

"You mean if something's going on at the lottery corporation?" Kate took a sip of coffee and put the cup down, relieved the discussion had turned to business.

"No…I mean what's going on when you moan and sigh like that, and how I can get you to do it some more?" He nodded cheerfully as if he really expected an intelligent answer to his question.

"I didn't *moan*, you fool." Thoroughly mortified, Kate fell back and pulled a pillow over her head.

"Yeah, you did—a few times. I thought Elvis was going to abandon ship, poor animal."

"You are so full of it," she said from under the pillow. "He didn't, though? Did he?" Kate sat up quickly and peered about. "Elvis, I mean, go overboard."

"Luckily, no. I think you've got some making up to do, though." Rhys shook his head. "All that noise aroused some kind of primal flight response in him."

Kate grabbed the pillow and dealt him a swift blow to the head.

"Violence. Another primal instinct. You should see someone about that. Or better yet, maybe I can help." He tossed the pillow aside, leaned across the bed and kissed her. Working a hand free, Kate reached up and pulled him down to her. *That cat's going to have to learn to live with it,* she thought.

★ ★ ★

Two hours later she disembarked onto the Granville Island dock. Late for work due to her morning lesson in primal behavior, she hurried up the ramp to shore and turned back to give an awkward wave to Wilson, who was busy tying up the boat.

Passing the Arts Club Theatre, Kate noted that their award-winning performance of War Horse had just wound up and she remembered how disappointed she had been when Matt refused to go. This crisp morning she found she didn't much care anymore. She was, however, wondering what she had gotten herself into.

She was pleased to see her little red car hadn't been towed and there wasn't even a ticket on the windshield. So he hadn't been giving her a line about the Island not enforcing the three-hour parking limit. Kate climbed in, started the engine, and paused for a moment to collect her thoughts. If anybody asked why she was late, she decided she'd tell them she had to stop at the printers to check an upcoming publication. That was true, too. As a matter of fact, she and Charm had done that very press check only a few days before. She chuckled, realizing she didn't care so much about Pacific Lottery anymore, either. Backing out of the parking spot, she wondered if her primal fight instincts had been drummed out of her for good.

Kate's thoughts were again on Wesley when, after a quick shower and change of clothes, she walked into the lottery office foyer at eleven o'clock. She was thinking things were looking pretty good for sneaking in unnoticed when she heard a familiar voice behind her. Feeling the colour rise in her cheeks, she slowly turned round to see Charm advancing on her, pulling a rolling tote of SAY trappings.

Charm took one look at her friend's flushed face and her own face split into a big grin. "Sorry I missed that press check this morning," she said loudly for the benefit of the guard at the security desk and anyone else who might be listening. "I was delayed at SAY headquarters and couldn't get free to meet you." Pushing past Kate, key fob in hand, she whispered, "You're just no good at this."

Humiliated, but definitely seeing the humor in being caught out, Kate cleared her throat, swiped her own fob, and caught up with her friend waiting in the hallway.

"The old 'press check pretext.' Always a favourite," Charm said.

"One day somebody's going to call us on it," Kate said and prattled on with other excuses they might use.

"Quit trying to change the subject. I'll get us a coffee and meet you in the boardroom—*my office*—in two minutes."

"No coffee for me, thanks." Kate shook her head. "Any more and my eyeballs will float."

"OMG! *You* don't want coffee? This is going to be *real* good." Charm pointed to the boardroom door, flashed Kate two fingers, and headed to the cafeteria.

CHAPTER 35

Her hands full, Charm pushed open the boardroom door with her foot. A smart-mouthed comment on the tip of her tongue, she stopped dead in her tracks when she saw Kate's grim expression. Righting the wheeled suitcase to stand on its own, she slipped into the chair opposite her friend. "What's the matter?"

"It's Rhys's friend, Wesley," Kate said. "He's dead."

"Oh my god. What happened? You knew him, didn't you?"

Kate nodded. "He was a really nice guy." She told Charm what she had learned the night before, while trying to stem the flow of tears.

Charm passed the box of tissues she kept at her desk. "And they have no suspects?"

"Not yet. But they only found him on Friday."

Charm's head nodded up and down as she tallied up the days that had elapsed. "But the most valuable clues are collected right away. Don't they know something by now?"

Kate leaned back in her chair and waved her hands back and forth in a defeated gesture. "I don't know . . . Rhys is going to try and get some info out of a cop he knows and call me later." She sniffed and stood up. "I'm late. I'd better get going."

"Tell me as soon as you hear something." Charm eyed her with concern. "Are you going to be all right?"

Kate nodded quickly, her lips pressed in a thin line.

Charm wrapped her arms around her friend.

"Whoa," Kate said. "If you do that, I'll start to cry again."

Charm stepped back and bit her lip. "I feel like a heel for what I was thinking earlier. That you'd slept with Wilson."

Kate stopped dabbing her tears, gave a labored sigh and leveled a telling glance at her friend.

* * *

Back at her desk, Kate powered up the computer and brought her e-mail up on the screen. First up was a memo detailing the corporation's new Code of Conduct. These measures were prompted, according to the memo, by recent acts of intimidation. Kate got a much needed chuckle over how Pamela and Trevor Edgar's passion to appear politically correct had resulted in a convoluted policy made even more confusing by loads of grammatical errors.

At one o'clock, Charm and Jim appeared to collect her for lunch and Kate reported that, "No, Rhys hasn't called yet."

"He hasn't had the chance." Charm nodded reassuringly. "He'll call."

At four o'clock, Charm stopped by with some written materials for Kate's approval and Kate had to admit he still hadn't called.

"So, call him." Charm dumped the paperwork. "What century are we living in, anyway?"

Kate felt foolish and she was feeling guilty about her relationship with Matt. First and foremost, she wanted to know how the investigation into Wesley's death was progressing but, was it unreasonable to expect Wilson to call after she had spent the night with him. They're all the same, she muttered as she packed her bag to leave at the end of the day. No texts, no e-mails, no phone calls. All the communications technology in the world isn't nearly as effective as a good swift kick in the ass when you're dumb enough to trust a guy. She zipped her bag shut and was plotting a quick exit when Jim stole in and dropped his ample self into the spare chair.

"I hope it's all right that I told Randy about Wesley. He wants to know if you are up to having dinner with us tonight?"

Touched by his concern, Kate gave him a small smile but shook her head.

"I just want to go home and have a hot bath. That British mystery I like is on TV tonight."

Jim quickened his sales pitch. "Come on. He finalized the purchase of the garden centre today and wants to celebrate. It'll be fun." Jim stood up and put his arm around her shoulders. "You need to get your mind off things and those shows are all reruns anyway."

Kate hesitated, then nodded her agreement.

"Great. We'll get Charm to come too," he said. "You know that woman's always up for a free meal."

"She's definitely got a hollow leg." Kate used the back of her hand to wipe away the tears that were trying to make a comeback.

Jim babbled happily on. "It'll be every man for himself when it comes to the food. You and I'll just have to be quick." He sandwiched her tightly to his side and marched her out the door. "I don't know if you've noticed, but that Randy's no slouch in the food mooching department either."

★ ★ ★

Kate was glad she and Charm had elected to leave the car home and cab it over to Jim and Randy's. Randy's dream had been to open a nursery for specialty plants and the get-together that night grew into quite a party as friends arrived to offer congratulations. They all stayed late and toasted the new venture a few too many times to ensure a safe drive home.

She arrived home shortly before midnight. Avoiding the bed where the rat had been found, she had rolled on her side trying to make herself comfortable on the couch, when she realized her mistake. She was staring right at the answering machine and couldn't avoid the glowing zero in the display. No messages. Wilson hadn't called.

★ ★ ★

The next morning Kate's phone rang, extra loudly it seemed, and she snatched it up quickly to make it stop.

"Good morning Sunshine," Charm said brightly. "How are you feeling today?"

"Urgghh," Kate responded.

"It was a blast wasn't it? More about that later. I can tell that I woke you up. Have you noticed the time?"

Kate glanced at the clock on the wall and groaned.

"Now don't think for a minute I'm swearing off my vow of irreverence, but it would probably be best if we were on time for Trevor Edgar's presentation on the New Code of Conduct. Your name is undoubtedly going to come up as an aggrieved victim and my mother would have some ancient Chinese pearl of wisdom for why we have to be there."

"Uh-huh." Kate's head was swimming.

"If we stop to buy lattes, though, we're going to be late. Pick me up on the corner and we'll have our special coffee at lunch. Clam chowder, that's what you need. Not the white stuff. Manhattan Clam Chowder's the ticket for a hangover."

She paused. "I didn't get that pearl from my mother. Mom never drank a drop. That's one from my personal collection."

* * *

Trevor Edgar, the private detective and self-appointed champion of women's rights, had reserved three seats at the front of the boardroom for the victims of the panty affair. With an audience of senior management and bureaucrats from the Ministry of Women's Affairs, he clucked industriously around Pamela, Kate, and Sabrina frantically trying to justify his position and the fee he was collecting. It was too much of an insult to her intelligence for Kate to play along, especially with the ghost of last night's celebrations haunting her, and she was glad when Jim, who was manning the switchboard, interrupted to say he urgently needed her advice.

She trudged out to the hallway, ready to thank Jim for the rescue, when she noted the grim expression on his face. Seizing her in a sideways hug, he walked her back to the communications department.

"You haven't seen today's paper, have you?" he asked quietly.

"No, we were pretty rushed this morning."

Jim cleared his throat. "There's something you should see and, I'm sorry, kid, but it's not good," he said, his voice trembling. He ushered her into the privacy of her cubicle where he had spread the front page of the Star out on the desk.

REPORTER INJURED IN CAR BOMBING

In what appears to be a targeted hit, Vancouver Star reporter, Rhys Wilson, was critically injured Monday morning by an explosive device planted in his SUV. Vancouver Police report that the detonation completely destroyed the vehicle. Also injured in the blast, but less severely, was tow truck driver, Francis Black.

Police are unwilling to release any details at this time but say it is lucky no one else was hurt in the blast that occurred just outside the Farmers' Market on Granville Island.

"Due to the early hour, there were few people around. Also in our favour was the fact that a number of shops on the Island are closed Mondays this time of year," says police spokesperson, Amanda Warrick.

The VPD believes this was not a random act of violence but that Wilson was targeted. Consequently, Warrick emphasizes the public need not fear for their safety. Homemade explosive devices have gained infamy in recent years in the Middle East, due to their ease in fabrication and their ability to penetrate heavily armored vehicles.

Rhys Wilson is an award winning journalist whose investigative reporting has often put him at odds with the seamier sides of society.

CHAPTER 36

Kate stared down the cluttered bottle-green hallway of 4West. She took a deep breath and was immediately sorry when the strong smell of industrial cleaner permeated her nostrils. She hated hospitals. Her dislike for them had turned to hate in her last year of university when her boyfriend had languished in a coma for two weeks after his motorcycle was broadsided. His family finally had to make the gut wrenching decision to take him off life support.

And here she was at St. Mark's Hospital again. After reading the news article, she had contacted Rhys's friend Colin Jones. The old editor knew few details, but he did know that Rhys was in Intensive Care at the 100-year-old hospital in Vancouver's downtown core.

Forcing herself to put one foot in front of the other, Kate proceeded unconsciously down the corridor, hoping she was mentally prepared. As she approached the ICU, a large policeman positioned himself across the doors, blocking her progress and snapping her out of her stupor. She introduced herself as a friend of Rhys's, explaining that she hoped to see him for just a moment. The guard stared through her with the assessing eyes of a seasoned veteran who has heard it all. Not a skilled manipulator at the best of times, Kate had exhausted her repertoire of sweet talking and was turning away when a familiar face appeared in the window of the ICU doors.

The doors opened with a soft "whoosh" and out stepped Phil, the purser from the Queen of Chilliwack. "Kate...he'd be so glad you came." Phil's face was splotchy red and there were deep circles under his eyes.

Kate's senses were on high alert for anything indicating Rhys's condition and the soft laughter filtering out of the ICU didn't jibe with the grave look on Phil's face.

He seemed to sense her confusion. "He's in a coma. His aunt and cousin thought it might help if we talked about old times. You know…reminded him of some of the fun we used to have." His gaze dropped to the floor. "I don't know what good it will do, but the doctors said it wouldn't hurt.

"It would mean a lot to him that you were here," he repeated, and Kate's alarm grew. He was talking as if Rhys were dead. Phil glanced over at the cop. "Can't you let her in?"

The cop scanned the two grieving people and his expression relaxed a bit. "You don't look like much of a threat to me, but no one's going in that room without my chief's OK."

Ignoring the cop, Kate turned back to Phil. "What happened? I only know what I've read in the paper."

Phil gave the guard a frustrated stare. "The nurses don't want too many of us in there at one time anyway. Why don't we get some coffee and I'll tell you what I know."

The cafeteria hadn't changed in the past eight years. One glance and Kate felt like she'd never left. Phil pulled a plastic chair out from a table and angled it in Kate's direction. He fumbled with another chair, its legs entangled with those on either side, but eventually won the battle and sunk down with a sigh. Kate forced herself to wait patiently until the exhausted man across the table was ready to begin.

"The cops haven't exactly been forthcoming with information," Phil said.

She nodded, willing him to go on.

"Monday morning, Rhys's cousin, Brad, got a call from Teresa, one of the managers down at Granville Island.

They've known her for years and she lets them get away with murder leaving their boats and cars parked there overnight." He looked wearily up at Kate. She nodded encouragingly again and he continued.

"Teresa was hysterical. She told Brad that Rhys had been blown up. She had just arrived at work when she saw him coming up from the dock to the car park. He had left his Jeep in a three-hour zone." Phil shook his head. "He does that all the time and, thanks to Teresa, he never gets a ticket. This time his luck ran out...Apparently he got to his truck just as a tow truck driver was hoisting it up.

"She said she was killing herself laughing—figuring he deserved it and all, when the Jeep exploded. It blew Rhys right off his feet and into the concrete bridge foundation."

Kate reached across and took his hand in hers, stopping the merciless drumming of his fingers on the tabletop.

"For years we've all wondered why he's kept at it—with all the threats and the lifestyle he's been forced to pursue."

"Because of his dad's gambling addiction?" Kate suggested softly.

"That was the original trigger for sure. But it was almost like he had a death wish and he used the threats to drive himself to uncover all the dirt he could."

Kate shook her head sadly.

"The cops know it was a targeted hit." He opened his eyes wide to illustrate an "aha!" moment. "Bomb in your car, how much more targeted can you get? The irony is he was being careful lately. He never stopped at the Island anymore." Phil sighed. "I can't figure out what he was doing there."

With a start, Kate withdrew her hand from Phil's grasp. "I'm the reason he was there, Phil," she said. "He met me at Granville Island because it's close to my apartment." Tears streamed down her face. "I'm the reason this happened."

Phil shook his head forcefully. "Kate, don't do this to yourself. All his friends have worried for years that something like this would happen. The man couldn't let sleeping dogs lie. He had a unique knack for getting himself into tough situations and making them even worse." Phil had resumed his finger drumming and was getting more animated.

Kate glanced about the cafeteria self-consciously and reached into her bag for a tissue to wipe her tears. "He wanted to raise awareness with his column."

"Maybe, or maybe he's just an ornery, muckraking bugger."

Kate clenched her lips tightly.

Phil groaned. "I'm sorry. But, damn it, I feel so helpless."

"Me too," she said.

He stared across the room, took a deep breath and seemed to compose himself. "The cop leading the investigation is Paul Lee, and I know he knows more than he's letting on. But he promised Rhys's auntie he's going to get the guys that did it and, I have to tell you, I wouldn't want that mean bastard looking for me."

"I know that name." Kate rubbed her forehead. "Oh, of course, he came to my apartment when I was robbed. He's also the cop that blew Rhys off when he reported threats before."

"I think they have a history," Phil said.

"I hope he's feeling good and guilty."

Phil gazed blankly across the room.

"Have you had anything to eat?" Kate asked.

"Let's see. Brad and I had coffee this morning across the street and we've been doing shifts with Rhys throughout the day. I think we forgot to have lunch."

"We'll go out later and get something hot to eat," she said.

"Rhys told me a couple of times that you are a good person, Kate, and he's a tough sell." Phil gave a strained smile and thoughtfully cupped his chin in the palm of his hand. "I'm not trying to be maudlin here but I think you are the reason he was being less of a martyr lately."

Kate blinked with surprise. "But I don't know him that well—"

"Irregardless my dear—" Phil stopped mid-sentence and snorted. "Oh, I can picture our wordsmith cringing when I say that...*Regardless* of what you may think, Kate, you mean a hell of a lot to him. He told both Brad and me that he was worried about you and we figured you are the reason he's been a slightly less belligerent bugger recently."

Kate didn't bother trying to brush away the tear that trickled down her cheek.

"Enough weepy talk." Phil reached across the table and patted her hand gently. "Time to put on my game face and get that coffee we came for."

They bought five large cups of coffee and the remains of the day's pastries. Stopping at the condiment counter for cream and sugar, Phil plucked one of his purchases from the takeout tray and banged it on the bar.

"Definitely seen better days," he said of the petrified doughnut, gaily festooned with pink icing and a few remaining sprinkles. He dropped it back into the box with a thunk, turned toward Kate, and did a double-take. "Can you watch this for me?" He indicated the tray. "I'll be back in a minute."

He walked briskly back to the cashier line-up and tapped the shoulder of someone in hospital scrubs. Kate watched as the man paid for his lunch and the two of them wound their way towards her through the maze of tables and chairs.

"Dr. Young says he knows you through your friend Matt, " said Phil.

"Hello Ritchie," Kate said forcing a smile. "It's been a while."

"Too long. I've been in the Middle East doing a little work with the Red Cross. Phil tells me you're a close friend of Rhys Wilson's."

"We've worked together," Kate faltered. Then, meeting Phil's eyes, "Yes, we're pretty close."

"Dr. Young is looking after Rhys," Phil interjected.

Kate inhaled and met the trauma surgeon's gaze. "Honestly Ritchie, what's the situation?"

Young put his sandwich and salad down on the table beside him. "He has severe internal injuries and he's lost a lot of blood. We removed his spleen and the shrapnel we could find. One leg was broken when he was thrown against the bridge." He continued matter-of-factly, "Don't ask me how, but even though he looks like hell, the cuts and scrapes on his face are minor and the shrapnel missed his eyes. I'm not quite so optimistic about his right ear. Right now, however, the main worry is his lungs. That's the big concern in blast injuries and there's nothing we can do but wait to see if they've been damaged...Forty-eight hours should do it."

Kate placed a hand on the table to steady herself and Young's face softened.

"Sorry. Reporting on this type of thing to the brass in the Middle East has become kind of second nature to me. Sometimes I forget where I am and whom I'm talking to."

"I wanted you to tell me straight." She sniffed. "Phil and I need to know the truth."

Young looked from Kate to Phil. "It's obviously not a good situation. Despite that, there is hope. He's young, he's strong, and the blast didn't hit him as it was intended to."

"What do mean?" asked Phil.

"To maximize the odds of taking out the driver, car bombs are designed to blow straight up," Young said. "Because Wilson was behind the car, not sitting in it, the impact of the blast wasn't as bad as it could have been. It would have blown right over his head, as would the balance of the shrapnel."

Phil and Kate stared at each other in stunned silence.

"My apologies again. I've just completed my third deployment and you have to keep things clinical in order to stay sane. What a pointless loss of young lives." Young shook his head, for the first time showing some emotion. "Vehicular bombs are usually designed to activate when a key is turned in the ignition. But these bastards used a 'tilt' detonator filled with liquid mercury that triggers when the vehicle drives off of a level surface."

Phil nodded. "When the tow truck driver hoisted one end up to tow it away…"

Young nodded. "Away it went." He reached down and grabbed his food. "As I said, there is hope. The fact that you're all here could make a big difference. Keep talking to him. Who knows what the subconscious can hear.

Anything we can try in a situation like this is fair game." He placed a hand on Kate's shoulder. "I'm sorry, but I'm late for a meeting."

"Thank you, Ritchie," Kate said solemnly.

"Hey, Dr. Young," Phil began, "the cop guarding the ICU won't let Kate in. If talking to Rhys might be helpful, Kate has to be there. Do you think you could convince him to let her in?"

Young snorted dismissively. "Not a problem. Come on."

As the two friends raced down the hall trying to match the long, loping stride of Ritchie Young, he turned to Kate. "How's Matt? When I last spoke to him he was hoping to go back east for an anesthetic course."

"He's there now," Kate said. "I think it's going well. He, ah, hasn't been in touch all that much."

"I understand there's quite a workload," Young murmured. He put his arm around Kate's shoulders, forcing her to scurry as he marched on.

CHAPTER 37

I mpassively reporting casualties was not the only skill Dr. Young had picked up in the Middle East. He'd also developed a no nonsense dictatorial manner that immediately had the ICU guard on his phone for supervisory approval and Kate through the door of the Intensive Care Unit.

While Phil delivered a cup of coffee to the nurse at the central desk, Kate got the lay of the land. Care had obviously been taken to make the ward more calm and homey since her boyfriend's stay. The lighting was subdued and the walls had been painted a colour that coordinated with the privacy drapes that quieted the monitoring devices and the rhythmic sounds of the patients' ventilators. She counted ten beds arranged around the glass-enclosed nurses' station.

"The nurse tells me there's been no change," Phil told Kate. "Are you sure you want to see him. It's pretty upsetting and he won't even know you're there."

"Of course I want to," Kate snapped, her unease giving her voice an unintended defiance.

Phil nodded slowly and led the way to the first space where he pushed the curtain aside and placed the take-out tray on a side table. "How's everybody making out?" he asked, overplaying the brightness card severely. "I've brought nuclear fallout from the cafeteria and, even better, I've brought a good friend of Rhys's—who I found cruelly harassing the kind guard at the door." He stepped aside and indicated Kate with a dramatic sweep of his arm. "Auntie, Brad, this is Kate Logan. Kate...this is Rhys's Aunt Ellen and his cousin, Brad Stewart."

Kate barely heard what Phil said, so stunned was she by the site of the broken figure before her. Despite the presence of Rhys's relations, she was sure Phil had brought her to the wrong bed, because this patient was unrecognizable as their friend. She glanced at Phil who took in her meaning and nodded.

Rhys was wrapped like an Egyptian mummy. It looked to Kate that skin had only been bared to accommodate a needle or tube. From a slit in his facial bandages peeked his partially open, un-seeing eyes—puffy and blackened by the blast. One leg was in a cast and a tube in the back of his hand dispensed a combination of drugs from bags hanging on an IV pole. Wide bands of tape secured an endotracheal tube to his mouth—the other end attached to a ventilator that hissed away methodically. Blinking computer screens reported vital signs.

The room had gone strangely quiet and everything seemed to be moving in slow motion for Kate as she tried to grasp the fact that the broken bundle of bandages and snaking tubes was the strong, vibrant individual she had waved good-bye to yesterday morning. The abrupt "buzz" of the automatic blood pressure cuff, kicking in for another reading, snapped her back to reality. She felt a soft touch on her arm.

"It's a pleasure to meet you, Kate," said Brad, who had shuffled around the bed to her side. She shook hands and murmured a greeting to Aunt Ellen.

"Phil, I was just reminding Rhys about that surprise birthday party of Cheryl's a few years ago," Brad said.

Phil groaned.

Brad pulled up a chair for Kate. "You'll like this story. It was another one of those times Rhys got to demonstrate the phenomenal native outdoor skills he inherited."

Aunt Ellen snorted and took the coffee Phil handed her. He wiggled the other cups free from the tray and passed them around.

"So," Brad took a deep breath, "it was Phil's girl-friend's birthday. Cheryl and her friends had hiked up to her dad's cabin on Cougar Mountain and we decided we'd get a cake and some beer and go up and surprise them."

"That was some cake," Phil said. "It had mountains on it and birthday candles that looked like little cedar trees. Rhys had that made up." He reached down and patted his friend's shoulder gently.

"Rhys and Wesley and I were waiting for Phil to get off work when he calls and says the ferry's behind schedule, so he's going to be a couple of hours late. Long story short, Phil arrives three and a half hours later and we figure our only chance of making the party is to take the old trappers' trail up the mountain. It's quite a bit shorter, but not used much anymore."

"I don't think I ever heard this story," Aunt Ellen said.

"There's a reason for that, Auntie," Phil chimed in.

"We lost the trail as soon as we set off. But—" Brad held up his index finger dramatically, "Rhys told us not to worry; he would use his celebrated tracking skills to get us back on the path."

Auntie groaned and Phil said, "Oh, it gets better."

"An hour later, we're way hell and gone lost out in the bush. It's getting dark. The beer's getting warm and the cake's getting droopy."

"You did drop it that once," Phil said.

"That wasn't my fault. He let go of it before I was ready," Brad said. "Rhys carried the cake most of the way but he handed it to me when he needed his hands free to feel the north side of trees for moss, sense the wind with a licked finger—and various other secret navigating techniques."

"Oh Lord," Aunt Ellen said. "Phil, we're going to need something a little stronger than coffee if this story goes the way I think it's going."

Brad made shushing gestures at his mother. "Anyway, we get to this clearing and there's an outhouse, which I took as a sign of civilization, and Rhys took a lot of credit for, saying we had found the trail. We tramp a little further on and he's 'feeling' and 'sensing,' and we run smack into a huge pile of bear scat, which Rhys hovers his hand over and declares pretty fresh, because it's still warm."

"I taught him how to do that when we were kids." Phil looked down at Rhys. "You want to argue that one buddy, you'd better get yourself out of that bed."

"Next we hear a great bloody roar and at the side of the clearing we spot a couple of cubs and a momma grizzly standing up on her back feet, sniffing the wind."

Ellen smiled. "I would have killed the bunch of you, had I known this."

"Violent mothers like you miss out on some of the best stories," Brad said.

"A griz with cubs," said Ellen. "To what do we owe your presence here today?"

"Ancient white man survival skills," Phil grinned. "We ran like hell and hid in the outhouse."

Brad nodded. "We stayed there all night."

"Eeeww," Kate said.

"Hell of a lot better than the alternative," Phil pointed out.

"As outhouses go, it wasn't bad. It obviously hadn't been used in years and it was a big one."

"Yeah, it was a double. We never did figure out what was up with that, did we Brad?"

"Nope. Why would two people go in together?" He looked thoughtful. "Even Rhys didn't have an answer for that one. But I remember how good that cake went with the beer."

"I remember hearing the bear sniffing around the outhouse all night."

"All this talk about cake's making me hungry. Anybody want to split a doughnut?" Brad asked.

"I'm not sure it's possible to get a knife through it," Phil said. He glanced at Kate, who shook her head. "It's all yours, my friend."

With some effort, Brad gnawed off a bite and nodded his approval. The silence that followed was broken only by the sound of him crunching.

"Well Rhys," Kate forced a smile and spoke loudly to the patient, "you're going to have to get better soon. I have full confidence in your backpacking skills and I want to hear your side of the story."

"I've got another classic Rhys-ism." Phil perched on the arm of Kate's chair. "Auntie, I think you've heard this one."

"If that's the case, it's probably pretty tame," she muttered.

"Do you remember when we had to put my grandma in that nursing home in East Vancouver? She couldn't live on her own anymore because she sometimes forgot to lock the door and turn the stove off."

Aunt Ellen nodded. "She didn't like the place one bit. She missed her neighbours and the mailman, and she missed her garden."

"Wasn't there something about her weeding the neighbours' gardens?" Brad asked.

"Yeah, that happened," Phil said. "She didn't always remember which garden was hers. The mailman usually spotted her while he was making his rounds and took her back home...Except that one time the posties were on strike and the cops called in the sniffer dogs to find her. Anyway, Rhys is a student in Vancouver at the time and he hears Granny's unhappy, so he starts taking her out to lunch every week."

"I remember hearing about that. She loved his visits," Aunt Ellen said.

"She had no use for me, her own grandson, coming to see her if it interfered with his visit, and I finally found out why. This bugger is taking her to all the best restaurants in town." Phil hooked his thumb in Rhys's direction. "When the hostess sat them down he'd say, 'Happy Birthday, Granny!' The light would go on, and she'd tell the waitress it was her hundredth birthday. The restaurants always made a huge fuss, pulled a birthday cake out of thin air, comped their meals, and, once, the two of them even made it to the six o'clock news."

"She celebrated her hundredth birthday every week?" Kate asked.

"Every week and ten years early. She was only eighty-nine at the time."

"Good for her," Kate giggled.

"They ate at every five star restaurant in town. We never figured out whether or not she knew it wasn't her birthday." Phil shook the box holding the remaining doughnuts in the direction of his friend, who declined.

The telling of the next escapade was preempted by a nurse who asked if she could interrupt them for ten minutes to check on the patient. Everybody looked from one to another and Kate had a feeling they were all thinking the same thing.

"Maybe we've talked the boy's ear off enough for today," Aunt Ellen said. "Brad, I know you need some time to take *Rock n' Roll* back to your marina."

"And feed Elvis," Brad said.

"Kate has suggested we go out for a decent bite to eat," said Phil.

"That's a wonderful idea, but you guys go ahead on your own. This old girl needs a nap." Ellen winked at Kate.

Brad lingered at Rhys's bedside after the others had filed out and Kate heard him warn his cousin he'd be smart to quit lying about worrying everybody and speak up and defend himself. "The stories I'm planning to tell tomorrow, we definitely never told our moms."

CHAPTER 38

The next morning Kate drew to the end of the block and stopped in front of a concerned Charm clutching newspaper and lattes. The night before, Kate, Brad, and Phil had rehashed the details of Rhys's situation over a subdued dinner at a bistro on Davie Street. She arrived home too late to phone Charm and fill her in. Judging by the expression on her friend's face, however, Charm knew Rhys's situation.

"Please tell me he's OK."

The intensity of her friend's stare almost made Kate break down. Biting her lip to stem the flow of tears, she slipped the car into gear and pulled out into traffic. "Let me find a better place to stop," Kate said. They drove a few blocks in silence before she pulled to the side of the road and told Charm what she knew. "I should have called you last night, but we grabbed something to eat after we left the hospital, and when I got home it was so late…and frankly, I couldn't bear to go over it again."

"Forget it. Jim told me where you'd gone. Do they have any idea who could have done it? I don't see anything new in this morning's paper."

"The cops aren't saying much. Phil thinks they know more than they're telling."

"I guess that's the smart thing to do." Charm passed the cooling latte to Kate, who nodded her thanks.

"From what Brad and Phil told me at the restaurant, there were a hell of a lot more people gunning for Rhys than he ever let on to me. I didn't know he'd worked in

London." She took a sip. "He uncovered a kickback scheme some politician had going that got the guy thrown out of Government. His wife left him and his father disowned him and willed this huge estate to the younger brother instead. The guy vowed he'd get even." When Charm inhaled sharply, Kate nodded and continued.

"After that, he went to Montreal where he investigated the effect gang activity has on regular citizens. The gangs were even forcing pizza joints to order truckloads more meat and cheese than they needed."

"Hunh?" Charm grunted.

"I don't understand how it worked, but the shops had to load their pizzas up with cheese and meat just to get rid of all the stuff they were forced to buy. Brad says the gangs were into everything and making millions."

"And his articles stopped it?"

"Apparently. Once they realized how prevalent criminal activity was, the citizens demanded the cops do something about it." Kate lifted her coffee in a toast. "And they did...the gangs moved out, giving up some very lucrative operations."

"How to make friends and influence people," Charm whispered.

"Yeah. The threats he's received here from over-extended, entitled stock promoters are just baby stuff."

"But don't you think it's more likely Rhys's bombing is connected to Wesley's murder? It's too coincidental."

Kate sighed and reached for a tissue from the box in the backseat. "I wondered about that myself, but Phil and Brad don't think they're connected. Phil's heard rumblings about native fishermen transporting pot up and down the coast. He says if Wesley knew that was going on, he'd try to put a stop to it."

"Maybe he confronted them last week and they shot him," Charm said.

"Maybe, and, to get back to your point, maybe he told the story to his best friend, Rhys, who stuck his nose where it doesn't belong one too many times."

"Yeah." Charm's voice was barely audible.

"Except." Kate raised a finger. "Brad says there is no way in a million years that anybody in Bella Bella would hurt Wesley. It's a close-knit community and he went to school with most of the fishermen and they all love him. He's the chief's grandson and his family has taken a lot of the kids in at one time or another, fed them, and helped them out. Alice even had extra bedrooms built on to her house to accommodate other people's kids, or people with nowhere to go."

"What a bloody situation." Charm blew out a sigh. "Are you going to go see him tonight?"

Kate nodded.

"I'll come with you if you like, but I'm not too good with hospitals."

"How about next time? It's really difficult getting past the police guard. They had to practically smuggle me in." Kate gave a half-hearted grin. "Did I miss anything at the meeting yesterday?" She put her cup in the holder and turned the ignition over. "If I hear any more about panties, I'm going to strangle somebody with the pair I was sent. Why doesn't Pamela just let it lie?"

"Crap. I forgot to tell you, Mardone noticed you were gone and kicked up a stink. He's anxious about something."

"Nothing new there." Kate checked her mirrors and pulled away.

"Maybe not, but two retired math profs were in to see him yesterday about the distribution of the winning numbers in Kinetic Keno. He was pretty rattled after they left."

* * *

The large note penned in childish script and taped to Kate's computer monitor came as no surprise. In heavy black marker, it ordered her to report to Mardone's 'offise' first thing. She removed her jacket and gave it an unsuccessful toss at the hook on the wall. Sighing, she was reaching to retrieve it when Jim slid around the door jam, scooped the coat, and hung it up. Stepping forward, he swallowed her up in a big bear hug.

"Oh, no...no hugging." She pulled back. "I'm OK until the hugging starts," she said, dabbing at her eyes.

Kate had just finished filling Jim in on the situation when Leah phoned, demanding to know where she was. "And like, don't try and say 'what meeting?' because I, myself, personally, taped a note to your screen."

"I'm on my way," Kate said calmly. She hung up the phone and pawed through the materials on her desk until she found what she was looking for. Then, glancing heavenward for Jim's benefit, she headed to Mardone's office.

Leah was working on what seemed a particularly stubborn cuticle when Kate stalked past her into her boss's office. The days where she waited patiently for the girl to acknowledge her presence had passed, as had the days where she took a back seat to Mardone's manipulating.

"I understand you had a visit from some people regarding the problem with Kinetic Keno," Kate said, as Mardone looked up with a start. "I thought you'd dealt with that."

"I...I," Mardone flubbed, then catching himself, stopped for a beat, eyed her harshly, and smiled an oily sneer. "There's no problem with Keno and I'm the one who'll ask the questions."

Kate stared back defiantly. "Those profs know some numbers have been drawn an inordinate number of times and others haven't been drawn at all, don't they? I've got the graph of the winning numbers right here." She held the paperwork out to him.

"I'm not interested in—" He backhanded the report out of Kate's hand, hitting her wrist hard in the process. "What I'd like to know is how you've become such an expert?" His eyes radiated hostility. "Doing a little dirty work for that loser reporter?"

"I know what a random number is," she said.

"So do I. Sometimes it turns up. Sometimes it doesn't. Case closed." He slammed his hand down on the desktop. "That's not why I wanted to see you."

In her peripheral vision, Kate saw Leah had assumed her usual eavesdropping position and she almost jumped out of her skin when Mardone bellowed. "Leah, put that damned nail file away and get me a coffee. Black, four sugars."

The young secretary sniffed, stuck out her chin, and marched off almost smashing into Tom, who also seemed to be lurking in the hallway.

"I want to know what you think you're doing walking out of here yesterday," Mardone yelled, his voice strangled. "Obviously you're not management material so you won't understand, but we're implementing Pamela's new Decisional Matrix around here and disseminating information is an important step in that process. Unfortunately, that involves you." He smirked. "At least until I get Jack Stec up to speed."

CHAPTER 39

Back in her office, Kate sank into her chair. Mardone had told her if she hoped to receive any bonus at the end of her contract, she had better shape up, starting with a media update on the corporation's zero tolerance policy on sexual harassment. His brave decision to "take the high road and move forward, despite the harm done to himself," was to feature prominently.

She had read through her first draft and was trying not to gag when she got an uneasy feeling. Spinning round, she was surprised to see an apprehensive-looking Trevor Edgar in the doorway.

He glanced left and right, scurried into her cubicle, and sat down. "I was wondering if I could buy you lunch?"

"Sorry, Trevor." She waved the press release. "I've got to get this finished."

"We could make it a quick lunch. I, uh, happened to notice you didn't return to the meeting yesterday. I thought I'd fill you in on what you missed."

"That's good of you. But Mardone pretty much brought me up to speed."

Edgar's shoulders slumped and he regarded her wordlessly for a moment, the muscles around his mouth flexing sporadically as if another invitation was forthcoming. Kate's mind raced as she tried to fashion another believable excuse.

"I read the news about Rhys Wilson." He leaned forward and lowered his voice. "I know he's a friend of yours. I just wanted to say, I hope he'll be OK."

Kate shot him the "drop-dead-and-die" glare that Charm employed with aggressive panhandlers. "You can report back to Pamela and Mardone that things are looking up Trevor," she said. "I can't see Wilson writing any more columns on Pacific in the near future, or—ever."

Edgar stared at her blankly then shook his head quickly. "Pamela didn't send me. I wanted to ask you myself...you know, how he's making out. There wasn't much information in the paper."

"First Mardone and now you. Why do you assume Wilson and I are friends? I don't know him." Kate's voice rose.

Edgar stood quickly, his face flushed. "I'm sorry. You're obviously upset. We'll do lunch another time."

"Can't see that happening." She bent to scoop up the press release that had fallen to the floor.

Edgar sidled warily towards the door, but his escape was thwarted when Tom's huge bulk blocked the exit.

"You OK, Kate?" he boomed.

"Yeah. I'm all right."

"Just a misunderstanding. Only a little misunderstanding," Edgar chattered. His gaze trained on the floor, he waved his wrist nervously at Tom to indicate he wanted to pass.

Tom ignored him and regarded Kate with concern. "You're sure everything's cool?"

Kate turned her back on the two men and pretended to be busy at her desk. "Fine, Tom. I'm just trying to get this finished."

Tom growled and stepped aside so the perspiring Edgar could scuttle past. Parking himself in the vacated chair, he blew out a huge sigh and levelled a look at Kate that said a real explanation had better be forthcoming.

★ ★ ★

"So you see," Kate said, summing up her visit from Edgar, "he's just pumping me for information so he can score some brownie points with Pamela and Gregor."

Tom rubbed his chin and sighed. "The guy's a worm, Katie. Don't worry about it, though. His contract's almost up."

"Mine is too. I guess we'll be pounding the pavement together."

"About that...I've talked to a few people...Told them you might be ready to make a move. I thought we could go over what I've learned at dinner tonight." He eyed her sideways. "After your reaction to poor old Trevor's kind invitation, I'm a little afraid to ask."

Kate eyed the mock apprehension on his face and let out a snort of laughter. "For Pete's sake. Yes. I'd appreciate your help on the job front and, if we must do it over dinner, OK."

"Tonight? Sushi?"

"Can't tonight," Kate said, sobering. "I'm going to the hospital to see Rhys."

"What *is* his condition?" Tom appeared stressed as he watched Kate struggle to compose herself.

"Not good, I'm afraid." She felt the corners of her mouth turning down.

"Don't worry. Stubborn beggar like him, I bet you'll find he's improved since yesterday." He patted her knee. "In any case, worrying doesn't help. You go see him tonight and we'll have dinner tomorrow."

She nodded.

"Koji's Sushi Palace. He's got a new inside-out roll. It's supposed to be sick."

"Sick?"

"Yeah. Charm says 'sick' means 'really good' now." He paused as Kate's expression registered with him. "Doesn't it?"

"You really can't pull that off, you know."

"Charm said I should practice using it in a sentence."

Kate shook her head. "Just get out of here. And tell me if this is OK, would you?" She held out the press release.

Tom grabbed the papers, saluted crisply, and marched off.

★ ★ ★

Kate and Phil had arranged to meet at five o'clock in the hospital cafeteria.

"Brad's going to meet us later in Rhys's room," Phil said as Kate took a seat across the table from him. "They're hosting a wooden boat show at the marina and he's tied up all afternoon trying to find moorage for latecomers."

Kate nodded absently. "I'm afraid to ask, but do we know how Rhys is doing?"

"I talked to Auntie around two o'clock and...damn it Kate...they had to take him back to the OR last night. He started bleeding again. They fixed the problem but, since then, he's taken a turn for the worse." Phil cradled his face in his hands.

Kate drew back. "I didn't think you were going to say that," she whispered. The two of them sat in silence for a while until Kate took Phil's hand. "There's still hope. Let's go upstairs and see what we can do."

Kate thought she was mentally prepared for the situation, but no one could have anticipated the scene when they entered the ICU. At the foot of the bed stood Alice, ablaze with colour in her native dress, softly beating a handheld drum. Chief Moses, Tina, Aunt Ellen, and Dr. Young chattered to each other while they industriously relocated tables, chairs, monitors, and IV poles. As a baffled Kate and Phil watched from the doorway, one of the ICU nurses marched up to Young and confronted him.

"Go ahead and write an incident report," he said. "This may be a little out of the ordinary but I don't recall anything in the hospital guidelines specifically prohibiting Spirit Doctors." He took the object Tina handed him and tucked it into Rhys's hand.

"Chief," Phil said, snapping out of his stupor, "you're doing a Spirit Search?" He strode toward the bed. Kate followed cautiously.

"Ah, Phil. You remember." Moses removed something that looked like an old rattle from a weathered leather bag and placed it on the bed.

"Of course...But, Dr. Young?" Phil shot a questioning look at the physician.

"It's worth a try. If we don't do something, he's going to go into organ failure."

Kate's hand flew to her mouth and she scanned the room desperate for a twenty-first century intervention. To her left, the same ICU attendant leaned against the nurse's station, her face a mask of scorn.

"Kate, so glad you could come. Can you give us a hand?" Tina clucked in a businesslike manner. "Doctor, we have to scootch him over a bit."

Young's eyes met Kate's and he jerked his head to the left, indicating she should come help. Tossing her purse aside, she grasped a corner of the sheet beneath Rhys and, on Tina's count, they pulled him sideways. Young shuffled to the head of the bed and checked to see the monitors were still correctly attached.

"What's going on?" Kate whispered to Phil.

"The Chief is going to search for Rhys's lost guardian spirit," Phil explained.

All eyes turned towards Kate and she coloured self-consciously.

"Don't worry, my dear," Aunt Ellen said kindly. "This isn't something you see every day. Do you want to explain, Phil, or do you want me to?"

Phil indicated she had the floor.

"We believe that a person becomes diseased if his guardian spirit leaves or is lost. It's the job of the Spirit Doctor to find it and bring it back."

Kate bit her lip and glanced at Young.

The physician looked tense. "Time is of the essence here, Ellen." He reached over to help Moses lower the safety rail on the side of the bed.

"We imagine each person's consciousness as a tree. Its roots represent the past, the tall trunk is the journey and its branches and leaves are the future. The Spirit Doctor lies down with the sick one, enters his altered consciousness through a gateway on the trunk, and searches for the lost guardian spirit. He may find the spirit in the roots or he may find the spirit has gone on ahead and is in the branches." As Auntie spoke, Alice and Dr. Young assisted Moses into the bed alongside Rhys.

"This shaker," Auntie retrieved the old rattle and handed it to Moses, "helps keep the Spirit Doctor connected to the present world. When he finds the spirit in the tree, he captures it in the soul catcher." She indicated the object, which looked like an old bone, in Rhys's lifeless hand. "Upon his return, the Chief will place one end of the soul catcher against Rhys and blow his spirit back into him. Since his body is no longer empty, illness doesn't have any place to hide."

Kate stared dumbstruck at Ritchie Young who returned her stare defiantly. He was spared having to justify himself when a piercing alarm sounded and he leapt to the monitors.

As Alice and Tina began pounding out an eerie beat on their drums, Kate turned and ran blindly from the room.

CHAPTER 40

She ran all the way to the basement parking level before she got control of her emotions and slowed her pace. But when the heavy door from the stairwell clicked shut behind her, Kate felt her anxiety rising again because she had absolutely no recollection where she had left her car.

Desperately wanting the privacy of her little vehicle, she wrestled her keys from her bag and pressed the alarm button. When the horn sounded a few rows over, she ran in its direction, jumped inside the car, and melted into the upholstery. All the helplessness she had felt when her boyfriend was hospitalized years before came flooding back. Her tears now flowing in earnest, Kate reached into the backseat for the box of tissues and felt the hairs rise on the nape of her neck. She peered out the rear window but, aside from an old Volvo with its interior light glowing dimly, there was nothing and nobody. An eerie, artificially-lit stillness met her gaze, which was as disconcerting as if someone had been staring back.

"Probably somebody annoyed at me for setting off the alarm," she informed the car as she turned the ignition over. She wiped away her tears the best that she could and gunned it for home, while she could still see.

Kate entered her building and spotted John, the manager, industriously organizing the residents' charity donations for tomorrow's pick up. As much as she loved the old man, she hoped the upbeat wave she gave him as she scurried to her door would keep him at bay for a while. She was still trying to come to grips with the scene at Rhys's bedside and was in no mood to make light conversation.

She was on high alert for intruders when she opened the door to her suite, but everything seemed just as she had left it, save for the flashing light on her answering machine, which she regarded warily. Good news was in short supply recently and more bad news she didn't need. After a moment, however, she marched over to the desk and punched the playback button.

"I wish you'd spend a couple of bucks and get a decent cell or listen to your voicemail. I've been trying to get you all day." Matt's voice burst from the speakers.

"Can you send my tux and dress shoes to me by overnight courier? One of my classmates has invited me to a charity ball in Palm Beach this weekend. Her father is CEO of the drug company that's hosting it. All of East Coast society will be there and it's a real opportunity for me to meet the right people." He paused for breath.

"I spent last weekend at their place on Long Island, sailing and hanging out with the old man." Another short pause.

"Good enough, then. You've got my address. Don't call me back because I'm trying to catch up on my rest.

"And seriously, get a new phone. I don't care if you are a contractor, Pacific should provide a good one for you. I may need something else and I want to be able to get hold of you."

The little beep sounded signifying the end of the message and Kate stared dumbly at the machine as the fussy female recorded voice asked if she would like to save or delete this message. The woman had to ask four times before Kate snapped to and punched delete.

"That narcissistic little toad," she muttered. Shaking her head, she strode to the kitchen and plucked a glass from the cupboard. "That unscrupulous worm." She reached further in for the bottle of scotch, which had recently proven so helpful for medicinal purposes. After a few swallows of the burning stuff and ten minutes of reflection, the curtain of indecision rose from her mind.

She marched into the living room and picked up the phone. When Charm answered on the first ring, Kate updated her friend on Rhys's condition. She also filled her in on Matt's phone call. She could hear Charm fuming.

"Don't you dare send him that tux, Kate Logan."

Kate sipped her scotch thoughtfully, pondering what she might send instead.

"Are you still there?" Charm yelled. "I've got an idea. Why don't you drop everything and come over here. We'll order something in for dinner."

"Why don't you come over here instead? I've got a glass of scotch with your name on it."

"Scotch? Yuck. I'll be right over."

Fifteen minutes later, Charm arrived at Kate's door with a box of utility grade garbage bags. For the next hour the two of them sipped scotch and stuffed Matt's belongings into the garbage bags.

"Perfect." Kate attached a twist tie to the last bag. "We'll put them out in the hall for John. He's getting a jump on the Christmas clothing drives." She cast a coy eye at Charm. "And here I was feeling like a heel because I had nothing to donate." She swept an arm toward the mountain of bags piled at the door. "Ta-dah."

"More like, 'touché!'" said Charm thoughtfully. "However, I don't think putting them out in the hall is a fitting end. I know you and, unlike me, you have a conscience. I wouldn't put it past you to cart them all back in here after I go home."

"And the scotch wears off," added Kate with a grin.

"Also a factor...Let's drive them to the collection depot right now."

"Super idea," said Kate. "But I think I'm too blitzed to drive and you don't—drive, I mean."

"Good point. I forgot about that." Charm poured another wee dram into her glass. "You know, this stuff grows on you," she said, eyeing the amber liquid.

"Let's ask John if he'll drive us."

They trotted out to the hall and assailed the building manager who was boxing up donations. After hearing Charm's rationale for the trip, and never having been a fan of Matt's anyway, he scurried outside to warm up his '74 Chevy station wagon.

★ ★ ★

The next morning Kate awoke feeling much better than she felt she deserved, after noting the empty scotch bottle in her recycle bin. After making their delivery the previous night, she, Charm, and John had completed packing up the rest of the tenant donations in the front hall and returned to her suite for Chinese take-out and a thorough re-hashing of recent events.

They all agreed that a physician like Matt, sworn to "Do No Harm," would be proud he had taken his oath a step further and donated his pricey technical outdoor gear, cashmere sweaters, wool suits, and Italian loafers to keep the homeless warm this winter.

Kate was fascinated to hear John's tale of witnessing a successful Spirit Search in the Yukon thirty years before.

The patient had survived not only his original illness, but the searching ceremony as well, John reported. Kate could have sworn she saw his nose grow as he gave the details, but his story gave her comfort and the nose lengthening was probably due to bad lighting, or too much scotch.

They didn't come up with anything too productive when brainstorming Kate's tenuous job situation except that Tom had indicated to Charm he might have a lead on positions for both of them. "He's got your back, you know," Charm said.

When Charm brought up the subject of the panties and the hiring of Trevor Edgar, Kate told them about her recent run-in with the "detective." "He's always been so backstabbing and sneaky, I just assumed it was more of the same," she said. "He seemed kind of sincere, though, and what could he hope to gain from taking me to lunch?"

John cast a glance at Charm who rolled her eyes.

★ ★ ★

"I've got to give Phil a call and find out what happened last night...and apologize for running out," Kate said as she and Charm pulled into the lottery parking lot the next morning.

"I'm sure he understands." Charm grunted and heaved her rolling shopping cart of SAY materials from the back of the car. "I'll be so glad when this stupid presentation is over."

Kate grinned and slammed the trunk down. Part way across the lot, she turned back to lock her car remotely with the key fob, and a familiar feeling of unease came over her. She glanced down the row of parked cars and spotted Trevor Edgar watching them from his twenty-year-old Swedish sedan.

Kate pushed the lock button and continued walking. "Edgar's spying on us from his car," she said.

"What?" Charm stopped dead in her tracks.

"Don't let on."

"Why the hell not?" Spinning on her heel, Charm gave Edgar a flamboyant wave, flipped him the bird, and marched off, dragging Kate with her. "Still think he's a good guy? I'd stay away from that creep."

★ ★ ★

Phil was just getting up after a long night at the hospital when Kate called and he wouldn't have any part of her apology, explaining that he could imagine how a Spirit Search appeared to the uninitiated.

"I have to give Dr. Young credit for being open-minded," he said. "I was afraid he'd get hell from his superiors, but he told me sometimes rules have to be broken."

"I think I understand a little better now, too," Kate said.

Phil said Moses was happy with the way the Spirit Search had gone. "It took a lot out of the old man. He looked and looked and finally located Rhys's guardian spirit high in the branches of his consciousness." Phil spoke matter-of-factly. "I guess he had one heck of a time capturing the spirit in the catcher. But he did, Kate. He did! And that's fantastic news."

Kate's newly opened mind wasn't quite prepared for the bounds of Phil's enthusiasm and she could feel it trying to inch its way closed.

"We didn't finish until around ten o'clock and Moses was exhausted. Brad drove them all over to Aunt Ellen's place in North Van for the night."

"I didn't tell Tina and Alice how sorry I am about Wesley."

"They know how you feel. I think it's Wesley's death that's keeping them going. Rhys is like a member of that family and they're damned if they're going to lose two sons."

Kate agreed to meet Phil and Brad at the hospital at five o'clock and hung up feeling a little less conflicted. She spent the rest of the morning incorporating Tom's suggestions into her press release on sexual harassment and avoiding phone calls from the growing number of reporters eager for a response to the math profs' "tweeted" accusations that Kinetic Keno was rigged. The old guys were skilled in social media and communications as well as number crunching.

Just before lunch she received a call from Charm begging for a ride to the shopping centre nearby. "I've had Pamela and the SAY conference up to the eyeballs and I think a little retail therapy and a couple pieces of pizza from that new Russian place would really help remedy the situation."

Charm chattered all the way to the plaza. Pamela had apparently hired additional inspirational speakers for the conference. "Fitting them in isn't the problem," she explained. "The problem is they won't stay at the same hotel as everybody else. They insist it be five stars. And get this, Pamela promised them a Whistler condo for the weekend and a chauffeured limo to take them up and back."

Charm steered Kate towards the food fair and was marveling at how those good looking Russian proprietors really knew how to toss their dough when Kate felt a tap on her shoulder. She turned to see two unshaven men, tall, broad-shouldered, and dressed in black. One wore a ski toque and the other a baseball cap on backwards. It wasn't until the one wearing the toque took a step closer that she recognized him.

CHAPTER 41

The familiar of the two put his index finger to his lips then turned the palm of the same hand toward the girls to reveal a police badge. Catching Kate's eye, Mr. Familiar angled his head toward the exit, then seized her arm and frog-marched her out the door as Charm scampered along behind.

Outside the shopping centre, his features softened slightly. "Take it easy. We just want to talk to you." He opened the front door of a dark sedan parked in the loading zone and indicated she climb in. The two cops then scanned the lot, nodded to Charm, climbed in the car, and peeled away.

"My apologies, Miss Logan. Sometimes I find things are easier to accomplish with less explanation," Detective Lee said from the back seat. "By the way, this is Don Larsen."

"Pleasure," growled backwards baseball cap, who had slowed the car down and was now discreetly cruising along with the traffic.

"What's going on?" Kate asked, needing quick answers to calm herself down.

Lee's response was interrupted by a squawk of inquiry from the police radio. Larsen listened and snorted with laughter. "You were right, Paul," he said, glancing at his partner in the rear view mirror before giving a coded reply to the dispatcher.

"In answer to your question, Kate, in light of recent events, we wanted to check in and make sure you are all right," said Lee. "It's good to see that people are watching out for you. Your friend, Charm, kind of renews my waning faith in mankind. She just phoned 911 to make sure you hadn't been kidnapped by a couple of dirty thugs.

"Don't worry," Lee said. "The dispatcher will tell her everything's OK." Lee cleared his throat. "We've been keeping a routine eye on you."

"I guess that's why I've felt like I'm being followed lately."

Larsen turned off the main street onto a narrow dirt track. They drove about half a kilometer to where the road ended in a turnaround strewn with garbage and cast off appliances. He killed the engine and her unease mounted. Cop, or not a cop, she could certainly see why Charm had described them as thugs.

"When did you think you were being followed?" Lee demanded.

"Last night at the hospital and in the parking lot at work this morning. But it was just Trevor Edgar this morning. He's doing some work for us." She looked from cop to cop. "Charm thinks we should steer clear of him, but he's more creepy than dangerous. And I might have been imagining things at the hospital. It was dark. It was a bad day."

"Get in touch with us immediately if it happens again." Lee handed Kate his card. "As you can see from Charm recognizing Larsen as a dirty thug, we're pretty good at what we do. If we are tailing you, you shouldn't be able to tell." He winked at her. "Granted, Don doesn't have to put too much work into his disguise."

Larsen cracked his chewing gum and smiled, his perfect white teeth the only thing inconsistent with his get-up.

"There hasn't been any more trouble since the break in?" Lee asked.

Kate shook her head.

"And you're making good use of your new lock?"

She regarded him wordlessly for a moment. "I get the feeling there's something you're not telling me."

The detective's impassive eyes met hers with a look she couldn't decipher. "We feel anyone associated with Rhys Wilson should be extra vigilant. And I want to know everything that happened Sunday night and Monday morning when you were on his boat."

Kate coloured but relayed the conversation she and Rhys had onboard, skipping events in the later part of the evening that she didn't think pertinent and figured they'd already guessed anyway.

"So he never indicated he was worried about his safety?" Lee asked.

"He's mentioned it in passing before and he warned me to be careful. That night, though, he didn't say anything specific. He was only concerned with what happened to Wesley."

Lee's thick fingers tapped the seatback and he exchanged looks with Larsen.

"He was pretty upset that the police up the coast considered him a suspect in Wesley's death," Kate said.

Lee waved his hand dismissively.

For ten more minutes they peppered her with questions concerning Rhys's friends, her past and present boyfriends, and the lottery corporation, then Larsen fired up the car and drove her back to the shopping centre.

As the car swung into the loading zone, Lee reached forward and placed his hand on Kate's shoulder. "Be careful and keep your eyes open. If Trevor Edgar bothers you or Charm anymore, I want to know about it. Are we clear?"

She nodded.

"One more thing: This meeting never happened. Don't tell anyone we contacted you," Lee said.

"Our dispatcher has told Charm the same. It would probably be a good idea if you reminded her," said Larsen.

Glancing from Larsen's to Lee's steely eyes, Kate caught herself automatically nodding in agreement, when she stopped. "How could this happen?" she spat. "You knew he'd received those threats. Why weren't you there?" She pointed her finger angrily. "All this talk about threats and surveillance. Why weren't you watching him?" Kate could feel her face getting hot and she was afraid she was going to lose it, but she didn't.

Lee stared at some object across the road for a long moment. "I was aware of the threats on Wilson." His eyes met Kate's with more compassion than she thought him capable of. "And in hindsight, yes, we should have had him under twenty-four hour surveillance."

"We tried, Paul," Larsen interjected.

Kate turned a questioning stare on the younger man.

"We kept losing him," Larsen said.

Lee chuckled with little enthusiasm. "We could never figure out if he knew he was being followed and purposely evading us, or if he was just that slippery."

Kate felt herself softening a little at their seemingly genuine regret.

"I'm not making excuses, but we have limited resources and he, himself, didn't seem that concerned."

Kate exhaled. "I can see how he'd be uncooperative. I shouldn't have blown up."

"Don't say that," Lee said. "You're right; we dropped our guard. Shit like this doesn't happen on my watch. I'll catch the guys that did this." He got out of the back of the car and opened Kate's door.

"How did you know I was on Rhys's boat?" she asked.

The corners of Lee's mouth turned up in a grin that didn't reach his eyes. "Like I said, if we're tailing you, you shouldn't know it."

★ ★ ★

Kate drove back to the office with her reluctantly muzzled friend. The two of them had sat in the food fair for forty-five minutes while Charm pumped Kate for information, all the while wolfing pizza. Kate had found herself hesitant to share everything, partially because she didn't think she could trust her effervescent buddy to keep her lip zipped, but mostly because she was concerned for her friend's safety.

Thankfully, Trevor Edgar wasn't lurking in the parking lot when they arrived and Kate couldn't spot any dirty thugs with badges either. Although the two women had overstayed their lunch hour on many occasions, with the "press check" excuse long exhausted, Kate was fretting over how to sneak in under the radar this time. With an exchange of winks and their attitudes sufficiently dialed up, they confidently reefed open the Pacific Lottery door—to cheers and the popping of flashes.

Gathered around an enthusiastic blue-haired woman clutching a colossal photo-op jackpot cheque were the majority of the lottery employees, kitted out as lotto balls— complete with numbered, spherical hats. Kate and Charm were trying to chart a discreet route past when Jim spotted them. Breaking away from the pack, Ball #5, which with Jim's bulk looked more like a genetically aberrant squash, lumbered over.

"You two really owe me this time," he spluttered.

Speechless, Kate looked from the monstrous "squash ball" to Charm and the two of them roared with laughter.

"What in the world's going on?" Charm managed to squeak out.

"It's one of Jack Stec's cutting edge marketing initiatives." Jim spoke in short gasps. "You weren't here Kate, so Stec and Mardone said I had to wear your costume. Needless to say, it's too small. I can't see. I can't breathe. And I don't think I'm going to be able to get it off."

A chorus of cheers went up from across the room. Kate saw all attention was now on a group of keen employees bouncing their spherical bellies and butts into each other, maybe simulating randomness, or maybe a complete surrender of their self-respect. She readjusted the glasses that had slipped down Jim's nose, gently took one of the arms that flailed from his sphere, and led him toward the main office door. Too short to support Jim's other arm, Charm bustled ahead and broke trail.

With both women participating, Jim was freed ten minutes later, breathing normally and sitting comfortably in Charm's office.

"I'm sorry I took your head off," he said, sipping a cup of tea. "Not your fault."

"We shouldn't have taken so long—" Kate began.

"I should have told Mardone and Stec where they could stick their lotto balls," he said. "I need that pension, though, you know?"

Kate patted his shoulder softly.

"Is this what we're paying Stec for?" Charm topped off their cups from the steaming pot she had fixed. "What do costumes like that cost, anyway?"

"Tom says you guys have to wear them whenever a big winner comes in," Jim said.

"He's on board with this?" Kate asked.

"Didn't do anything to back me up, just kept complimenting Stec. Neither one of them saw fit to put one on himself, though." Jim glanced over at the lotto ball getup jammed between two chairs to keep it from rolling away. He was blowing out a long sigh when he abruptly stopped and turned to Kate.

"A call was put through to my desk while you were at lunch. Phil, Wilson's friend, says he thinks it would be a good idea if you came to the hospital a little earlier this afternoon. He thought you should know things aren't the best."

Kate felt herself go cold.

"He told me to tell you everyone will be there." Jim spoke quietly. "I'm so sorry, kid."

Time slowed to a stop for Kate. She stared unseeing at the dumb costume and felt herself devoid of all senses and emotion in the vacuum the room had become.

★ ★ ★

The scene in Rhys's hospital room was somber. Phil, Moses, Tina, Alice, and Aunt Ellen sat quietly in chairs they had pulled up to his bedside. Ellen absent-mindedly patted the one hand of the patient that was unencumbered by IV lines. Kate was shocked at how much worse he appeared. He seems to be fading into the bed covers, she thought.

A haggard Phil was the first to notice she had arrived and he walked quietly across the room to her. "There's been no progress," he whispered. "And, there's something else." He bit his lip. "They've decided to disconnect the respirator."

Kate stared at him, stunned.

"Brad's talking to Dr. Young and the ICU team right now."

"I don't know what happened," said Moses in a small voice. "His was a stubborn spirit. It must have been too far up in the branches for me to capture."

Kate attempted a smile for the defeated looking old chief.

"I was sure I had it, though." Moses eyed Kate and Phil blankly, his thoughts obviously elsewhere. "I was sure."

The door behind Kate opened with a swoosh and Brad and Dr. Young entered. Ritchie Young walked over to Kate and wrapped his arm around her tightly.

"You've heard?" he asked.

She nodded.

"We don't know what will happen. He's shown small improvement in some areas, but overall…" Young's voice trailed off.

"Is there no chance he'll recover?" she asked meekly. "I didn't think you'd take a breathing tube out so soon."

"We're not taking it out. The tube stays in. We're going to turn the *respirator* off."

Not seeing how this bit of information made any difference, Kate glanced from Brad to Phil and back to Young.

"Sorry, guys," Brad said. "I didn't explain that correctly earlier. I'm not sure I understand it myself."

Young marched over to the bed and examined his patient and the monitors. "These new machines let us adjust the volume and saturation of oxygen while leaving the endotracheal tube in. We can turn it right off to see if he's capable of breathing on his own. If he's not, the tube is still in place and the machine kicks in with little 'puffs' of assistance." He looked into the worried faces of everyone assembled and, in his customary blunt fashion, said, "Shall we give it a go?"

Kate's heart almost stopped when Young first dialed the oxygen down. Rhys's gasping and choking were horribly distressing but, as tearful family and friends fled the room, she stood strangely impassive by the doctor's side as he calmly scrutinized the monitors. After an hour, things had settled down and everybody had been encouraged to return. Rhys still needed the respirator, but Young said he was pleased.

"We're not out of the woods by a long shot but he's a strong young guy and I'm satisfied with today's progress." He conferred briefly with the ICU nurses then patted the patient on the shoulder. "Keep on fighting, Rhys. It seems you're pretty important to a lot of people."

Kate stayed for another hour, the few incidents of panic quickly quelled with supporting puffs from the respirator. When she felt the situation was stable, she excused herself to meet Tom for dinner. Brad had just launched into a story about the time Rhys's mom had purposely stranded teenaged Brad and Rhys on Little Orca Island for a week when she learned they were skipping school.

"Remember how hungry we got, Rhys?" Brad said. "Those were fun times, eh?"

Kate bent down to give the patient a kiss on the forehead. "I want to hear your version of this story," she said.

"I'll walk you to your car," Phil said, putting an arm around her.

"She left them on an island way up there, by themselves?" Kate whispered.

"Oh yeah. You didn't want to get on the wrong side of Rhys's mom. She was madder than hell." He grinned at

Kate. "I was skipping school with them, but they covered for me." He glanced back at Brad who was reminding Rhys how cold it had gotten when their matches got wet and they couldn't build a fire. "And for that, I will be eternally grateful."

★ ★ ★

Tom had a window table and was halfway through his warm sake when Kate arrived at Koji's. She grinned when he stood as she approached.

"Wow, who does that anymore?" she asked, taking her seat.

"I'm practicing up. Charm tells me chivalry isn't just dead, it's buried six feet under. I'm gonna prove her wrong." He settled his large self back in his seat. "Am I wrong in thinking you're in a brighter mood than you've been lately?"

"You are absolutely correct. Some good news today and I could sure use one of those." She indicated his sake.

"Your wish is my command...Domo Kyoko," he said to a kimono-clad woman who discreetly placed another flask of sake on the table.

Tom reached across and poured the rice wine into Kate's cup. "Kanpai," he said and held his drink aloft. "What is it we're drinking to?"

Grateful for a friend and the chance to regroup, Kate took a sip of the strong drink and filled Tom in on the improvement in Rhys's condition.

★ ★ ★

"So, he's not fully recovered by a long shot, but he's improving," Kate concluded.

"Do they know what happened?" Tom asked.

263

She shrugged. "You know as much as I do."

"I'm glad to hear he's doing better. I've been a little hard on him in the past, but I know he's got a job to do. I'll even admit he's pretty good at it. And...I'll drink to that, too." He winked and signaled for another round.

"Hey, this is strong stuff. I think we'd better order some food, don't you?" Kate pointed to the menu. "I missed lunch."

"No lunch? What were you doing over your extended lunchtime, missy? I know you weren't around when the lotto ball costumes were handed out."

Kate smiled and sidestepped. "Are those dumb costumes an example of Stec's marketing acumen?"

"The whole thing's ridiculous," Tom said. "What a way to disrespect your employees. But what are you going to do?"

Kate shot him a disparaging look.

"He's Gregor's stepson. Have you met the mother? She wants her kid to have a job. Poor Gregor has to keep the peace." Tom grimaced. "Believe me, he has to...Didn't you think Jim was cute as lucky number five?"

"I think we sometimes forget how old Jim is."

"Ahh, he'll be all right." Tom pushed aside the folder in front of him to make room for the second round of sake.

"Could I get my usual, Kyoko, love?" He pointed a finger at Kate, then himself. "But make it times two, tonight." She bowed and left the table. "You'll love this stuff. They've got some special rolls they make only for me."

Kate refilled their sake cups. "I leave it to you Thomas-san."

"Maybe I should order extra if you missed lunch?"

"I'm sure we'll have more than enough. Some of Pamela's demands at this morning's SAY meeting left

Charm in need of some retail therapy. I'm afraid we were so busy scouting for organic hair colouring that we lost all track of time."

Tom patted his balding pate. "Something I can *totally* relate to."

"So you figure we're stuck with slimy Jack Stec?"

"Don't you remember the lessons I read to you at lunch not long ago: 'How to Succeed as a Bureaucrat'? These people are masters at the system. You bet we're stuck with him. Unless he gets thrown in jail, of course. But that's what I wanted to talk to you about."

"Throwing Jack in jail?"

"That would be handy." He snorted. "However, what I want to discuss is *us* working the system to get *you* a new job. Your contract's almost up and I think we can both agree that a renewal doesn't seem likely."

"You think not?" she asked with a sarcastic grin.

"If you have any brains, and I know you do, you don't want to stay anyway. So…" He pushed the folder across the table to Kate. "I've been casting about and I think I've found something for both you and Charm. Yes, it's at Transit, but it's a whole new division and you'd be running your own show."

Kate flipped open the folder and scanned the job description.

"It's a perfect fit for you and I've set them straight as to who said what in the panty affair."

"So they don't think I'm Ms. Politically Correct trying to grandstand?"

"Nope."

"Charm too?"

"Yup. I don't think Charm wants to continue to be Pamela's gopher while she justifies her position with these

'Employee Empowering Seminars.' The future of every employee is threatened at Pacific. Jackieboy's mommy isn't going to be satisfied with him working in the lowly communications department," he said, eagerly tucking into his spinach and sesame salad. "That's why Pamela was so thrilled when she thought Gregor sent her those panties. She has to have a friend in Gregor, or Jack's going to have her job, and she's going to be out on her self-actualized toosh." He slowly enunciating the last word and chuckled. "She's got a real good thing going there. I mean do you know what she's getting paid?"

Kate didn't and waited with chopsticks at half-mast for him to spill the beans. Kyoko, however, interrupted with a sushi creation that was named after Tom and caused him to lose the thread of the conversation. Grabbing a ricey round and decorating it generously with wasabi, he plunged in for a toast to the senses, pausing only to mop away the sweat that trickled down his broad forehead into his eyes.

"Deciding to move on might be a little tougher when you hear about some of the other pricey seminars Pamela has planned for employee development," he said.

Glad for a laugh and knowing Tom wouldn't disappoint, Kate nodded encouragement.

"The first is a personal trainer who prefers to be called a 'sports scientist.'" He flexed a chubby bicep. "As far as I can see, this guy's talent is his ability to flatter his clients while he counts their sit-ups and they swap wine recommendations."

Kate snorted and attempted to add a comment.

"Hold on. I haven't told you about the rest of these life coaches." He waved his rice-encrusted chopsticks in the air.

"Also on tap is a 'reservations professional' who, for a hefty fee, will phone the restaurant of your choice and reserve a table for you. Bloody amazing." He tried unsuccessfully to coax a few more drops from his sake flask and Kate obligingly poured him some of hers.

"Next, we're going to be privileged to hear from a couple of half-baked Olympians who didn't quite make it to the Olympics. But they have reasons for that—a lot of them. However, they're good looking ladies, now billed as life coaches, and they want to *advise and impart inspiration.*"

Kate tried to break in with a guess at the Olympians' identities, but was shushed.

"What I'd like to know is what these two chicks, at twenty years of age, know about life and the skills required to get through it? My favorite employee empowerers, though, are..." He eyed Kate shrewdly. "I shouldn't tease you. I wouldn't want you turning down the Transit position because you can't bear to miss this. Oh all right, I'll tell you. It's the 'Declutterers.' Not just one, but a whole herd of them. They are going to tell us what to throw out of our closets. For an extra charge, plus travel time, they will adjudicate your fridge for high fat foods. Now, decluttering is not my area of expertise, but don't you think sitting in judgment of a guy's fridge is treading on sports scientist turf?" Tom pushed away his empty plate. "However, if it leads to infighting and Pamela is involved, oh boy, I want a front row seat."

Kate started at the loud ring of her cell phone. Embarrassed, she glanced at the other diners. "I forgot to put it on vibrate," she said, diving into her purse.

"It's Phil," said the caller. "It's about Rhys—"

CHAPTER 42

Kate gave a couple of short honks and blinked the car's lights as she pulled into the curb to pick up Charm.

"Bit more spring in the old step this morning, I see," Charm said, clicking her seatbelt in place.

"Rhys started breathing on his own late last night and Dr. Young says his lungs weren't damaged by the blast." Kate eased the car into traffic and continued rapid-fire. "I've got so much to tell you. Remind me to fill you in on Tom and hair colour in case I forget."

Charm raised an eyebrow then listened eagerly as Kate told her what had happened at the hospital the previous night.

"I'm so glad he's getting better. I've missed our verbal jousting and his Machiavellian trickery," Charm said.

Kate laughed. "Why don't you come with me tonight and tell him that?"

"You want me to abuse a defenseless sick person?"

"Absolutely. We're all doing it. His cousin says if he's got an issue with what we're saying, he can wake up and tell us."

"Hmm, sounds intriguing. I'd like to meet these people I've heard so much about. Especially Moses. He sounds like my type of guy."

"We'll have to get you by the police guard. I'll get hold of Dr. Young and work something out." Kate stopped for a light and grinned at her friend. "Do you think you could wear a hat? The hair spikes might be perceived as a little neo-Nazi by the officer."

Charm stuck out her chin defiantly and patted her head. "New growth is always rather *vertical*." She flipped down the visor and inspected herself in the mirror. "I may have gotten a little heavy-handed with the styling last time. Sometimes my head gets so cold, it aches. Bald guys must have a hell of a time." She giggled. "So, what about Tom and hair colouring?"

Kate relayed to Charm the discussion she'd had with Tom at dinner, including the job opportunity for the two of them.

"I don't see how I can say no," Kate said. "Are you interested?"

"Definitely. Even if it is Transit. I've had enough of Pamela the Great, Gregor, and the whole lottery scene."

"I'll tell him it's a go, then." Kate signaled to turn into the lottery lot. "As for hair dye...I couldn't very well tell Tom we were late returning from lunch because I got hijacked by the cops, so I told him you were searching for an obscure hair dye."

"Perfectly plausible," Charm said. "No worries. If he asks me, that's what we were doing...It was a tough brand to find. Tough colour. A real irridescent one."

"Geez, don't elaborate. That always screws up a cred-ible white lie."

"Don't worry about me. I've got your back." Scrambling out the passenger door, Charm yelled, "Edgar check," and pantomimed an intense scrutiny of the parking lot.

Kate said a silent prayer and climbed out of the car.

The two women had arrived early and the building was unsettlingly quiet until they drew near Charm's office-in-a-boardroom from which came the staccato hum of an animated conversation. Drawing nearer, Kate spotted

Pamela and a number of senior management types seated inside. When they halted in front of the open door, Mardone stretched an arm back and slammed the door in their faces.

"Well a very good morning to all of you, too," Charm said. She moved her head from side to side as if she had been struck. "What's that you were saying earlier, Kate? Change jobs?" Kate wrapped her arm around her friend and walked her down the hall to the communications department. "You wanted to know if I was interested," Charm prattled on. "I get treated with such respect at the lottery corporation that it'll be a tough decision. I'll have to think long and hard."

Kate snorted with laughter as they turned the corner and ran smack into Tom who, for a change, was moving at a rather high rate of speed.

"Morning, ladies and sorry about that." He picked up his papers from the floor. "I usually figure I have free run of the place until eight thirty."

"Where is a morning sparrow like you off to at such a clip?" Charm asked.

"Pamela's called some emergency meeting." He winked at Charm. "Maybe one of the SAY presenters has actually made it to the Olympic team and won't be available to give her speech."

Charm groaned. "Oh please, not that. I'd have to find a replacement."

"I don't think you've got much to worry about." He gave her a knowing glance. "I've got to run, but on my desk, you'll find more information on that matter we discussed last night. I know Lucas threatened to withhold your bonus, Kate, so I've also included the contact info for a good lawyer that I know. Have a peek. I think it's a great opportunity for you both." They nodded their thanks and he dashed off.

A few minutes later they stood behind the disaster that was Tom's desk.

"There it is," Charm said.

Kate pulled her prying eyes from papers reporting Dragonfly Casino's impressive performance. Moving aside the pill bottles which she assumed were acting as paperweights, she grabbed the manila envelope with "Kate" scrawled across it.

"Geez, what is all this stuff?" Charm was scrutinizing the labels on the prescription vials. "He could open his own pharmacy."

Kate glanced nervously out the door and was convinced no one was watching. "What's in them?" she whispered.

"I can't understand what they say. But they're almost all empty."

★ ★ ★

"I'm not much of a friend," Kate said, perching on the edge of her desk. "I've been so wound up in my own affairs, I haven't asked Tom how he's feeling or how he's doing with the weight loss." She grimaced. "Although, if last night's dinner and drinks are any indication, his health isn't his first priority."

"I'm going to bring him in some healthy vegetarian meals. Jim and I are following this blog that's got some delicious recipes. Tom can take them home at night and just microwave them."

"We've got to keep him away from Jim's cookies," Kate said.

Charm was nodding when Kate's phone rang. "I'm going to go hide the cookies," she said and scurried out.

Ten minutes later, she was back. "Jim and I are going to do the diet, too. Give the stubborn old fart some company." She picked up the envelope containing the job info. "Let's go over this at lunch. In the meantime, you'd better put it away. Any one of these nosy people around here could be snooping through the stuff on your desk." She slipped the envelope into Kate's bag and turned to look at her friend. "Whoa. What's happened? Nothing's wrong with Rhys, is it?"

Kate shook her head. "That was Rhys's editor friend, Colin Jones. He wanted to know how he's doing and he wants to figure out who's behind the bombing."

Charm's mouth dropped open. In two long leaps of her short legs, she was at the cubicle doorway peering right and left. "All clear," she whispered. "What'd he say?"

"He didn't say anything. I stopped him."

"You did what?"

"I think it's better if we talk in person."

"Of course. That weasel, Edgar, is probably a first rate phone-tapper. Are you going to tell the cops?"

Kate looked thoughtful. "That's what I'm trying to decide. Colin's getting on in age and he sounded a little shaky. I'm going to meet him tomorrow night in Horseshoe Bay to hear what he has to say. He might be upset or imagining things."

Charm was in the process of inviting herself along when Jim burst in. "Hey you two, how come Tom's still pissed at me? I just tried to ask him a question and he shoved right past me...practically knocked me over."

Kate shrugged. "I can't keep up anymore." Her phone rang again and, with a glance heavenward, she reached to answer.

"Pamela wants to see me," she said replacing the receiver.

Jim and Charm pulled an identical grimace.

"Make yourselves at home," Kate said. "I'll be back in a minute."

Kate returned five minutes later, accompanied by a grim faced security guard carrying a filing box. She winked at Jim and Charm and, with her head held high, plucked a few personal possessions from her desk, placed them in the box, and was escorted from the building.

★ ★ ★

"Why don't you tell Rhys what happened at work today, Kate?" Brad settled himself gently on the end of his cousin's bed.

Kate looked from Charm to Brad. "Might be upsetting," she whispered.

"Lay it on him, my dear." Moses winked at Kate. "This one has a stubborn spirit. He needs a bit of fire lit under his keester."

Still doubtful, but at everyone's urging, Kate gave a brief rendition of her firing from the lottery corporation for: 1. unethical behavior and failure to adhere to Pacific's Code of Conduct, 2. failure to fit the corporate culture, 3. insubordination. She blushed as she itemized the charges and explained that now she wouldn't receive the end of contract bonus that was due her.

Murmurs of disbelief and sympathy came from those gathered in the room.

"Can they do that, dear?" asked Alice.

"They can withhold my bonus if I'm fired." Kate gave a wry grin. "Because of a joke poster we gave our boss, Tom, and because I didn't climb on the bandwagon and make an issue of the panties, they're saying I condone sexual harassment."

"That's bloody ridiculous," Phil said. "I know how hard you worked for that stupid outfit. And Rhys has mentioned this Tom to me before. Come on, *you* sexually harassing a guy like that?"

"And then for him to complain about it?" Moses's statement brought the conversation to an abrupt halt and everybody burst into laughter.

Kate looked in astonishment at the crumpled old chief who grinned sheepishly back and shrugged his bony shoulders.

"Tom didn't have anything to do with it," Charm said. "He was so upset at Kate being fired that he stormed out of the meeting and no one's heard from him since."

"It was past time to move on." Kate grinned. "And Tom gave me the name of a lawyer who specializes in situations like this. So I'm optimistic something can be done about my bonus." It felt good to be able to vent to these people who she had known for such a short time but realized she now considered her closest friends. Kate watched the bedcovers rise and fall as Rhys breathed strongly and evenly. His colour was better and the swelling had gone way down.

The squeak of rubber soles and an explicit "Ahem" announced the arrival of the ICU nurse. "I think it's time you folks gave the patient a little rest. I can appreciate your 'modus operandi,' but if he's going to get better, he'll have to rest between lectures." She winked at Moses, who winked back.

"Say, ladies," said the old chief as he used the bedrail to pull himself to his feet. "The girls and I have been asked to dinner at the longhouse on the reserve in North Vancouver. The Band is very kindly having a function in my honour and serving up the visiting chief's favorite meal. Would you like to come along?"

"That sounds awesome, Moses," Charm said. "What's on the menu?"

"Geez Charm," Kate cringed.

"No worries. That's a good question." Moses raised his wrinkled old paws and helped Charm slip on her jacket. "Liver and onions."

"No way," Charm said. "My absolute favorite."

"The stubborn one likes it, too," Moses said loud enough for Rhys to hear. "But you can't properly enjoy a fine dish like that from a hospital bed." He winked again at the nurse and whispered, "One for the road," as he shuffled past her.

CHAPTER 43

The girls were warmly welcomed at the longhouse and Moses and Charm declared the food exquisite. Kate's doubts that liver was Charm's favorite dish were dashed when she found her friend swapping a recipe for a Chinese variation of the dish with one of Moses's favorites. Kate, herself, couldn't get past the homemade blackberry pie served for dessert.

Over dinner, the group discussed plans for Wesley's funeral on Tuesday in Bella Bella, and Kate volunteered to be liaison with the Museum of Anthropology on the memorial service they were planning in the summer. It seemed to her that hope for Rhys's recovery was helping Wesley's family and friends cope with his loss. When dinner concluded, two young members of the Band presented Moses with a gift.

The old man tore at the bright packaging with a vengeance.

"It's a beaut," he said, eyeing a top of the line metal detector. "I've always wanted one." With the help of the kids, he lifted the unit from its box then flailed away with his arthritic limbs trying to sling the thick carrying strap over his shoulder. "Not much treasure up our way, but there should be lots on the beach down here. Let's go see what we can find."

"Can I give it a go, Moses?" Charm's eyes shone. "I'll carry it for you."

"Thank-you, my dear. Be careful though, eh. It's a very sensitive piece of equipment."

"She'll be careful." Tina winked at Charm and helped her dad thread his skinny arms through the sleeves of his jacket.

Brad drew Kate aside. "I hate to call you away from such an exciting event but is there any chance you could drive me over to my marina? I'm off to Bella Bella tomorrow but I have to move *Rock n' Roll* out to anchor in the bay tonight to make room at the dock for the wooden boats in the festival. And I have to show my assistant what to feed Elvis—and how to protect herself from that possessed animal."

Kate extracted Charm from the animated group of treasure hunters and told her she'd be back shortly.

"That cat is one ornery beggar," Brad said, holding the heavy cedar door open for Kate. "He knows something's wrong."

* * *

"Nice people," Kate said as she and Charm left the reserve later that night. She made a left turn off Capilano Road towards the Lions Gate Bridge and Vancouver.

"I know. They sure don't deserve all this crap that's happened to them," Charm said.

"You should see Brad's marina. It's huge. This festival is going to be a real hit."

Charm's voice came slowly and evenly from the darkness of the passenger seat, "Moses thinks Wesley and Rhys might have been trafficking drugs."

Kate's eyes flew from the road to her friend and she almost hit an on-coming car.

"Watch it," Charm yelled, steadying the steering wheel. "Geez, keep your eyes on the road or I'll have to find myself another chauffer."

"Sorry." Kate took a deep breath and fixed her eyes firmly ahead.

"Moses didn't want to do much detecting down at the beach. He wanted to talk." Charm reached forward and snapped the stereo off. "He told me Wesley's had troubles with alcohol and drugs before and was acting strange recently, staying out late with the seeder young guys in Bella Bella. Apparently, even though his motorboat had broken down and the weather was terrible the day he was murdered, he insisted on going out in his kayak. Moses thinks he was heading to a prearranged meeting and was ambushed."

"That's a bit of a stretch, isn't it?"

"I told him that. So he told me about an e-mail Wesley sent to Rhys and accidentally copied to Moses. In it, Wesley tells Rhys they'll need some money to get their operation off the ground, but that local transport won't be a problem as they have enough boats. Transport to Vancouver and Seattle, he says, could be a challenge initially and he asks Rhys to forward him contact information on the 'guys he knows.' Wesley wrote that, after he works the kinks out, things should run as smoothly as Rhys's group and the only problem will be finding a big enough laundromat in Bella Bella. Moses says there was a smiling emoticon after that."

"Rhys told me that Wesley was arrested for smoking pot years ago," Kate said. "He didn't sell it though." She turned right onto Denman Street and parked at the curb. "I can't believe any of this is true."

"Moses wasn't sure Rhys was involved, but he says he has serious doubts about Wesley's innocence. But if Rhys wasn't involved, why did somebody try to kill him?"

"There are a whole bunch of people who would like to kill Rhys for a whole bunch of reasons. It could be any one of them. He would also definitely stop a friend of his from dealing drugs."

Charm was uncharacteristically silent.

"I just made it sound like Wesley is guilty when I don't for a moment believe he is," Kate said.

"Moses doesn't know what to do. He said he can't tell Alice or Tina or anyone else until he knows for sure...I guess he had to confide in someone."

"You're a good listener."

"I guess I'm far enough away from the situation, but with you guys as friends, I've got a stake in it." Charm went silent again for a long moment. "I'm sorry, Kate."

"There's no reason to be sorry. Once Rhys wakes up, we'll get the story straight."

"Moses says Phil is the eyes and ears of the coast, so he's going to get him to see what he can find out."

"Good idea. I've seen Phil in action. He'll figure out what's going on."

They sat silently for a moment in the dark car, then Kate turned the engine over and they headed home.

* * *

Kate slept a fitful sleep and woke the next morning with a blinding headache. Late last night she realized she had forgotten to turn her phone back on after leaving the hospital's "no cell zone." She had pushed the power button and watched the screen fill with the calls and texts she had missed. Almost all from Matt. All demeaning and demanding. Incensed, Kate texted back that she would forward his tux after she received six months of postdated cheques for his half of the mortgage payment. Recalling this the next morning, she smiled. She knew she wouldn't have to scour Goodwill for his formal wear because she knew she wouldn't see the cheques. Mysteriously, her headache abated.

She measured coffee into the machine, pressed brew, and climbed into the shower. Emerging from the invigorating suds and ready to face the future, Kate poured herself a strong cup, grabbed pen and paper and a seat at the kitchen table. Ten minutes later, she examined her to-do list, now ordered and fleshed out with relevant notes, and was satisfied she had a reasonable plan of attack. Throwing on a pair of jeans and a sweater, she headed to the bank with two goals in mind: opening a line of credit to pay lawyer's fees and convincing her account manager to be a little flexible with the next couple of months' mortgage payments.

CHAPTER 44

Two hours later, Kate left the bank and mentally checked the first two items off her to-do list. Unbeknownst to her, there was provision in her mortgage agreement that allowed her to delay one or two months' payments and the account manager was also more than willing to open a line of credit...with Kate's new car as collateral.

Next door to the bank, the shiny new phones in a wireless store beckoned and Kate decided there was no harm in a quick peek. The phones were capable of a lot more than the old one she was using and the aggressive salesman told her they were a much better deal. She was only able to extricate herself from his clutches by promising to return in a couple of weeks when he assured her even more deals could be had.

She walked four blocks down the street, partially to distance herself from the salesman and partially because she had a coupon for a free breakfast sandwich and coffee at the fast food outlet on the corner. She sat down at a table, took a bite of the bacon and egg creation, and pulled out her to-do list for an updating.

Kate had no idea what fighting the corporation was going to cost in legal fees. In any case, she now had access to $20,000 via the new line of credit, although the thought of using it made her cringe. Maybe this lawyer of Tom's worked cases on a contingency basis? She tossed aside the thought of calling Tom right then to inquire, instead jotting down a note to contact him in a couple of days. Having to deal with his impulsiveness at the moment would certainly interfere with the productive agenda she had set for herself.

She skipped over the next item on her agenda: Rhys/Wesley and Drugs? deciding that tackling item number four, Questions for Colin Jones, would better sustain her positive frame of mind. Rhys's old mentor had suggested meeting for dinner at a pub in Horseshoe Bay, which was close to his home. Eager to meet him and hear what he had to say, Kate agreed on seven o'clock.

She and Charm had decided against reporting Moses's suspicions to the cops.

"No way," Charm had retorted. "Those cops seem to think we're obliged to tell them everything and they never tell us anything...*You*, I mean. They never tell *you* anything. I guess a person could argue it's none of *my* business. Aren't the cops getting paid to find the facts?"

Kate was pondering if she should fill Colin in on the drug rumours when her cell rang. "Not in the mood today," she muttered to herself when the display indicated Caller Unknown. On the third ring, forgetting what it did to the cat, she let curiosity get the best of her.

"Is this Kate Logan?" asked an accented voice. "It's Alastair Fawkes. Don't hang up. I call in peace."

Kate groaned, but stayed on the line.

"Are you still there?"

"I'm still here. What do you want?"

"I called to see how you are." When this attempt at camaraderie was met with stony silence, he yelled, "Are you still there?" With Kate's reluctant assurance that she would hear him out, he went on to say he had called the lottery yesterday—admitting the reason for his call was to pressure her on the Keno fiasco—and was told she had been fired.

"You and I have had our differences, but you were the best communications liaison they ever had. I know all about the infighting at Pacific and although you were a little wet behind the ears at first, you very aptly managed the tug-of-war between all of them, and us." He chuckled a raspy smoker's laugh. "I bet it'll take ten years off your life."

Not going to be goaded into saying anything she'd read in tomorrow's paper, Kate murmured, "Uh-huh," and, thinking a few notes would be prudent, flipped her notepad open to a clean page.

"I know a few people on the inside who tell me that self-serving Pamela Luther was lying in wait to exact revenge on you for that daft Pantygate affair. Those bastards think the rules don't apply to them. They screwed me too, you know."

Fawkes broke off a few times during his rant to ask Kate about Rhys's condition and to express what sounded like genuine concern for her welfare. Then, when she thought he was finally running out of steam he said, "I guess those math profs have got some pretty good proof Kinetic Keno is rigged. Have you got any comment on that? That's Mardone's responsibility, isn't it?"

Kate pinched the bridge of her nose. "You almost had me believing you cared, Alastair."

"Kate...that was harsh of me. What can I say? 'Reporter's reflex.'"

"Have you ever considered the number of people, besides me, that you piss off? I don't really count because I don't have a gun or know how to build a bomb. But it seems to me you ought to watch your back. Could be someone's declared a 'journalist jihad' and you're next.

"Alastair?" Kate asked sweetly. "Are you still there?"

"Touché, my dear. Maybe I do deserve to have my knuckles wrapped. But I'm not going to change who I am or what I do and, despite what you think, I do care about Rhys, and I am on your side."

"In that case, you may quote *me* as telling *you* to 'get on your bike,' an adage you may recognize from your childhood." Fawkes's giggle filtered back over the phone lines and she clicked "End."

★ ★ ★

At seven o'clock that evening, Kate angled her car into one of the parking spots bordering the park in Horseshoe Bay. She had found The Very Nice Cat without any trouble, but figured everybody else must be lost. There wasn't a soul about and it was cold, wet, and strangely...yellow. She switched the car off, peered out from her toasty encampment, and realized it was the streetlights reflecting off huge piles of fallen maple leaves that were casting a golden Halloween glow all along Bay Street.

Inside The Nice Cat, a cozy fire burned and there was lots of action. The barkeep, who had evidently been watching for her, waved a greeting and pointed to a tweed clad gent at a table close to the fire. *Definitely got Fleet Street in his veins,* she thought, taking in the blazer, Mackintosh raincoat, and Wellington boots. Colin stood as Kate approached and they shook hands and introduced themselves.

"What a popular place," she said. "But there isn't a car parked outside. I wasn't sure it was open."

Colin inclined his head towards the front door. "Mostly locals." A group of four, laughing and joking while they held each other up, was heading home.

"Safer for everyone if locals walk," he said with a smile.

Kate snickered and reminded herself she wasn't a local and had to drive home. "I have never thanked you for writing that letter to the editor," she said.

Colin chortled. "My pleasure. They edited out some of my best stuff, but I was surprised they printed it at all."

After the waitress dropped off two sleeves of beer and took their orders for halibut and chips, Kate filled Colin in on Rhys's condition. "He hasn't made the progress the doctors were expecting since yesterday's improvement, but when I was at the hospital this afternoon, they impressed upon me that every case is different." She tried to put on a brave face.

Colin was grave. "Journalists often get pleas to hold something back because it might jeopardize political relations, a police investigation, someone's character, or ourselves. It's happened to me and I know it's happened to Rhys." He sat back in his chair to enable a big orange cat to leap onto his lap and curl himself into a comfortable position.

"Most often these requests are not in the best interest of the public," he continued. "It might be 'nice' if we didn't report some things but, in most cases, the public is far better served when we write honestly. It would be a slippery slope if we started censoring ourselves." Tough talk but the devastated expression on his face indicated self-doubt.

"He hasn't relapsed." Kate hoped she sounded upbeat. "That's important. And he does look much better." For a long moment, the only sound was the snapping and popping of a wet log in the fire. "That's a very nice cat you have there," she said after a while.

"Humphrey is a *very* nice cat. I'm told they even named a pub after him." Colin rubbed the cat's cheek and his purring could be heard over the sounds of the fire. "And he's fat and stubborn and may even have a couple of fleas." He looked at Kate and they both laughed.

"C'mon, my girl," he said. "Let's put on our thinking caps and nail these bastards." He flipped open a coil pad. "I've made a few notes."

Over the next couple of hours they pooled their resources and racked their brains to make sense of the situation. Kate was relieved when Colin pooh-poohed the idea of drugs as a motive.

"I know better than anybody that you can't judge a book by its cover," he said. "I couldn't count the number of church-going, soccer coaching, devoted family men I've written about who've committed murder. But I also know there is absolutely no way Rhys would traffic drugs." His agitation roused the cat and earned Colin a golden-eyed glare. "Sorry, Humph." He softly patted the big tom, who settled back down.

"Rhys figured he was onto something with this Vertex group," he said. "He originally ran into them in Montreal, or was it London, a few years back. I'll check into that and get back to you. I can't remember how it all got started." He flipped to a clean page in his pad and jotted down a reminder. "I know he was pretty suspicious when they showed up here."

"They've managed to get the contract to operate all the new casinos." Kate's mind flashed back to Rhys's black eye at the Museum of Anthropology. From what she'd learned about Hans Niedermeyer of Vertex, it seemed he would be capable of such a thing. She scratched down some notes of her own.

"Maybe that's what he was sticking his nose into." Colin tapped his pen on the table. "I know he went to visit a local slot machine manufacturer."

"I know the guy; real charmer," Kate said, recalling her conversation with the hot-tempered president of Jackpot Manufacturing.

"As I recall, the VLT guy told Rhys the contract hadn't been put out to tender as is required by law, but had just been given to Vertex," said Colin. The waitress brought him another drink and removed their plates. "Rhys said the local guy was paid to build a couple of prototypes, but he felt he'd been thrown a bone to keep quiet."

CHAPTER 45

"This fabric is perfect for my wings." Charm stretched a portion of the gauzy material taut between her hands and held it up to the sunlight streaming through the country café's window.

Kate sipped her Americano and nodded. "Very fairy-like."

"Scary-fairy," Charm corrected. "That's why it has to be black."

"How did you ever come up with the idea of being a scary fairy?"

"I stole it from Jim. That's what he was for Halloween last year." She took a dainty bite of her sandwich. "He doesn't mind, though. It was actually his idea that my costume emphasize more scary and a little less fairy, and I think he's absolutely right on. What do you think?"

Kate held her face in her hands for a moment then let one eye peek out. "You know, sometimes...no, pretty much all of the time...I can't believe you people."

Charm grinned and tucked the wing material back into her shopping bag. "What are you going to be for Halloween this year?"

"How about an unemployment statistic with a big mortgage?"

"We can't have talk like that on such a beautiful day. Things are on an upswing. Rhys is getting better and Tom's going to come through for us job wise." She signaled the waitress who detoured over to their table.

"Tell me," Charm asked, "do you always have such great weather for the Artisan Market?" When the waitress answered in the negative, Charm said, "I didn't think so. And that is reason enough to celebrate with a couple of glasses of that black currant wine you guys make?"

When their drinks were delivered, Charm raised hers in a toast. "You've had a few stresses lately, my friend, but things are going to get better. I can feel it in my bones. Here's to the future." They clinked glasses and sipped the concoction, which went down especially smoothly, prompting Charm to declare the alcoholic content of berry wine remarkably low and order another round.

"You mentioned your mortgage. Couldn't you work something out with the bank?"

"I was just stressing. The account manager was actually pretty understanding. She said they're having to make allowances for a lot of people lately. It's kind of a worry, though. Matt seems to be more interested in staking his place in society than paying his bills." She told Charm about his barrage of unpleasant calls.

"Change your phone number. Sell your place and move in with Hank and me till you find something else."

"That's the thing. The condo's in both our names and he won't consider selling. He wants to keep it for an investment."

Charm tapped her fingers angrily. "He wants to keep all his options open in case his new chums dump him and his societal 'coming out' doesn't 'work out.'"

"I know. I thought this lawyer Tom recommended might be able to help me with the situation." Charm extended her arm across the table in a high five and Kate slapped her one back. "On a lighter note, did I tell you I talked to Alastair Fawkes yesterday?" She returned Charm's grimace with a positive nod. "He wanted to let me know he's on my side."

"Still pissed at Pamela scooping the big pay, big pension VP job from him, eh?"

"Seems like it."

"You don't work for Pacific anymore. You don't have to put up with guys like Fawkes calling you on your private cell. Change your number. Get a new phone."

"Don't get your fairy knickers in a twist. He might be a good person to have on my side. You never know." Kate regarded the increasing intensity of her friend's tapping and fuming and put her glass down. "I've got an idea. Can you get the address for Jackpot Manufacturing on your phone? They're around here somewhere."

Charm's thumbs scampered deftly over the device. "Got it," she said, leaping up battle ready. "They're not far at all. Let's go." She grabbed her purse. "What are we going to do when we get there?"

"Probably not much. It's Sunday; they won't be working. Colin says Rhys paid them a visit and I'd like to take a look—see if it's a mom and pop operation or if it's actually capable of producing the number of units Pacific is after."

"That doesn't sound like a very exciting plan. I'm more of an action kind of gal."

"That you are." Kate retrieved the shopping bag Charm had forgotten. "And one day soon, you and I ought to sit down and go through an ADHD checklist." The two friends threaded their way between chairs and tables and out of the restaurant.

"Funny you should say that. An old boyfriend once suggested it to me."

Kate beeped the door locks open and put the shopping in the back.

"I understand a lot of very creative people have ADHD," Charm said.

"So I've heard."

★ ★ ★

"There it is." Charm pointed to a group of low industrial buildings surrounded by chain link fence and topped with razor wire. "Hey what are you doing?" she yelled as Kate motored past. "The gate's open. Drive in."

Kate pulled the car over on the narrow shoulder a couple of hundred meters down the road. "I wanted to size the place up. I didn't intend to go in."

"Well, that was it. That doesn't tell us much."

The two women peeked back at the compound. After a long moment, they twisted back around in their seats and their eyes met.

"I didn't see a No Trespassing sign," Charm said sitting taller.

"What about all that razor wire and the fact nobody else knows we're out here?"

Charm stuck out her chin and bit her lip as she digested this bit of information. "I didn't see any guard dogs."

It was Kate's turn to bite her lip. "I suppose we could always say we're lost and need directions." Charm nodded and Kate popped a U-turn. "But we stay in the car until we're sure it's OK." A metallic thud announced she had engaged the door locks.

The girls bounced down the rutted access road in the little sports car, Charm fighting the confining seatbelt to peer about and take everything in, Kate nervously checking left and right to make sure she had ample space if a quick U-turn was called for. The driveway ended at the largest of the metal buildings. They sat there for only a moment before a pot-bellied man in blue jeans and a lumberjack shirt emerged with a dog.

"It's a Lab," said Kate.

"A meth lab? I knew it," Charm whispered. "Let's get out of here."

"No, a Lab *dog*, action gal. They don't make a miserable one." Kate gave a cheery wave to the man who appeared a little dumbfounded, and climbed out of the car.

Charm, following a little reticently, watched Kate introduce herself to man and dog.

"We've spoken on the phone," Kate said.

"Have we?" He laughed and gave Charm's hand a hearty shake. "Sorry if I seem a little out of it. Jack told me you'd be coming by but I didn't expect you so soon."

Charm looked sideways at Kate thinking she detected a slight crack in her friend's newly found confidence, but Kate just nodded as if to say: Hey! It's a surprise to us, too.

"Come on in you two. Jack said Pacific would want some background on me and the company for your article. I'll put on a fresh pot of coffee and we'll dig into the box of doughnuts he brought."

An hour later, their heads swimming with information and more questions than when they'd arrived, the girls waved goodbye to Jerry, the president of Jackpot Manufacturing, and his dog Nicky, rattled out the driveway and through the gate.

"Holy crap on a cracker!" said Charm. "What's that all about?"

"According to the conversation we just had, Jackpot is manufacturing the VLTs for the downtown casino. The funny thing is Jerry thinks he's got the whole order, but he doesn't realize the scale of this thing. He's only making about one quarter of the VLTs that Pacific is installing. So the rest of them are coming from somewhere else, and I'll bet it's Vertex. Somebody at Pacific doesn't want Jerry tattling to the press about how it hands out big money contracts and is creating a smokescreen to keep him quiet. It would also be a good way to hide the real number being manufactured, wouldn't it? In any case, what business is it of Stec's? That's not—"

"Not his job," Charm finished. "And him promising Jackpot an additional contract to manufacture VLTs for corner stores. He can't do that, Kate."

"For at least three reasons. It's not his job. The contract has to be publicly tendered, and slots in corner stores are 100 percent illegal."

"He's starting up his own slot machine business and Pacific's paying to manufacture the equipment," Charm said with a gasp. "We have to tell Tom."

"Don't go all ADHD impulsive on me. We've got to think this through."

Charm slouched down in her seat and chewed her lower lip. "Maybe we should tell the cops."

"You're the one who didn't want to give them any information. 'What are they getting paid for?' I seem to recall you saying."

"I guess you're right. By the way, what's with going all commando back there?"

"Commando?"

"You know what I mean."

Kate blew out a sigh. "I don't know. When I saw Jerry come out of that building, all I could think of was the phone conversation we had, how rude he was to me, and I was so damn mad for all the times I was chewed out and taken advantage of at Pacific. I just saw red and thought I'd go on the offensive...And I figured the dog wasn't going to bite."

"He was a nice dog. Turned out old Jerry was pretty hospitable, too. Good doughnuts. Asked if we knew how Rhys was."

"It didn't hurt he thought we'd been sent to write a story profiling his business. And I think the amount of money Pacific is paying him is going a long way towards repairing the psycho flaws in his personality." Kate changed lanes to pass a slow moving van. "What was it he said about Rhys again?"

"He said he hopes they catch the guys that did it and that he shouldn't have given Rhys the bum's rush when he came out to the plant. He also said he asked a lot of questions, but he was nice enough about it."

"Right. Jerry said he thought it strange when Rhys asked if Pacific had ever made any funny requests like wanting invoices split up or billed to a subsidiary. I think we should tell Colin Jones about this."

"Good idea. We can trust him." Charm reached forward and redirected the heat vent. "You know, you may have something with this ADHD. All I was thinking about when we were talking to Jerry was that I had to call Tom right away and fill him in. Could be, 'shoot first and ask questions later' isn't always the best plan." Charm's thoughtful insights were interrupted by Kate's cell ringing through the car's hands free system.

Dutifully following her new "think first" maxim, Charm waited for Kate's OK before poking the answer button. After a short pause and a throat clearing, someone said, "Hello, Kate? Trevor Edgar here."

Charm inhaled sharply.

"Er, hi, Trevor," Kate said to the microphone on the dash.

"Just a courtesy call, babe, to say I'm terribly sorry how you've been treated by Pacific."

"Thank you." A silence followed which Kate was careful not to fill.

"I'm always eager to help out my lady friends any way I can and I think we should meet for a drink."

Sounds of a serious gagging problem came from Charm's side of the car.

"Bring along your resume," he continued, "I'll proof it for you and tell you what skills need improving."

The gagging was replaced by rustling sounds as Charm retrieved Kate's purse from the backseat and pawed wildly through it.

"This Wednesday works well for me," Edgar said. "I'll call you with the meeting time and place. Till then, try and not be too sad. I'm here to help."

Kate poked 'end' on the dashboard at the same time Charm located the phone in her friend's purse. Without a word, Charm opened the window and hurled the phone out. Through the rear-view mirror Kate watched her cell bounce off the highway and arc gracefully into the ditch.

Charm closed the window and smiled. "I can't help it. Impulsivity floats my boat."

CHAPTER 46

After their visit to Jackpot, Kate and Charm drove to the hospital where they received the upsetting news that Rhys's recovery seemed to have stalled.

"Right after Moses and the Aunts left this morning for Wesley's funeral, I sensed something was wrong," Phil said.

Kate had to agree Rhys seemed "greyer."

Despondent, they left the hospital, picked up some take-out from Charm's favorite Lithuanian pizza eatery at Broadway and Fir, and drove to Charm's to eat.

★ ★ ★

When the phone shrilled at her place the next morning, Kate started so suddenly from her fitful sleep that she fell off the couch.

"Morning, Kate. I'm calling to get your new address so I can send your final cheque," said Samantha of the lottery's HR department. "Your cell didn't go through so I gave this number a try." There was a pause. "I didn't wake you, did I?"

Kate shook her head to clear the cobwebs and explained her cell phone's sad demise. In answer to Samantha's inquiry, she gave a quick recap of Rhys's condition. "Don't tell anyone, OK? I'm probably being stupid, but I'm starting to see demons at every corner and I don't think everybody needs to know what's going on."

"That's not stupid at all. Don't you remember what I told you that night at The Flying Otter? You've got to watch your back. I know you communications people are in the business of disseminating information, but you have to learn to put a cork in it sometimes—for self-preservation." She groaned. "And, right after I say that, I remember that Charm and Jim were your colleagues. Good Lord, you never had a chance."

Kate punched the pillow behind her into a more comfortable position. "Don't you think we need more people who tell it like it is?"

"In a more moral world." There was a long silence. "But those people wouldn't last long at Pacific Lottery." More silence.

"Easier on a person, though."

"True. You don't have to remember to whom you told which lie."

Kate laughed. "When I started working at the lottery, I was pretty naïve about the political power game. I didn't know what I was getting myself into. I understand it a lot better now. But—it's too late." She snorted.

"You've come along very nicely and I'm proud of you. If I wasn't so damn close to retirement, I'd say what I think about a few things around here and be proud of myself, too…I had an idea you'd moved after the break-in?"

"Only to the couch. I'll never sleep in that bed again. Please send my cheque and any other funds and care packages you can find to the address you've got on file. It would be much appreciated."

"I'll have it in the mail today," Samantha replied. "Also, seeing as I'm being so bossy telling you to keep your mouth shut, allow me to open mine and fill you in on a few things going on around here."

Kate's eyebrows rose.

"Further to our conversation at The Otter, I thought you'd be interested to know your friend, Jack Stec, is on probation."

"What?"

"Please don't think I stuck my nose in his business, especially after Gregor telling me very succinctly that background and reference checks wouldn't be required. Before I even got the chance, lo and behold, I received a call from Jack's parole officer checking on his employment status. Holding down a job, I'm told, shows you're a stable, participating member of society."

"I'll be damned," Kate said. "Tom told me he smoked a lot of pot. What did he do? Was it something to do with drugs?"

"Unfortunately, I had no success weaseling the nature of his indiscretion out of the parole officer—close mouthed old so-and-so. The little jail-bird is taking over around here, though. You weren't even out the door before he was moving office partitions, usurping your space for his own secretary. And my dear—the secretary. I thought Mardone's was a dizzy dandy. You should see this one. I think she's still spinning from her last job dancing around a pole."

After Samantha hung up, Kate showered, dressed, and headed down to the corner café for a latte and, because old habits die hard, the morning paper. She had just spread the news out on her table and was savoring the first sip when an article at the bottom of the front page leapt out at her. Alongside the beaming visage of Gregor raising his glass to the future of gaming ran the headline: "Thousands of Lottery Players Robbed of Winnings." The article went on to explain how a glitch in Kinetic Keno is estimated to have cost thousands of lottery players, hundreds of thousands of dollars in winnings. There were several barbed quotes from the retired mathematicians who had joined forces with the citizens' group PAGE, People Against Gambling Expansion.

"If the government won't admit to the facts and shut the lottery down, at least let's have some transparency and accountability," said one of the professors.

"Certain issues have come to light," the article quoted Mardone. "To say they came as a tremendous shock for Pacific's senior management would be the understatement of the century. However, in the proactive style so typical of your lottery corporation, our lawyers have already taken steps to rectify the situation. We are urging people to come forward and we will ensure they get their rightful winnings.

"As far as accountability goes," Mardone continued, "on Friday, Pacific Lottery dismissed Manager of Communications, Kate Logan, whose flagrant disregard for her colleagues and participation in incidents of sexual harassment is no secret to *Star* readers, and whose role in tampering with Kinetic Keno is currently under investigation."

CHAPTER 47

After reading the defamatory article, Kate tramped the avenues of huge homes that bordered the commercial section of Granville Street, concentrating solely on putting one foot in front of the other. Only when she stopped to pat a big black and tan dog that followed her to the park did she feel her blood pressure slow.

"David," she said, spying the dog's name on his tag, "what am I going to do?" Her eyes welling up with tears, Kate sat down heavily on a wooden bench and David parked his head on her knees. She explained the situation to the friendly dog, who didn't say much in response, but stared back reassuringly with his brown eyes. They sat this way for an hour, patting, explaining, and not responding until Kate had come to some conclusions.

"I've got to move on, Dave. I can't stop them telling lies about me, but I can stop letting it get to me. And I need a job. I don't need a $400,000 condo." At this, David raised his head and gave a woof, which Kate immediately recognized as affirmation.

"Matt can buy me out. Otherwise, if I refuse to pay my half, I think he has to make the entire mortgage payment. I'm not sure that's right, Dave," Kate whispered. "But I seem to recall it is and I'm going to check into it. And...to hell with him, too. It's time I told him it's over. What a ridiculous situation. He's always been a selfish pain in the ass." Another woof and she knew she was on the right track.

Back home, Kate fired up the little laptop Charm's boyfriend, Hank, had kindly loaned her. She soon had the information she wanted, and a call to UBC's free student law services confirmed it. If one borrower couldn't come up with their half of the mortgage, the other one was responsible for paying the entire amount. If Matt didn't want to pay the whole wad, he would have to come around to Kate's way of thinking and sell. Armed with this new info and a reference page of legal fine print, she dialed Matt's cell and explained the situation.

"Funny you should bring that up," he said. "Just last night over a brandy, I was discussing my real estate holdings with Emily's father and he has volunteered to buy your half of the condo. He's such a great guy. This is just beer money to him." Matt laughed merrily, then his tone changed to a sterner one. "At market value, of course. Don't even think of trying to gouge him. This guy's smart. Did you know that if *you* died, with that insurance we bought, I'd get the whole thing for free."

Dumbfounded at the ease with which Matt had agreed, and by what could be perceived as a death threat, Kate nonetheless remembered her high school Business Ed. teacher's advice: When you've successfully made a sale, don't embellish the product, chat further, or blather on— SHUT UP.

"By the way," Matt twittered, obviously thrilled someone was paying his bills with their bar change, "what's the best number to get hold of you at? I gave up on the cell but now the landline doesn't work."

One glance at the solid red light on her answering machine and Kate knew the device was bouncing incoming calls because the voicemail queue was full.

"Call me on the home number. I'll fix the problem with the phone. And there's one more thing," Kate said.

"I think you'll agree that with us living on opposite sides of the country, there's no point in pretending we have a relationship."

There was a pause. "Huh?"

"I think we should take a bit of a breather, Matt. Break up."

"Well, like yeah. Didn't you get my text? That's why I'm buying you out of the condo."

Thanks to the tacit advice of her four footed friend, Dave, a grin spread across Kate's face. "You sent me a text to tell me you were breaking up with me?"

"Didn't you get it?"

"No. But I've sure got it now." She shook her head and her grin grew bigger. "I'll tell you what, I'm going over to the bank right now to arrange the details of this sale. You tell Mr. Big Shot to call me tonight at seven o'clock, Vancouver time, and I'll tell him my price." She hung up and felt like the weight of the world had been lifted from her shoulders.

★ ★ ★

"Make sure you get the price *you want,* and then wash your hands of the whole thing. Good riddance to the bunch of them," Charm said when she stopped by after work. She took the mug of tea Kate passed her. "What a day for you. First that bloody piece in the paper, and then Matt, the texting jackass. I wonder how he manages to punch the little letters with his big hooves?" Perplexed, Charm settled herself on the couch.

"I've got a new mentor who advises me things are on an upswing."

"Hmm," Charm said. "Do tell."

Kate was about to spill the beans about the strength she drew from patting an introspective dog when the phone rang. She snatched it up, listened for a while, then fell back on the couch clutching the phone to her ear. "That's fantastic, Phil. And Ritchie said things are really improving?" Kate gave Charm a thumbs-up. "I'll be right in. Oh damn it, I can't. I have to be here at seven o'clock." Her eyes strayed to the wall clock. "I'll come after that. To hell with visiting hours. See you when I get there."

"I think I got the gist of that conversation," Charm said, throwing her arms around Kate.

"He had some bleeding that had gone undetected. They did a procedure last night and he's been improving ever since."

When Charm spontaneously broke out in an ADHD rendition of a happy dance, Kate ducked for safety and headed to the fridge for something to toast with.

"Oops, I better not have anything to drink before I talk to Emily's father," Kate said.

"Yes, you had better be on your toes for someone so *important* and *moral* and *principled*, judging by the "if Kate were dead we'd get the whole shebang comment." Charm danced over to the fridge and pulled out a half bottle of Pinot Gris. "Me, I can be flat on my ass, and it won't matter at all." She dumped her tea down the sink and slopped in some white wine.

They clinked mugs and flopped on the couch.

"I forgot to tell you that Tom has been frantically trying to get hold of you," Charm said. She held up an open palm in a "just relax" gesture. "We're not going to let this worry us on such a beauteous day, but I'm afraid the boy is somewhat pissed because he had arranged for you to meet with the president of Transit earlier today and he couldn't get hold of you to tell you." She ripped the last few words off at warp speed, glanced sideways at Kate and cringed. "Probably because someone drowned your crappy, but still kind of functioning cell phone in a ditch."

Kate pointed at her answering machine. "If I'd cleared my messages, he could have gotten through to me here. Don't worry about it. I'll call him and straighten it out."

"On a lighter note, let me share some 'most exciting gossip' with you." Charm cupped her mug of wine in two hands, savoring the moment. "Detective Lee and his jolly sidekick paid a visit to Mardone today." She nodded in response to Kate's astonishment. "I guess that's more of an observation than juicy gossip."

"Interesting, though," Kate said.

"Keno perhaps? Oh, to be a fly on the wall." Charm grinned. "They were still there when I left. I hung around for a bit, but thought I was being a bit too obvious, so I scrammed."

They were considering the possibilities when Charm's cell phone vibrated across the table. She snatched it up and glanced at the screen. "Hank's downstairs in the car. Come and tell him about Rhys. He'll want to hear it from you."

★ ★ ★

"That's great news." Hank grinned from inside his hybrid two-seater.

"Find out if it's OK for Hank and me to visit tomorrow, would you?" Charm added, climbing in.

"I will." Kate shut the door with a flourish, automatically checking the street for oncoming traffic before the little car pulled out. "By the way..." She bent down to Charm's window. "Did you happen to notice that old Volvo on the other side of the street?"

All three turned their attention to a sedan where the driver, unsuccessfully trying to shield his face with a newspaper, was sinking lower and lower in the seat.

"Why that little—" Charm threw open the car door and marched across the street. "You slimy worm." She snatched the tabloid he was clutching and glanced at it. "Catching up on three-month old news are you?" She hurled it back at him. "That does it. I've wanted to call the cops on you before, but Kate wouldn't let me. Not this time."

Trevor Edgar struggled to sit up. "No need, no need, Charming. Just concerned about Kate. Yup. Stopping by to confirm our date for a cocktail."

He looked so outgunned and pitiful with his left arm raised in case Charm got physical that Kate found herself feeling sorry for him.

"I couldn't get you on your cell, so I thought I'd spin by," Edgar yelled, peeking above and below his arm. "To confirm our date."

"Look, Trevor," Kate said, prying Charm away, "I don't think I can make it. Some things have come up." Slipping away from Kate's grasp, Charm pranced aggressively toward the car. Edgar quickly turned the engine over and screeched off down the block.

* * *

"I can't apologize enough for screwing up after all the trouble you went to," Kate said the next evening over dinner with Tom. She explained how phone troubles, times two, had put her out of the loop. "I hope I haven't blown our chances with Transit?" She chewed her lip while regarding Tom's unsympathetic face.

"I'll admit I was pretty pissed off. I have to be able to get hold of you. I felt like a dumb ass, telling Michael from Transit how talented and ambitious you are and then not being able to contact you." He sipped his sake. "However, he's a pretty decent guy and seems to understand." Tom smiled for the first time that night. "Provided that is—" He stared at her with an exaggerated intensity, "You tell me you're free to meet him at noon on Friday."

"Yes, yes. I'll be there."

"Awesome. Let's drink to that then." They clinked sake cups. Tom gulped his and Kate sipped hers. "Sorry if I was a little snippy, but I don't know Michael all that well and I just want things to work out for you." He smiled more broadly and seemed to relax. "By the way, so that doesn't happen again, I got you a present." He placed a small cell phone on the table in front of her.

"It's just a cheapo one," he said when he saw Kate's hesitation. "They work well enough and, if you lose it, you just get another one."

"I insist on paying for it."

"Not going to happen. I want to be able to contact you if an opportunity comes up. I feel bad about the way you were treated at Pacific, Kate, and that dirt in yesterday's paper was the final straw." He caught her eye. "Everybody knows you didn't mess with Kinetic Keno."

"That's just it. Everybody *doesn't* know. You and I and Mardone know I had nothing to do with it, but a whole hell of a lot of people who read the newspaper believe everything in it is true." She shook her head then stopped abruptly. "I'm forgetting that I'm not letting bad press get to me anymore."

"No?"

"Nope. I have a new mentor and 'life coach'—very worldly and knowledgeable—who advises me that ruminating over this crap is bad for my health and won't get me anywhere."

"Sage advice." Tom unfolded his napkin and smoothed it in his lap.

"'Get rid of anybody and all things negative and move on' is as close to a direct translation as I can manage." She sipped her drink. "Sometimes David doesn't communicate his point all that well. But I got the gist of it."

"David, eh?" Tom asked. "ESL?"

Kate nodded.

The server came to take their order and got into an involved conversation with Tom, who wanted something not on the menu. When they finally came to a decision, he insisted on a couple more sake also.

"You're not the only one that's interested in my well-being." Kate filled him in on her strange run-in with Trevor Edgar. "He's creepy, but I'm sure he's harmless, so I talked Charm out of calling the cops. Besides, she pretty much scared the bejesus out of him. He'd be insane if he turned up again."

"Really got riled up, did she? I'd like to see that... from a distance." They both laughed. "Don't report him. Just ignore him. Trevor's been unsuccessful solving the horrifying Pantygate debacle and he's trying to prove he's got some worth so that Pamela will keep paying him. He's probably hoping little tidbits of info about you will keep him on the payroll. I'll talk to him tomorrow and tell him to lay off." He paused for a beat. "You're spreading yourself a little thin with admirers, aren't you, Katie my girl?

First Wilson, then Edgar, and now the mysterious David."
He winked.

"Speaking of Wilson, he showed some real progress yesterday. And he's doing even better today."

"That's terrific. The way things go in hospitals these days, they'll probably kick him out the door and send him home tonight." Tom grinned and topped off Kate's sake cup. "Seriously, though, you've got to tell him to ease up a little on the reporting. I'm so glad he got lucky this time, but what about next time? We don't want to see this happen again."

She nodded half-heartedly. "Part of me hopes he's learned his lesson and realizes one obstinate muckraker, armed with laptop and newspaper column, can't take everybody on. At the same time, though, don't you think we need more transparency? Don't journalists represent the public's right to know what their officials are doing? With today's technology, you can run, but you shouldn't be able to hide."

"Maybe my most favorite corporate maxim, 'Keep your head down, helmet on, and mouth shut,' needs an updating for the twenty first century." Tom roared with laughter and signaled for more sake.

CHAPTER 48

The next day, Phil, Brad, and Kate perched expectantly on their chairs waiting for Rhys to wake up and join the party. Late the night before he had opened his eyes and squeaked out a few words. The nurses had removed the facial bandages and tidied him up and Kate thought he looked a thousand times better.

"I feel like a baby bird waiting for mother to fly in with a worm," Phil said.

Kate chuckled and got up to stretch her legs. She picked up the card beside a beautiful flower arrangement on the dresser and inhaled sharply. "With every wish for your speedy recovery. Lucas Mardone," she read from the card she held loosely between thumb and forefinger.

"Your tax dollars at work," said a labored voice.

All three swung round to see Rhys grinning feebly at them. "...Tough to talk 'cause of the tube," he said, referring to the endotracheal tube which had been down his throat for days.

"We've brought Kate with us this morning so we don't have to put up with your whining and lying about," said Phil.

"For Pete's sake, Phil." Kate seized Rhys's hand. "Dr. Young tells us you're doing much better. How do you feel?"

"Better than I look, but that's not saying much." Rhys slowly slipped his hand from her grasp and thumbed the control mechanism, which raised the head of the bed. "... Think I needed the rest." He dropped the gadget on his chest and took Kate's hand again.

Kate reassured him that she was fine and that Francis Black, the tow truck driver, was doing much better and had been released from the hospital.

"…Heard that was the case…good."

With Rhys nodding off every now and then, over the next half hour they filled him in on what they knew of the investigation into his attack.

"It's all a blank…and Wesley…did they catch who did it?" Rhys's eyes moved to Brad. "Did I miss the funeral?"

Brad explained a small funeral had taken place the day before, but a memorial next summer would be the real celebration of his life. Rhys nodded again and closed his eyes.

A long silence was broken when the nurse walked in with a lunch tray and orders to eat up because physio begins today. Rhys cringed and the visitors snickered.

Kate was pleased to see he managed to get down almost all the liquefied hospital food, including the mysterious stuff none of them could identify. She had kissed him goodbye, promising to bring a strawberry milkshake that evening, when the door swung open.

"Anybody home?" rang out in plummy accented English. "Isn't there supposed to be a guard on this damn door?" Colin Jones strode in confidently, despite the yellow chrysanthemum decorated with Halloween cobwebs and little witches he held in one hand. When he spotted Rhys grinning at him, he made a show of stopping and staring. "You're just too bloody stubborn to die."

"Thank-you for your kind words, Colin," said Rhys.

Kate giggled and placed the plant on the dresser, shoving Mardone's to the back. "Brad, Phil, this is Colin Jones. Colin, this is Rhys's cousin, Brad, and his friend Phil."

Everybody shook hands and Colin placed his leather gear bag on the foot of the bed and his hands on his hips. "Seriously, you dumb sod, how are you?" he asked.

Kate listened with half an ear as the four of them rehashed the matter one more time, tuning back in when she heard Colin say he had some interesting new information.

"I haven't heard back regarding that incident you were involved in in London. But that nob would have gotten to you before now if that was his intention. However, the chief thug you tangled with in Montreal was let out of jail a year ago. Since then, because of the city's crackdown on organized crime, he and his gangbangers have all moved out here." Colin popped a pair of reading glasses on the end of his nose and scanned a sheaf of notes he extracted from his bag. "According to Sergeant La Rose of the Montreal Police, the chief gangbanger now resides only 30 kilometers outside of Vancouver.

"I was originally told he had an alibi, but I've just learned that the girlfriend who alibied him has recanted. La Rose says our cops are picking up the investigation." He snorted. "That's a comforting thought." Slapping the papers down in his lap, he turned to Kate. "I had to charm and cajole people clear across the country to get information I should have been able to get from our own cops."

"That could be our guy," Phil said thoughtfully. "All the more reason to make sure this room is secure." He walked to the door and peered in both directions for the guard, apparently not finding him, for he set off down the hall, the door whooshing shut behind him.

Kate, Brad, and Colin stayed a few minutes more, finally chased from the room by a trim physiotherapist who arrived armed with a smile and a determined glint in her eye.

"Time to get you up and moving," she said. "No more lying around. We need the bed."

★ ★ ★

Kate returned home after arranging to meet everyone that evening at the hospital. She was energetically pitching all clutter and anything that remotely reminded her of Matt when the phone rang and Emily's father ordered her moved out in two weeks' time. Thankful for the legal advice she had obtained, her recent soul-searching, and for Samantha who had advised her to "grow a couple," Kate informed him she might be able to accommodate his "request" but, as it was contrary to the terms of the legal agreement they had struck, she would require a cash incentive. After some condescending remarks that devolved into childish threats that Kate struggled not to laugh at, he grudgingly agreed to her demands.

She had returned to her job with renewed vigor when the phone again interrupted her therapeutic tossing.

"Charm tells me you're moving and I won't be able to reach you at this number anymore. So I was hoping to get new contact info in case I have official HR business to discuss. I hope you don't mind Charm filling me in on your affairs?" asked Samantha.

Kate laughed off her concerns and passed on the information.

"You're not upset about this thing with this girl, Emily, and her father, are you?"

"Are you kidding? Delightful family."

"Charm, June and I think it would be kind if you popped Emily a short e-mail thanking her for being so understanding about Matt's herpes," Samantha said.

"What herpes?" Kate asked, bewildered.

"C'mon. Use your imagination. It would be fun. On another note, I thought you might be interested to know that Jackieboy is on probation for smuggling cold medicine."

"They do that?"

"They use it to make crystal meth. He should have gone to jail but, with Gregor's pull, he got probation, provided he went to a rehab center. Of course he didn't need "rehabbing" at all. The plan was to make it look like they'd taken some action, while they got him out of sight, out of mind 'til things cooled down."

"I'll be damned."

"There's more, and it's worse."

Kate shoved the clutter from the couch and sat down.

"A few years ago, he and some of his fraternity brothers were hauled in on a rape charge at some posh college back east. It took me a while to dig this up because he was using the surname of his stepfather-du jour, Norman Scott. It turns out mother Sharon has been married at least three times and Jack uses whatever surname suits him." Samantha paused to let Kate catch up. "It was obvious to everyone that the immoral, spoiled assholes raped this girl. But the poor young woman committed suicide after the lawyers and social media attacked her, and the charges were dismissed for lack of evidence."

After Samantha's troubling call, Kate continued packing her Goodwill boxes, giving the decision 'to toss or not to toss' much less consideration than before. Later that night she discussed the events of the day with Charm and Hank over dinner. They had visited Rhys earlier, thrilled to see his progress and to see the police guard back at his post.

"That bugger, huh," said Hank. "Two days out of a coma, one leg in a cast, and he wants to go home."

"Is it possible to get around a boat on crutches?" Kate asked.

"He wants to go home and, come on, we *know* he'll manage." Charm daintily wiped dipping sauce from her lips. "And, like Rhys said, the water's calm at Brad's marina. It won't be so tippy."

"Tomorrow's a bit soon though. Maybe Saturday," Kate said. "Elvis will be mad at him."

"His cat," Charm told Hank. "Not a feline you want to desert."

"Brad tells me he and Elvis are getting along famously," Kate said.

"Hah! Phil told me that Brad's scared stiff of the cat and won't go on the boat to feed him without Phil riding shotgun." Charm giggled.

While they were visiting Rhys, Kate had mentioned the dirt Samantha unearthed on Jack Stec and his many aliases. On the drive home, she brought it up again. "All the awful things going on these days, don't you sometimes wonder if you blinked and were dropped on another planet?"

"A corrupt, creepy, narcissistic planet," Charm said, as Kate brought the car to a stop.

Hank climbed out and reached in to pry Charm from the back seat of the small car. "The two of you can't be out of Pacific Lottery soon enough, as far as I'm concerned," he said.

"Oh, that's right. Don't forget you have a lunch meeting Friday with Tom and the senior transit dude about our new jobs," said Charm.

CHAPTER 49

Kate sprang off the couch the next morning, secure in the fact she was headed in the right direction. The driver wasn't arriving until late morning to collect her clothing donation and she decided there was time to take in an aerobics class.

That's been part of my problem she told herself as she laced up her shoes. Not enough exercise. "At the very least, you always feel so good when you stop."

She arrived back home two hours later, stiff but happy, and was turning her key in the lock when the phone rang. Racing inside, she plunged headlong into the stack of donation boxes. She limped to the phone and glanced at the call display that read "unknown."

"That's the next thing to go," she muttered, grabbing the receiver.

The caller took a breath and slowly exhaled. "Hi," he said in a playful tone. "I thought you might like to get together for a drink."

Kate's thoughts immediately flew to Trevor Edgar, but the voice was wrong.

"I, myself, would never condone an inter-office romance, but now that you're no longer working for Pacific, what's holding us back? Not Rhys Wilson, that's for sure." There was a snicker.

"Who is this?" she asked.

"Like you don't know..."

Unnerved, Kate's finger hovered over the "end call" button. "I said, who is this?"

"It's Lucas…Lucas Mardone, Director, Pacific Lottery Corporation," he continued. "A-ha! Now she remembers."

Kate felt her stomach muscles tighten and she had to make a real effort not to hurl the breakfast she had just treated herself to.

"What do you say? We don't have to pretend to ignore each other anymore."

Kate's finger went into a dogged dive bomb, poking the end button over and over even after the connection had terminated.

★ ★ ★

After the charity's driver collected her boxes, Kate went for a walk to clear her head, hoping she would run into David. She was comfortable thinking Mardone's call was a practical joke and that he and his over-pierced secretary had called on the speakerphone in order to get a reaction out of her. The fact was, though, it was easy to tell when the speakerphone was on. It hadn't been. And Mardone had seemed "sincere"— manipulative and smarmy, but sincere. The thought made her shiver and she glanced thoroughly about to make sure she wasn't being followed before headed down the street.

★ ★ ★

After a half hour of brain-cleansing pavement pounding with no sign of David, she sat down on a park bench and called Brad.

"They're discharging him tomorrow," he reported. "And he wants to go home to *Rock n' Roll*. I'm not sure that's such a good idea."

Kate thought for a moment before she heard herself parroting Charm. "I guess he just wants to go home. He'll manage."

316

"You're probably right. The cops say they won't be responsible, but the marina security guards can keep an eye out."

"How about if I come over later this afternoon and tidy the boat up a little? I've been on a bit of a roll lately when it comes to cleaning and sorting. Tomorrow night we can all have a bite to eat on board."

"That sounds great. I'll try and get the stove fixed by then."

★ ★ ★

Brad met Kate at three o'clock at the Marina and rowed her out to *Rock n' Roll*, anchored a short distance away from the vessels docked at the wharf for the Wooden Boat Festival.

"Look out! It's the psycho attack animal." Brad yanked back the arm he had extended to Rhys's boat. Kate grabbed the swim platform before they floated off. "Watch out. He'll tackle your hand," he yelled.

With a snap of his bushy tail, Elvis sashayed across the platform to where Kate held fast to the boat, lowered his head and rubbed his cheek along her knuckles. She patted his head with her free hand and the cat purred loudly.

"Now I've seen everything," said Brad in disgust as he hauled in the oars.

Aside from a few sanitary duties associated with the psycho attack animal, Kate didn't have to do much cleaning. She mixed up a fishy dinner concoction for Elvis, freshened his litter box, gave the table and counters a once over, and made the bed, which was in a bit of disarray after her last visit. The cat seemed to appreciate the attention and, while Brad tried to fix the pilot light on the stove, Kate scored some brownie points with Elvis.

★ ★ ★

The next morning, she had just parked her car in the underground lot of the 18 Carrots Gourmet Food Store, intending to pick up some delicious, ridiculously costly items to complement the wine she had purchased for dinner when she felt the hairs on the back of her neck stand up and stay there. Panicked, she slammed down the door lock button and was frantically checking the rear view mirror when there was a loud rap on the driver's window.

CHAPTER 50

"Police. Step out of the car please." A flashlight clicked on, illuminating Detective Lee's face. Behind him, his partner Don Larsen, flipped her a finger wave.

Kate reacted slowly, not because she was following any TV police directives, but because she was mad. She exhaled a few deep breaths as her flight or fight response abated then, with a "move out of the way" flip of her hand in Lee's direction, climbed out of her car and into the back of theirs.

"We have a couple of matters we'd like to discuss with you." Lee settled himself beside Kate and closed the door.

"You could have phoned," she retorted. "You don't have to scare the living daylights out of me." Even in the dimly lit car park, Kate could make out Lee's eyes staring right through her.

"What do you know regarding Wilson's activities in Montreal a few years ago?

"I don't know anything about his *activities* other than he did a couple of articles on gangs which resulted in some of them going to jail." She tried to draw information from their well-crafted blank expressions, then gasped. "Did they plant the bomb?"

Kate saw Lee and his partner exchange glances and a message pass between them.

"My first priority here is not who planted the bomb in your boyfriend's car. And don't accuse me of holding a grudge. I know journalists have exposed criminality where the police have overlooked it and I know they often pay with their lives," said Lee. "My uncles were journalists in China. One disappeared; the other was murdered. But what we have here is a sociopath masquerading as a journalist. Wilson is not the martyr he makes himself out to be. He's got a past which includes assault, drugs, conspiracy and, as far as Montreal goes, the evidence points to him manufacturing methamphetamine."

Kate started at the second mention of meth in as many days. "So you think he got what was coming to him." Her hands wrapped more tightly around her bag in her lap. "I don't believe any of this."

"Suit yourself," said Lee. "He and his friend were dealing dope on the coast, which resulted in his friend being tried and convicted."

"Only Wesley was charged, and it was for smoking pot, not selling it."

"Come on, Kate. Wilson was guilty. He just got lucky. Then there was his assault of a respected ferry captain—"

"He was never charged in that and I bet you don't even know what happened—"

"You're right. The charges were dropped. Speculation was there were threats against the captain and his family which caused him to change his story."

"That's not what happened at all. Rhys told me—"

"A month ago a tourist was murdered up the coast, near a place called Namu," Lee said.

Kate hoped he didn't think her loud gulp suspicious.

"Wilson was quick to rush to the suspect's defense, shut him up, and hook him up with a slick Vancouver lawyer." Lee's voice was getting louder.

"They're old family friends."

"Sure they are. They also traffic drugs together."

"That's impossible."

"It's not impossible at all," Lee said.

"Hard to prove is what it is," interjected Don Larsen between snaps of his chewing gum.

"Dumb, he definitely is not," agreed Lee.

Kate's fingernails dug further into the leather of her purse as she recalled Moses's suspicions that Wesley and Rhys were trafficking dope.

"What do you know about this friend of his, Wesley Baker?"

"I met him a couple of times and I liked him." She cleared her throat. "You're wrong about Wesley. You've got to be wrong about all of this."

"Wilson murdered Wesley because he backed out on some business arrangement. We received an anonymous tip."

"If I wrote press releases based on information like that, I'd get fired."

"You were fired," Lee snarled.

"I'm not listening to any more of this crap." Kate fumbled to find a door handle in the cruiser.

"Hold on a minute. I'm not finished." Lee sounded slightly more considerate. "The fact is we thought you were involved in Wilson's 'accident.'"

"What?" she gasped.

"There are some 'less than model citizens' at Pacific Lottery who we felt might coerce you to get close to Wilson in order to get rid of him. He was planning something with someone there, but it seems there was dissension in the ranks.

"They parted ways with a big bang," Larsen piped in.

Kate ignored him. "What makes you think I'm innocent now?"

"CCTV footage on the Island shows no one tampered with Wilson's car Sunday night, and our forensics guys say the bomb could have been planted days before," Lee said.

"If you were trying to get rid of him and knew about the bomb, you'd have to be pretty stupid to be riding around in the car when it was armed and ready to blow," said Larsen.

Kate shivered at the thought. "You're really chasing your tails with all your plotting and accusations, aren't you? Maybe I'm on the other side, working with Rhys in this 'drug ring.'"

Lee cleared his throat. "In the process of trying to tie you to the case, let's just say we might have done a little eavesdropping."

"You bugged *Rock n' Roll*," Kate gasped. "That's how you knew I was there the night before the explosion." She thought back to everything that had taken place that night. "Nice," she said with disgust.

"You're either a *very* good actor or you don't have anything to do with this," Larsen chirped.

"Did you ever get the feeling Wilson knew any of the other lottery employees personally or did he pump you for inside information on Pacific's operations at any time?" Lee asked.

"You mean when we weren't on the bugged boat? No, he did not."

"I hope you're telling the truth, Kate. With Wilson being discharged from the hospital, we're eager to prevent a fire fight."

"Rhys once told me you were a decent guy and to call you if I was in trouble," said Kate. "I thought sociopaths like him were supposed to be more astute judges of character than that."

Lee cleared his throat but remained silent.

She took a deep breath and exhaled. "With the possibility of violence, I assume you'll be providing protection for him."

Larsen made a dismissive clicking noise. "He makes it pretty hard, on a boat like that."

"You had no trouble accessing it to plant a bunch of bugs."

"The marina has security," said Lee. "That should be sufficient."

"No risk to innocent civilians on city streets," Larsen interjected. "That's important."

CHAPTER 51

T roubled by her discussion with Lee and Larsen, Kate's meal plans for Rhys's homecoming fell to more of a subsistence level of sandwiches and cut vegetables. She set the catering platters down on *Rock n' Roll's* little table and smiled as Elvis threaded himself between her legs. Kate sat down and he jumped into her lap, purring like a motor. "I bet you know more than you're telling. You've probably overheard stuff that would make or break Lee's case." Hopefully *break* it, her inner voice said, but without as much conviction as she would have liked.

"I may be the worst judge of character ever put on this Earth, Elvis. But I'm going to get some answers out of the three of them tonight. So, let's go outside and light a welcoming lantern, shall we?" With the cat close on her heels, Kate walked out back to where she had tied the dingy, lit the hurricane lantern, and lowered the glass chimney. When her cell rang, she put the lantern down and raced inside to grab the phone, her feline shadow in close pursuit.

"Kate, I looked into the shifting alibi of that thug from Montreal," Colin reported. "It seems that since moving to our west coast lotus land, our suspect has become a devotee of hot yoga and is head instructor at one of those pricey retreats in the Gulf Islands."

Kate listened half-heartedly to Colin's tale as she debated whether or not to fill him in on what Lee and Larsen had told her.

"He got his girlfriend to say he was in town with her because he didn't want his former associates to know he's on an island keeping company with downward dog and the yogis. She recanted because she caught him with a female instructor in a less than yoga-like pose. But all that doesn't matter because the cops now know he was on the island at the time anyway, and he has been for months. So we're down one promising suspect. It's a good story, though, isn't it?"

Kate removed the metal dome from the sandwich platter and was careful to set it down clear of the flickering pilot light Brad had lit the day before. "Nobody else in the gang could have done it?" she asked.

"Apparently not. Rhys is being discharged today, isn't he?"

"Phil's bringing him home tonight. They've been delayed because Doctor Young got hung up in the operating room and he wants to see Rhys before he leaves."

"Give him my best would you Kate? I'll be by tomorrow."

After Colin hung up, Kate gave Elvis a scoop of the special cat food she'd brought him and uncorked a bottle of white wine. Pacing herself, because she had a lot of issues to clear up that night, she had taken only a couple of sips when a rough jolt at the stern shook Elvis from her lap and Kate from her thoughts.

★ ★ ★

"There are no coincidences in my business, but there's a whole hell of a lot of information that only falls into place if you're the linchpin," growled Paul Lee.

Sitting in a chair at the end of Rhys's hospital bed, Phil stared open mouthed at his friend and the detective.

"You spent a lot of time on the reserve in Montreal," Lee continued.

325

"I was doing some research."

"Come on. That's not what you were doing," said Larsen.

"You can read the articles. They ran in the paper for two weeks."

"We read them," Lee said. "Small time money laundering. Pretty insignificant when you know what was really going on."

"You seem to know far more about it than I do," Rhys said.

"They're manufacturing crystal meth on the reserve," Lee snapped.

Rhys gave Phil a level eyed stare that said "keep calm" and, with effort, lifted one bruised arm and rubbed the back of his neck.

"Funny how that didn't make it into your articles," said Larsen.

"In journalism, you've gotta stay on topic," Wilson said evenly.

Lee and Larsen exchanged glances; sweat ran down Phil's brow.

"All of the pressure to legalize pot these days. That would be a hell of a shame for you, wouldn't it?" Larsen shifted intimidatingly to the edge of his chair. "We've got a witness that says you were there to see how you could turn your grow op into a meth lab."

"Well he's been smoking something pretty strong," Rhys countered.

"And when the pros in Montreal pointed out your new meth products are going to result in even bigger profits, you had a new problem," Lee continued. "So you befriend Kate Logan, a rather naïve young woman, and then get next to Lucas Mardone who's got that good thing going rigging online games. It's all part of your plan to use the lottery corporation to launder the money, isn't it? What happened with Wesley Baker? He refuse to go along with your plans? Liked things the way they were, did he?" Lee gave Phil and Rhys a well-practiced "let's get real" gaze.

More accustomed to purser duties on the ferry than to warfare, Phil perspired quietly, eyes ping-ponging back and forth between combatants.

Wilson, his eyes narrowed, jaw set in anger, met the senior detective's accusing stare for a long moment then said, "Are you out of your mind?"

Larsen extracted a smart phone from his jacket pocket and glanced at his boss who nodded.

"This was phoned in to our tipster line," Lee said. "Play it, Larsen."

"We'll need some new channels. I'm getting behind. Gotta get it flowing. Get it legitimate. All this bloody cash is becoming a real pain in the gut."

"If that's the case, how are you gonna handle more? They want to know, positively, how much you can handle."

"Listen. Listen, Scott. Big money stuff is no problem. I've been doing this for years." There was a muffled sound like something being moved.

"They start hauling in real serious cash…I can do it. No problem."

"What about wire?"

"Wire'll cost them less."

"I think I should get one of my native contacts from back east out here."

"No need bringing in someone we're not sure of." Chuckling. *"Our home-grown native has taken care of everything."*

"Seriously? This other guy, he's good."

"We'll see. My guy's pulled everything together. The building's all finished now and the one remaining complication will be removed, if you know what I mean. Dumb bugger."

There was the sound of laughter.

"Should I tell them you have some plans for them?"

"Absolutely. I can process increments of five million easily."

"Camouflaged so they don't have to worry?"

"It'll all be legitimate proceeds from gambling and investments. I'm not going to camouflage anything. It'll all be goddamn legitimate."

"OK, OK. We figure to move a couple hundred million a year, cash and wire."

"No problem. I've got great investments. I've done well in wineries recently and my telecom deal just went from eighteen cents a share to $1.75. Big, open markets. I get in and get out and no one's the wiser. That's the secret. Tell them not to worry. It's totally legit. I can explain it all to them."

"What about our little lamb? My friends are concerned she's gotten too close to the man." There was a pause. *"They want all loose ends tied up."* Another pause.

"I may have made a bad judgment call there. I thought she would be useful. Not to worry. I'm keeping a close eye on things and, if they don't resolve, they'll just need a little nudge . . . All part of the package."

Lee and Larsen stared intently at Wilson who stared impassively back.

"Mardone doesn't seem to be one of your biggest fans. Although he was willing to trust his 'home grown native' to handle some things at this point in the game," Lee said. "What did you do to piss him off?"

"I think it's time to call the men in white coats or, at the very least, my lawyer," said Wilson, grabbing his cell phone.

"We've got evidence of Mardone's involvement and yours." Lee's voice grew louder. "What I want to know is, who's Scott?"

"Rhys," Phil said, "make the call."

Wilson punched in his speed dial code for the newspaper's lawyer and handed the phone to Phil to explain the situation. Exhausted, he lay back on the bed and rubbed his temples. "It sounds to me like somebody has been very good at planting evidence. So good in fact that, when I prove you wrong Lee, I'm not even going to gloat…much."

On the phone in the corner of the room, Phil was rapidly explaining the situation.

Wilson gazed up at the ceiling. "In the first place, that's not Lucas Mardone on your tape. I've heard him rant so many times I'd recognize his voice in an instant. Mardone is pronoun challenged. He says 'myself' instead of 'me,' or he'll say 'me and him' rather than 'he and I.' Sounds stupid, but it's a pet peeve of mine and he *always* does it." He cleared his throat. "Also, when he gets worked up, his Newfie accent surfaces. The guy on your tape gets flustered a couple of times, but he doesn't lapse into Newf, and his grammar is pretty good."

"And he's your partner, so that's what you'd say. That's just lame, Wilson." Larsen roared with laughter and looked to Lee for support.

"Play it again," Lee said tersely.

Grudgingly Larsen played the clip two more times.

Lee looked thoughtful. "If it's not Mardone, who is it?"

"Hell if I know," Rhys said.

Phil handed the phone back to his friend. "Your lawyer suggests you put a sock in it 'til he gets here."

Still reclined on the bed, Wilson made an OK symbol with his finger and thumb.

"Would you still say that wasn't Mardone on the tape if I told you he was the one who planted the bomb in your Jeep?" Lee stroked his chin with his left hand.

Startled, Rhys snapped his head round and stared at Lee. "Yep."

"Interesting. What would you say if I told you he was dead?" Lee asked.

"Based on what you just told me, I probably wouldn't be too upset." Wilson forced himself to a sitting position and eyed the detective critically. "We can play all the games you want, but I'm telling you, you've been had." He hopped on his good leg to the chair beside Phil. "What happened to Mardone?"

Still guarded, Lee said, "Last night...refused to stop for police...wrapped his car round a telephone pole."

Phil cringed.

"His daughter was in the car with him. She's in surgery right now."

"Why were you chasing him?" Rhys asked.

"We wanted to take a look at his laptop and phone." Wilson made a summoning motion with his hand and, reluctantly, Lee complied. "After the crash, we searched his condo and found his computer. You really should have picked a more trustworthy partner. I guess you realize that now." He indicated Rhys's injuries. "But I'm referring to the fact that he didn't even try to hide the plans for your meth operation. He's even got pro forma income statements on his hard drive."

Wilson nodded his head dismissively. "Get past it, Paul. It's a bunch of crap. What else did you find?"

Lee seemed to consider Wilson's comment. "A .22 handgun, small pipe bomb, three kilos of weed in an old computer case and a downloaded do-it-yourself course on how to build a bomb just like the one the lab figures blew up your truck."

"How coincidental," said Wilson.

"That's what I said." Larsen nodded confidently.

"I thought you said there were no coincidences." Wilson glared at the cops. "Can't you see how pat this is. Somebody's set this whole thing up, either because we're a threat to something big, or to get me." He gazed at Phil. "It just seems like an awful lot of trouble to go to in order to do me in."

"Play it again, Larsen," Lee said.

Larsen rolled the wheeled table into the centre of the group, put his phone on it, and played it a fourth time. They all leaned in, listening intently for any gem they had missed. When the discussion on the tape drew to a close, Wilson snapped his fingers and his eyes met Lee's.

"Jack Stec's last name used to be Scott," he said.

CHAPTER 52

"You missed lunch, Katie, my love, so I thought I'd stop by for a little dinner."

Kate scrambled from her chair, alarming Elvis who spat and ran downstairs.

Tom's face was red where it should be white, and white where it should be red. His tie hung loose and his shirt was partially unbuttoned. In his right hand he held a gun, which he had trained on Kate.

He stumbled in from the stern of the boat and, straining his huge girth, bent and peered down to the sleeping quarters. "Wilson not here?"

Kate managed to shake her head.

"Too bad, but nothing I can't deal with later." He collapsed into Rhys's plush chair. "Well...it's just the two of us. How cozy." Nodding with satisfaction, he gazed over at the table. "Ah, food. Good. I missed lunch." He stretched over and tugged the little window curtains closed. "There's something romantic about a boat isn't there?" He waved the gun toward the stern. "I've got a boat too. Mine's bigger and much newer. Too late now. Your loss."

"What's going on, Tom? What's with the gun?" For Kate, everything seemed to have gone quiet and slowed down. Rigid with fear, she could hardly talk.

"Sit, sit." He waved the gun from Kate to the chair and back again. Pulling out a handkerchief, he mopped his forehead, stuffed it back in his pocket, and sighed. "I'm sorry it's come to this Kate, but I want you to understand the scope of my problem. I'm a simple man with simple needs and everything is getting so goddamn complicated." He extracted the handkerchief for another quick wipe. "How about I have one of those sandwiches?" With a grunt, he reached over and grabbed one.

"Umm, not too bad. I was getting a little light-headed from hunger," he said, then sneezed with a roar, splattering bits of smoked salmon all over Kate's pant legs. "When I hired you, I wasn't just thinking, 'Here's someone who can do the job.' I was also thinking, 'Hey, here's a nice little piece of stuff. I think I see a future here.' I'm talking money, boats, exotic vacations, lots of pampering." Kate's mouth dropped open and Tom held up his hand. "Let me finish." He cleared his throat. "When you walked in my door, I thought it was karma! You're sweet, gorgeous, and so organized—a little bit naïve, but I figured I could fix that. You had the juice. You just needed some guidance."

Through the loose weave of the curtains, Kate saw the lights of an approaching boat and mentally willed it to stop. The boat chugged passed.

"You missed our lunch meeting again today. Michael, from Transit, is starting to think it's quite amusing, although I don't think he'll be signing any paycheques for you in the future."

"Is that what this is all about? I'm sorry, Tom. You wouldn't believe the day I've had." Kate flashed him the brightest smile she could muster. "How about we do lunch Monday?"

"Now how exactly is that going to work, my dear protégé?" He patted the gun with his free hand. "Charm was quite concerned when I told her you'd stood me up again today, and, true to form, once she started making excuses, she fell all over herself filling me in on everything you guys have been up to."

Kate groaned inwardly. "Did she tell you where I was?"

"Yup. But I already knew that." He licked cream cheese off his fingers and pointed a stubby finger at the cell phone he'd given her. "It's got built in GPS. You can run, but you can't hide…Got anything to drink?"

"Do you really think you need something to drink? Maybe part of the problem here is mixing booze and those pills of yours? Have you ever considered that?"

"Nope, but I have considered I need a drink. *You've* got a drink, but you won't offer your guest one. There's hospitality for you." His wild eyes scanned the boat. "I'd be much more relaxed if I had a drink."

"All right, I'll get you a drink." Kate found herself quite irrationally getting angry in the face of the waving gun. She stood up and, with surprising speed, Tom repositioned the gun on her. "I have to get you a glass, unless you'd rather chug it right from the bottle," she said.

"No need to be spiteful, Katie. Just don't try anything. I went out of my way to come over here and it'd spoil everything if I had to shoot you before I told you *why* I had to shoot you."

She snatched a glass from the cupboard and heard a murmur of irritation.

"Haven't got any red, have you?" She glared at him. "Hah. Wilson isn't much of a host, either, heh-heh." He grabbed the drink from her and with a flick of the gun barrel indicated her chair. "I now know from my informative conversation with Charm that you are not partner material." He pulled a sad face, sticking out his lower lip.

"Maybe you could cut to the chase and tell me what this is all about, because I haven't a clue."

"Let me open by saying I blame this all on Wilson." Tom lurched towards her, his dilated pupils making his eyes serious and scary. "Incidentally, he's not going to make it, is he? Those fireworks cost me a couple of garbage bags of some really excellent stuff."

"What fireworks? Do you mean the bomb? Are you saying *you* planted the car bomb?"

"Me? Nah...I got some kid to do it."

Stunned, Kate felt her anger skyrocket and her fear plummet. "What in the hell did you do that for?"

"It may be his job to snoop around, but he was getting too close, and I didn't like him snooping around *you*." He indicated his empty glass needed a fill up. "You were supposed to be *my* partner. I knew that because you always say good morning to me."

"I say good morning to everybody."

"You should watch that. People will get the wrong idea."

"You're out of your mind." Unable to believe her situation, Kate reached for her own glass and took her first drink since he'd arrived. "So, you're guilty of attempted murder. What else have you been up to? I think you owe me an explanation."

"Right on the first point and on the second. I'll say it again; you've got the juice." He waggled his empty glass back and forth and she slopped some wine in. "Really, Kate, conspiring against me with cops and newspaper reporters. Alienating my affections with Matt, Wilson, and now this David?" He clucked a disapproving sound.

"Not that it's any of your business, but David is a dog and what do you mean conspiring against you?"

"For some time now, I've been having you followed."

Kate's eyes widened.

"Yup, the services of your good friend Trevor Edgar fell handily into my lap when Pamela hired him to solve Pantygate." He snickered. "Desperate little bugger will do anything for a buck. His fee fell even further when I threatened to tell Pamela he'd been arrested for exposing himself to joggers on the trails at the university. He's a pretty fast runner, apparently. Some of them gave chase, but it was months before he was caught."

Kate took another needed drink. "Did you get him to break into my apartment?"

"Are you kidding? I would never let that maggot invade the privacy of your home. Did that myself—channeling talents from my misbegotten youth. I had lost my customer list and I figured I must have misfiled it in that Vertex file you lifted from the office. I couldn't have you passing that on to lover boy. Thought I'd have a friend of mine take a look at your computer while I was at it." He let out a wet belch. "The rat was a little warning." He shook his head. "Sometimes you don't catch on all that quickly, though, do you?"

Kate's thoughts flashed back to the helpful cops the day her condo was broken into and the same cops, significantly less helpful this morning, in the underground parking lot. She tried to remember what it was one of them had said. Tom continued talking.

"For some time now, I have had a nice little business going alongside my official lottery duties." With some effort, he freed his index and middle fingers from grasping the gun and the glass and traced quotation marks in the air to emphasize "official." "A small business with great personal service. Very nice, very neat." He gave her an exaggerated wink. "You don't have a clue, do you? I make a pantload of coin laundering money."

She nodded slowly. "It's got something to do with the winning number reports, doesn't it? That's why you were always on Jim's case about them."

Tom bobbed his head up and down dramatically, his mouth open a mile. "That's the juice I'm talking about." He downed a big swallow of wine. "When my clients tell me they've got some cash to get into the system, I check our list of winners and tell them who's just won and how much. They contact the people and offer them more for the ticket than they'd get if they claimed it. What are the ticket holders going to say? 'No, I don't want the four mil, I'd rather take the three million the lottery will pay me, thanks very much.'" He sneezed. "Everything shipshape and I take a percentage." Unable to grab his handkerchief with both hands full, he ran his runny nose up the right arm of his jacket and sniffed aggressively.

Kate glanced quickly at her watch. Judging from the ETA Phil had given her, he and Rhys wouldn't be arriving for some time. It was obvious Tom wasn't going to let her go, and she could see there was every possibility he was going to kill her. But she was damned if she was going to make it easy for him.

"Between you and me, I'm branching out," he continued. "Don't want to put all my eggs in one basket, so I'm helping my clients invest their money, too. I've also got my geeky friend working on reprogramming Kinetic Keno so it'll draw the numbers I want it to."

"I wouldn't count on that. Haven't you been keeping up with the papers?"

"Oh, that. My geeky friend got the code a little brass-backwards the first time we went online with Keno. But it's all good now, and don't you worry about those nosy grey-haired buzzards. Their time is passed. Can't compete with the new technology."

Kate shrugged. "People are listening to what they have to say."

Tom waved his gun. "If it blows up in our faces, my hacker friend is going to make sure Mardone gets the blame. That'd be sweet. Wouldn't it? Come on, smile; you'd like that."

There was a low growl as Elvis sashayed back on deck, his tail snapping back and forth. With a yell, Tom kicked his leg out. Elvis spat viciously and retreated behind Kate's legs.

"I hate cats," he said. "They have no soul, and I think I'm allergic to them."

Kate reached down and stroked Elvis gently. "So what was my role going to be in this?"

"Ho-ho. Now you're interested. Too late, Katie girl. This really isn't going to turn out well for you. But seeing as you asked..." He lifted his glass to his lips and regarded it quizzically as if wondering where all the wine could have gone.

With a set to her jaw, Kate leaned forward and filled it up again.

"I'm a much better storyteller when I have a full glass. Shut up, cat," he said when Elvis growled.

"In answer to your question, business is brisk and I just can't micromanage everything anymore...This problem with my gut, maybe surgery, could lay me low for a while and customer service is important to me. If the need arises, I need someone to be able to do pretty much everything I do. There have also been a few hiccoughs with my expansion plans." He held up the palm of his gun hand.

"It happens in every business. Nothing that can't be dealt with."

Figuring she had nothing to lose, Kate said, "What did you fuck up?"

The glassy eyes turned ruthless in an instant. "I'd remember who's got the gun, if I were you." He cleared his throat. "Now, where were we? Ah, yes. Out of kindness, I made the mistake of hiring Jack Stec to do a bit of grunt work. This situation you and I find ourselves in today is *his* fault. His and his greedy mother's." He nodded. "And a little fuel was added to the fire by those bleeding hearts who want to legalize weed. If that happens, it's going to put an end to a fine business."

Kate glanced at her watch. "It sounds like these valued customers of yours are drug dealers."

"Some big guys, some mom and pop operations. What can I say, I'm a popular guy. Legalizing pot is on the horizon, though, and I just wanted to do a few more deals and retire to that pampered lifestyle I hoped to share with you. Then everybody starts getting greedy."

Elvis emerged from between Kate's legs and strutted protectively between her and Tom. Tom trained the gun on him.

"No," she yelled, leaping from her seat to grab the cat.

Tom laughed. "Stec, who doesn't appreciate the importance of customer service, decides we ought to ditch our existing customers and get into the meth business." He arched his back and shifted in the chair. "I don't know about you, but pot people are my kind of folks. Laid back, thoughtful, into nature, that's pot people. I bet if the Doc had laid out a nice course of treatment of medical marijuana for me, I'd be on the mend by now. But this meth shit, I don't want any part of it." He flashed the palms of both hands as best he could. "Call me a control freak, Type A, what have you—guilty as charged. But this is my operation and I'm not relinquishing the reins to some little snot. So sue me." He sneezed violently three times and glared at Elvis.

Kate emptied the rest of the wine into Tom's glass.

"I made a mistake not knocking Stec off right away, but I was in a jam. Business was good. I had too much cash to handle and, in the beginning, he was useful. Unfortunately, his mother, Elsie-Sharon, found out and the three of them got a little too big for their britches and figured they'd take over."

"Who's the third?"

"What?"

"Stec and Sharon make two. Who's the third?"

"Oh, right." He gave his wineglass a look of accusation and wedged it between his legs. "Do you remember a while back when the cops found that ticket reseller in a closet?" Kate nodded slowly. "Good girl. He was my original partner. He and Stec went behind my back to bring Vertex in and try to turn *my* business into a meth operation. Of course I couldn't have that."

"Didn't the paper say that guy was dismembered?" she asked in horror.

"Katie, you of all people should know not to believe what you read in the paper. It wasn't dismemberment as much as an attempt to illustrate a theme." He scrunched up his face. "I had had 'Hear no Evil, See no Evil, Speak no Evil' buzzing around in my head for days. Well, I managed to chop off his lips and ears quite professionally, but I couldn't bring myself to tackle the eyes." He made another

340

face. "I'm sure you can imagine. I mean, a little harsh, eh?" He looked for confirmation to Kate, who had just remembered the cops telling her the boat was bugged. Hoping they were still listening, she decided to buy herself some time and nodded sympathetically in appreciation of his predicament.

"Anyhow, I realized it was his tendency to dip his hand into the cookie jar that irked me the most. So..." He slapped his thigh with great gusto. "Bob's yer uncle. I chopped off his mitt and stuck it right in the old canister. Only problem was the dumb cops didn't get the symbolism.

"I hadn't meant to kill him, but things got heated...I'm thinking of checking my medication with my doctor. I feel it might be making me a little less patient. Ach—you know." He shrugged his shoulders. "What can you do?"

Kate glanced down at her watch.

"Late for something, Katie girl? Somewhere you've got to be?" He let out a braying laugh. "Relax, you're not going to make it."

Kate fought the chill that ran down her spine and continued to play for time, willing the cop cavalry to come to her rescue. "What about Gregor? He must know?"

"That horse's ass. He has *no* idea. He actually believes the wife furnishes that tasteless display of consumption of a house of theirs with the proceeds from her knick-knack store."

"What's the deal with that store? I've been in it."

Suddenly seeming anxious, Tom glanced towards the back door, then pushed the curtains apart on the window behind him, and peered out. Apparently satisfied, he grunted and turned back to Kate. "It's amazing what you can get away with. I won't deny it was somewhat Stec's idea—mostly mine." He extended a hand and snapped his fingers. "I think I'd better have another sandwich. Pass 'em would you?

"The store is another way we legitimize clients' funds. That's the reason I brought Stec in. I wanted him to manage some nail salons. It would have worked nicely but he didn't think it was manly enough and tattled to mommy, who immediately wanted a piece of the action."

Kate took a sandwich for herself. "I don't get it."

"She legitimizes my clients' money by depositing it in the knick-knack store's bank account as if it were sales receipts. I get my cut. Sharon and Junior take theirs. If anyone gets suspicious, you've got to admit it's pretty hard to place a value on that weird shit she has in her store. It's worked brilliantly up 'til now." He shifted uncomfortably in his seat and his eyes bounced around the boat. "Stupid Sharon is such a show-off. That bloody house, the cars, the clothes, the jewellery. I warned her only amateurs show off and that she's going to get us all caught."

Elvis jumped from Kate's lap and began to walk in circles between them, making a haunting primordial sound.

"I know a smart girl like you will understand why one last body doesn't make any difference...Actually, you won't be the last. I'm going to dust Stec—personally. Outsourcing isn't proving to be all that efficient. And things wouldn't be complete if I didn't nail his greedy mother, too." He brayed again. "Gregor can thank me later." He sneezed four big wet ones in quick succession, almost shooting himself in the face when he tried to stem the river of snot with his sleeve.

"God damn that cat. It's going overboard." His eyes and gun still trained on Kate, Tom leaned heavily on one arm of the chair to lever himself up, spilling the wine glass wedged between his legs.

"No! I'll put him out back." Kate leapt up and grabbed Elvis, who struggled to get free. Seeing her opportunity, she made a big show of the trouble she was having to calm him. With one hand she grabbed the cat by the scruff of his neck, swore, and quickly pulled her other hand back as if she'd been scratched. She pretended to stumble and with her free hand pushed the metal dome of the sandwich tray directly over the pilot light on the stove, sealing the burner off.

Tom was using both hands to push himself to his feet and, for the first time, Kate saw the gun wasn't trained on her. The cat dangling from one hand, she bolted out the back door, picked up the flickering hurricane lantern, and hurled it as hard as she could at the stove.

CHAPTER 53

Detective Lee was rocking back and forth on the back legs of his hospital chair, contemplating the feasibility of Stec's involvement, when his cell phone rang. He snatched it up, listened for a moment, and turned open mouthed to Rhys.

"Your boat's on fire, Wilson. Yours, and a bigger one, have blown up."

Phil's face went ashen. "My God, Rhys. Kate's on the boat. She wanted to surprise you."

CHAPTER 54

Rhys shifted anxiously in the uncomfortable metal chair. The furnishings in this hospital room weren't quite as plush as they had been in his intensive care unit. It seemed a long time ago that the recovery room nurses had assured him it wouldn't be a long wait, and he was starting to worry something was wrong. He reached for the pair of crutches propped against the wall and did a couple of laps around the austere room to work out some kinks.

★ ★ ★

After Lee and Larsen had bolted to the boat fire the night before, Phil had piled Rhys into a wheelchair and raced him to the basement where Phil's car was parked. They had arrived at Brad's marina just as Kate was being loaded into an ambulance. Hobbled by his crutches and broken leg, Rhys couldn't get close enough, fast enough, to ask her condition, and had watched helplessly as the ambulance screamed off.

Phil, however, with two strong legs and a background as a 'can-do' ferry purser had leapt down the bank to the waterfront to see how he could help. While the marina's fireboat doused the last burning embers of the two torched boats, more police arrived, some stomping down to the beach where they conferred with Lee, Larsen, Brad, and members of the Fire Department, others erecting crime scene tape and training bright white lights on the black water.

Rhys watched Brad pass the bundle he was holding to Phil, then climb into a zodiac and head back out on the water.

Swinging his free arm for momentum, Phil hiked back up the bank and with a half-smile presented Rhys with a towel wrapped bundle of soaked, indignant, and howling Elvis.

★ ★ ★

Just when Rhys was contemplating a practise sprint down the hall, the door burst open and Dr. Young marched in, followed by a wheeled hospital bed and the orderly providing the muscle power. Young gave a thumbs-up to Rhys who breathed a sigh of relief and hobbled out of the way so they could swing the bed into position.

"It was just as we suspected," Young said to the patient in the bed. "And after we got you warmed up, we removed all the shrapnel." He patted Kate's shoulder. "The burns should heal with minimal scarring. I'll have one of the plastic surgeons stop by later today and take a look."

Rhys hopped over and eased himself onto the side of her bed. "Elvis is eager to see you but Dr. Young won't let me bring him in." He grinned at Young. "I thought after hosting a native healing ceremony, smuggling an old tom cat into a hospital would be a snap."

"If the damn animal would quit all that yowling, it would be child's play," Young said as he checked Kate's monitors. Then, with one final pat to her shoulder, he instructed the two of them to give him a break and stay out of trouble for a while, and left for his next case.

"Probably better if I see Elvis in a few days." Kate smiled weakly. "It'll take at least that long for him to forgive me for jumping overboard with him." She shuddered. "God it was cold in that water. I tried to yell, but nothing would come out. It was Elvis' howling that led them to us. I couldn't have held on to that log any longer."

"He's a hero of a cat. And I think he knows it." Rhys took her hand. "Are you really all right?"

She sniffed and turned away. "I killed a man, Rhys."

"And made the world a better place." He gently rubbed the back of her hand with his thumb. She closed her eyes, sighed deeply and told him what had happened on the boat.

"I should have been there," he said, grimly.

"Would have been worse. You'd have been too much of a threat and he'd have shot us both right away."

Rhys was quiet for a long moment seemingly absorbing what he'd heard. Then he leaned over and kissed her cheek. "Did you tell anybody else why the boat blew up, Kate?"

She shook her head slowly.

"I think we should keep it simple for the cops, leave out the part where you threw the lamp at the stove, and blame the blast on me."

Kate frowned.

"Lots of people can corroborate that stove was faulty. The gas didn't stop flowing if the pilot light went out." He smiled at her. "But then, I guess you figured that out."

"Brad lit it when he was trying to fix things earlier, and he forgot to put it out," Kate said.

"It's perfectly believable that it blew up. It happens all the time. Even Elvis padding around the counter could have done something to cause it to blow." He grimaced. "I never thought of that 'til now. God, that was stupid of me.

"What I'm trying to say is...I don't trust Lee. He seems to have a problem telling the bad guys from the good guys, and I don't want you accused of anything." He lowered his voice. "Maybe Tom tried to light a cigarette off the pilot light and that caused the stove to blow. What do you think? Plausible?"

She squeezed his hand hard just as the door swung open and Lee and Larsen walked in.

Rhys bristled. "Great. It's the Keystone Kops. Kate just got out of surgery. Why don't you come back tomorrow?"

Kate shook her head softly and gave Rhys what he hoped was a complicit wink before telling the two detectives a newly edited version of what had happened the night before.

"Berwick behind the whole sordid mess, eh?" Lee said. "That pretty much dovetails with what the search of his house turned up. Garbage bags full of 20s, lottery tickets, and three loaded handguns, as well as a home pharmacy of oxycodone, stimulants, and other prescription pills which Charming Wong informs us he chased down with alcohol. The police divers can't find anything to autopsy down at the marina but I'll lay you odds he was higher than a kite last night."

Lee glanced at Rhys. "We talked about a number of things yesterday."

"I remember it well."

The detective held up his hands defensively. "I apologize for thinking you and Wesley were involved. I hope you can understand that from our point of view you had a history, and you were always in the wrong place at the wrong time."

"Always?"

"A whole hell of a lot of the time," Lee growled. "In any case, since our discussion, our analyst has uncovered some irregularities with the incriminating evidence on Mardone's computer. It looks like it was planted. We also found an external hard drive hidden on top of his kitchen cabinets that contained a draft letter to the RCMP. In it Mardone details his suspicions the Keno game is being hacked and says he thinks someone in the lottery's IT department is responsible."

"Tom bragged about a hacker friend," Kate said. "But he never said who it was."

"We're following up," Larsen chimed in.

"If Mardone wasn't guilty, why'd he take off when you tried to question him?" Rhys asked.

Lee cleared his throat. "It has come to light that the passenger in his car was not his daughter."

"He doesn't have a daughter," Kate said. "What are you talking about?"

"He attempted to flee the scene and wound up smashing his vehicle into a pole at 140 kilometers an hour because he didn't want us finding a fifteen-year-old prostitute in the car with him," Lee said.

"What?" Kate pushed herself up on her elbows.

Lee updated her on Mardone's fate.

"Mardone dead, too? I don't know how this could get any worse," she said.

As if on cue, Rhys and Lee shrugged their shoulders and exchanged glances with Larsen.

After a short silence, Lee said, "Did Berwick mention the names of any of the drug dealers he was working with?"

Kate shook her head.

The detective clicked his tongue. "Based on information we received this morning, I'm pretty sure we're going to find his biggest clients were the guys running the grow op at the old cannery in Namu."

Confused, Rhys glared at Lee.

"I've known about it for a while, but it's not my juris-diction and every attempt I made for a joint operation to raid, it was blocked," Lee said. "We finally got the go ahead yesterday and the boys are still at it. They tell me it's the most high tech operation they've ever seen."

"Brand new building hidden in the hillside," Larsen said. "All guarded by dogs, laser beams, electrical fences, and booby traps."

"How did you know they were growing pot in there?" Rhys asked.

Lee tapped the heel of one of his heavy boots on the floor while seeming to wrestle with a decision.

"Just over a year ago we were alerted to some strange activity at a garden centre on the west side of the city. A woman phoned to say she didn't think the centre's clien-tele with their dual wheeled pickups fit her neighbourhood and she thought we should tell them to shop elsewhere. We sent a unit out to pacify the old girl, but after listening to a bit more of her story, decided to keep the shop on our radar." Lee raised his eyebrows at Kate. "Long story short, we wound up slipping a couple of small GPS units in some bags of fertilizer and tracked them to Namu.

"The problem was the authorities on the coast couldn't get any cooperation from the Ministry of Native Affairs," Lee continued. "They were told they'd need a lot more evidence before they could go tromping all over sacred native land." Lee looked at Kate. "I think they were waiting to see if the government legalizes pot."

Kate looked blankly back.

"It would dictate how hard to come down on them," Lee explained. "The press would make mincemeat of us if we spent millions on a bust, jail, court time, and lost resources for something that isn't a crime two months later."

"On the other hand," said Larsen. "If weed remains illegal, the government would love to take credit for a drug bust of this size, 'making streets safer,' 'saving families,' etc."

Rhys broke in. "Well the 'sacred native land' rationale is a bad one. Some distance inland, yes, but not at the cannery."

"In any case, they're saying they've never seen anything like it. Must have been lucrative as hell. And they found a bunch of winning lottery tickets in a locked file cabinet." Lee shared a nod with Kate.

"I knew there was something suspicious going on at Namu. If you'd told me this earlier, rather than playing silly bugger, I would have checked it out."

Larsen and Lee shrugged.

Rhys scowled at the two of them. "I've got contacts all over the place up there. Only this morning I got a call from a guy I went to school with who's now a cop in Bella Coola. Wesley told him he thought the local kids were up to something late at night in their boats and asked him to keep an eye out. Wesley took his role as the Chief's grandson very seriously and he would have felt it was his duty to go over to Namu and check things out and..."

"Get shot in the process," Kate finished.

"If we'd been warned ahead of time, Wesley wouldn't be dead and Kate wouldn't be lying in this bed right now," Rhys said.

Larsen attempted to share another scowl with Lee, but the senior detective seemed to be carefully examining the toes of his boots. After a long silence he said, "I'm very sorry for the pain and suffering you've been through and I'm pleased to see you're both on the mend."

"It's strange, isn't it," Larsen said. "Don't you think so, Paul? The whole boat goes up, two of them actually, and Kate here only catches a few pieces of shrapnel."

"Quite a few pieces, and second degree burns," Lee clarified.

"If the pilot light went out on the stove, the valve didn't stop the fuel from flowing like it was supposed to," Rhys said. "It sounds like Berwick snuffed out the pilot light when he lit his cigarette, the gas kept flowing, and the lit cigarette ignited the whole works."

Lee met Rhys's eyes and thoughtfully nodded agreement.

"It was lucky for me Tom insisted I put the cat outside. The second he took his eyes off me to light that cigarette, I jumped." She shivered. "I knew it was the only chance I had." Recalling what Young had said concerning the directionality of blasts, she added, "I guess it blew straight out the back door and nicked me in the leg as I went over the side.

"I remembered your listening bugs, you know, and I tried to keep him talking as long as I could, hoping you'd hear."

This time it was Larsen who looked sheepish. "Budget concerns. Didn't have the manpower to keep monitoring."

"What bugs?" Rhys asked.

"I'll tell you later," Kate said.

Rhys regarded them quizzically for a few moments then snapped his fingers. "The audio clip. It must have been Stec and *Berwick*. Have you caught Stec?"

"We apprehended him at his parents' home last night, smoking pot and playing video games with his friends.

Maybe we were fortunate to catch him in the laid back state he was in because he admitted to everything including having that discussion with Tom on his boat." Lee stood up. "Miss Logan, we should let you get your rest."

Kate turned to Rhys. "What audio clip?"

"I'll tell you later," Rhys said while nodding his tight lipped goodbyes.

CHAPTER 55

Ten Days Later

"We're in here," Rhys yelled from the family room of his aunt's house.

The kitchen door slammed shut and a moment later Charm spun into the room. "Hi, guys. Wow. What a great place."

"Beautiful yard, too," said Hank ambling in after Charm. "Great for kids."

"You're sounding a little domestic, today, Hank." Kate lifted her injured leg off the footstool to make way for the visitors.

"Yeah." Charm cuffed him on the arm. "What's up with that?"

Blushing, Hank sunk onto the sofa.

Charm hooked a thumb over her shoulder towards the kitchen. "We've brought sustenance for the injured."

"Umm. That's what smells so good." Rhys reached for his crutches.

"Sit, wounded people. Sit. I'll fetch it." Charm tossed her coat on a chair. "Can I use some of your aunt's plates, Rhys?"

"Take whatever you need. She'd want you to make yourself at home."

Hank got up to help Charm. "We've got a real feast tonight. Charm's Lithuanian pizza shop is expanding into curries and ribs."

"And some interesting Lithuanian appies," Charm piped in from the kitchen.

"Great combo." Rhys nodded.

Charm set a stack of plates down on the dining table. "Of course we also brought the regular Tuesday Night specials: Habanero Wing-Dings, Hail Caesar Salad and Paparazzi Pepperoni Pizza." She retreated to the kitchen and returned with napkins and a handful of forks. "Isn't Aunt Ellen home, Rhys? I'd hoped she'd sample some of this stuff with me."

"She insisted on going to the drugstore to pick up the prescription for my burn." Kate took the glass of wine Hank offered her and nodded thanks. "I'm starting to feel pretty guilty, being waited on like this."

"Don't," Rhys said. "She told me she's grateful for the company. Ever since my uncle died and Brad moved out, she's been lonely in this big old house."

Charm perched on the arm of the sofa. "Cheers to the two of you. Thank God you're OK."

The four of them clinked glasses.

"I must tell you that besides bearing a sumptuous buffet, I have tidings from the office," said Charm. "Jim and I went through Tom's desk. I didn't expect to find much because the cops were there before us, but we did find a pair of G-string panties."

"I always figured him for the panty perp," said Kate.

"And get this, we also found the receipt for all of the pants stapled to an expense form. Seems he was planning to claim the panties were souvenir scarves for dignitaries at the Dragonfly opening."

"I've never seen these infamous panties," Rhys said. "Worth expensing, were they?"

"Oh they were quite nice. French lace," Charm said. "I mean if you're in to that sort of thing." She cleared her throat. "OK, so that's just a little teaser. I've got juicier, more serious news. While we are nosing around Tom's office, in walks Sabrina." She levelled a stare at her audience and paused for effect. "She's the hacker. Tom screwed her into doing it. He knew her husband had left her, her mom was sick, and he knew she needed money to look after little Cooper."

Kate's mouth dropped open. "Sabrina has an autistic son who requires constant care. Her husband took off a while ago and left her with all the bills and no child support," she told Rhys.

"Tom promised if she'd do what he wanted, she could keep her job and he'd get her a raise. If she didn't, he said he'd see she was fired," said Charm.

"Oh no," Kate said.

"She's blaming herself for Mardone's death. She told Tom that Lucas was suspicious something was going on with Kinetic Keno, hoping he'd stop mucking with it. Instead of letting things lie, though, he insisted she plant incriminating info on Mardone's hard drive. Other than being a most supreme asshole, Mardone wasn't guilty of anything."

"If it's any consolation, she's not responsible for his death," Rhys said.

"That was his own doing," said Kate. "Where is Sabrina now?"

"The cops nabbed her just as she was making us promise to give you her apologies."

"Maybe we can explain her situation to Lee," Kate said.

Charm nodded. "She also wanted me to tell Rhys she's sorry she wasn't more forthcoming with the info she'd been leaking him. She was too frightened to say more."

"So that's who it was." Rhys reached for the wine and filled everybody's glass.

"Fill 'er up," Charm said. "I've got more news."

"I'd better get those appies." Hank headed for the kitchen.

"This next story is more upbeat, I promise," Charm yelled after him.

"Get this. Right after the cops take Sabrina away, Gregor comes into Tom's office with his dog. He's brought the dog to the office and he's looking completely out of it." Charm did a quick check of her audience. "I don't mean stoned. He was just absolutely wiped out, like bewildered." She smiled. "I gotta be sure and clarify who's stoned and who's not, these days. It seems to be going around big time." She tapped Kate's knee. "So, Gregor asks me to see if I can convince you to come back. He says he'll double the original bonus you're entitled to. In the meantime he wants me to head up the Communications Department." She slapped her thigh. "Can you believe it?"

Hank slid the appetizers onto the table. "Don't forget the part where he told you that, with Kate, Mardone, and Tom gone, you were his only option."

"Oh yeah," Charm said quickly. "That wasn't his greatest moment."

Rhys and Kate roared with laughter.

"You do know I'd throw something at you if you weren't already so messed up," Charm said to Rhys.

He raised an arm in defense.

"What's so funny, you guys?" Aunt Ellen stuck her head into the family room.

"Hurray! You made it. Don't pay any attention to them," said Charm. "Just having fun at my expense."

Still laughing, Kate said, "Ellen, please come and sit down and let me wait on you for once. Charm and Hank have brought dinner." She followed Charm into the kitchen. "I shouldn't have laughed. It was the way you said it."

"What was funny was the look on Gregor's face when *he* said it." Charm chuckled. "But I do seem to be the hub of communications lately." She glanced sideways at Kate. "I also took a call yesterday from somebody who's been trying to get hold of you."

Kate leaned against the counter and eyed Charm suspiciously. "There was a time when a line like that wouldn't have worried me...now, however—"

"Matt called," Charm said.

"What?"

"He said he saw your picture in the paper and everyone back east is very impressed that his girlfriend is such a hero." Charm pursed her lips.

"Girlfriend?" Kate whispered.

Charm nodded. "He wants you to give him a call at his new number. He lost his old phone when Emily kicked him out. She's taken up with the CEO of some company in Silicon Valley."

A smile spread across Kate's face. "Things are going to be a little awkward for him—co-owning a Vancouver condo with Emily's father."

"He says he's concerned about you and he'd like to help." Charm turned her head aside and was working her way up to one of her best gagging performances when there was a rap on the door.

Perhaps it was the possibility of Matt making an unwelcome appearance that made Kate inch the door open cautiously.

"Guess who?" a voice rang out.

"Larsen," chastised another voice. "Vancouver Police . . . Hi, Kate," said Paul Lee. "Can we talk to you for a minute?"

Relieved to see Lee and Larsen rather than the alternative, Kate exhaled a big sigh and opened the door.

"I thought you might want this back." Lee handed Kate a laptop. "We found it at Berwick's house. Seems to be in full working order."

Kate nodded her thanks. "How did you know where we were?" she asked, as Rhys swung into the kitchen on his crutches. He gave them an accusing stare that might as well have asked, "More bugs?"

Both detectives looked at Charm.

She groaned. "I thought it was OK to talk to them now."

"Oh dear, what's wrong?" Aunt Ellen padded her way into the kitchen, a worried expression on her face.

Larsen grinned, indicating the crestfallen Charm. "We have that effect on people."

Lee snatched his hat from his head and motioned Larsen to do the same. "Nothing, ma'am. We thought Ms. Logan and your nephew might like an update on the situation. I'm sorry to intrude on your home."

Charm gave Larsen a thin-lipped smile, shoved a bowl of curry and a serving spoon at him and pointed to the table in the family room.

Realizing they were about to eat dinner, Lee seemed genuinely upset. "I don't want to interrupt. We'll come back another time."

"Don't be silly. You're more than welcome. Go on in and sit down," said Ellen. "Rhys, get a couple more chairs from the other room."

Rhys gave his Aunt a loaded stare which she returned full bore. "You know the chairs I mean," she said. "Go get 'em."

"I'll help you," Larsen said scurrying along behind. "Pretty hard to move furniture on crutches."

"Detective, you sit here on the sofa beside Kate. She'll sit on that side so she can put her leg up." Auntie tugged the foot stool over to the correct spot. "There. That'll work fine."

Kate put two big dishes of food down on the table. "We understand you've arrested Sabrina," she said. "I hope you realize what her situation is with her son and how Tom manipulated her into doing what she did."

"We're learning about it," said Lee.

"Charm and I would like to vouch for her."

"And Jim, June, and other friends in the office," Charm yelled from the kitchen.

Lee held up a palm. "I know. I know. Early days yet, but I'll see what can be done."

Larsen returned with a chair under each arm as Aunt Ellen entered the room with a couple of bottles of champagne and two more glasses.

"I've been holding on to this since I thought Brad was going to marry that nice girl from Victoria. Gentlemen?" Ellen asked, holding up the glasses.

There was a pause, then Lee smiled broadly. "Thank you. Why not...Larsen, you're driving."

"Oh," Larsen said, retracting the arm he had extended for a glass.

Hank grabbed a coke from the table and tossed it to him.

"We'll do our best for your friend Sabrina," Lee said. "We know Berwick was a master manipulator and we're finding out he was also a master criminal. So far we've uncovered two more aliases with criminal records to match and I have an idea we'll find more."

"Any other murders?" Rhys asked.

"Not yet." Lee paused. "But never say never."

"I still find it hard to believe," Charm said. "In retrospect, I guess there were signs that something was going on with him, but we always put it down to job stress or his health." She handed Larsen a plate and told him to help himself to dinner.

"He never said what was wrong with him," Kate chimed in. "But I know he had to lose weight before they could operate."

"We figure that's why he was horsing down the amphetamines," Larsen said. "Kind of a self-styled 1960s slimming plan."

"Not a good combo when mixed with oxycodone." Lee took the plate of food Charm passed him. "We also found bags of pot and every indication that he was using that, too."

"Geez. About the only thing he didn't do was smoke regular old cigarettes," Charm said. "Remember how he went after the Prize Payout clerks when he caught them smoking, Kate?"

Recalling the cigarette-based reason they had trumped up to clear Kate of any accusations, both Kate and Rhys stiffened. Lee's smiling eyes made contact with theirs and the unspoken innuendo hung in the air.

"Absolutely right. We didn't find any cigarettes," Lee said.

"Would have been healthier for him if he'd ignored the Surgeon General's warning and risked lung cancer," said Hank.

"The kids have tried explaining it to me, but I still don't get what this Berwick was up to," Aunt Ellen said.

"It's not something law abiding citizens would understand," Lee said. "Money laundering is what criminals do to disguise the illegal sources of their wealth, prevent a trail of incriminating evidence, and turn their illegal funds into something they can spend. When the process is complete, they usually wind up with a little less than they started with, but they can spend what they've got without raising suspicions.

"Berwick has been laundering money for years. With Kate's information added to what we already knew, we've been able to piece things together. He used the lottery corporation, Sharon Chernin's store, an olive oil store, a nail salon, and a line of rental RVs called 'Fly and Drive' to wash his clients' dirty money." Lee wiped wing ding sauce from his mouth. "That way, if one channel got too hot, he had others to use."

Aunt Ellen nodded but her brow was furrowed.

"What was probably his undoing was his recent decision to become a bigger player. While continuing to launder money for his original clients, he got involved at the ground level with this grow op at Namu."

"I have a friend who'd really like to know how they got hold of that site," Rhys said.

"I'm on it," Larsen said between bites. "This is delicious, Charm. Where'd you get it?"

Charm pushed a napkin imprinted with the name of the restaurant across the table towards him.

"Yes, Larsen's looking into it. Details of the purchase are well hidden in layers of bureaucracy," Lee said. "But, you can see it smelled from the beginning."

"That'll make Phil happy," Kate said.

"Oh, he'll have something to say about it," Rhys grimaced.

"Namu is so isolated," said Aunt Ellen.

"Perfect for them," said Lee. "They were able to transport dope to the U.S. by water. Anything bound across the country, they paid the native kids to deliver to Bella Coola—"

"And they stashed it in secret compartments in the Fly and Drive RVs," Larsen interrupted.

"Then," Lee said loudly, reclaiming the tale, "it was transported by vacationing families who were totally oblivious to the fact they were drug mules. Fly and Drive rental associates across the country juggled the loaded RVs so they went to the required destinations. They had marijuana leaving the Port of Montreal for Europe, Prince Rupert for Asia, and crossing over into all the U.S. border states."

"I remember seeing those RVs in Bella Coola and there were so many at Dragonfly Casino, they had a special place to park them," said Kate.

Larsen nodded. "If a new opportunity opened up, they designed a cheap vacation package that people would really jump for, which terminated at the new market. The vacationers happily did the driving for them. You've got to give them credit," he said, oblivious to Lee's glare.

"So, how was becoming a bigger player his downfall?" Hank asked, reaching to fill everyone's glass.

"It seems to have become more than he could handle and he was starting to self-destruct. From what Kate told us, we now know he murdered his original partner, the ticket reseller, for going behind his back with Jack Stec to manufacture meth and take over the operation," Lee said.

"But once the guy was dead, Berwick was short some manpower. He hoped to bring Kate into the operation to take some of the pressure off of himself."

Charm patted Kate's shoulder. "She's always in demand."

"He must have thought Jack Stec would also be useful or he would have gotten rid of him earlier, too. Meth meant more money and continued opportunities, if pot was legalized." Lee sat back in his seat and crossed his arms. "It doesn't seem to have worried Stec that Berwick was capable of murder and had already done away with one partner. He brought some individuals from Vertex Gaming into the Namu operation and together they were turning the Dragonfly Lake casino into their own little fiefdom to skim profits and launder money."

Lee thanked Charm when she collected his empty plate and turned to address Rhys. "We now realize that we misinterpreted an e-mail Wesley sent you where he discussed starting up a soccer league for the troubled youth in Bella Bella, like you did in Vancouver."

Everyone stared solemnly at Rhys who nodded. "He wanted to do something similar, maybe get the kids down to Vancouver and Seattle for a few games."

"All the evidence we've found indicates he was just trying to keep the teenagers in Bella Bella out of trouble," Lee said. "One of the punks we arrested told us Wesley was caught nosing around the cannery, but we don't know who killed him. Apparently, there were some strangers there that day. We're going to keep digging."

At the mention of Wesley, Aunt Ellen had wiped her eyes and hurried to the kitchen. She now stuck her head into the family room, apparently thinking it safe to return, and asked if anyone would like dessert. "I stopped by Black Bear Bakery and picked up some treats," she said. "There's more than enough for everybody."

"I'm coming, Ellen." Charm gave Kate a direct order to stay seated, snatched up the dinner plates, and scurried into the kitchen.

"You guys are fantastic hosts." Larsen shoved the last of the pizza crust into his mouth. "I'm glad we stopped by."

Lee caught Kate's eye and looked heavenward.

"Can I tell them about Vertex?" Larsen asked.

"Why don't you go ahead?" Lee grabbed his drink and eased further back into the couch.

"Well...Vertex is actually a legit operation," Larsen began. "But there are a few bad apples and one strange coincidence to connect them to Pacific Lottery. I bet you'll never guess what it is."

Rhys and Hank exchanged glances and shook their heads.

"Hans Neidermeyer's mother is Sharon Chernin's cousin. Twenty-five years ago, Sharon, who was then 'Elsie Bach,' met Gregor Chernin at a lottery convention in Europe. She married and divorced a couple of times before running into Chernin again and marrying him." Larsen gratefully accepted the dish Aunt Ellen handed him. "Her grandfather started Vertex Gaming in Germany and it was a huge success. But, like the old saying goes, the first generation makes it, the second generation saves it, and the third squanders it. Once Stec got scheming with Neidermeyer—"

"Poor old Tom didn't have a chance," Kate said.

"Vogel, the German fisherman murdered near Namu, was a senior Vertex manager who, we figure, refused to go along with what Neidermeyer and his crew were doing," said Lee. "We think he was probably snooping around the grow op facility and had a heart attack when he touched the electric fence. The coroner noted tissue damage to his hands."

Rhys grimaced and recalled the conversation in the plane to Dragonfly on that evening that seemed so long ago. "It was appalling the way they spoke about their colleague who had just been found dead. But it all makes sense now."

They chewed away for a few moments, digesting dessert and what they had just learned, until the silence was broken by a loud meow. Kate snorted and glanced at Rhys as Elvis sauntered in, tail swishing.

"If any of you are allergic to cats, the door's that way," Kate said. "I learned my lesson."

Elvis checked out each visitor with a penetrating stare before leaping to the back of the sofa and padding along to where Lee sat. The detective plucked a bit of pastry from his plate and passed it over his shoulder to the cat, who took it gently.

"I didn't think he'd eat that," Lee chuckled.

"Anything and everything," Rhys said.

Eyeing what remained on the plate, Elvis reached a paw forward and cuffed Lee gently on the ear.

"Elvis. That's no way to treat guests." Aunt Ellen got to her feet. "Come on and I'll get you your dinner." The cat jumped onto Lee's lap, pounced to the floor with a thud, and padded after Auntie.

Lee grimaced. "He's a tank, isn't he?"

"He doesn't take too kindly to diets," said Rhys.

Kate gathered up the dessert plates and carried them to the kitchen.

"What about the audio clip? You said it was definitely Stec and Berwick?" Rhys asked.

"Stec was trying to ascertain if Berwick could handle the amount of dirty money that the meth op would bring in. The 'little lamb' they referred to as 'needing a nudge' was Kate."

Kate returned to the room and perched on the arm of Rhys's chair. "The tape," she said. "Rhys told me about it."

"Not everything." He put a hand on her knee. "I couldn't remember all of it."

"Just a sec," said Larsen. He closed his eyes and squinted hard. "They said, 'The building's all finished and the one remaining complication will be removed…if you know what I mean…the dumb bugger.'"

"That's right," Lee said, seemingly unsurprised at his partner's recall. "We know the building they referred to was the new one in the hillside at the cannery, but we don't know who they were calling a dumb bugger. Berwick's partner was already dead."

"Also," Larsen said, his eyes still squinty, "we never figured out who they were referring to as 'the home grown native.' I mean, once we decided it wasn't Rhys they were talking about." Larsen gave a thin-lipped smile.

Rhys nodded pleasantly, as if to say, "Understandable error. I can see how that could happen," and turned to Lee for a more definitive explanation.

"Stec says he can't recall what that was about." Lee scratched his upper lip. "I don't buy it though. They were planning a murder."

"Where did this tape come from?" Charm asked.

"Trevor Edgar," said Lee.

Kate's eyes almost fell out of their sockets. "What?"

Lee made a tsk-tsk sound with his tongue. "Trevor Edgar has recently come forward and claimed he's the one that recorded it and phoned it in to our anonymous hotline after making several failed attempts to report his suspicions. I'm afraid he didn't get too far in the system, which, the good news is, is causing a rewrite in protocol."

"He tried to tell you what he knew, but nobody listened?" Hank asked.

Lee sighed. "Edgar is pretty well known to the boys in Vice. He's never been violent—"

"Just *demonstrative*," Larsen interrupted with a grin.

"He's been arrested several times for exposing himself, peeping, public nudity, and working as a private detective without a license. He's an attention seeker and will basically say anything if he can hold centre stage," said the senior detective.

"He was the genuine article this time, though," Larsen said. "He says Berwick asked him to keep an eye on Kate and report all her activities to him."

"You should have listened to him," Charm said.

Lee smiled a small smile. "He also told us he followed Kate for some time before realizing she was in love with him, switching loyalties, and trying to contact us."

"Oh," Kate said quietly.

"Yech." Charm said loudly.

"Definitely a miscalculation on our part. I hope you can understand the position we were in," Lee said.

All eyes turned to Kate who shrugged. Rhys looked less forgiving.

At this point, Elvis sashayed back into the room trailed by a strong eau de fish and went straight to Lee for a pat on the head.

"We mustn't take any more of your time." Lee stood and Larsen followed suit. "Mrs. Stewart—"

"Ellen, please. It's Ellen."

Lee smiled broadly. "Thank-you for your hospitality, Ellen. We hadn't intended to be wined and dined, but I sure appreciate it."

Larsen nodded vigorously, pocketing the napkin with the pizza shop's information.

"We have yet to locate Sharon Chernin." Lee picked up his toque and tossed Larsen his cap. "But she won't get far." He shook Kate's hand then turned to Rhys. "I want to apologize for my confusion earlier," he said. "And I promise you, I *will* find out who murdered Wesley." The two men's eyes held a silent conversation until Rhys extended his hand and they shook.

CHAPTER 56

S haron Chernin stretched out on the softly cushioned chaise lounge, reaching back to free her long blonde hair.

"Champagne, darling?" asked a cheery male voice.

"Why not," she said. "Don't you love it when the biggest decision you have to make is, 'Hmm, what shall I drink today?'"

With a wild grin he pulled a long saber from where he'd held it behind his back.

"I also love a man who knows what he's doing," she purred.

In one well-practiced motion, he slid the sword down the neck of the champagne bottle and sliced off the cork. "Your wish is my command." He filled two champagne flutes and handed one to her.

"Would it still be if I weren't sitting on twenty-five million freshly laundered bucks?" she asked, batting her long eyelashes.

He shoved the bottle into the ice bucket. "My dear," he said icily, "you forget I'm sitting on a few myself. How many yachts do you think I need?"

"Take it easy; I was just messing with you," Sharon said. "You really can't take a joke." Her crystal glass sparkled in the sun as she took a sip. "And, in answer to your question, the more the merrier. One might run out of gas, get beached, or one of the many other nasty things that befall yachts."

He smiled wickedly, reached down, and clinked his glass against hers. "Do remember my darling, *who* it was that shot the native kid, and *who* it is that knows *you* did it."

"You'd be wise to remember how much of a hardship that could be to you—a death sentence even." She batted her eyelashes again. "You know as well as I do that he was getting too nosey, and he was Wilson's best friend. I seem to recall it was *you* who dumped the kid's body and Vogel's as well. I was long gone. It was also *you* who tipped the cops that Wilson dusted the guy, and *you* who told them he was getting set up to manufacture meth."

Her companion looked at her with a mixture of hatred and admiration.

"Scootch that umbrella over a smidge, would you?" she said. "I'm in the shade."

He jumped to do what she asked. "Seriously though, isn't there something we can do for Jack? At the very least, we should get him a good lawyer," he said.

Sharon removed her oversized sunglasses and glared at him. "How can you say that? Don't you believe me when I tell you that he and Berwick were going to get rid of you? He might as well be dead to me."

"He is your son."

"It's called tough love." She replaced her glasses and exhaled loudly.

He snatched up his glass, strode over to the deck railing, and peered out at the cable cars inching their way up the line to Sugarloaf Mountain. They drank in silence for a few moments. "I guess we make a good team."

"The best, darling. Never a dull moment. Like Taylor and Burton."

"I hate leaving loose ends, though." He shaded his eyes to catch a better view of the near-nude sunbathers below, then, remembering Sharon's temper, quickly redirected his glance back to Sugarloaf.

"Don't worry about Wilson. He's nothing," she said.

"He never gives up, you know." He anxiously ran his tongue back and forth along his upper lip.

"Don't bore me. I want to party." Still luxuriating on her chaise, Sharon lifted her arms in the air and jived back and forth in a kind of seated samba.

Leaning against the railing, Richard Stahl, the Minister of Native Affairs, cupped his jaw in his hand, calming his anxious tic, and stared out to sea.

72938072R00211

Made in the USA
San Bernardino, CA
30 March 2018